Lies Beneath the Sand

A Novel Out of Africa

Samantha Ford

Published on Amazon Via KDP
All Rights Reserved.
Copyright © 2025 Samantha Ford
(ISBN 9798307438046)

No part of this book may be reproduced or transmitted in any form or by any means, graphic, electronic, or mechanical, including photocopying, recording, taping or by any information storage or retrieval system, without the permission in writing from the copyright holder.

The right of Samantha Ford to be identified as the author of this work has been asserted in accordance with the Copyright, Designs and Patents Act 1988 sections 77 and 78.

This is a work of fiction. The characters and their actions are entirely fictitious. Any resemblance to persons living or dead is entirely coincidental.

******

Also by Samantha Ford

The Zanzibar Affair

The House Called Mbabati

A Gathering of Dust

The Ambassador's Daughter

The Unexpected Guest

A Widow in Waiting

Hidden in Full View

She whispers through your dreams at night, carried on a warm breeze from another land, bringing memories of a place so far away now, a place you knew and loved.
This unforgettable place called Africa.

The world is ever changing – probably more so now in 2025. There are wars raging, unimaginable natural disasters, political instability, and a sense of hopelessness and despair.
Hope is all we have now.
I trust my story brings you joy, and memories of days gone by, a few hours where you can escape to another place.

South Africa
2005
The Wild Coast –Eastern Cape Province

There was silence there, amongst the endless sand dunes. The heat was intense, stultifying. The whispering breeze lifted the powdery sand and moved it to another place, making no difference to the desertscape with its undulating slopes of shapes and outlines. A map-less place, a place unchanging in its constant shifting. The waves of heat rising from the sand creating a mirage, leaving ripples and ridges of hard sand.

The motionless silent figure was a dark outline, faceless, against the shimmering gold and apricot yellow of the sand, as he watched the woman from afar. The hot desert distorting his shape with its wavering heat.

She stood and watched the pounding thrashing fury of the boiling sea moving towards her as the tide turned, then leaving for a moment, before coming back, hungry for her.

The Wild Coast, in South Africa, is aptly named. There was no stillness there once the silence of the dunes descended into the roiling waters of the angry furious sea.

The watcher hunkered down and waited.

The tall woman's dark hair was being whipped around her face and body. She wore a long white dress which hugged and danced around her slim frame. Across her chest was a leather bag which she kept close to her heart.

She lifted her tanned arms, in salutation, then slowly walked towards the boiling sea, unaware it was waiting for her. Once more coming back for her and this time it would take her.

The watcher waited; he was a San man. A man who only knew the shape of the desert into which he was born. His body strong and resilient. He had lived in the desert all his life, he knew the whispers and moods of the shifting sands, he knew the unforgiving sea and its ways. His other senses were as keen as the animals in the Kalahari, in another place far from here, where his ancestors had come from.

His loin cloth was made of antelope skin, his necklace of beads and shells clicking softly, his arms and ankles decorated with anklets made of more beads and shells of red, white, blue, turquoise, yellow, and green. His soft cape draped over his shoulder, his pouch of deadly arrows warm against his back along with herbs, leaves and dried strips of meat. The heat of the afternoon brought sweat to his brow, captured by the band of animal skin around his forehead, keeping his cap of tight curls close to his head. The sun caught his high cheekbones and the deep greenness of his slanted eyes.

He knew where she would be. He had been chosen to track her.

He watched her and the other figure. The woman turned, seeing the tall man, and started to run towards him, stumbling through the soft sand, calling to him and waving her arms. The man lifted his arm as though in greeting.

The sound of his gun shattered the silence of the desert.

The woman fell forward. The man bent down and reached for the soft bag she was carrying.

Instinctively the San man drew his arrow from the pouch behind his shoulder. His aim was straight and true, the arrow with its deadly poisonous head made its mark and the man, too, fell onto the soft sand.

He loped silently towards them, moving over the ground as lightly as an antelope, with natural grace, his delicately proportioned limbs and finely muscled body moving with ease, as the bubbling scum of the incoming tide began to make its first claim. Small crabs bubbled up out of the sand then once more disappeared into their secret places.

He hunkered down next to the woman and gently turned her over, the blood from the wound in her head turning pink with the greedy meeting of sand and sea, her startled eyes slowly closing. He hissed through his teeth, then turned to the man.

He was a white man, tall and strong, his skin not as white as the skin of the woman, but he was a man who had spent many years under the harshness of the African sun. He removed his arrow from the man's body but left its deadly head embedded in his heart.

He searched through the pockets of the man's khaki uniform. Something round with strange signs and thin arms that moved, wrapped in the thick skin of an animal he did not recognise, held together with a metal clasp. He thought the round thing with its leather covering had been able to help him find the woman and kill her. He found the dead man's identity book and put it in his pouch with the round object.

He looked at the gun, the harbinger of death, and threw it far out into the sea. He had no use for weapons such as this with its loud noise. His own weapons were silent and deadly.

The end results the same.

He turned back to the woman. Around her neck was a delicate necklace glinting in the harsh sunlight, with a life still of its own…carefully he removed it. In the soft leather bag, he found the hard squares of something he had never seen before. His brow furrowed as he turned one over and over in his hands. He felt another object and lifted it out. A small book with writing and nothing else.

Cautiously he lifted one of the hard squares to his mouth, could it be some kind of food the white people carried with them? It tasted of metal, he spat the taste of it into the sand, then put them in his skin pouch along with the book with the writing and the thin necklace and the ornament it carried. The small cotton bag, with its precious contents, he also put carefully away in his pouch, along with her identity document.

The tide was coming in, the pounding furious sea would not care what it carried back out into the endless oceans. The sharks would be waiting, hungry as always along this coastline, the most dangerous waters for sharks in the world. They would both be taken to another place where their ancestors waited.

He watched them as the greedy incoming tide made its presence known.

He had failed in his mission to watch out for the woman. But he had taken the life of the man who had killed her. Her ancestors would be happy it was so.

Tomorrow they would both be gone.

Chapter Two
KENYA
1965

Christiana Palmere was considered odd by the aristocratic Kenyan society. She lived out on a remote farm near Naivasha, her house was simple and basic, she had built it herself with the help of some of the local Africans. A meandering add-on of random rooms, all thatched with a wrap - around veranda. The garden was a wilderness of green and brown plants and wildflowers.

She was not part of the scene of Nairobi's vibrant social set.

Christiana was French, by birth, from a family of eminent doctors and scientists, she could have moved easily into the social scene of Nairobi. But she had chosen a different path. She wanted to be more than a social butterfly, there were far too many of them in Kenya. She preferred to study the ones with colourful wings.

Christiana was more fascinated by the wildness of Kenya, the local tribes, the flora and fauna, and the wildlife. She had had no formal training, no degree in botany or science, but she had taught herself. Listening and watching the local Africans, observing how they lived, what they ate, how they healed themselves with indigenous plants. Different tribes used different methods for healing. Christiana was hooked with this other world. A world of natural healing which she felt could teach her more here, than all the white-coat wearing scientists in their sophisticated laboratories in cities somewhere else in the world.

Her two girls, Fleur and Helene, played happily in the bush, their little feet creating a soft dusty path down to the compound where their nanny, Patience, family lived. Here they mixed with the African children, learned to speak their language, Swahili, and the ways of the bush and the animals around them.

Their young strong bodies, dressed only in shorts, were bronzed by the fierce sun, their blonde hair a long tangle of curls, rarely brushed, shot through with gold as they ran wild and free, their two dogs of undetermined breed, followed them happily wherever they went. Patience ensuring they didn't venture into the lake where bad-tempered hippos lurked beneath the surface.

They became used to seeing their mother, wearing a large white sunhat to shade her face from the burning sun, digging in her garden, collecting specimens in glass jars, waving vaguely and smiling at them as they raced past with their African friends in tow. They were unused to discipline, disinterested in hugs and bedtime stories. They had everything they needed dancing around them every day, out there in the bush.

That time, in Kenya, was the happiest Christiana could remember. Her housekeeper was called Noah, but she had no idea how old he was, nor did he. He became invaluable for his knowledge of plants. When he had finished his work around the house, he would take her out into the bush and explain the medicinal properties of plants, bushes, tree bark and berries, roots, tubers, bulbs, fruits, rare flowers, and seeds, and which ones were toxic or poisonous and to be avoided.

Sometimes, leaving the girls with Patience, Christiana and Noah travelled farther afield in her battered, but mostly reliable, old Volkswagen, visiting remote villages and meeting the traditional healers and medicine men.

Christiana recorded everything meticulously in her large leather notebook. After Noah had made dinner for the family, he would join her and show her how to mix her various specimens, explaining their value and for what they could be used.

She wasn't an absent mother, by any means. She loved and adored her girls, but knew they were happy, well looked after, and never left on their own. They too participated in her research, bringing insects, unusual tiny flowers, sometimes a snake or a lizard, for her inspection, after a day running wild in the bush.

Christiana had never married, but she had had a five-year affair with Jean-Clive. He was the father of her two girls but tiring of life in Kenya, where he had worked as a ranch manager for a wealthy cattle farmer, he had returned to France. She had never seen him again or been in touch with him. They both agreed it would be easier to continue their lives this way and better for their girls' future.

Kenya society turned its back on Christiana. Two children born out of wedlock and a lover who left her? It was scandalous! Her parents, living in France, were equally horrified.

As far as the gossip was concerned, she was quite mad and spent far too much time than was decent with the locals. Her house, it was said, over gin and tonics and canapes, was not only run down but she allowed African children and their parents to visit whenever they wanted. It simply wasn't done. Her two girls, they gossiped, were as wild as the natives they played with. And, it was said, this woman Christiana had a problem, probably with drink, she was given to fainting, or passing out, they said gleefully, once at the Nairobi Club library for goodness sake, and it was only eleven in the morning!

The years rolled by, but eccentric as Christiana was, she home schooled her children and any other children from the compound. Teaching them to read, write, and speak both French and English, thereby giving them a good, but somewhat erratic, educational platform from which to grow.

Her parents, in France, had been appalled to see the photographs Christiana had sent them of the girls. They looked like wild jungle creatures with their untidy hair, ragged sun-bleached shorts, and bare feet. They urged her to send the girls to boarding school, either in France or the UK.

They would be happy to pay for the further education of their grandchildren, in either country. They needed a decent education, they argued, in a civilised country, where children wore sensible shoes and clothes, it would not be acceptable for them to grow up with only a basic education.

Reluctantly Christiana had agreed. Her girls had been educated, by her standards, but Fleur was twelve now, and her sister Helene ten.

It was time to let them go. She was aware of the tumultuous political changes occurring in the country, where many whites saw no future for themselves.

Perhaps there was no future here, for her two girls. But she had no intention of leaving. Christiana had come to Kenya as a young woman, during her gap year, before university. Fallen in love with it and decided to stay and stay she would.

She had chosen to send her girls to be further educated in the UK rather than France. She thought they would have a more rounded, international education there, and better opportunities in the future.

Chapter Three
England

Fleur and Helene were bewildered with their new lives in England. Their grandparents had secured them places in one of the finest boarding schools in the country. Their mother, Christiana, had always been a somewhat distant and vague figure for their entire childhood, but they loved her, missed her, and missed Patience, Noah, and their African playmates even more. And the dogs, the wildness, the freedom and the blueness of the sky, the warm sun on their skin.

The first few years were difficult as they squeezed their bare splayed toes into tight shoes, wore school uniforms with ties around their necks, thick jumpers and coats, and wondered when the grey skies would ever lift, and they would feel the heat of the sun in that cloudless, endless, blue sky they remembered so well.

They lay in their beds at night staring at the beige walls of their dorm, bereft of the pale green tutting lizards they were used to seeing on their bedroom walls at home, lying in wait for passing mosquitoes.

But like all young children they adapted to their new life, making new friends, and embracing this unknown world they had been plunged into. Despite their erratic education in Kenya, they did well with their studies, mixing with other children from all over the world.

They had found another tribe to be part of.

Christiana lived on the meagre allowance her parents sent from France. When the school holidays rolled around, her parents insisted the girls came to them in Nice, to further educate them in a different culture.

Reluctantly Christiana had to agree, after all they paid the extremely high school fees which she could never have afforded on her allowance, she also couldn't afford to fly them both to Kenya for the school holidays. The girls and their mother exchanged frequent letters, but all three felt the years passing and realised they had grown apart and gone their separate ways. They now moved in different worlds. Christiana had only managed to visit her two girls twice over the years.

So, it was the two girls became more European than Kenyan. They loved their school they even, grudgingly, became to accept the strict rules and regulations imposed upon them, giving them more stability than they had ever had, growing up wild and free in the bush.

The years rolled past, and their school days came to an end. Both girls achieved excellent results and were accepted into university.

Helene opted for a teaching degree. Fleur wanted to study medicine.

Then the news came from Kenya. Their mother, Christiana, had died.

Chapter Four
Kenya
1980's

Their grandfather had broken the news to them. "You will be met, in Nairobi, by a car from the French Embassy, everything has been arranged to make this difficult journey a little easier for you both. There are some complications, but all will be explained to you in due course. I'm so sorry. Your grandmother and I share your grief, but it will be harder for you. You must be strong for all of us."

Both girls peered out of the windows of the plane and looked at the country they had left behind so many years ago. It was a new country now, an African country, with an African President, no longer run by the colonial whites.

As young girls they only vaguely remembered Nairobi. Their mother had taken them there when she made infrequent visits to the library to pursue her research. It seemed a long way from the small holding at Naivasha where they had grown up. The city's skyline had changed beyond recognition.

Both their grandparents had decided not to attend their estranged daughter's funeral, they were elderly now, and felt the flight from France to Kenya would be too long, emotional, and arduous.

The years had passed, they did not know their daughter anymore. She had become a stranger to them with her unconventional life out in the Kenyan bush. Christiana had been their only child, but they had lost the essence of her as a little girl to the place she had called her home. Kenya.

Fleur and Helene watched the passing countryside from the windows of the air-conditioned car. There were many cars on the road leading from the airport into the city. Some old and battered, their engines belching black clouds of smoke, compared to the sleek and highly polished imported cars which glided past them with their tinted windows, leather interiors, and anonymous passengers.

Modern shops, rose high next to the old traditional and familiar buildings which had been there for decades, throwing them into shadowed forgotten shapes. A curious mix of then and now. Traditional markets were selling fresh produce, handmade crafts and colourful bolts of material, vendors sold drinks and cigarettes from their carts. The streets lined with dust covered flowering trees and avenues of vibrant coloured bougainvillea and jacaranda trees, where haughty cranes goose-stepped high in the branches. They perched like overlords above the exhaust fumes and belching traffic, and the cacophony of endless noise from motor bikes weaving their way through the heavy traffic, and the booming African music vibrating through the brightly hand painted taxis.

Pedestrians manoeuvred expertly through the seething mass of vehicles. Stately mothers, some carrying firewood on their heads, with babies tied securely to their backs, sleeping through the chaos surrounding them.

The modern supermarkets icy with air conditioning, their shelves bulging with imported foods and shiny trolleys to take it all away in. Muted music played through hidden speakers, the shadows from the modern buildings dwarfing the simple *dukas* throwing them into the dark shadows of alleyways, almost lost in time.

Fleur had met the sons and daughters of wealthy Kenyans at university in England. Some had accrued their fortunes with fat government contracts, passed through familiar hands. Some may call that corruption – others called it commission. But it enabled them to send their children across the sea for expensive educations.

The wheel had turned.

Fleur had read many modern-day books about the early days in colonial Kenya. The characters who had worked long and hard to tame the African bush in their attempts to make it more European. Those stories now only a whisper on the wind, the written words fading with each passing year. Words written by hurricane lamps way out in the bush, recording the day's finds and events, the lamps attracting moths, mosquitoes and other insects as the author worked laboriously into the hot humid night.

Old statues had been removed by the new African government; the dusty old cowboy town was no more. The colourful characters who had walked and ridden down the dirt roads, the names of which had gone down in history, good or bad, were but a lingering memory. But they too were part of the history of Kenya.

The Herbert Baker designed law courts cowered in the shadows of tall new builds that glinted in the sunshine, dwarfing the old stone buildings of yesteryear, leaving them in the gloom of the past with their memories and ghosts.

The colonial homes of the wealthy aristocratic white people who had developed Kenya, and made it what it was today, were standing empty and derelict out in the African bush. Wreathed in silence, the bush stealthily claimed a little more back as each year passed.

No more the sound of laughter, music, or clinking crystal glasses, wild parties, and even wilder behaviour of the chosen few with titles and money. A few of their descendants still lived there, but not many.

Although some had survived, the owners still working the land, others had turned their homes into game lodges and hotels with a colonial history which international tourists loved but had not paid the price the original owners had paid in blood, sweat and tears as they tried to tame the land.

Yes, Kenya had changed, but films and books about those heady days still lingered. The scandals, the characters, their lifestyle, would always be part of the Kenyan landscape. Tourists flocked to the country from all over the world, seeking that long-lost heady world, and imagining it in their mind as they sipped their sundowners and thought about the people who had once lived in these splendid colonial houses, sitting in their chairs, and lying in the beds of those long dead extraordinary people who had shaped the country.

But one thing had not changed. The brutal and spectacular beauty of the land, the wide-open expanses of the bush and the animals who roamed there and had done for thousands of years. Here time had stood still. Some things cannot be bought and sold, and so it was with the untamed defiant bush and the animals who inhabited it.

Fleur pushed the hair back from her face and thought about her mother. Some things stay in your mind she mused, like her childhood, which nurtured the soul of her memory and sometimes blotted out the reality of where she lived now.

Like nature they stay with you, like all recollections. They may make you weep sometimes, but those memories are yours and yours alone. Never to be owned, or imagined, by anyone else.

She hoped, one day, to have children of her own and when she did, she would bring them back to Kenya, show them the stunning magnificence of Africa. Help them understand her better, show them the different life she had been brought up in. She would pass on her stories to her children and know they would never forget her or the country she had loved and still loved.

Yes, Kenya had changed, of course it had. But the essence of the country had not. Mother Africa was still there and always would be.

Helene looked at her big sister. "So, what do you think Fleur?"

Fleur turned and frowned. "People say it's a mistake to go back to a place you loved, a place you were brought up in. But that's only if you expect it to be the same, or worse.

"Getting off the flight, smelling that dusty pungent smell, which is so unique to Africa, feeling the sun prickling my skin, it all felt familiar to me, all the smiling Africans, the energy of the place. I truly felt I had come home. How about you – what did you feel?"

Helene shook her head. "Your recall is obviously sharper, and more romantic, than mine. I felt nothing at all. It looks chaotic, it's not a place which evokes any strong feelings in me. Only another place. I prefer London and France, to be honest. That's where I belong, not here. But here we are and there are things we must do. I'll remember more when we get to the house where we grew up. I'm not looking forward to that, or the funeral either. I hardly remember our mother…"

She shrugged her slim shoulders. "But that's what happens when you send young children off to a boarding school in a country they've never been to. Children think they have lost their parents, been abandoned, but it's the parents who lose their children. The bond is broken, especially in our case, well, certainly mine. I feel Grand Mama and Papa were more my parents than our own mother."

The car pulled up outside the Norfolk Hotel, the driver assuring them they had a room booked there, and he would be back for them first thing in the morning, to take them out to their mother's house at Naivasha.

The sisters checked in and wandered through the gardens, passing the old canvas covered wagons from a time long ago, heading towards their cottage room. A peacock spread its glorious tail and squawked at them indignantly.

"So, Fleur, what shall we do for the rest of the day? Hang out here, or do the tourist thing?"

Fleur turned her head sharply. "I'm not a tourist, Helene, this is my country, where I was born. I'm going to sit out at the Lord Delamere terrace, have lunch and people watch. Are you going to join me?"

Helene tossed her head in dismissal. "No. I'm going to look around the shops, I'll see you later."

Fleur made her way to the terrace and found an empty table, although the place was busy with locals and tourists. The locals were easy to pick out, their casual clothes, the easy way they spoke in Swahili to the staff, their tanned faces and bodies, some of the men wearing elephant hair bracelets or colourful beaded ones.

The tourists were different, their pale necks festooned with cameras, their new safari clothes still creased from their packaging, their slight nervousness at being so far from wherever they came from to a place called Africa.

Fleur ordered a sea-food platter. Something which would have cost a fortune in London. She bit into a crispy garlic prawn and closed her eyes as she savoured the taste.

She thought about her sister Helene. They had been close as children, as close as two sisters could be. But after they were sent away to boarding school, she saw her sister change. Helene was already holding a place at a prestigious school in London, teaching French and English.

Helene had adapted to a new way of life in England quickly, whereas Fleur had struggled to make sense of it all. Perhaps, she mused, her sister either didn't like the place she had been born in, or worse, hadn't approved of their mother's way of life, her obsession with things other than her children. Helene thought her mother had cast them aside to achieve what she really wanted to do, follow her passion for traditional healing.

"Excuse me?"

Fleur startled out of her reverie and thoughts of her sister, turned at the sound of a very English accent. An attractive man, in his late thirties, tanned, blond and dressed in army uniform, was looking at her, his cap under his arm.

"It's getting a little crowded in here. I don't wish to intrude but may I take this spare chair? You don't have to talk to me, I promise?"

Fleur gestured for him to sit. "Of course. My sister has deserted me, I don't mind talking to you at all. After all you're wearing your credentials."

She held out her hand. "My name is Fleur Palmere."

He shook it. "Captain Michael Bennett. Thank you." He placed his cap on the table and sat in the vacant chair.

A waiter hovered over the new guest. Michael ordered a beer and a hamburger from the menu. Then turned back to her.

"Off on safari then?"

Fleur shook her head. "No. I've come from the UK to attend my mother's funeral."

Michael waited until the waiter had placed his beer in front of him. "I'm sorry to hear that. It must be a difficult time for you. My condolences."

She looked at him and frowned. "Why do you say that? You don't know me or my mother?"

Michael took a sip of his beer. "You're right, a trite thing to say, but one has to say something, not so? Bad manners not to."

She smiled at him. "Sorry if that sounded rude, I'm a little edgy at the moment. So, what are you doing here? I know they have a British army presence here in Kenya and I see from your epaulettes you are with the Medical Corps. Are you a doctor?"

"Indeed I am. Been here for four years now. Love this country, so vibrant with life, well unless you're dying of course. I love it so much I bought a simple beach house in Lamu. When I leave the army, when I retire, I shall spend the rest of my days there. It's where I want to be, but not where my family want me to be, unfortunately."

He took a sip of his beer. "Might be a bit of a scrap about that. But duty calls, as they say. I only have a month or two left on my posting here, then I shall no doubt be sent somewhere else and try to adapt to a duller sort of life."

Fleur leaned over, and without thinking, helped herself to one of his chips crowded around his hamburger. "How so?"

Michael chewed happily on his excellent hamburger and gestured for Fleur to help herself to more chips, amused at her audacity but finding it quite endearing in a stranger and a young woman at that.

"Well, I shall continue with my military career as a doctor, go wherever I'm posted, not to any hell holes, I hope. The world is a dangerous place and always has been, more so now. But eventually my family will expect me to go back to the UK and take up the reins of my inheritance. Anyway, enough of me. Tell me about you."

Fleur looked out from the terrace, watching the tour buses off-loading their safari passengers, after days in the bush. "I was born here, looking back after years at boarding school in the UK, I suppose I'm English now. My mother was French and lived here most of her life. Our holidays were spent with my grandparents in France. I don't know who my father was, she never told me. But she wanted us to be educated in the UK."

She grinned at him. "My mother was considered somewhat odd when I look back on it all now. She was fascinated by the medicinal and traditional benefits of local herbs, berries, bugs, bark, and a multitude of other things. She wandered around the bush with Noah, he was our housekeeper, and his wife, Patience, who was our nanny.

"Noah introduced her to all sorts of traditional healers and, what they called them then, witch doctors. I have a sister called Helene. She has no interest in Kenya, the UK is her home now, as it is mine, I suppose."

Fleur paused. "It's odd really, but I feel a deep connection to this country. It will seem empty somehow without her here anymore."

Her eyes filled with unexpected tears and Michael quickly moved to safer ground.

"So, Fleur, what are you studying?"

She grinned at him. "I'm not anymore. I'm a doctor like you."

Michael smiled. "Excellent field to enter into – exciting times ahead for science and medicine."

Fleur waved her hand in front of her, against a persistent fly who was more interested in the chips on Michael's plate than she was.

"Yes. But I don't want to be any old doctor, doing the hospital rounds. I want to learn about how to cure diseases. Working in an NHS hospital is hard work with little time off. On call twenty-four hours a day, mountains of forms to fill in to ensure no angry patient, or their families, decide to sue for malpractice. It wasn't what I expected, tiptoeing around being careful not to say the wrong thing and offend someone."

Michael glanced at his watch, then to an army jeep which had just pulled up outside. "I must be off, I'm afraid, my driver has arrived," he paused, picking up his cap. "Perhaps your mother had a greater influence on your life than you realise. There's a surge of interest in alternative medicines now. Even Prince Charles has become involved. I, personally, even though I'm a medical doctor, think there's some merit in some of those findings. But we need scientists, botanists, with a solid medical background, to go out into the field, to study plants, like your mother did, collect specimens and learn about the traditional use of plants for healing, or using them in tandem."

He paid the bill, dismissing her protests that she should pay for her own lunch, then reached into his shirt pocket and gave her his card. "I shall follow your career with interest. Something tells me you may well discover more than you know about yourself." He paused, "and perhaps your mother."

He hesitated. "Look, you'll feel drained after your mother's funeral. You and your sister are welcome to use my place in Lamu, take a little time out, perhaps, before you fly back to the UK.

"There's an old hotel there called Peponi. Everyone knows it, been there for years. The guy running the beach bar is a chap called Peter; he knows where my house is. I have someone who looks after the place, his name is Ali. He'll take good care of you."

Fleur looked up at him. "That's very kind of you, but my sister and I both need to get back to London. But thank you for the offer. Another time perhaps?"

Michael smiled at her. "Any time. I often invite friends to stay there, Ali needs something more to do than stare out at the sea day after day.

"Anyway, it was nice to meet you despite the sad circumstances. Good luck."

Michael Bennett thought about the woman called Fleur, she was probably no more than thirty or so, he was ten years older, but he had found her quite beguiling and most attractive. He felt it would not add to anything if he'd told her he had heard about her mother.

Gossip had always been rife in Kenya, and although he and his regiment lived a life apart, at the military base in Gil Gil, he had heard the stories of the slightly mad French woman who travelled around in her old beaten-up car, accompanied by her housekeeper called Noah, and there were stories about him too…what exactly was their relationship?

But he had been intrigued by the French woman called Christiana, the woman who had dedicated her life to trying to find alternative cures for so many diseases prevalent today.

He had been confronted by how enormous it all was. Why were so many people suddenly stricken with various forms of cancer? Alzheimer's and Dementia had become a very real problem, not seen decades before. Yes, older people became a little forgetful, it had always been like that, but not on this scale. People in their fifties were diagnosed with Dementia and other related diseases. Scientists, doctors, and specialists, all over the world, used all their knowledge and expertise to explore why it was so.

From what he had studied and read; it was not the case in many other countries of the world. It seemed to be a more western dilemma. Perhaps it was caused by loneliness. Parents left alone as their children departed for other destinations, maybe it was the despair of wondering what their place had been in their children's lives. Who they were now. Grandchildren they had never met. Their children had left them far behind to sit and watch the flickering screen of a television as night descended on yet another empty day, another one yawning in front of them tomorrow.

And he was ashamed to admit, the only winners were the big pharmaceutical companies…he knew they had first class scientists and doctors working with them on the effects of medicine, sponsored by highly qualified research teams. But even so, few cures had been found for the many diseases prevalent today.

Chapter Five

Fleur and Helene presented themselves at the French Embassy the following day. They were led through to the office of a young *attaché* who had been tasked with explaining the repercussions of their mother's death.

"You see, *mademoiselles*, it has become a little complicated. I understand you have come to Nairobi to attend the funeral of your mother, *Madame* Christiana Palmere?"

He shuffled the papers in front of him. "It is my unhappy duty to inform you your mother died some time ago, almost a year now. She has already been buried. Your mother was most specific about where she wanted it to be."

Fleur and Helene looked at each other, aghast.

"It was only a few weeks ago we were informed of her death, from someone who worked with her for many years," once again he shuffled through the papers in his file.

"A Noah Kamanti came to us here. He had with him an envelope which contained a copy of her will and within the document was where she wished to be buried. He was the one who informed us she had died some time ago. There was a signed letter, with the papers, from a mission station deep in the bush. Noah took your mother to the priest there. Noah was not an educated man, but he knew he had to have some certificate for when Europeans died.

"The priest confirmed her death and signed it off on a mission letterhead. Noah told the priest he would take your mother back to her home where the family would attend to her burial."

Fleur felt the blood drain from her face. Helene seemed unmoved.

The *attaché* continued with his difficult task. "This also seemed to be in order, the family would take care of all the funeral arrangements. However, we didn't realise at the time that *Madame's* own family lived overseas, and it would be Noah and his wife Patience who would arrange things."

Fleur leaned forward. "Noah? Yes, I remember Noah and his wife Patience, she was our nanny. But why did he wait so long before he informed the authorities of her passing?"

The young *attaché* mopped his brow with his handkerchief, and wished he were anywhere but here. He suddenly had a deep longing for the long fields of lavender, spread in front of him in Provence, where he was born. The cool breeze from the Mediterranean Sea, the different seasons, the lilt and nuances of his own language and the food of his country. Summer could be hot there, but not as relentless as it could be here in Africa.

Kenya was a true challenge, where things were never what they seemed. An obvious case in point as he sat across from the two daughters of the deceased sitting in front of him.

He drew a deep breath. "According to Noah Kamanti, *mademoiselle*s, your mother was bitten by a venomous snake as she worked out there in the bush. Noah was with her, but he was unable to save her life. They were deep in the bush, far away from anyone who could have helped him. He did his best, but it was too late. I'm sorry."

Once more he dabbed his forehead. "In his own simple way, Noah brought the proof. He brought the dead snake with him in a glass jar. Of course, there were legal procedures to be followed, but the letter from the priest, and signed by him, was enough for us here at the Embassy."

He cleared his throat uneasily as he continued. "Exhuming her body was not an option. I'm sorry to be so brutal but that was the situation. We, here at the Embassy, have a duty to any French citizen, to investigate the death of one of our own here in Kenya. However, her will was certainly legal and her wishes upon her death most specific. *Madame* Palmere clearly trusted Mr Noah Kamanti to carry out her wishes, so much so she left her home to him. It's all here in her will. The letter from the priest was genuine and we accepted it after we had checked this was indeed so. *Madame* Palmere was killed by a snake.

"The Embassy contacted your grandfather who agreed no further action would be required and your mother should be left in peace as per her wishes. We, of course, went to your mother's house to ensure if there was anything suspicious which should be further investigated. But we found nothing unusual. Mr Kamanti was a simple man, but he could not read or write, his grief over her death seemed genuine, we had no reason not to believe what he told us was the truth. I'm sorry."

Helene had asked no questions. She seemed to listen, detached, to the facts of her mother's death but had not re-acted. But Fleur felt differently.

"Therefore," she said, "there will be no funeral my sister and I have travelled so far to attend?"

"No, I'm sorry. The answers you are seeking lie with the family who inherited your mother's property at Naivasha. They will be able to tell you what happened in more detail and the circumstances surrounding her death."

He closed his file. "We will, of course, take you there. An Embassy car will collect you tomorrow as arranged by your grandfather and take you to where your mother is buried."

Chapter Six
Naivasha

Fleur and Helene were driven back to the Norfolk, consumed with their own thoughts. There was little or no conversation.

They dined in the hotel restaurant that evening and after a glass or two of wine, Fleur decided it was time to discuss the whole sad story of how their mother died, what her wishes had been, and how they should proceed from here.

"Look, Helene, we must talk about this. Yes, it was a shock to hear *Mama* had died some time ago, but there is nothing we can do about it. We must go back to the house and speak to Noah and Patience and get a more accurate account of what happened."

Helene stabbed at her steak, then threw her knife and fork down. "Let me tell you something Fleur? I personally don't care about the whys and the wherefores. *Mama* has gone. Nothing can change that, as you say.

"We both have copies of her will, from the Embassy. She made it quite clear how she wished to be buried and where. The house and its contents she left for Noah and Patience. She also stipulated, quite clearly, she did not want either of us to come to her funeral, which was unconventional to say the least.

"So, let me tell you another thing Fleur. I hardly remember her; I can't remember her spending a great deal of time with us. We grew up wild, don't you remember that? Then, when it suited her, we were packed off to another land and chucked into a boarding school – we didn't see her again, well, twice perhaps when she came to the school, and that was embarrassing, with her bare legs, her ankle and wrist beads, wearing sandals. Other mother's wore pearls or expensive jewellery, dressed in their country attire. We never came out here again for holidays but were packed off to the grandparents in Nice. She didn't even come and see us there!"

Fleur calmly patted her lips with her napkin. "*Mama* didn't have the money for that," she said softly, "she was dedicated to her work. How do we know what she felt when her daughters left the country? How do we know how hard it might have been sitting there every night on her own with only Noah and Patience for company during the day. She most certainly didn't float around the social scene of Nairobi – she was an outcast to them – somewhat eccentric they thought?"

She took a sip of her wine. "She wrote to us, Helene, was so proud of what we had both achieved, she was always interested in our lives so far away from hers. Some people don't have the choices to live the life they want. *Mama* didn't have choices. She did the best she could. She saw no future for her daughters here, but she most certainly realised the opportunities for our future careers were in the UK or Europe. She chose the UK for us."

Helene gave a dismissive shrug of her shoulders. "Well, you might be proud of what she did, I, personally don't care either way. As I told you, I don't remember her, can't even remember her voice. For me she died years and years ago. She abandoned us, as far as I'm concerned."

She picked up her fork again and poked at the steak on her plate. "I've thought about it often afterwards. Only in my case she didn't abandon me, I abandoned her. Forgot about her. I only wrote to her because it was the rules of the bloody school. Every Sunday we had to write to our parents.

"That was another thing I can never forgive her for…we don't even know who our father was! How can that be acceptable? Who was he? Where is he? Surely to God we have a right to know?"

The tears of anger and frustration were welling up in her eyes. "There's even a blank on our birth certificates where his name should have been. I mean what kind of a woman was she?"

Helene pushed her plate away. "Reception changed my return flight to London. I'm leaving tomorrow. If you want to make this ridiculous rite of passage and see her grave – well, go ahead and do it. But you'll be doing it on your own. A mound of dirt won't bring her back, it won't make any difference to me."

Fleur looked at her younger sister. "Helene, you should come with me out to the house, see where *Mama* is buried. It might help to bring closure, acceptance. I've studied all this, it's part of the medical curriculum, learning to deal with death and its long-term consequences. It might help you come to terms with who you are now?"

Helene shook her head. "No, it won't." she snapped. "Since she sent us off, I've had a difficult time dealing with relationships. Closure and acceptance don't exist in my vocabulary. I got through the boarding school stuff, but afterwards when I met a boy I liked, or, as now, a man, I was always waiting for it to blow up in my face. So, I didn't give myself completely to anyone, I always kept back a big part of myself, a bit of insurance if you like, in case they dumped me, like *Mama* did."

Fleur felt her own eyes fill with tears. "Oh, Helene, you're so angry and bitter. It was how it was then. It's what parents did, they sent their children off, not because they didn't love them, but because they wanted them to have a decent education which wasn't available in Kenya then…" Her voice trailed off.

She took a deep determined breath and continued. "I mean look at you now! You have your teaching degree, and ended up in that illustrious school, teaching French and English. You'll meet a like-minded person who will fill all those empty spaces in your heart and give you hope for a future."

Fleur dabbed at her eyes. "You'll marry and have children, and they'll fill those gaps with all the love you think *Mama* deprived you of. Once you have children of your own, you'll understand your mother, why she made the choices she did."

Helene stood up, pushing her chair back angrily, throwing her napkin on the table. A waiter hurried forward to stop the chair from toppling over and disturbing the other diners.

"Goodnight Fleur. Don't wake me up when you finally come to bed. I don't want to talk about any of it anymore. I hope you find what you're looking for when you head off for Naivasha tomorrow. As far as I'm concerned that chapter of my life is closed. I never want to come back to Kenya again."

Chapter Seven
Naivasha

With the warm glow of the rising sun promising another gilded day in Nairobi, Fleur set out on the road threading its way through the Kenyan countryside. The driver was silent as he manoeuvred through the traffic, as though sensing her aloneness, her wish to be with her memories of a place left far behind, and a mother who had gone forever.

From the back seat of the Embassy car, she caught the occasional glimpse of giraffe, zebra, and antelope in the distance. She opened her window and breathed in the scent of wildflowers mingling with the dust of passing cars. There were clusters of shops, markets selling fresh vegetables, precariously balanced on hastily erected temporary structures of plastic crates and planks held up by even more plastic crates. Vegetables temptingly displayed, blood red tomatoes, oranges, bananas, paw paws, melons, carrots, and potatoes scrubbed and washed to enhance their appearance.

There were other stalls, colourful clothing rippling in the breeze with their riotous colours. Stalls offering household items, bars of soap, cigarettes by the packet, or individually, plastic containers filled with cleaning products, feather dusters and neat piles of colourful washing up cloths.

Then the mountain of eggs balanced precariously, but artistically displayed, and the caged chickens who had produced them. Ready for eager buyers, dead or alive, preferably alive. They stood, jam-packed, pecking at each other with frustration at the lack of space in their cages, their yellow beaks agape, tiny pink tongues vibrating, as they struggled for air.

Goats, with their flat yellow eyes, tethered, their pathetic bleating with no guarantee of any long-term future.

Dotted in between these busy rural markets were simple eateries offering soft drinks and basic foods. Braziers with their glowing coals offering corn cobs and sizzling meat. No restaurants, no waiters, no seats to sit on – no, they would become the fast-foods of the future. The take-out industry of things to come. The drive-ins where you collected your cooked dinner.

In the far distance she could see the Aberdare mountains like ancient sentinels watching over the horizon, the vast expanse of Lake

Naivasha glittered like a carpet of silver, nestling in the heart of the Great Rift Valley, surrounded by lush vegetation and acacia woodlands, its surface occasionally broken by sprays of water and the grunting, belly laughs of the many pods of hippo who lived beneath its depths.

When the sun started to set in the evening the surface of the water would be transformed from silver to softer hues of amber, cream and gold, shot through with orange and red, animals would come to drink, and the exotic melodious water birds would return to their homes in the thick reeds to roost for the night amongst the tangled dead branches. A mother duck leading her ducklings home into the shallow darkened reeds leaving only the slightest of ripples behind them.

Fleur smiled to herself as all the memories of the lake returned to her when she had been a child playing with her friends, under the watchful eye of Patience, along the shores with its gentle lapping water but hiding the dangers beneath.

Finally, the car turned down a deeply corrugated dirt road and stopped at her mother's house. A dog limped towards the car, its rib cage showing through its dull coat, and gave a half-hearted bark of warning, before moving towards the shade of a tree, panting with the heat, its long pink tongue hanging out of the side of its mouth.

Her mother's simply built house looked sadly neglected since Fleur last saw it, so many years ago. The thatching on the top of the three *rondavels* sagging in places, the white paint of the walls, splashed with the red soil from the rain of the land it was built on. The once green polished floor of the veranda surrounding the haphazardly built main dwelling now faded, barely recognisable, and dotted with bird and chicken droppings. Four goats wandered around, their yellow eyes watchful, their mouths masticating making their straggly beards quiver with the effort.

Fleur suddenly felt unsure about coming back. What she remembered as a wonderful childhood home, had been claimed and degraded by time. The encroaching bush eager to take back what had been taken from it. Despite the state of her home, it still held within the two people who had loved her mother; the two people she herself had loved. Patience and Noah.

Having heard the car arrive, and the barking of the dog, Patience hastily made her way to the front door, swinging brokenly on its original rusting frame. She squinted against the bright sunlight, holding her hand above her eyes, watching the passenger alight.

"Who are you, mama, who do you seek. Are you lost?"

Fleur smiled. Patience was older, of course, had gathered a great deal of weight, but her face was the same, rounder now, a face Fleur had grown up with, a face she had loved as a child.

She held her arms out. "It's me, Patience. Fleur!"

The tears ran down Patience's face as she held the child she had known and loved once more in her arms. "You came back, my little *toto*, you have come back. I thought you had forgotten us, Noah, and me."

Unexpected tears also ran down Fleur's face. "No," she said softly. "I never forgot you, how could I?"

Patience looked over Fleur's shoulder. "But where is your sister, Helene? Why is she not here with you?"

Fleur extricated herself from Patience's fierce hug. "Helene found it too hard to come back. But I have come to see you. I came to find my mother, to say goodbye to her."

Patience took her by the hand and led her into the house. "I will make you some tea, or perhaps a glass of milk, as before?"

Fleur smiled at her. "I've gone beyond milk. Tea would be wonderful. Where is Noah?"

"He has gone to talk to your mother. He goes there every week to place flowers and remember her. He loved her you see. He remembers her every day. He goes there to talk to her of many things."

Whilst Patience bustled off to make the tea, a wide smile on her face, Fleur looked around what had been her mother's sitting room. The furniture, now faded, was still the same as she remembered. She wandered through to her mother's bedroom, running her hands over the thin bedspread of the now sagging bed. There was the same bookshelf made of planks and bricks.

Fleur looked at the faded black and white photographs of herself, her sister, and her mother. Nothing had been removed or taken. She leaned forward and smiled sadly. Yes, they certainly looked wild and unkempt with their tangled hair, wearing only shorts, no shoes. Her mother smiling broadly from beneath her wide brimmed hat.

There was another photograph of her mother bent over a pestle and mortar, looking sideways at the camera with a frown on her face.

Fleur made her way to the tiny annexe to the kitchen where her mother had kept her jars of samples, all labelled meticulously. She caught her breath – the shelves were bare. Nothing left.

Patience was calling her. Fleur returned to the sitting room, recognising the chipped cups and saucers, the old brown teapot. She was carrying the rusted frame of the photograph of her mother.

"Would it be alright if I took this photograph, Patience, something to remember her by?"

Patience beamed at her. "Of course. Come, child, let us have our tea and I will tell you about your mother. How life was for her when her *totos* left for this place across the sea. *Eish,* your mama cried many tears during this time, this she tried to hide, but not from Patience. I saw more than she knew. But, later, Miss Christy found joy and comfort in her work again and her tears dried."

Fleur was more than surprised. "She cried when we left?"

Patience nodded, "Many times, she was missing you so much. Sometimes she is going to the bush alone, without Noah. I am thinking she was not looking for her plants, I am thinking she was looking for you both amongst the shadows of her mind. Looking for your little footprints in the dust. It was hard for her to be alone without her babies."

Fleur held up her hand, although she wanted to hear more about her mother. She remembered the ways of the Africans. It was courteous to ask after their own family first, how the crops were doing, when the rains might come.

"Tell me, Patience, how is your life now? Where are your children? Is Noah in good health?"

A shadow crossed Patience's face. "Noah has another job now, he is a gardener at a farm not far from here, but it is a long way on his bicycle, he must leave when it is still dark to get there, it is also dark when he returns. But the money he is making is enough to bring food to the table. I grow vegetables but not many. Noah takes them to the village near where he is working and sells them there. Miss Christy, your mama left us this house so we would have a place to live. *Eish,* she was a good woman, always good to us, we miss her very much." She wiped her eyes with the back of her hand.

Fleur sipped her tea. "Your children? Your daughter who I played with, Noni? I remember her."

Patience stared out of the dusty cracked window and paused before replying. "You know, little missy, my childhood, before I came to work here, was happy, much happier than for children now. I was content working in my parent's *shamba*, playing my part for the family. Nobody was alone, we were a close family, grandparents, brothers, and sisters, with many cousins, aunties, and uncles. Each one of us had our place, there was much love and affection and no fear of tomorrow."

Patience wiped the corner of her eyes again with her sleeve. "Today families want more than we had. Our children leave, following their dreams of money and power in the big city Nairobi, leaving what they have always known behind, thinking they would be happy somewhere else. But happiness can only be found inside yourself not in another place."

Patience took a noisy gulp of her tea from her chipped cup. "Some of my friend's children went across the seas to another country, where it can be very cold. These children are grown up now, some even have grandchildren, have bigger families they have married into. They live in places with little rooms, in another land where there is no room there for us, their family. We are forgotten and broken now. They have gone far away."

Fleur nodded her head, knowing full well about broken family ties, fleetingly she heard her own sister's words when they had had dined together at the Norfolk.

"My mother, Patience, was she happy here on her own, after we left to go to school in another country?"

Patience beamed at her. "Oh yes. Very happy, but crying also, as I told you. Happy you had gone to another place for learning, better than here in Kenya. She missed her *totos* but loved them enough to let them go. It is what a mother does, little missy, a mother who thinks more of her children and their new lives, than she does of her own old one.

"Miss Christy was so proud of her girls. Helene a teacher of language and you little missy, a Doctor of Medicine. This she told us. She would read your letters to us, so we could follow you and not miss you so much. Ah, here is Noah!"

Fleur stood up and held her hands out. "Noah! Look at you. The same as I remember."

Noah stared at her in surprise, his face breaking into a beaming smile. "Ah, missy Fleur, it is good you have come back to see your mother now, and where she is. It is where I have been today, to sit with her and talk about all we learned together. I have been waiting for you, knowing one day you would come back. I am telling her you will come soon."

He looked down at his dusty feet with their cracked heels and split yellow toenails. "Come missy, I will take you to her now, she will be pleased to know you have come back to see her."

Fleur followed him, asking about his life since she left, the little girl she used to play with, his daughter, Noni.

"*Eish*, missy, she is leaving many seasons ago, as you did. Noni is living now in a place called Tanzania with her own husband and four children. She is too busy to come and see us, it is costing much money to get from there to here. But she is a good daughter and sends a little money when she can, it is true we need the money but also it would be better to see Noni, more so than money."

They climbed a small hill, not far from the house. "Here she is, missy," he said softly.

Fleur gazed down at the mound of rocks, there was no cross, no plaque saying who was lying beneath, only a simple bouquet of wildflowers Noah had brought earlier. Towering over the grave was an ancient baobab tree its upside-down branches reaching for the cloudless sky. In the distance she could hear the deep belly laugh of the hippos from the lake.

He hunkered down next to the grave and pointed to a log. "Here is where I am sitting when I come to talk to her, you may sit there now, as her daughter, although it is my own seat."

Fleur stared at the mound of stone in disbelief. "Tell me what happened, Noah?" she said quietly, her eyes wandering over what was left of a monument to her mother.

He sighed heavily. "We always walked in the bush together, she would show me things and I would tell her what the plant was and how it could be used, or not, some of these things growing from the ground are most poisonous. Miss Christy was busy in the deep bush. The snake came silently and quickly, looking and finding her there."

A tear slithered down his cheek. "I could not save her, there was no plant or leaf nearby which I could use to stop the poison. It was a bad snake, but I killed it anyway."

He stared at the mound of rocks. "Your mama died quickly, missy. I drove her to the mission station, many miles away, in the old car, also with this dead snake who had taken her.

"The priest was a kind man and gave me a piece of paper, which I could not read. But I knew European people must have such a piece of paper. With Patience helping me we made a bed for her from plaited reeds. Before the sun was setting, we carried her here, wrapped in this bed. Patience kept watch over your mama, as I made the hole in the ground."

He paused for a while remembering that time. "With me I had carried all her medicine bottles we had found together. When she was lying quietly there, I emptied all the bottles over her, so she could take her work with her to the next place where her ancestors were waiting."

He wiped another tear from his eye, then gestured around him. "There are many big stones and rocks here, missy. I collected these and covered her with them. There are also wild animals here. I wished for your mama to be safe from them. The hyena is always looking and looking for bones to eat…it is calcium they seek so they may survive."

His voice trailed off. "She was safe from them, as she is now. She is not lonely; I am here many times to talk about the plants and leaves we discovered, the secret things not wanting to be told. She was safe with me, but not so safe when I could not stop the snake from taking her."

He pointed proudly at the stones. "See here, missy, the plants and seeds she collected for her work have not forgotten her. I buried them with her and already they are starting to grow, in time it will be green and alive again. But not Miss Christy, it is true they will remember as we do."

Fleur reached over and placed her hand on his bony shoulder. "Why did you wait so long before you went to Nairobi to let the Embassy know what had happened?"

He shrugged. "This is what she wished for. Miss Christy did not wish to be taken from here and be buried in a land far away, where nobody would care about her, where she would not have a Noah to talk to her and look out for her, as I do. We talked about death and what should happen should this come, which it surely does. She is telling me that is what she wanted if she died here in Kenya, a place she loved. She is telling me to wait before going to the French place in Nairobi. It is where she wanted to rest, where she could hear the laughter of the hippos from the lake. The roar of the lions, the sneezing and grunts of the antelope and the call of the owl as he waited for his mate."

He frowned. "Miss Christy said I must take the papers in the brown envelope in her drawer to Nairobi. She wanted Patience and me to own this house she called her own, so we will be able to visit her and be with her. It is what I did. I am also taking the snake to show these people from another land what had killed her. I am also telling them they must not disturb her sleep – they would find nothing there for examining."

He looked at her helplessly. "I did what she asked, missy, maybe it was not right, but I thought it was so. I forgot about the brown envelope in her drawer. Miss Christy said it must go to this French place in Nairobi, but she did not tell me when it should be done."

Fleur stood up. "I think you were right Noah," she said softly. "You knew my mother better than both her children did."

Noah looked at the frayed edges of his trousers and poked at some of the red ants busy around his bare cracked feet.

"Perhaps it is so. But the thought in someone else's head is only known to them unless they wish to speak of it."

Fleur glanced at her watch. "I must return to Nairobi; the Embassy will be wanting their car back. I must say goodbye to Patience. But please give me a few moments with *Mama*, I want to say goodbye."

Noah nodded. He understood. It was why she had come back to her mother, back to her childhood home and all her memories.

Fleur placed her hands on the cairn of warm stones and rocks. "I came back, *Mama*, I came back to see you, but you have gone. I was too late. I loved you, *Mama*, I love you still. I thought of you so often here in Kenya. This is a lonely place to be buried, but Noah tells me it is what you wanted. I must respect that. I'll come again to visit you. I don't want to leave you here alone without your family, without your daughters."

Tears spilled from her eyes, as her words were carried on the soft wind which swayed the wildflowers Noah had left on her grave. Her own posy of white roses which she had brought with her from Nairobi and placed on her mother's grave looked wrong. To conventional, to modern for a woman who had led her own life amidst the wildness and beauty all around her.

"I'll arrange for a plaque to be put here, with your name, because I'm so proud of you *Mama*, for all the work you've done over the years. I'll not let you be forgotten.

"Goodbye, *Mama*," she whispered to the soft echo of her mother's voice around them both. She leaned forward and retrieved the posy of white roses. "You would have hated these. I'll give them to Patience. Noah's wildflowers are more to your liking, more like you."

The car stood with its engine idling, Patience held her close, as she had always done, the tears spilling over her round cheeks. "Go well, my child, my little *toto,* take care of your sister far from here and remember us, think of us. We shall watch over your mama; she is safe here with us, as she has always been."

Fleur hesitated briefly, then pulled away and held onto her nanny's plump arms. "Patience, I can help you with my own medicine. Noah needs it, I can see by the way he walks he's in pain."

She wiped away the tears from her old nanny's eyes. "You are finding it hard to see clearly anymore, this, with modern medicine, can help. Will you let me help you both?"

Noah had silently entered the room; he shook his head. "No, missy this is what must be. What good will this modern medicine do? It will only stop, for a short time, what is already coming? We have no need of your medicine from over the seas."

He lifted something from the table, something wrapped in a simple sack cloth. "I have kept this for you. Your mama has written many things in it, over the past seasons. She asked that I give the book to you when you came to see where she is resting. She knew you would come to find her again."

He removed the simple sacking and ran his hands over the leather cover. "I have looked after it well, because she has written things, I have helped her with," he said proudly, "and to be sure the pages of her important written words would not be eaten by the hungry moths and insects who are liking to eat paper and the words written on it. Without the book her story will only be whispered by the acacia trees and sink into the red soil of the land."

Fleur looked at him speechlessly. She remembered her mother's big leather book, how she spent hours meticulously recording her findings.

Noah cleared his throat. "I am thinking she has found something important. You have the same eyes as your mama, you must use them well to seek what she was looking for."

Carefully he unwrapped something from a piece of newspaper and held it out to her. "She is also wishing for me to give this to you. She knew you would come home one day. Miss Christy said to tell you she always held it close to her heart, as close to her heart as her two *totos*."

Fleur looked at the simple gold necklace and the worn round pendant hanging from it. She pressed the tiny catch at the side, and it opened. Black and white photographs of her daughters as small children.

Fleur and Helene captured in a time so long ago.

Chapter Eight

Fleur, from the rear window of the car, looked back at her mother's old house, saw the ancient baobab tree outlined against the sinking sun, and tried to imagine her mother lying there. But too much time had passed to many gaps yet to be filled with empty memories.

She saw Noah standing next to her mother's grave, his arm raised in farewell. She choked back her tears; it was an image which would stay with her for the rest of her life. Noah watching over her beloved mother as he had always done.

Before she left Kenya, she would arrange for a plaque to be made and delivered to Noah at her mother's house. He would place it on her grave.

The Embassy car pulled up in front of the Norfolk Hotel; holding the leather-bound book in her hands she headed to the Delamere terrace for a glass of ice-cold wine.

Helene had already left the country.

Fleur stared out into the night, watching the lights of the city of Nairobi, overwhelmed with the visit to her mother's final resting place and all she had learned from Patience and Noah of her final years.

"Well, hello again!"

Fleur looked up to see Captain Michael Bennett smiling at her. "May I join you?"

She lifted her shoulders. "Yes, please do. I could do with some company. It's been a difficult and emotional day."

Michael signalled to the waiter. "Let me buy you another glass of wine, then you can tell me about it, if you wish. Are you sure you don't want to be alone for a while?"

Fleur shook her head. "No, I don't want to be alone. You see, there was no funeral," her voice faltered. "My mother died some time ago, I'm not sure when, only nobody told us about it. But I did see where she was buried – it wasn't easy. No cross, no plaque, only a mound of rocks and stones. It's hard to deal with, but in a way I know that's how she wanted it. A sort of Kenyan way. All a bit of a shock now that I'm back in Nairobi."

She looked down at her hands. "Out there speaking to the old house staff who looked after her, well, it seemed okay, seeing her grave out in the bush…well, it doesn't seem okay now.

"To make things even more difficult, my sister, Helene, refused to come with me on the journey to see our mother. She left for London this morning. So, I have more than enough to deal with now."

Michael nodded and gestured to the large leather-bound book on the table in front of her. "That looks quite old, did your mother leave it to you?"

Fleur took a sip of wine and felt for the chain and pendant around her neck. "Yes. It's all her notes and observations on the powerful effects of using natural remedies to cure various ills. *Mama* spent years and years out in the bush and recorded everything in there."

Michael Bennett leaned forward. "May I take a look, if it's not too personal a question to ask?"

With care she pushed the book towards him. "Of course, but it's written in French I'm afraid."

Michael smiled at her. "I speak French, so shouldn't be much of a problem. Looks like quite a tome…"

He turned a few pages and seemed absorbed in her mother's findings. She watched him.

He was older than she was, but there was something about him she found attractive. He was tall and slim and walked in a loose-limbed way, a confident way, as though he knew where his place was in the world. His blond hair was cut short but hugged the shape of his head, his eyes were a deep blue, fringed with thick dark lashes. His mouth full and sensuous. But it was his hands she noticed, strong and capable, his fingers long, his nails short and square. Capable hands, the hands of a doctor or a pianist. Sensitive hands. Healing hands.

She looked out at the night, watching the traffic, making its way back home, her thoughts in turmoil by the events of the day. Tomorrow she would fly back to London and fix other people's lives, although she knew she would leave her heart here in Kenya.

Michael closed the pages of the old leather book and gently pushed it back towards her.

"It seems to me there are years and years of valuable research here, things perhaps the world is not ready for, or perhaps even more importantly, won't take seriously. You must take great care of it."

He ran his fingers through his hair. "Look, I'm a doctor, as you are. I can see you are in a heightened emotional state, which is understandable under the circumstances. It's a lot for anyone to accept.

"I want you to think about my place in Lamu. Instead of rushing back to London, where you will be plunged back into the world of medicine, why not take a few days away, take a break. You need to process the legacy your mother has left you; you need to think about your relationship with her and what today meant to you."

He placed his hand over hers. "Take some time out, learn about your mother, don't you see it's what she wanted? All her work? She has given this journal to you as a gift. Take some time away from everyone and everything. If you think her work, over all those years, has no merit, then so be it. But you owe her one thing, as a gift from her to you. At least read her book, then make your own decision."

Fleur stared through the window as the plane began its descent on its approach to Manda Island. Here the dhow would take her across to Lamu, the sea impossibly turquoise dotted with the darkness of seaweed and other life within its depths.

She carefully navigated the crumbling steps of the dock and boarded the ancient wooden dhow. The ride across the channel took little more than ten minutes. En-route they passed other ancient wooden dhows gliding by in silence, with timeless elegance, their greying sails turning to seduce the wind, as they had done for hundreds of years.

The dhow docked and she scrambled with the rest of the passengers onto the dirt quayside, clutching her overnight bag. Open air restaurants faced the water, tourists, and locals, she presumed, sat watching the endless traffic on the water. Sad faced donkeys, their heads bowed down in submission, struggled with their heavy-laden burdens as they daintily picked their way through the crowds of fisherman, heading for the dark, shadowed, narrow alleyways of the island's interior.

There were no cars on the island of Lamu and there were no dogs. The island was deeply Muslim and had been for thousands of years.

A young boy tugged at her sleeve. "I take you somewhere. You ask? I take?"

Fleur smiled at him. "Peponi. You know the place?"

The boy smiled at her. "Of course, only place famous here in Lamu for drinking. I take. You follow."

Peponi had been standing on the island for decades. Many Kenyans had chosen to retire to the simple way of life, here in Lamu, finding their own people amidst the hundreds of tourists who visited the island. Peponi, with its view across the tranquil water, it's terrace bar laden with heavy boughs of bougainvillea, it's easy laid-back atmosphere and years and years of history, welcomed locals and tourists alike.

Fleur made her way to the bar to look for the man called Peter. Michael had told her he would show her the way to his simple dwelling on the island.

A cheerful young man, with sun bleached hair down to his shoulders and wearing only ragged shorts, called out to her. "Are you Fleur? Michael's friend?"

Fleur nodded. "Yes. Perhaps you would show me where his place is? Are you Peter?"

"Sure. My name's Peter: he said I should expect you. Only five minutes away from here, give me a minute and I'll take you there."

Fleur turned to the boy who had brought her to the hotel. She rummaged in her bag and found some money. "Here you are, thank you for bringing me here."

The boy's face fell. "You don't need someone to show you Lamu?"

She patted his shoulder. "No. Some journeys are best made alone…"

He looked puzzled but happy with the money she had given to him.

He laughed. "Okay. You need me, you find me where you found me before?"

She watched him leave, such a simple life with no expectations. She almost envied him.

Peter, a thin white towel thrown over his bare tanned shoulder, led her to Michael's house and introduced her to Ali, Michael's caretaker. "There you go. Come and have a drink at the bar later, you'll meet all the locals. Michael tells me you're a doctor?"

Fleur nodded. "Yes, I am. But, right now, I'm not up to meeting anyone – I need to be on my own for a while. I have things to think about…"

Peter left with a cheerful wave of his towel. Fleur, aware of Ali waiting for instructions, looked around.

Michael's place was more than simple. It had a thatched roof, and a spacious veranda surrounded by a low wall of white stone. There was a squat square table held up by elaborate iron legs. Four planters' chairs surrounded it, designed to accommodate your entire body: their long arms readily available to rest your drink upon at the end of a long day as you watched the sun go down.

In one corner was a lush deep green palm in a curvaceous long white pottery holder, in another an assortment of woven baskets of various sizes holding dried grasses.

In the centre of the table was a hurricane lamp and a shallow wooden bowl holding an assortment of shells collected from the shores of the island.

Above the table a rattan fan turned slowly, enough to keep the flies and mosquitoes away, but hardly enough to freshen the hot humid air of a summer's day.

Down one side of the veranda, from the roof, sheltering it from the heat, was a glorious display of greenery and blood red bougainvillea and hibiscus, a stark contrast to the low white walls.

In amongst the blooms was a narrow stone table, sheltered from the heat, holding a sturdy square woven basket, with an assortment of bottles of alcohol and glasses. This, she suspected, would not have been approved of by Ali, with his long white *kanzu* and white embroidered cap of his religion.

But like all things in life, the strictly religious Muslim community, had taken cognisance of the world, which was changing around them. The island of Lamu could not survive on religion alone.

Their religious leaders, despite their reservations, knew the future lay in tourism, something they would have to come to terms with, but without losing their own personal identities or their faith.

Ali, with a wide smile gestured for her to look around. There were four rooms. Two bedrooms, an open area with cane chairs, a wooden table for eating at, the wide veranda looking out over the tranquil sea and a basic bathroom with an outside shower.

There were no paintings or pictures on any of the bare walls, no books anywhere. Nothing to remind anyone of a previous life with any memories. She smiled, yes, a perfect place to remove yourself from all that had been before. There were no carpets, no hard stone floors – only sand.

She wandered into one of the bedrooms. A stone-built bed base with a mattress, pillows, cushions, and a snowy white mosquito net and that was it. Rattan blinds shielded the room from the harsh sun.

This she assumed was the main bedroom. At the foot of the bed was a large chest, elaborately carved with brass studs, her overnight bag next to it. A fan moved slowly overhead, paddling the hot humid air, and fluttering the folds of the mosquito net.

Beneath the mosquito net, was a neat pile of *kikois*; the brightness a splash of colour against the pristine white sheets and pillows of the freshly made bed. *Kikois* she knew was probably the most versatile of fashion. They could be used for sleeping in, entertaining in, used as a towel, a cover up after a day on the beach, wrapping a baby up to sleep on the sand, used as a tablecloth or shading your face from the sun. They came in a riot of colour and designs and were the very essence of a staple wardrobe in East Africa and instantly recognisable.

Outside the coconut palms rustled and clattered with the placid wind from the tranquil sea.

Ali, hovered in the kitchen, waiting anxiously to serve her. This too, was basic. A few pots and pans, a sink, a fridge-freezer, a gas stove, and a modest cupboard which, she presumed, held cutlery and crockery and not much else.

She turned to Ali. "It's perfect."

"Doctor Michael has said to look after you well, which I will. He said you will find your way here in his place. I will make food for you if you tell me what you wish for. I will go to the fish market and buy this?"

Fleur smiled at him. "I'd like some fish and salad. I'd like to explore the heart of this place before I eat tonight. Is it safe for me to go out alone to do this?"

Ali beamed at her. "Of course. You will be quite safe." He hesitated briefly. "Perhaps, cover your shoulders with something. This is a Muslim place, one of the oldest in the world. We must respect the old traditions of our ways."

Fleur acquiesced. Opening her luggage, she found a light cotton scarf and threw it around her shoulders.

Ali nodded his approval. "I will go to the fish market for buying your dinner tonight, Doctor Fur."

Fleur made her way through to the wide shady town square. She saw shops down darkened alleyways with their doors flung open, selling fruit, silver jewellery, spices, and freshly squeezed fruit juices. An old man tended his meat on a brazier, cheerfully calling out for customers.

Old men in their long pristine white robes and embroidered white caps on their heads, sipped their coffee and talked the hours away in the small square with its shady trees, and cement benches, which seemed to be the heartbeat of the ancient town. Cats, thin and gaunt wandered beneath the trees, or found a spot pooled in sunlight where they languidly licked their bony bodies and fur as content, it seemed, as the old gentleman sipping their coffee.

Women swathed in black buibui glided past returning from the markets, their kohl rimmed eyes, sometimes hidden, sometimes not, behind an elaborate framework of mesh, their baskets held close, carrying food for their families for the evening meal.

Fleur ventured further into the old alleyways; tiny shops where craftsmen continued practicing their skill; designing elaborate, highly decorative lamps, the ancient art of brass studded carved doors, exquisite heavy silver jewellery decorated with blood red stones. Ancient crafts, still practiced here, but gone from other worlds now. The shops were dim, poorly lit, with only lanterns, as the craftsmen bent to their work, as they had always done through the ages.

She stopped at one of the dimly lit shops, she wanted some memento of Lamu. The owner smiled at her and gestured for her to look around, then he bent back to his work. Fleur picked up a black, intricately carved lantern, it was exquisite, and she knew she wanted it, wanted to take home a memory of her time here. Fleetingly she wondered if her mother had come here, then dismissed the thought; she would never have had the money to make such a journey.

Fleur would find a place for the high domed lantern in her own home; would watch the shadows of another place flicker and light her London flat, whispering its recollections and bringing memories of a place far away.

There were no designer shops here, no international companies shouting out there glittering labels, no Mayfair boutiques, or Fifth Avenue in your face modernity, no high-rise buildings. It was as it was. As it always would be, as it always had been.

Fleur smiled to herself. No celebrities would visit looking for the latest fashion and sleep in a place where the beds were made of stone and the floor was pure sand. It would never happen. Let them go looking elsewhere…

There would be no private jets coming here delivering a pot of caviar for their spoiled guests.

This was the essential essence of the place. A place that would never change, would remain as it was, true to itself. The place asked for nothing more. Yes, it wanted tourism, needed it, but on their own terms…a place in time, but it would not buy into the new world, would not tolerate the excesses and would not tolerate half naked women frolicking on their beaches, the loud music and alcohol consumed in their own piece of the world. It was their world; their place and they would keep it that way.

As it had always been.

As she walked through the shadowy alleyways, she glimpsed through half opened brass studded doors, cool open courtyards, the soothing sound of soft fountains of waters with archways leading to other shadowy adjoining rooms, cascades of tumbling bougainvillea, a riot of colours, softening the stark whiteness of the walls.

She squeezed her back against the wall as a man on a bicycle waved cheerfully at her, a basket of coconuts balanced precariously on a rack behind him.

The aroma of coffee was everywhere. Elegant brass pots sat on top of charcoal braziers, with tiny round silver cups lined up ready for thirsty customers.

Early in the evening the peace of the island would be shattered by the amplified muezzin wail from a mosque, calling the faithful to prayer, followed seconds later by other mosques. Oddly comforting, she would find.

Fleur, feeling the heat and humidity of the now late afternoon made her way back, with some difficulty, as one alleyway looked very much the same as the others. Now hopelessly lost she asked one of the locals for the direction to Peponi, once there she would easily be able to find her way to Michael's beach cottage – which she did.

Kicking off her shoes she stripped off her clothes, had a shower and wrapped one of the *kikois* around herself. Picking up her mother's leather book she settled into one of the planters' chairs and carefully opened the first page and was soon lost in yet another world of secret plants and herbs way out in the African bush.

In the background she was aware of Ali quietly going about preparing her dinner. As the sun began to set Fleur closed the leather book and put it carefully on the table in front of her.

She watched the turquoise sea change to gold and then red. In the distance an old wooden dhow floated silently and majestically by, its few lanterns already lit for the dark hours to come, and the fish they hoped to catch.

Ali padded out to her. "*Mama,* sorry to disturb. Will you be going for drinking with the white people at the hotel? Or, perhaps, you would like some refreshment from the fridge? There is a white wine there for the doctor's guests," he pointed to the sturdy basket holding bottles of spirits, "or perhaps the gin and tonic, the doctor himself is liking this when he sits where you sit now, to watch the sun going down?"

Fleur smiled at him. "I would like a glass of wine, thank you, Ali, then dinner. I haven't eaten anything all day."

Ali padded silently away and then returned and placed a glass of wine reverently on the table in front of her. "I will prepare your dinner now, *mama,* it is my pleasure. Perhaps you wish to eat out here, it will be cooler I am thinking."

Fleur sipped her wine and thought about her mother. The years and years she had spent under the unforgiving sun out there in the loneliness of the bush. The African sun is harsh, it has no recollection of yesterday and what might have happened, it only sees today, as her mother had.

Without any doubt her mother had been totally dedicated, but more than that she had believed in the extraordinary ability of nature to heal, a hidden plant with no name with the power to cure, either on its own or mixed with others. From what she had read so far, Noah had his own African names for some of the plants. If her mother had been a qualified botanist, she might have been able to give some of the plants their Latin names – but she had had no training whatsoever.

Instead, next to the description of the plant or herb, she had meticulously described what it could be used for and then sketched it in astonishing detail.

Fleur had spent seven long years training to be a doctor and had worked at one of the finest hospitals in London, the Chelsea and Westminster, and it was one of the busiest in the city. She knew science and medicine were making great headway, experimenting with new drugs to find cures for so many illnesses, but it was a slow process, it took years to have some of the new drugs passed through the legal process and approved before they could be used on patients.

Working for the NHS as a junior doctor, was a brutally hard job. Most of the doctors had no social life, they were on call twenty-four hours a day with barely enough time to snatch a meal in the canteen. Any weekend or holiday plans could be scuppered in a second if their bleepers went off and they were called back to the hospital.

They snatched ten minutes when they could, sometimes sitting upright on a chair as they dozed, desperate for some sleep or slumped across a desk with exhaustion, their heads on their arms. The hours were erratic, and Fleur sometimes worked eighteen hours a day, staggering home at the end of a shift too tired to eat, all she wanted to do was sleep.

Going from ward to ward, sometimes on her own if she was called, or trailing along behind a senior consultant, filled every hour God gave her. But the hardest thing was seeing the patients lying in their crowded wards, desperately hoping for a cure, or an operation which would give them their lives back.

Or queuing at the dispensary waiting to have their prescriptions filled out, the pharmacists as busy as the doctors as they dished out thousands of pills every day to the desperate patients who would take anything for a few hours without pain or a better quality of life – but, most of all, they had hope. Hope that the pills would perform some kind of miracle to give them back the lives they had taken for granted before they were diagnosed.

After two years on the wards, the brutal erratic hours, human drama playing out every day and families who had lost a loved one, the mothers who had lost their baby, the tears, the ragged grief, and the tragedy all around her she had finally decided it was not what she wanted to do anymore.

The end of a shift didn't mean her work was done for the day, there were still mountains of reports and notes to write up before heading for home. The legal papers which had to be signed off so the hospital could not be sued by the family for any kind of malpractice should a patient die. It wasn't the world she had thought medicine might give her, it was more about not being sued, the rigid rules and regulations of the hospital, and less about the well-being and terrifying fear of the patients who lay there in their beds.

Fleur had thought long and hard about it. There were multi-national pharmaceutical companies in the city. Her mother's dogged determination for finding cures for different illnesses was in her own blood she realised, after studying her notes and illustrations in the big leather book.

Fleur's passion had always been researching possible new drugs coming onto the market and to this end she had approached one of the wealthiest pharmaceutical companies in the world and had been accepted as one of their top researchers. The company was more than impressed with her first-class credentials and the fact that she had worked for the NHS for three years. The Foundation ploughed its profits back into research and this had appealed to her.

When news of her mother's death came through, the company had granted her two weeks of compassionate leave to fly to Kenya and put her family affairs in order. And here she was.

Ali lit four hurricane lamps, bringing them to where she was sitting, and set the table in front of her for dinner. He brought through the freshly caught fish he had bought down at the harbour, accompanied by a crisp green salad and golden chips. Fleur's stomach rumbled with hunger and anticipation, she thanked him and ate hungrily.

The only sounds around her were the rustling coconut palms, the hissing of the hurricane lamps, the sizzling of a moth or other insect drawn to the light, and the gentle sound of the sea as it lapped at the water's edge.

Ali cleared the table, topped up her wine glass and said goodnight. "*Lala Salama, mama,* I will see you tomorrow, Allah willing. I will bring you breakfast once you have woken."

Fleur wished him goodnight and reached once more for the leather book. Pulling the hurricane lamp closer she continued to read, twirling her mother's necklace through her fingers, narrowing her eyes as the lamp flickered. She hadn't taken it off since Noah had given it to her.

Buried deep in the pages of the book she found a yellowing bookmark.

NAIROBI CLUB LIBRARY – PLEASE DO NOT REMOVE THIS MARKER.

Fleur smiled, her mother was oblivious to rules and regulations. No doubt the library book had never been returned – or its marker.

An hour later she rubbed her eyes, closed the book, and made her way to the bedroom. Next to the bed Ali had placed a square plastic bowl of water and a towel. She smiled tiredly. At least there would be no sand from her feet beneath the sheets.

Fleur burrowed under the mosquito net, tucking it in behind her. She lay back on the surprisingly comfortable bed and sank into the mountains of soft pillows.

Within minutes she was asleep.

For the next two days she studied her mother's findings, making her own notes next to her mother's.

For illness in African society there is an explanation. This is what they believe. Natural, cultural, or social, angry Gods and spirits. They believe the traditional healer will heal them.

Traditional healers hold onto their powers, nothing is written, but only passed down from generation to generation. Sometimes in the rural areas, they sacrifice dogs and cats, or goats, to heal the afflicted.

Fleur raised her eyebrows at this, but read on, slowly turning the now fragile pages of the journal.

The traditional healers have effective remedies for treating malaria, stomach ailments, respiratory problems, rheumatism, mental problems, fertility etc. They study the animals in the wild observing how they know what to eat when sick.

Fleur was fascinated with her mother's astute notes and made notes of her own as she read on.

The World Health Organisation has seen something… if they can combine traditional and modern medicine to produce drugs, well, it would be a winner.

Finally, she closed the book, holding it close to her chest and took a deep breath.
What had her mother meant with her final sentence?

After all my years of research and talking to sangomas, traditional healers and medicine men and women, I have discovered something. But I was looking in the wrong places for what I really wanted to find. It is in another country, South Africa. As far as I can ascertain this plant is only found in one area of that country.

Fleur frowned. South Africa?

I travelled there, only briefly, because money has always been a hindrance to any plans I try to make. There is a region there called the Eastern Cape, there are people in South Africa called the San. They mostly lived in the desert. They are nomadic and have lived on the African Continent for thousands of years. They live extraordinary long lives and live off the land, using only their own traditional cures to treat diseases and ailments, these people guard their secrets well.

My years of research are held here in my book. I think it is invaluable information and must be guarded closely, kept carefully away from anyone and everyone.

I plan to return to South Africa to explore all the possibilities there. To find and meet these San people wherever they may now be. I shall write my findings here in my book.

But first I must find what I am looking for…and I shall.

Chapter Nine
London

Arriving back in London, after her few days in Lamu, Fleur had contacted Michael, thanking him for her stay there and giving him her contact details in London.

"The least I can do is buy you dinner, Michael. I'd like to see you again and tell you about my time at your beach house, which I thoroughly enjoyed, despite the circumstances. My *Mama's* tome, as you called it, made for fascinating and intriguing reading. Let me know when you're back in the UK."

Without any hesitation Michael had agreed to their dinner date on his return, and the many more that followed.

Now she watched the flicker of the candle which threw intricate patterns on the walls of her bedroom from another Lamu lamp she had found in a shop in London, but without the delicate touch of a master of that craft, more likely, she had thought when she saw it in a shop on the King's Road, made in China. She turned towards him and ran her fingers softly down his face.

"How long will you be able to stay this time, Michael?"

He ran his hand over the curve of her hip and pulled her close. "A few days, my darling, only a few days."

"Then where will you go?"

"The Middle East is looking dangerous, but having said that I could be posted anywhere, the world is in a mess. But it will never be my choice. I must go where the regiment sends me. It could be anywhere where the British have a base, the Middle East, the Far East, Cyprus, Gibraltar, Germany the Caribbean. It's a little-known fact that the British and the Americans have discreet bases on many a deserted coastline, watching and noting the movement of ships."

Fleur wriggled free from his arms. Pulling her *kikoi* around her, not wanting to think about him leaving again, she smiled at him. "Come, darling, we must eat now. Lovemaking makes me hungry for reality. I've prepared dinner – may I tempt you to finally get out of bed?"

Michael and Fleur had become lovers. The age difference of ten years had made no difference to either of them. His parents had sold the ancestral home in Dorset to an international American corporation who had been looking for a base in England to entertain their investors and shareholders. They planned to turn the pastures and farming land, which had been there for centuries, dotted with cattle, hay bales and sheep, into a world class golf course.

His parents had moved to a modest town in Portugal, a place they had visited on many occasions over the years, bought a simple house out in the country, far away from the tourist spots and settled happily there, relieved of the huge burden of mounting debt it took to run a country house in England.

Although Michael knew he still had a base with his parents in Portugal, he rarely had the time to visit. When he took leave from the army there was never enough time to travel to Europe – there was someone else he was keen to see and spend his precious time with.

Someone he had fallen in love with and wanted to marry and have his children with.

Fleur.

He made frequent trips to see Fleur in London and their relationship had flourished, based on the many things they had in common. He used to stay at a modest hotel but then one evening, after they had had dinner together, she had invited him back to her place for a nightcap.

He found he no longer needed to stay in the hotel…

Michael found her compact flat enchanting. Fleur had created her own little piece of Africa in Notting Hill. It was filled with light during the day and in the evenings she would fill the darkness with her ornate Lamu lanterns; he had bought her two more on his last trip to Lamu.

These were of a different design and turquoise in colour, tall and elegant with their square glass sides, throwing even more light into the darkness. These she had placed either side of a *faux* fireplace which warmed the room and created the illusion of a flickering fire.

A low white table with a cream sofa and two matching armchairs surrounded the fireplace and tall lanterns, each scatter cushion, embroidered individually with the face of a young lion or a cheetah cub on a cream background, on each one of them.

The large pictures on the walls were photographs of an exotic looking Bedouin safari camp somewhere in Kenya. The rich colours of Persian rugs, the copper tables and the hurricane lamps scattered throughout the lounge area, the dining tables with their snow-white tablecloths and many lit candles, a 1920's record player, its large, flared copper horn, catching the flickering candlelight, and the beige tented canopies, gave the place a magic all its own.

The curtains throughout the flat were muslin and pure white, sometimes softly moving like restless ghosts, not enough to keep the cold air of an English winter out but brought back recollections of another place far away. The rain, though cold here, spat and hissed against the windows, but from the cosy interior of the flat it reminded him, once again of Africa – it rained there too, but the rain was warm and welcomed and often more violent than here in England.

It was hard to believe you were not somewhere out in the bush but here in the heart of London, despite the lack of velvet nights peppered with endless stars.

In one corner of the room a bookcase was crammed with medical and research books. Her mother's leather-bound book taking pride of place in the centre, sitting on the piece of sacking it had been so carefully wrapped in when Noah had given it to her.

The kitchen was simple but practical with a modest round dining room table and two zebra patterned chairs. The handles of the cutlery decorated with the colourful and instantly recognisable exquisite bead work of the Ndebele people of South Africa.

The bedroom, when he finally got to see it, was simply furnished. The focus was the large double bed festooned with a light mosquito net; he had smiled at that; no mosquitoes in London as far as he knew. Low tables on either side, with lamps shaped to look like hurricane lamps.

As he would soon come to learn, the bed was as inviting as its sole occupant.

Now they chatted easily over dinner, discussing politics, medicine, books, and a myriad of other topics.

Michael watched her as she talked. It was her eyes he had always remembered when he first met her at the Norfolk Hotel. They were large and expressive, but it was the colour of them which was so arresting. They were blue, a blueness he found hard to describe. In the evening, he had come to learn, they became darker. Her hair was long and dark, not blonde, which was normally associated with blue eyes. She was tall and slim, her legs long and shapely. But although he found her irresistibly attractive it was her strong personality, her inquisitive and questioning mind, and her tenaciousness which he admired. Fleur, he knew, was driven by something. Something which consumed her life.

He had met lovely girls in Nairobi, dated many and had a few affairs, but found his interest waning after a few dates. Nairobi had a vibrant and carefree social life, the endless cocktail parties, dinner parties, house parties, safaris, weekends at holiday homes in Mombasa, polo, and horse racing. It was all about who you knew and the next social event. A gilded life indeed.

He would never say life and relationships were cheap there, but it seemed to him there was something fundamentally different. Few seemed to be concerned with the real meaning of life, what was going on around the globe. They seemed, overall, to flit from party to party, affair to affair, their social lives full, and it seemed to him they lived for the moment, a form of escapism from a troubled and frightening world. Something he sometimes envied.

There was nothing wrong with that, he knew. But at some point, the reality of life had to hit home, what was going on in the world; what the future held. But it had always been the magic of Kenya, he knew. People did indeed, live for the moment.

Fleur, he knew, had dated other men, had had one or two affairs she had told him about. But he felt she was living a life which would not give her what she truly wanted. Her medical and research work consumed so many hours of her days and nights.

At the weekends she would spend all the time she had at the Physics Gardens in London. The gardens were over three hundred years old and had the foremost collection of medicinal and herbal plants, collected by young botanists for decades, who had travelled the world and brought back to England exotic plants and flowers from around the globe.

Here, using the knowledge she had gained from her mother's book and her exquisite drawings, Fleur had managed to identify dozens of plants and flowers, with the enormous knowledge of one of the head botanists, and given them their correct Latin names. But there were still many gaps of plants they had not recognised but were keen to do so.

But she would not hand over her mother's book or allow anyone to copy the notes and drawings. Always she would hear her mother's warning whisper.

Be careful.

Fleur came from a different world, he knew. Her childhood, her close relationship with her mother, her difficult relationship with her younger sister, Helene, whom he had yet to meet; and her relationship with him.

His own life had followed a pattern of tradition; his father, like him, had been a military man. In that world there had been order and discipline, a moral compass to follow, a life dictated by what was happening in the world. An acceptable standard to live by with its rules and regulations.

Michael knew from the stories his father had told him that decades ago life had been different for a military man. In those days, the postings were exotic, exciting, but still following the strict rules, and dictates of military life. Postings to India, the Far East, to places like Malaya, Hong Kong, Ceylon, Africa and all over the world where the British had interests. There were lovely houses supplied for them, fully furnished with a plethora of staff to keep things running smoothly.

The social life was heady stuff for those who had never left the UK. It was a complete and unexpected life, a wonderful *entre* into a world they could never have imagined. Military personnel took their wives with them, and they too lived a gilded life. They brought their children up there with house staff and nannies available, schools provided for them, following the British curriculum, leaving them to pursue a heady social life they had no idea existed.

But within this giddy world of an expatriate life, relationships fell apart. In many ways it was too easy, too tempting. Without the strict protocols and the rigid military lifestyle they had adhered to in England, they found a new and exciting way of life – and they took it, grabbed it with both hands, oblivious to the consequences which would follow them for the rest of their lives.

But, Michael mused now, he doubted any of them had any regrets of the risks they took, as they sat under the grey and heavy skies of England, less years ahead than behind, alone with a long-ago world now lost to them. A vibrant world of colour, of laughter, exotic food, and a whirlwind social life. A feast for the senses.

He thought it must be a lonely and empty life they were living now. Memories, he knew were precious, as individual as the person who had them. Some which could be shared, but others that could never be shared with anyone; everyone had a secret life. But a world which would seep back into their minds as they trudged down the aisles of supermarkets with their wobbly wheeled trolley, recognising certain fruits from long ago when they were a normal thing to eat and not an exotic fruit, with a suitable price to match.

Today, he knew, military postings were different. Regiments were sent to dangerous places; the Middle East was a case in point. Soldiers marched on; their families stayed behind in England. There was no place for social niceties. No cocktail parties, no social life – only the brutal recognition that it was now war with an unknown enemy – a war with many facets. A faceless enemy.

Fleur watched Michael against the faltering flickering remains of the candlelight. She had been successful so far in the world of medicine, and Michael had enhanced her entire life. But still she wanted more…

Her sister Helene she didn't see as often as she would have liked, hardly at all when she was working in the hospital. Helene had changed considerably, she seemed to have shrugged off the trauma, as she had perceived it, of her childhood in Kenya, her years in boarding school, and embraced her life as a young and very attractive teacher in a prestigious school in London.

"You see, Fleur," she had said when they had dinner two months ago, "I've changed." She took a deep swallow of her wine. "I've accepted everything now, my childhood, my absent mother, the years in boarding school, because something changed.

"From thinking I must be ugly, unattractive, not worthy of love, well, it took a while, but suddenly I found men really liked the look of me and it opened a whole new world for me. I had something they wanted. They wanted me." There was a challenge in her eyes as she looked at her sister.

Fleur narrowed her eyes. "What on earth are you trying to tell me, because I'm not sure I want to hear it?"

Helene's blue eyes, the same colour as her sister's, the same colour as their mother's, closed briefly, then opened.

"To be *wanted* was all I ever craved. Men want me, they like me, they like the fact I don't want anything from them. I have discovered the world of passion and sex, with no strings attached!"

Fleur shook her head firmly. "No, you're wrong. You're also taking a lot of risks with sexually transmitted diseases. A new one called AIDS, which there is no cure for, is spreading quickly. You won't find what you are looking for by sleeping with men and having affairs."

Helene waved her wine glass around the restaurant. "Oh, but I will. I don't want to get married, but the one thing I do want is a child of my own. Someone who will belong to me and only me."

Fleur nodded. Her sister was in an aggressive mood assisted by the amount she was drinking.

"Well, I don't care if you approve, or disapprove of my lifestyle, Fleur. After all you have your cosy little life with the Captain from Kenya, don't you?"

Fleur nodded. "Yes, I do, Michael is my whole life, I love him, very much. But he's away a lot, I'm not sure about the long-term future. I'll have to wait and see."

Fleur took a sip of her wine. "So, with the many lovers you have in your life, who might, should you become pregnant, be the father of the child you so desperately think will save your life? Don't you think he would have the right to know?"

Helene laughed bitterly. "Don't you think we had the right to know who our father was?"

She caught the attention of a waiter and pointed to her glass. Fleur frowned. "Don't you think you've had enough? Three gin and tonics before dinner as well as a bottle of wine and now you want more?"

Her sister grinned at her. "Yup. Then when we've finished dinner, I'm meeting some friends. We're going clubbing where I shall drink as much as I like without you glaring at me with disapproval. I know you don't take any prescription drugs, but at these wild parties I go to they have drugs, no prescription required, they make me happy, very happy, they take me away from the world for a few hours."

She took a large gulp of her refreshed glass of wine. "You should try to loosen up a bit, Fleur, have a bit of fun now and again. You're boring you know, always poring over books and down the lens of microscopes. But maybe your Captain from Kenya is as boring and it's why you get on so well together.

"What happens if the good captain wants to marry you and have a family. You'll have to give everything up, won't you? The long hours you work won't leave any time to bring up children, the captain, no doubt, will spend a lot of time fighting his wars, so where will that leave you?"

Fleur stared at her sister. "Don't be a bitch Helene," she snapped. "We haven't talked about marriage or children. He's ten years older than me, the army is his whole life, he's as dedicated to military life as I am to my research. Anyway, you're drunk and I'm not enjoying the conversation one bit."

Fleur stood up then bent to kiss her sister on both cheeks. "Take care Helene. You need to look after yourself…you're treading a dangerous path here with your health."

Chapter Ten

Michael returned from the Middle East on his way to Portugal. He spent one night with Fleur, and she was concerned at how tired he looked, how thin he had become.

"It's so good to see you, my darling, I need you now even for a brief time, before I must fly to Portugal. Something happened to my parents."

His eyes had filled briefly with unexpected tears. "They're dead, Fleur. A wildfire was spreading across where they were living, up there in the hills, it was a scorching hot summer. They didn't have time to escape before the fire engulfed the house. They're gone.

"There are things I need to do, legal things, insurance etc. The army has given me a week of compassionate leave, then I must return to the regiment. But first I must go and see what happened in Portugal."

That night their lovemaking was intense and raw. She held him in her arms as he wept at the loss of his parents. "You're all I have now, all I have left Fleur. I want to marry you, I need you. I want to have children. I want to have a more real life, away from the horror of what I've seen, the devastation, the dead bodies of my men, blown up by roadside bombs, picked off by snipers. I want to wake each day and have you next to me, be my anchor, and give me hope."

Fleur could feel the claws of sadness and loss as they bit into him. "Hush, Michael. We can talk about marriage and children some other time; this is not the right time. Go to sleep now. You need to rest before you confront the reality of tomorrow."

She stroked his back. "I met you in Nairobi at a bad time in my life. I'd lost my mother. You helped me through that, letting me confront what had happened to her, at your house in Lamu. You were kind and compassionate and I thought a lot about you during that time.

"I'll never love another man the way I love you, my best friend, my lover, my life. Now sleep, my darling. I'll always be here for you; I'll wait for you for as long as it takes. You're safe here with me, far away from the terrible things you've seen."

Michael didn't have the time to return to London and see Fleur, but he called her before he left to join his regiment once again.

"It's all gone, my darling, the house is no more, my parents' bodies were never found," his voice broke briefly. "There was no funeral. I'll have to live with that, as you did. All the mementos of our life together, all the photographs, the things I remember from our home in England – all gone.

"The house was not insured. There's nothing left of our lives as a family together. You're my life now. I'll hold on to that to carry me through the war and count the hours before we can be together again; start to rebuild my life, our lives. I'll write to you. I love you, Fleur. The thought of us being together, being married, having children – it will keep me going and give me hope for the future.

"We'll spend time in Lamu, watching the children play, watching them grow up, we'll be happy there, you and me. The world is changing, becoming dangerous, but there in Lamu, things will remain as they have done for thousands of years. It's a good place for us to be, a peaceful place far away from the modern troubles of today."

He paused for a moment. "It's where I want us to be."

Chapter Eleven

Fleur thought about Michael constantly, knew what he was going through, from seeing the terrible news coverage of the wars in the Middle East, and knew how much he needed to hear from her. She wrote to him every week, telling him about her work, how she was trying to assimilate it with the research her mother had done, how overwhelmingly important it was becoming to her. Her letters had to go via his regiment's headquarters, leaving her with no idea of where he was.

Michael returned wearily, from time to time, and spent precious moments with Fleur, but she sensed that this time he had a lot on his mind.

"You're off again soon aren't you, darling. Where to this time?"

Michael turned towards her and held her tightly in his arms, feeling the warmth of her next to his naked skin. "Not a good place, unfortunately, it's back to the Middle East."

He pushed back the hair from her forehead and kissed her. "I've decided to resign my commission when I get back. I want to be with you, Fleur, it's the only thing I want.

"I can find a job here in London at one of the hospitals, as a civilian, a doctor. Or better still at one of the Military hospitals out in the country where they treat soldiers who have had their arms or legs blown off, their minds shattered; a rehabilitation centre, where they try to heal the body and the mind."

He lay back. "I could be useful, having seen the effects of war myself. Many soldiers have come back from the war zones not only with missing limbs and other terrible injuries, but also with shattered minds, it's something I would be keen to be involved in."

He paused for a moment. "I've given this a lot of thought, my darling. You could move out of London and work with me, go back to what you were trained to do – practice medicine. We could get married and finally be together, work together, until we decide to start a family."

He propped himself up on his elbow and looked down at her. "What do you think?"

Fleur looked away at the candle flickering next to the bed. "You need to give me time, Michael, it's a lot to think about. I'm not sure I want to practice medicine again; I love what I'm doing now – the research and all the possibilities I see.

"But I need to go back to Africa and follow up on my mother's work there. Whatever she found seems to be of paramount importance and I want to continue with that search, not in Kenya but South Africa. You do understand, don't you?"

He smiled at her. "Yes, of course I do. My dreams of one day returning to Lamu and living with you there can be put on hold until you come back from foraging in the bush."

He lay on his back. "Maybe think about going whilst I do my tour of duty in the desert. It seems I'll be there for a year at least. But I can handle it if I know you're also doing what you need to do. But how will you fund such a trip, Fleur. Where will you stay and how will you pay for it all."

Fleur sighed. "I'm not sure yet. I had a modest inheritance from my grandparents, but I blew most of it on buying a place in Lymington, in Hampshire. It's rented out, so that will help. But I'll have to resign from my job at the pharmaceutical company, I'd already made plans to do that anyway."

Michael was quiet for a moment. "I want to help Fleur. I also have my inheritance from my parents, from the sale of the country house. I haven't done anything with it yet."

He turned her face to his, running his fingers across her lips. "Let me become involved in your mother's journey and yours. Let me finance it, let me contribute something to the world of science. I need to know you'll be safe. If you agree, I'd like to have a monthly amount put into your account, so you don't have to worry about money?"

She buried her face in his shoulder. "No wonder I love you so much, darling, always doing so much for everyone else without giving much thought to your own needs. Yes, I accept your offer and thank you. I want to continue with my mother's journey and now I'll have you beside me every step of the way, being a part of it, being with me."

He gazed down at her. "You will marry me one day, won't you Fleur?"

She pulled him down to her. "Yes, my darling, of course I will. It's what I want, it will keep me going as well, knowing you'll be waiting for me, when I come back. I'll always love you, never forget that. Always. Now come here…"

Sometime later, Michael glanced at the clock next to the bed. "Okay. Let's get dressed and go out for dinner. We can discuss all of this in a more upright position, my Fleur."

Over dinner they discussed the next year, what they both might be doing and how they would go about it.

Michael watched her as they ate; she looked preoccupied he decided but put it down to the marriage plans they had now put into place, of course she was preoccupied, as he was.

He took a sip of his wine as the waiters removed their plates. "There's something else I need to discuss with you. Our family lawyer, my parent's lawyer and now mine, has his office here in London in Knightsbridge."

He signalled for his bill. "His name is Jeremy Foxton. Decent sort of chap, old school. He knows my family well," he stumbled briefly. "He knew my family well. As a serving officer in her Majesty's Armed Forces and all other personnel, we're required to have a lawyer with our wishes carefully detailed in case of any unforeseen circumstances.

"I want to talk about your mother, Christiana. Her years of research and what she discovered could be valuable. If her leather book fell into the wrong hands, well, her name would never be mentioned again, and a pharmaceutical company would become immensely rich with her findings, taking all the credit, as you well know."

He tucked his credit card back in his wallet. "I know you're not using any of your mother's information in the research you're doing now, so all of it remains your property and not the company's. When do you think you will resign and set off for South Africa?"

Fleur shrugged. "It's a big decision but I think I'll resign in the next day or two and leave for Africa soon after that. The timing seems right. I don't want to stay in London if you're not going to be here – it will seem too empty somehow.

"I've already warned the Chairman that I'll be leaving, he's started looking for a replacement for me. He has someone in mind, a Kenyan doctor, very clever by all accounts, and well qualified to replace me, but I will need to spend some time with him to ease him into to my old position."

Michael reached for her hand. "Don't take the book with you. The Armed forces have embraced technology, still in its infancy to some extent. I'll be stationed, for a few weeks, in a place called Bovington, down in Dorset. If you agree, I can take the contents of your mother's book and have the information put onto a floppy disc. You need to type up all the information, take photographs of her drawings and add your own observations. It would be easier, and safer, to take discs with you rather than the book."

Fleur twirled her wine glass as she listened. "Start your own book, Fleur, then you can add to the information of your mothers on the floppy disc when you get back. I would strongly suggest you leave your book with Jeremy. It'll be safe there, away from prying eyes.

"If anything should happen to either of us, Jeremy will know what to do. It will, of course, be totally up to you. You may instruct him to destroy the book or donate it to a company you trust."

He reached across the table and took her other hand. "Why the tears, my darling. I think it's a good and sensible plan."

She stood up, steadying herself with the back of her chair. "I need to visit the ladies. Give me a minute or two will you Michael?"

He sat back and watched her make her way through the tables. There was something bothering Fleur. Perhaps she was dreading the time when they would have to be apart again, as much as he was.

Their brief time together came to an end. As Michael had suggested she had spent many hours typing up her mother's research and findings, had taken photographs of her exquisite illustrations of the plants, bulbs, and flowers she had found. These she had given to Michael.

On their last night together before he began his posting in the desert, he'd given her the details of his lawyer, Jeremy Foxton, and the floppy discs which held her mother's life of research in the African bush.

He held her close for their final goodbye. "You will write Fleur won't you. I'll live for your letters and enjoy reading about all your adventures in Africa."

Fleur pulled away from his fierce embrace and held both his hands in front of her, unsuccessfully trying to hold back the tears.

"Of course, I will, although I'm not sure where you'll send yours. But I'll sort something out when I get settled, I doubt the postman will deliver mail in the middle of the bush, but I'll find a post box somewhere in the nearest town.

"I love you, Michael. I'll live for the day when we can be together again. Whatever happens I will always know where to find you.

"Lamu."

Chapter Twelve

A few days later the CEO had come into her laboratory. "Fleur, this is Doctor William Mwanga, he's from Kenya and joining our team. I'll leave you to it then, shall I?"

Fleur held out her hand. "Hello Doctor Mwanga, I'm delighted to meet you."

William gave her a wide smile. "I believe we both have a history in Kenya. I heard about your mother when I was a boy. I recognised your name immediately. Palmere, right?"

Fleur stared at him. "Yes, Christiana Palmere was my mother. Did you meet her then?"

"No, unfortunately not. But her name is well known, a name whispered through the years. I understand she was an extraordinary woman?"

Fleur felt her stomach flutter with pride, her eyes prick with tears. "They remember her then?"

William smiled. "Indeed, they do. But, of course, without meaning to offend, she was considered a bit eccentric by the Europeans then, however, we Africans saw what she was looking for, understood the old ways of medicine which she had found. Unfortunately, it has no place in the world today."

Fleur gestured for him to sit down, containing her emotions, as he continued. "There are some research companies who have tried to listen to the old ways of Africa, but mostly it's only mumbo-jumbo, to them. Not fit for purpose in the new world. Far more money to be made with synthetic drugs."

William looked around the laboratory with its high technology. "Medicine, research, science, well, it's galloped ahead, which is a good thing, not so?"

Fleur frowned. "I don't agree. Traditional medicine has a place in the world today. I've always believed that, as my mother did."

Mwanga removed his glasses. "It seems the old ways have no place in the new world. People want a quick fix with a brand they respect, produced by a respected pharmaceutical company."

Fleur crossed her arms, feeling anger at the way he had dismissed and insulted her mother's belief in her work. "So, what are you going to research here in the laboratory then?"

He grinned at her, his perfect teeth white against his African skin. "The use of traditional medicine has prompted the World Health

Organisation to explore and experiment with combining traditional and modern medicine to produce drugs. In South Africa, for instance, eighty percent of the rural Africans who don't have access, or the money to go to city hospitals and clinics, use what they call *muti.* Nothing is written down in their world but passed down. There are no safety regulations in place."

He put his glasses on. "International pharmaceutical companies are racing against each other to incorporate the old ways with the new. To find the secrets of that old world. That's what I'm here to do; to help them replace the old with the new."

Fleur glared at him. "You do realise, of course, for those rural Africans it's about more than that. It's about their absolute faith in nature and the traditional healers…The mind is a powerful thing."

She sat back in her chair. "You think a packet of pills with a long stream of paper explaining all the side effects and compounds of the drug, the cost of such pills, do you really think it will turn them more towards western medicine? Half of them can't read for a start. The long list that comes with the pills will mean nothing to them, surely you can see this. All that printed information is to protect the big pharmaceutical companies from being sued, they must list every possible remote thing that may go wrong."

She shook her head. "Those Africans who can read or get someone to read the long list for them, will be more terrified of the side effects of the drug than its healing properties, and let's face it, it's only putting a temporary band aid on the problem. The problem will return if they don't continue to take the pills – exactly what the big pharmaceutical companies want."

William grinned at her. 'Well, that's what they're paying me to do here, using my extensive knowledge of traditional medicine and formulating it into something more scientific and produce a pill which will cure all the old ailments."

Fleur shrugged. "I wish you well then. In a way you are betraying your people with your brave new world, fooling them into believing what has yet to be proven."

He shook his head. "I'm not betraying my people; I'm trying to help them and millions of other people around the world. Traditional healers will eventually die out, technology is the way forward. Western medicine is leading the way. Sick people have complete faith in the white man's medicine. People are leaving the rural villages of Africa and heading to the cities – looking for jobs, looking for a better way of life, difficult to find traditional healers there. They pop a pill and have utter faith it will cure them, or at least help them cope with the pain."

Fleur took off her white coat. William's words had struck a sour and angry chord with her – their philosophies on traditional and modern medicine were poles apart. She doubted very much, should any cures be found for any rare diseases, the local people would not benefit in any way. The cost would be out of their reach.

"Well, good luck with your new job William. I have to say I don't like your arrogance. You'll find all my research files, my findings. Make what you will of them."

William looked confused. "Where are you going?"

Fleur started to empty her drawers, selecting a few of her own personal files from the cabinet, then covered her microscope with its protective cover.

"I'm leaving. It's all yours now. There are six other experts in their field working here, I hope they'll go along with your misguided philosophy."

The other members of her team kept their heads down feigning deep concentration as they listened to the fiery exchange from their boss Doctor Palmere and the new arrival.

William looked at her over his glasses. "I hope within all your files, papers, and records, I'll be able to pursue some of your mother's findings. She must have recorded them somewhere, given them to you when she died?"

Fleur glared at him. "Yes, of course she did. But they belong to me and only me. You won't find any trace of her here – perhaps an anecdote or two.

"You follow your path William – but you're not taking me, or my mother, with you. Is that perfectly clear to you?"

As the door of the large laboratory slammed behind Doctor Palmere, one of the research assistants stood up and came towards him. "I was waiting to be introduced but it seems our Doctor Palmere is having another one of her hissy fits. Not easy to work with I have to say, but she knows her stuff. Been here for some years now. I'm Hansie."

William turned and held out his hand. "Have you worked with her for long?"

"Yup, about three years. More admin and transferring information to the computer, it's all about technology now. Tedious but necessary work," he gestured around the room. "You have some interesting scientists to work with here, they come from different parts of the world. China, India, Europe, Africa."

William smiled at him. "Where are you from then?"

"South Africa. Studied botany at the University of Stellenbosch, then spent a few years in the bush as a game ranger up in the Sabi Sands, but the money was poor, and I got fed up with the endless game drives twice a day. Tourists only wanted to see the big five and were not particularly interested in plants, flowers, and bits of bark."

He rubbed his face. "Got fed up with it all actually, changed lodges a few times, but tourists are the same with their stupid questions, like, 'what time will we see the lions' I lost respect after a while. Africa was a place to visit on their bucket list. Once when some American asked me if she could get out and stroke some of the lions, I just lost it.

"I was tempted to tell her to hop out and go right ahead. Plenty more tourists out there. That was the moment I knew I had to do something more worthwhile."

He laughed. "Being a game ranger is not a glamourous life believe me."

William Mwanga studied him. "So, you gave it all up, came here to the UK, joined the company and pursued your love of botany, right?"

"Yup. That's what happened. I learned a lot from the feisty Doctor Fleur, she had a lot of information which she learned from her mother in Kenya, but she wasn't going to share any of it. To be fair she made a huge contribution to the company, but I always felt she was holding something back, something she obviously felt was important, but clearly didn't want to share with anyone. That woman trusted nobody. But I know she was onto something, something important, she mentioned it a couple of times without giving any details. But I have a pretty good idea of what it was and where she was looking for more information. South Africa."

Doctor Mwanga polished his glasses, feigning disinterest. "A cure for cancer perhaps?"

Hansie laughed. "No. For years doctors and scientists have ploughed millions into trying to find a cure for cancer including us. Still haven't found it, or maybe one of the big pharmaceutical companies have found it and want to keep that information to themselves. Billions of dollars of revenue come from treating cancer patients."

Hansie looked at Fleur's now empty desk. "No, Doctor Palmere was onto something else, something truly astonishing, but she wasn't going to share that information with anyone until she was satisfied, she had indeed found the cure for whatever it was.

"Anyway, let me introduce you to the rest of the team."

After doing so Hansie watched the new doctor sit down in Fleur's chair and adjust the levers on the side to suit his tall frame.

Hansie grinned at him. "Well, I hope you enjoy your new position, I'm thinking of resigning as well, going back home for a bit of a different climate, these dark low clouds, the rain, and the cold are not good for my soul, or well-being. But I wish you luck. Doctor Palmere will be a hard act to follow."

William made a quick decision. "I'd like you to continue to work in this department. You'll be able to contribute a great deal from what you learned from Doctor Palmere, plus, you are a South African and from your years as a game ranger, well you'll know the country more than most, know the bush and all the areas."

Hansie nodded. "*Ja*, I certainly do."

William kept his face devoid of any emotion. "From what I can gather Doctor Palmere had turned her research from Kenya to South Africa. You're a South African, you're a botanist and you have worked with the good doctor for some years." He paused. "Or perhaps you are planning to meet up with Doctor Palmere and work with her?"

Hansie looked at him in astonishment. "Absolutely not, hasn't even crossed my mind!"

"Good. You know the lie of the land there; you could be a valuable member of the team. If Doctor Palmere plans to go to South Africa in the future, then she will be following some important knowledge, which our company have shown a great interest in, but she has been reticent about what it is. As far as I can gather she has used none of the equipment or used her time here to work on whatever it is she is working on. Therefore, she is not legally under any obligation to discuss anything with the company which she clearly considers to be private information gathered from her mother. The company cannot make any claim to it."

Doctor Mwanga adjusted his glasses. "I'd like you to stay and work with me. Then, we can decide how to move forward, perhaps a promotion within the department might persuade you. How does that sound to you. Something more interesting which will give you the incentive to stay on, my assistant maybe. Perhaps a field trip to South Africa now and again?"

The South African nodded his head. "Happy with that. Hey, how about we go down to the local pub, have a drink, Will?"

Doctor William Mwanga looked at the eager face of the South African. He knew many great doctors and scientists were South African born, including the legendary Chris Barnard who had performed the first ever open-heart surgery, he had the greatest respect for them.

He looked at the solid, strong looking South African in front of him. He had taken an instant dislike to him and his strong accent, his familiarity with his future boss, but he also saw how useful he might become as a botanist out in the field.

The ex-game ranger stood. "Shall we go then, have a couple of pints. I want to know how those white Kenyans ever got to grips with handing over their country of milk and honey to the blacks, hey. Long time ago now, most of the whites have left and gone to wherever, from what I remember."

Doctor Mwanga held back his temper. "Actually, the European people who were born in Kenya and the generations that came after them, are still there. President Kenyatta encouraged them to stay after Independence, many of them did. They had no-where else to go. Our people and white Kenyans may have complaints with how the country has changed under a Black government, the older ones. But the new generations live happily and content, mixing easily as one people. Blacks, Europeans, Indians, after all they are where they want to be, is that not so?"

Hansie heard the change of tone in the Doctor's voice, now with an edge to it.

"You have big troubles in your own country, young man. I think you personally may have problems with adjusting to this. You'll have to adapt, as the whites did in Kenya...but I fear you Afrikaners will have a problem with it."

William stood up. "I have no wish to join you for a drink; I do not partake of alcohol. I shall recommend to the board of directors that you are appointed my assistant. Meanwhile you will address me by my correct name which is Doctor Mwanga.

"We will work together, and you will follow my instructions, is that clear? Also, I should tell you I am not particularly fond of South Africans or their politics, nor do I wish to join you in any social activities."

Hansie shrugged. He had nothing to lose. He still had a future with the new head of department of research with this international company. If things worked out, or didn't, he could return to the country he loved, and work from there. Doctor Fleur Palmere had been a hard person to work for, her standards impossibly high. In her world speculation did not exist. She wanted hard facts and proof.

Hansie knew instinctively she would now turn her sights to South Africa and go on her way to find what she was searching for. He had an idea of what it might be. Although she had never discussed it with him or anyone else in the company.

He put on his coat, wrapped his scarf around his neck, picked up his rucksack, wished Doctor Mwanga a pleasant evening, not that he cared either way if he had one or not.

He was off to the pub to meet up with his fellow South African mates and watch a bit of rugby, speak their own language, Afrikaans, and not care if they offended anyone or were politically correct with their conversation.

Chapter Thirteen
London

Fleur tossed and turned in her wide empty bed. The phone next to her rang, it was two in the morning. She knew it wouldn't be Michael calling her, he had been in the desert somewhere for a month now. It could only be her sister Helene; she groped for the phone.

"Fleur? I need your help?"

Fleur sighed. "You're drunk, Helene, that's all. Take a couple of aspirin and call me again in the morning, okay?"

"No, Fleur. I'm frightened what I might do to myself, worse than I've already done. Please come, I'm in my flat. I need you."

Fleur sighed again and sat up. "Alright, I'm on my way; stay calm alright?"

Fleur sat across from her sister Helene. Her hair was lank and greasy, her face puffy from drugs and drink, her grubby dressing gown wrapped tightly around her thin body, the remnants of past take-outs spattered down the front. Her hands shaking as she tried to clasp them together in front of her.

"I've been fired, Fleur, they don't want me anymore, just like *Mama* didn't. I was drunk during one of my classes, but it appears it wasn't the first time. Even my wild party friends have abandoned me. Nobody wants me. Not even you."

Fleur leaned forward. "That's not true, Helene, you're my sister and I love you, as I always will, despite everything. But I've watched you over the years, despaired with your drinking and drug problems, your wild party life. Your endless affairs, and, yes, sleeping around, always trying to find something to make you find yourself again.

"Nobody will ever be able to give you what you're looking for. Only someone who really cares for you, someone who will always love you come what may – that's me."

Fleur stood up and paced around her sister's chaotic flat, seeing the take-out boxes piled on the kitchen floor. The mountain of unwashed dishes scattered around the kitchen. The empty bottles and full ashtrays everywhere. The place smelled bad, the bedroom with its stained sheets, the bathroom smelling of drains.

"Look at this place, Helene, it's disgusting."

Helene covered her face with her hands, tears seeping through her fingers. "Will you help me, Fleur? I don't want to be here anymore, really, I don't. Nothing seems to work for me."

Fleur sat down again and took her sister's hands in her own. "Helene, if you carry on like this you'll destroy yourself, you'll never find what you're looking for. I'll help you, but I need to take you out of London, far away from the crowd you're mixing with. You must give up the alcohol and the drugs. It doesn't help you; it only blurs the edges for a few hours. It's not the answer and never will be."

She pushed her sister's hair back from her face. "You need to heal your own body, nurture it with good food, not take out junk. You need to face the reality of who you are. Not what you are trying to do to ignore it by drowning yourself in booze and drugs and unstable relationships."

She paused for a moment, knowing she was being tough on her little sister, but also knowing it was the only way in the circumstances. "You've lost your job, no other private school will take you on, not now. Word travels fast. We both inherited money from our grandparents. You I have no doubt, have blown it on drugs, booze, and parties."

She looked at her sister and frowned. "You're not pregnant, are you?"

Helene leaned back in her chair. "No, I don't think so, I'm not throwing up in the morning," she gave a wobbly smile, "only when I've overdone things a bit the night before."

Fleur shook her head in despair, her mind suddenly made up. "You said, one day, you wanted to get out of London and live on the coast. I looked for somewhere on the coast and found a place you might like. It's called Lymington, in Hampshire. I bought it some years ago and rented it out. Why not think about going there and starting a new life, away from this one you are so caught up in?"

Fleur took a deep breath. "I want you to come away with me for a few months, just the two of us. I'll put you back together again. It won't be easy for you, I know, but I'll help you.

"Hand in your notice on this flat. You won't be coming back to London, that I can promise you."

Helene looked at her sister. "What about your job here in London?"

Fleur took a deep breath. "It will suit me as well. I resigned from my job, and I need to plan what I'm going to do next. You're not the only one with obstacles to overcome. But, I think, we can do it together."

Chapter Fourteen

Fleur found a place where she could take her sister. It was a simple farmhouse in Yorkshire, hidden amongst the windswept desolate Dales. Miles from the nearest town of Pickering. Helene, she knew, could not drive, she herself would have to shop once a week and leave her sister alone at the farmhouse where she wouldn't be tempted to fall back into her old bad habits.

Helene was beginning to look better, healthier. It had been brutal for her in the beginning as she fought with her demons, but her health had improved considerably. Her anger and frustration with life had subsided. She had been given another chance, by her sister, and she was eager to start a new life somewhere else. It wouldn't be easy. But like her sister Fleur, she was determined to make things work. Determined to have a new life somewhere else.

The remote farmhouse was perfect. They had no visitors, no distractions from the outside world. During the day they would walk for hours, sleep in the afternoons, and spend the evenings reading, watching television, or playing card games, and talking long into the night about their futures.

The baby came a little sooner than either of them had anticipated. With guidance from Fleur, the little girl was placed in her sister's arms.

"Something of your own, Helene. What will you call her?"

Helene looked down at the tiny baby. "I shall call her Lucy."

Helene took the baby back to her sister's place in Lymington, and there she put her life back together.

It had everything she needed to bring up her baby. Helene took her out every day, pushing the pram through the old town, through the weekly open-air markets, and down to the quay where she would sit and whisper quietly to the child as she looked out towards the distant island of the Isle of Wight, watching the ferries go back and forth.

She joined the library, became involved with the church there, gradually building up her own little social circle. She found a place for Lucy at the local crèche and offered her own services, free of charge, to look after the children.

There was a good school there and, in time, Helene started to teach the little ones, going back into the world of teaching that she had loved.

Helene had finally found her own way home. She was content with life although it had come at a heavy price.

Fleur had given notice on her flat in Notting Hill before they went to Yorkshire. Her tenants, in Lymington, had been given notice and she had moved all her own things there. The Lamu lamps, the furniture, and the pictures on the walls.

Fleur had already planned to go back to Africa. To find her way back to where she came from. They had spent months before Lucy was born planning their futures.

Many years later Helene had to confront the truth. The price had been a high one to pay, perhaps too high. But like all major changing decisions in life, it was only when you looked back you realised how much it had really cost you.

Helene had lost touch with her sister. Yes, she knew she was in South Africa, out in the rural areas, following in the footsteps of their mother. Communication was impossible.

Helene had looked down at her sleeping daughter. She knew she had been given another chance at life, and she was going to take it with both hands, whatever the price might be.

But the ultimate price would be high.

Chapter Fifteen

Fleur looked at the carefully written letter to Michael. Reading it again and again, before folding it and carefully sliding it into the waiting envelope.

My darling Michael,

I am sending this to your military base, knowing they will send it on to you, wherever you might be in the Middle East.

My sister Helene has recovered well and given birth to a little girl. I've never seen her so happy or content. She has no idea who the father is, but she doesn't care much about that, she has finally found what she was looking for. Someone she can truly call her own and pour all the love and care she has been holding back for so many years. Helene and the baby, Lucy, have moved into my little place in Lymington.

This part of the letter is unbearably hard for me to write.

I won't be coming back to you Michael. Africa has always been my home, difficult to explain unless you were born there, as I was. But it's where I want to be.

I love you dearly, and I always shall, but marriage and children will never be enough for me. I must follow my destiny.

I have to let you go.

I know you have dedicated your life to the army, and I understand it's your whole life. You were prepared to resign your commission to be with me, but I don't think it would have made either of us happy, it would never have been enough. You would be doing something in a civilian capacity in England, and I don't want to ever work in a hospital again or be part of a big company who dictate what you can do and what you can think.

I want to be me. I want to find what my mother seemed to be so close to finding. I want to go back to Africa, where I truly belong.

My little hut in the middle of the bush where I shall be working is on a private reserve. There are other game lodges in the area, but this is the only one I could find where they would allow a scientist to reside, for a modest fee. But no mingling with the guests! The area where my little dwelling will be is called Jumba, but it's only going to be a temporary place before I move on again. I tried to find Jumba on many maps but can't see it anywhere, maybe the place is indeed remote. But I have been assured I will be met at the airport in a place called Port Elizabeth and transferred to the camp.

So, you see, as you wander around, following your wars, I shall become as nomadic as you, following what I believe is possible, hoping to make a difference, as you want to, fighting my own wars in a place far away.

I will think of you, of course I will, you will never be out of my thoughts. I love you and always will.

I have wrestled with other solutions to keep you close to me, but I know that you have a calling, as I have, and I know, without doubt, you would not be happy wandering around the bush with me.

You need to be where you can help and heal others who have been badly wounded, their minds shattered.

You have a gift – and you must use it to help others, as I, myself, hope to do.

I arranged a meeting with your lawyer, Jeremy, as you advised, and left my mother's book with him for safekeeping. I have my discs with me with all the information you downloaded. I doubt there will be any computers out in the bush for me to download and refer to, but all she has written, all her observations, well, I remember them all.

I shall keep my own record of what I discover.

As I don't yet have a bank account in South Africa, I asked Jeremy to handle the monthly payments you so generously offered to help me with my research. He will take care of things until I am more settled and can give him my new bank account details.

But perhaps after reading this letter you might change your mind, if you do, I shall completely understand.

Go well, Michael, keep me close to your heart. I doubt either of us will ever experience what we had together with anyone else, but who knows what the future might hold? Perhaps in the years to come when I've found what I'm looking for, I'll return to London, I just don't know now?

Maybe, we might see each other again, but I don't want to give you hope. I want you to have those children you want so badly and follow your dream of living in Lamu. I want you to be happy, I truly do. But I want you to keep loving me as you do, keep me close, know I am still with you. Fall in love again but remember nobody will ever love you as much as I do. Nobody.

I will always be with you, right next to you as you go through your life.

I have had to make many hard and difficult decisions in my life, but this is the hardest one. It has broken me.

Should fate decide differently I know where you will eventually go – Lamu. I know I will find you there.

My love, as always,
Fleur.

Chapter Sixteen
Early 1990's

Fleur caught her connecting flight from Johannesburg to Port Elizabeth. She stared out of the window of the plane at the confusing, diverse, and wide-ranging environments below her. Coastal plains, rugged mountains, lush forests, dense vegetation and towering trees, the hills with glaringly white rocky outcrops, what looked like long dry riverbeds, waterfalls, canyons, lakes, and the endless stretch of the remote bush.

She had spent many hours poring over maps, searching for information in the local library, made notes, learned about which people lived where. It was a vast and incredibly beautiful country.

Doggedly she had narrowed her search down to the Eastern Cape to begin with. Here, she decided, would be where she would start her journey. The place her mother had mentioned in her leather book.

Fleur collected her luggage from the carousel and made her way to the arrival's hall. The airport building was small but clean and functional. She already had her visa which she had collected from the South African Embassy in London. The immigration official had smiled warmly at her as he stamped her passport, wishing her a pleasant and successful stay in his country.

She looked around anxiously for the lodge manager, someone dressed in khaki she had presumed with the name of the lodge, Jumba, emblazoned on his shirt.

All the passengers had departed, and she stood there alone with her suitcase and her black medical bag, unsure of what to do next. An African approached her and half raised his hand in greeting. "You are the doctor?"

She smiled at him with relief. "Yes, that's me, I thought you might have forgotten my flight details. Anyway, I'm pleased to meet you. What's your name?"

He lifted her suitcase. "I am Abel. Come I will take you to the camp."

The dilapidated Land Rover stood forlornly in the now empty car park, its sides splattered with dried mud, there was no lodge logo on the door. The passenger seat had a large tear in the middle and empty cans thrown carelessly on the floor. The smell of cigarettes was overwhelming from the overfilled ashtray. Hastily she wound down her window. With some difficulty she reached for her seat belt, dismayed to see it was broken. She fumbled for her sunglasses.

Abel, she decided, was a man of few words, his face sullen and unsmiling. If she asked him questions about the town of Port Elizabeth, or questions about the camp, he only grunted and lit another cigarette. She hoped the lodge owner, Chris Malherbe, would be more forthcoming with information than Abel who, she assumed, must be one of his trackers or rangers, or perhaps he was just a driver; he certainly, so far, had not shown any people skills which he would need for the lodge's guests.

Abel reached the outskirts of the town and turned right onto a dirt road.

Fleur looked around for some signage indicating where the lodge might be, then finding none studied the bush around her. It looked dry, parched, and dense with bushes and spindly trees, which scraped against the sides of the vehicle, as it bounced and bucked over the rough rutted dusty track, swerving to avoid potholes. She felt the sweat begin to trickle down her back, her teeth juddering with every bone jarring bounce of the vehicle.

She turned to Abel, the fine dust and cigarette smoke already swirling around the inside of the vehicle. "Is the camp far from here?"

He looked at her, his eyes hard, his face still unsmiling. "Yes."

Fleur could feel her temper rising. "Look Abel, I'm a paying guest. I must close the window, and I would ask that you don't smoke any more cigarettes. Do you understand?"

She struggled to get the window up again, a sharp branch with thorns tore at her arm and she gasped with the sting of it. Blindly she searched her bag for a tissue and the small bottle of antiseptic she always carried with her.

Fleur dabbed at the scratch, at least the smell of antiseptic dissipated the stench of stale cigarettes.

They drove in uncomfortable silence for the next two hours. Suddenly the bush parted in front of them and the vehicle stopped.

Fleur got out, removed her sunglasses, rubbing her stinging eyes and stared. The ground was bare and dry, harsh sunlight filtered through the leaves of a tree highlighting the clumps of dried withered grass. The ground in front of her was surrounded by sparsely leafed trees and heavy rocky outcrops.

A few ragged tents were set back in the shade of other trees, their faded torn sides held together by rusting broken zips. The ripped canvas streaked with bird droppings. Vines clung viciously to the original framework.

Tarnished cooking utensils lay forgotten near a long-abandoned fire pit now overrun by weeds. A broken stool leaned against a termite infested table.

Fleur turned to Abel, horror and disbelief etched on her face. But he had disappeared, already anticipating the camp would not be to her liking and not what she had been expecting. He had heaved her case and black medical bag out of the vehicle and dumped them in the sparse shade of a tree, then driven off into the bush.

Fleur looked around her, spotting her luggage she walked slowly towards it and sat down on her case. This camp had been deserted many years ago, she calculated. Abel, the surly driver, had disappeared. Around her was only the silence of the bush with the occasional sound of a bird and a faint rustle in the bushes.

She was tired. The long flight from London already taking its toll and combined with the hideous drive through the bush in the disgusting vehicle, and the sullenness of its driver, she felt herself beginning to unravel.

In the distance she heard another vehicle, she stood up and looked towards where the sound was coming from. A swirl of thick dust indicated it might be coming her way.

She sat back down on her case, straightened her back and took several deep breaths. If it was the owner of the camp, Chris Malherbe, coming to welcome her to his so-called camp, she was more than ready for him.

The vehicle came to a stop and, indeed, Chris Malherbe got out and came towards her.

"Well, hello, Fleur. Chris Malherbe. I'm thinking perhaps you may be a little disappointed in my deserted camp – sorry about that." He grinned at her.

Fleur tried to contain her anger and outrage at what she was confronted with. "Your information promised me everything I was looking for, a place next to your so-called luxury, but rustic, camp, a place for me to continue my research…" Her voice trailed off for a moment. "I paid you a lot of money, a deposit and three months up front for my accommodation."

She gestured towards the deserted camp. "The information pack you sent to me was misleading in the extreme. I shall take legal action against you; you can rest assured of that, and I want my money back."

He scratched his dark beard. "I'm afraid I won't be able to return your money, it's all gone. It went into my friend Jumba's account, and he's now closed it. So, no trail there for your legal buddies to follow.

"South Africa is a big country, lady, with all sorts of attractive borders to explore, places to disappear to without a trace. The post office box where I received mail has also been closed. So, a bit of a dead end."

Fleur thought quickly. Surely, he wouldn't leave her here in the middle of the bush with no food or water. But she knew if he did, she would die there, and all his problems would go away.

She lifted her shoulders, feigning capitulation, and mustered up a weak smile. "Alright, Mr Malherbe. Look, I have some American dollars, very much valued here against your own currency, would you take me back to town, to a hotel, so I can make other plans. There's clearly no point in trying to take legal action against you, so let's call it quits, shall we?"

Malherbe took only a few moments for him to agree. "Okay, done deal. I'll load your luggage, and we can be on our way. I'll accept two hundred US as payment."

Three hours later, with little or no conversation between them, Malherbe dropped her at a derelict and completely deserted camping site.

He lifted her suitcase and placed it at the entrance of the camp site manager's office. "Well, I'll be off." He held out his hand eager to grasp those precious US dollars.

Fleur looked at him and raised her eyebrows. "You believed I would give you more money, Malherbe? You're a bigger fool than I thought you were. It was an empty promise, like the one you gave me on your illegal information pack. You'll not get one more single cent from me."

Blood suffused Malherbe's face – she had outwitted him. Almost.

Fleur glared at him. "So, what are you going to do about it? Oh, you have a serious problem with your blood pressure and circulation, it's only a matter of time and it will kill you – heart attack, nasty experience. I hope it's long and painful.

"You only know me as a scientist, but I'm a fully qualified medical doctor. Your so-called ranger, Abel, is also on the way out. It's not the cigarettes which will kill him – he's more than likely got Aids. I wouldn't worry too much about improving his PR skills, or customer service in the hospitality industry, the skills he is sadly lacking I have to say. Bad long-term investment. But always a price to pay isn't there?"

Fleur watched his vehicle depart in a cloud of furious dust, his exhaust belching out black fumes. She looked around the empty site which had clearly been closed for some time, then turned and knocked on the door of the camp site manager.

A puzzled black face greeted her. "I need to stay here for a couple of nights can you fit me in somewhere?"

"Ah, *mama*, this place is now closed, there is nothing left here anymore, only myself, watching and keeping things safe until the Bank is coming tomorrow, then I too must leave, but I will help you if I can. There is a small *rondavel*, it is basic but clean. I have a little food here, some meat for a braai perhaps?"

Fleur closed her eyes with relief. "Not sure what a braai is, but will you help me?"

"Of course, *mama*, it would be my pleasure. We still have some vegetables in the garden, I will make you a salad should you wish? But you are looking tired, you come from a faraway place I think?"

"Yes. I do. I'm very tired. I need to sleep, desperately need to sleep, thank you."

"My name is Simon. Let me take you to the place for sleeping. When you wake, I shall be here to help with your dinner."

Fleur looked around and spotted her suitcase covered in dust thrown down in front of the crumbling house. She looked around wildly. "Where's my bag, it's small and black. It has all my papers in it, my medicine, my passport, and personal records. My wallet and all my identity papers. My credit cards and money?"

Simon patted her shoulder. "Have no fear, *mama*, while you sleep, I shall search the bush for this important bag. I will find it for you. But you must rest now."

Fleur woke six hours later, groggy and disorientated. Her tiny room was clean and had a shower. She relished the dark brown water spitting in spurts and starts, the tepid water washing over her hair and body. So far, the trip to South Africa had been a complete and utter disaster, enough to make her want to fly back to London on the next plane, go and find Michael, tell him she had changed her mind, she wanted to share her life with him, a safe and loving world with him beside her.

But she kept hearing her mother's voice in her head. She had to keep going – but where to next? Who could she trust now? Where was her bag with all her personal documents?

Fleur stepped outside her room and saw the glow of a fire, crackling and spitting into the clear night, spotted with stars, a warm wind was blowing through the deserted camp site.

Simon was carefully tending some meat over his fire. He had lit a lantern, its warm glow throwing a warm and yellow light across his grill. A rusty table was at his side, a bowl containing a salad caught the light of the lamp with its glistening dressing. A candle lighting a place for her with a single plate and a knife and fork.

She felt her throat tighten. He had seen something in her, somehow wanting her to feel safe. She made her way towards him and sank down on the torn canvas stool he had placed there for her.

"Simon, you have no idea what this means to me, and I want to thank you for taking care of me. I'm not in a good place at the moment, but you have given me hope. Thank you. Did you find my black bag?"

Simon shook his head. "I searched but I am thinking whoever left you here is taking the bag with your money and documents."

He turned the meat over on the braai. "Hope," he said softly, "is a small word with much meaning. Sometimes the only word which will keep people going as the days and years go by. I have hope for my own country, it will always be my home."

Fleur frowned, trying not to think about her missing medical bag. "Is this not your country then?"

"No. My country is a place far away with a new name now. I only knew, from a child, it was called Rhodesia. I grew up there, it was a peaceful place, a beautiful place which could snatch your breath away before you knew it. Black and white people lived there with respect for each other. We were one people.

"My family, where I was born, lived on a farm outside of a place called Bulawayo. They were good people, who owned the farm, they worked hard on their land. We Africans were happy there."

Fleur had already picked up that his accent was softer than that of the driver Abel. He seemed gentler when confronted with a white woman. Abel had given her the impression that he wasn't fond of white people at all, he had been surly and aggressive.

Simon continued. "We had our compound, with houses, with water and electricity. Each month along with our pay we received meat and mealie meal and other food to keep our bellies full and our hearts happy. It was the law of the white government. The *memsahib* there took care of our children, teaching them to read and write, a gift from God. She was our *mama*, and we loved her."

Simon poked at the embers of the fire. "If there was sickness or injury, she would take care of this too, as she would her own, her name was *mama* Mary. She had four of her own children, we grew up together, playing in the bush, but she was fierce this *mama* Mary." He laughed. "We had to go to her school before we could go and play again."

Simon turned the meat over once again and removed it to a plate, indicating she should eat now.

Fleur felt her stomach rumble in anticipation, she was starving for food, already feeling her teeth rip into the meat before her. But she hesitated.

"Look Simon, this looks delicious, but I don't care to eat alone. Will you not join me. There's more than enough for two?"

Simon smiled at her, the flickering flames of the fire caressing his gentle face. "I would like it very much, thank you."

It was his own food he had prepared for her. The cupboards and the cold box for meat was now empty. He had gone hungry many times before, but this woman had a greater need than he had now. He returned to the fire with another plate and knife and fork.

They sat together in silence, eating what some people would consider a basic meal. The lamb chops were crispy on the outside and pink with tender meat on the inside. The potatoes skin was tough but inside light and fluffy.

Fleur sucked at the bones of the lamb chops and devoured the glistening salad. "Tell me more about the place you come from, it's called Zimbabwe now? Why did you leave?"

Simon looked at her. "I didn't leave. My country left me, and I took myself somewhere else. But not my heart and my soul, they stayed behind in the land where I was born."

He cleared the plates from the table and took them to what she presumed must be what used to be the camp manager's kitchen. He returned minutes later and indicated to his seat again. "It is permitted I sit once again?"

Fleur smiled at him. "Of course it is. Tell me more about your family? Tell me about your country?"

Simon poked at the fire until he was satisfied with the warmth it exuded. "As I was telling you, I was happy there. *Baas* Peter and *mama* Mary made us all one family. They had four *piccanins* of their own. I myself had two brothers; we all grew up together…"

Fleur turned her head at the lonely giggle and cackle of something in the bush. Her body stiffened... "What's that?"

Simon gave her a reassuring smile. "It is a hyena but have no fear he will not come near the fire; you are safe here with me."

He stared off into the bush, his mind seemingly somewhere else.

"Go on," Fleur encouraged, "tell me what happened to the family and why you are here so far away. Why did you leave them behind?"

Simon sighed deeply, his dark gentle eyes watering. "I did not leave them; they were taken away. We had heard there was trouble coming but did not know it was coming to us out there in the bush. But when trouble is looking it will find you. It found us there that night many years ago now.

"There were many soldiers, but not white ones who we did not fear. These were Africans with their uniforms and guns. They were not gentle people; they were angry and shouting that our farm was to be taken and belonged to their people."

Simon stood up abruptly and paced around the fire. "That night I shall never forget. They pulled *baas* Peter and *mama* Mary from their beds, then the children, they were screaming, very much frightened. Out in the compound they tied the wrists of the children's mama and papa, the children were crying very much. *Mama* Mary tried to soothe them, but her gentle voice was lost in the blackness of the night and the shouting of the soldiers."

He wiped his sleeve across his eyes. "They watched as the soldiers shot their small children. Then they made the parents kneel and shot them from behind their heads, so they fell forward, their blood joining the blood of the three children."

Fleur was speechless at hearing of such graphic and savage behaviour, her knuckles white on the edge of her chair, the food churning in her stomach.

"But you said there were four children, Simon, where was the other one when all this was happening?"

Simon stopped his agitated pacing and returned to his rusty torn seat. "It is to my shame I had heard from others the farm was to expect big trouble from the soldiers. I did not tell the family, for I did not wish to frighten them. I thought they would be left alone; they had done nothing wrong, only the right things. It was not a rich farm, no herds of cattle, only vegetables for selling in the shops and market, many fine vegetables."

He poked the fire again. "Before the sun was setting, I went to my grandmother, who also lived with us all in the compound. Each evening, she would go to the big house and bath the babies of the family, tell them stories, and sing them lullabies. They waited for her every night; they loved her you see. Then they would sleep and take her stories and songs with them to another world where the people who sleep go to each night.

"The youngest child was called Poppy, she was but two years old, I am thinking and followed my grandmother when she was in the family home. My grandmother loved her more than the others perhaps because she was the youngest. Poppy was always smiling and laughing with no fear of what was watching for her in the shadows of that night and waiting for her.

"She had a dog, small as a cat, with white fur. This little dog also listened to the stories my grandmother told the children at bedtime and would fall asleep next to the little one in her baby bed."

Simon pulled his face down with his hands and looked up at Fleur, his cheeks wet with grief. "It was that night I told my grandmother, after she had given a bath to the children and read them their story, she must take the baby Poppy to a place deep in the bush, with the small dog. I told her there was big trouble coming that night.

"She laughed at me and asked how she would explain to *mama* Mary one of her children was missing, and the dog, and how must she carry a baby and a dog? She laughed again then stopped and looked at me."

Simon was quiet for a few moments. "You see *mama,* we African people have another sight, we have instincts passed down from generation to generation, it is how we have survived through the years. My grandmother saw something in my eyes and felt some long ago instinct, it was my fear she was seeing.

"When it was dark she placed the baby girl, Poppy, on her back, wrapped the small dog in a blanket and disappeared into the thick bush. The child was asleep, it made no sound. My grandmother's back was a place known to her for she had been carried there many times from when she was born. The child would not see what would happen to her family, when suddenly she did not have one anymore."

Fleur wiped the tears from her eyes. "Where were you when all this happened, when the soldiers came?" she said softly, her voice breaking.

Simon avoided her eyes. "It is to my shame I was a coward. I, too, hid in the bush, behind some rocks, where I could see the house. I saw what happened. I could do nothing but watch as the soldiers killed the family I loved.

"The soldiers set fire to the farm, there was nothing left, only a black burnt place with smoke rising. No bodies to bury – nothing left."

Fleur shook her head. Yes, she had seen people die in the clean and sterile confines of a hospital ward, yes, she had seen the victims of car accidents and all the rest. But the savage killing of innocent people, of little children in a world such as he had described was beyond her comprehension.

"Did you find little Poppy again, and your grandmother, Simon?"

He smiled sadly at her. "Yes, I found them where I knew they would be. When it was safe, I took them to a mission church in Bulawayo, my grandmother, little Poppy, and her white dog. It was a long way to walk. Taking some days. My grandmother carried the baby on her back, and I carried the dog with the short white legs.

"My grandmother was broken to hear she too had lost her family. I was the only one left. But, because of the child she loved, and the white dog, she followed me to safety. The child did not see the many tears she cried."

Fleur swallowed the lump in her throat. "Oh, Simon…"

He shook his head at the memories. "I myself had no job now, nowhere to go, no family left because the soldiers killed the white family, but they also killed the rest of my own family, calling them traitors to the cause."

He prodded the dying embers of the fire, with eyes Fleur knew, still held images of the family he had lost.

"So, you came here then Simon?"

"Yes, *mama*, I came here. I found this job at the camp site. I have been here for over twenty years now. The money I made, which was little, I sent to the mission church where little Poppy and my grandmother stayed. My grandmother was already old before the troubles, but she loved the little Poppy she had brought up and the small white dog with the short legs. When it was her time, she died."

Fleur could hardly contain herself. "So, what happened to little Poppy?"

Simon gave her a broad grin. "She is grown up now. There is a place near Bulawayo where they take injured wild animals, mostly abandoned babies. Poppy is working there now, helping save the ones who could not save themselves. She has no memory of her life on the farm that was burned along with her family. She is living her own half-life, but she is missing my grandmother and the little white dog with the short legs.

"This is where I shall be returning. Poppy has found a job for me there, caring for the animals who never hurt anyone, only man has inflicted these injuries. The little dog had only ever known much love from my grandmother and Poppy. This dog, like Poppy, only knew love with no memories.

"Poppy knows nothing of my past connections of the family, only that I had sent money to the mission to help her and others. I will stay there and watch over her as I have always done since that night. She will always be safe with me. I will never leave her again because she is the only family I have now, as I am the only family she has."

Fleur looked at him with tears of respect in her eyes. "Will you tell her, one day, of what happened to her family?"

Simon shook his head vehemently. "No. What good would it do now, so many years later? She remembers nothing of her family, it is better that it remains this way. Some memories are good, some not so good. Why fill her thoughts with the bad things that happened that night. She remembers nothing. It should remain so. Let her live her life with hope, and not horror of something that happened so many years ago now."

Simon stood up. "I must go now, *mama*. I must collect my few things and be ready for when the truck comes to collect me tomorrow before it is light. There are people who will be coming here to sell this place, the bank now wishes to have back. Perhaps someone who comes will see you and help you, I cannot do this."

Fleur stood up and took his hands in hers. "Go well, Simon, you are a good person, a fine Rhodesian man. You should be proud of what you have done for Poppy." She fumbled in her bag strapped across her shoulder. She withdrew two hundred US dollars and pressed them into his hand.

"Take this money, it will help you on your way back to Poppy and your new job. I ask only one thing from you. Buy her a gift and tell her it comes from someone across the seas, who wishes her well on her journey. Will you do that for me?"

Simon looked at the money, then looked at her. His eyes filled with tears at this unexpected gesture from a stranger. "What gift would you like to give to my little lost sister Poppy?"

Fleur smiled sadly. "The gift of life. Faith, hope, courage, and much love. You will find something."

Chapter Seventeen

When Fleur woke the next morning, the camp was eerily silent. Sometime before dawn she had heard a vehicle and presumed it had come to collect Simon.

She lay back on the pillow and recalled their conversation around the campfire. She had read about the history of Rhodesia in her research of African people on that continent. A proud and fearless people, fighting alongside each other for something they believed in. She had also read the graphic accounts of what shocking things had been done to the people there, both Black and European, slaughtered in their hundreds.

Last night she had heard first hand from someone who had lived there and gone through such an ordeal. Her own problems had faded away in comparison. Simon had faith and hope in his future, despite his shocking past and he would go on, as she knew she must.

She closed her case and left it outside the deserted manager's office. The utter quietness of the place, with the soft calling of doves, had a calming effect on her. She decided to sit at an old picnic table she had noticed, under a tree at the edge of the camp site, some way from the main house, almost hidden from view by a thickly leafed tree, and wait for the officials to arrive who would without doubt be now taking over the future of the place. They would come by car; she would get a lift back to the nearest town and make another plan from there.

Three long hours later as the sun was at its hottest, she finally heard a vehicle in the distance. She stood up, shading her eyes from the sun before fumbling for her sunglasses.

Five cars had arrived, the men dressed in shorts and shirts with one or two in business suits, this she presumed would be the bank officials and a possible lawyer or two. She sank back down; this was not the moment to announce her presence. Her suitcase still stood outside the manager's office, but nobody seemed to have noticed it. Her black medical bag was nowhere to be seen.

Fleur watched the men with their clipboards as they conducted the business of officially closing the old camp site down.

The sun was now unbearably hot, and she felt her eyes begin to close, she put her arms on the chipped and dirty cement table in front of her, ignoring the spattering of hard dried bird droppings, and felt the familiar greyness, then darkness surrounding her mind. Then nothing.

Sometime later she lifted her head and looked around. Once more the place was deserted, all the cars had left. She looked wildly around as panic once more set in, she lifted her hands to her face, the tears seeping through her fingers. The thought of sleeping on the ground, with no shelter, no food, and no water, surrounded by cackling hyena and other predators was more than she could take. Simon had gone, taking his hope, and hers, with him.

Then she heard a gentle voice. "Hey, who are you and what are you doing here. How did you get here?"

She looked up, her eyes brimming with tears. "Oh, God, I'm so pleased to see you."

Fleur stood up and threw herself into the arms of a complete stranger, burying her face in his shirt.

The man patted her back awkwardly. "Hey, it's all right. Come on pull yourself together and you can explain what you're doing here. Crying and carrying on isn't going to help you. Let me get you back to the old manager's house, you look as though you need water and some shade. You sound English?"

Fleur looked around wildly, she was weak with lack of food and water and doubted her legs would carry her the short distance to the manager's now deserted house.

She stumbled along next to him trying to take deep breaths to calm herself, but the intense heat put paid to that, she felt the familiar greyness coming back, and then the dark, as she collapsed at his feet.

Blake Hemmingway carried her onto the veranda and lay her down on a long rusting sun lounger. He went into the now empty kitchen and found a ragged cloth, turning on the tap he waited for the brown rusty coloured water to jerk its way out of the tap. It wasn't clean but it was cool. He bathed the woman's face, her wrists, and her ankles, then returned and repeated the whole process several times. He had bottled water in his vehicle, it was warm but pure, sourced from a crystal-clear waterfall in the high hills of the Eastern Cape, and this he poured carefully and gently into the woman's mouth, sip by sip.

He saw her case propped against the wall and bent to examine the luggage label. *Doctor F. Palmere.* He sat back on his heels, more confused than ever. The British Airways tag loosely attached to the handle. What was a British doctor doing here at an abandoned camp site with no car?

He looked at her, some colour was returning to her face, her breath was becoming steadier. She was slight, as he had discovered when he picked her up from the dust around his safari boots.

Her hair was dark and tangled, her limbs smooth and with the occasional redness where the sun had burned her. Her loose-fitting trousers and short tee shirt were grubby with the signs of a long journey.

He reached into his pocket and withdrew a clean blue handkerchief; he poured water from the bottle and gently dabbed the rust stains from the tap water from her face. It was a pretty face, not classically beautiful, but attractive, he thought she was probably in her mid-thirties, maybe a bit younger, it was difficult to tell.

Doctor Palmere started to stir, and he reached for her hand. Patting it gently, he spoke to her soothingly. "You'll be all right, had a bit of a bad experience. But I'll take you into town, to a hospital, they'll be able to put you back together again. Can you hear me, Doctor Palmere? Not many women have fainted at my feet, but I'm flattered you chose to do so."

Fleur heard his voice from a faraway place, it was soft and comforting, mellifluous; she floated up to meet it.

She opened her eyes and found the voice. He smiled at her, his breath catching in his throat. He had never seen eyes the colour of hers, the blueness flooding the whiteness which should have been around them. For a moment he was mesmerised.

"Hello Doctor Palmere, my name's Blake Hemmingway. I suggest you drink this bottle of water, slowly, and take a few moments to get your thoughts together."

He handed her the bottle, and she drank from it greedily. Her eyes beginning to focus again; he still held her hand, gently stroking it.

She struggled to sit up, brushing his hand aside. "No, doc, take it easy for a few minutes." He pushed her gently back.

"I don't know where you've come from or how you ended up here in the middle of the African bush, but something happened to you which brought you to your knees, at my feet."

He smiled at her. "You're safe now, it's all over. Okay?"

Fleur nodded. She could see him clearly now. He was tall and well built, his skin tanned by the African sun, his grey eyes matching the greyness at the temples of his short close-cropped hair. He was dressed in khaki shorts and a shirt, his face clean shaven with deep lines across his forehead and the sides of his mouth, these deepened as he smiled at her, she thought he was probably in his late thirties.

She swung her shaking legs over the side of the rusting sun bed and took a deep breath. "Thank you, did you say your name was Blake?"

He nodded. "Yes, Blake Hemmingway. This camp site used to belong to an Afrikaans couple; it was a simple place, not built for international tourists, only the locals with their caravans, looking for somewhere out of the cities where they could just be… but it was a money loser. I'm with a team of developers who want to buy it and build some kind of fancy game lodge here.

"So, what's your name. I know your surname, but you surely have a Christian name?"

"My name is Fleur."

He glanced at his watch. "Look, the whole place has now been sold and everywhere has bloody great padlocks on the doors. We can't stay here, and the next decent town is five hours away. We should go there, and I'll take you to the nearest hospital so they can check you out. You have been taking your malaria pills, I trust, being, I presume, a medical doctor?"

Her smile was tentative. "Yes, of course. But…."

"Yes, I know. You don't know if you can trust me. I understand that. Would it help if I told you I'm English, as well, and I was born in Brighton?"

Fleur thought she might start to weep again at the sheer force of speaking to someone from her own land. But she pulled herself together, relief flooding through her body. "I don't care where you come from, but you've helped me, and for that I'm truly grateful. But the fact you come from Brighton gives me hope?"

Blake frowned, then laughed. "Hope?"

"Yes. Hope. A little word I learned from someone I met recently…"

Blake stood up. Yes, indeed, he was tall, an ex-military man she suspected, judging by his straight back and the way he was already taking command of the situation in hand. She saw a fleeting glimpse of Michael in him.

"It's going to be dark soon and I need to be on my way, with you, of course. My truck is parked behind here. I travel a lot through the bush and spend many nights under the stars. The back of the truck has a fitted mattress, it's comfortable I can assure you. It has bedding and a warm duvet. I don't think you're up for a night bouncing through the rough bush in the passenger seat. I'm not sure what happened to you and how you ended up here, but first you need to sleep somewhere comfortable and safe.

"Tomorrow, you can tell me your story. I've already put your suitcase in the truck, so let's go shall we."

Fleur looked at him nervously. "I'm not sure…"

"Okay, if you're not sure, I'll retrieve your suitcase and leave you here. Is that what you'd prefer?"

She shook her head in despair. "I'm sorry, I'm not thinking straight. I don't want to stay here on my own. It's kind of you to offer to help me. I'll come with you."

He grinned at her. "Well, I wasn't going to leave you here anyway. Come on."

His truck stood under a tree, she could hear the night birds making their way back to their homes to roost, heard the hideous giggling cackle she had heard the night before, from the hyena coming out to hunt, and other grunts and calls from other predators, and felt her legs begin to buckle again.

Blake dropped the tailgate of his vehicle and turned towards her. "Up you get… whoa, looks like you're going to faint on me again."

He lifted her up and settled her on his makeshift bed, plumping up the pillows around her head and covering her with his duvet. Her big blue eyes opened again. "Thank you," she said softly. "I need water."

Blake gestured to his right. "There are bottles of water here, within your reach. I've left a chicken pie next to them. I always pick one or two up on my travels. The one I bought this morning should be all right, cold of course, but tasty. Eat a little if you can, otherwise drink plenty of water."

He patted the duvet around her body. "Right, we must get going. Once I start the engine a dim light will show the bottles of water you need to drink, otherwise try and sleep."

Fleur felt the movement of the vehicle as it made its way through the black night, she was warm and comfortable, the nightmares which had followed her receded. As hard as she tried to get her thoughts together, the more they evaded her. The man called Blake had saved her life, she could hear the noise of the engine but filtering through was the soothing sounds of Beethoven's music.

She felt herself falling backwards again and let go.

Chapter Eighteen

After the endless and rough ride through the bush, as the sky turned grey and pink with a new day dawning, Blake had stopped in the town of Graaff-Reinet and had Fleur checked out at the local hospital.

He had been assured by the doctor, De Klerk, his passenger, although still in a state of shock, was dehydrated and needed nourishment to help build her strength, she was also running a fairly high temperature which he wanted to keep his eye on. He wanted to keep her in the hospital for a couple of days under observation, although Fleur argued this was not necessary. She was a medical doctor and could take care of herself. But the doctor and Blake Hemmingway were not having any of it.

Doctor De Klerk had given her a strong sedative to calm her down and eventually she allowed herself to be tucked up in a private room, all the fight had left her. Blake had sat next to her bed, watching as she tried to ward off the effects of the sedative.

"Listen to me, Fleur. You have nowhere to go, nowhere to stay and no one to look after you. You need a couple of days here so you can think things through, okay?"

She had turned her extraordinary blue eyes towards him then looked wildly around the room. "Where's my bag, what have they done with it."

Blake smiled at her; concern etched on his face. "Your bag is safe, you were wearing it across your chest, remember." He lifted it off the back of the chair and handed it to her. Here it is, quite safe." He hooked it over her head and through her arm. "There, will you now calm down a bit?"

Fleur sighed with relief and held out her hand. "So, are you going to leave me here. Where will I go, I don't even know where I am?"

He cleared his throat. "Of course I'm not going to leave you here. I'll stay with you; I can sleep in the back of my truck. When the doc gives you the all clear you can decide what you want to do, and we'll take it from there. Now, go to sleep, will you. I need a bit of sleep myself. I'll come back in a few hours and check on you."

Fleur nodded. "Okay," she murmured woozily. "I must admit I don't feel good, I think I'm running a fever. I'll feel better when I wake up I must have fallen over or fainted at some point."

Blake watched her drift away and tucked her hand back under the blanket.

He took a long hot shower at the hospital, changed his clothes, then drove around the old town with its church towers, and neat shops. He knew it was one of the oldest towns in the country with a wealth of historic charm; well preserved Cape Dutch architecture, whitewashed buildings with thatched roofs and gabled facades, the streets lined with quaint homes and churches reflecting its long history. Their chiming bells ringing out over the town as they had done for so many decades, bringing a sense of belonging and reassurance in a troubled world.

He headed for the nearest filling station on the outskirts of the town. After living in South Africa for many years and travelling thousands of miles across this mighty country he knew the best place for a decent breakfast was always next to a filling station.

After a satisfying breakfast and three cups of coffee he made his way back to the truck and parked under a large, leafed tree in the grounds of the hospital. Crawling into the back of his truck he slept for five hours.

When he awoke, the sun was beginning to set. He made his way to Fleur's room. A single lamp threw a warm glow around the room. The monitors above her bed beeped and blinked. Her body a slight mound under the bedding.

He had bumped into Doctor De Klerk as he'd finished his rounds. "Ah, Mr Hemmingway, may I have a quick word with you."

Blake followed De Klerk to his rooms and sat down. "How is she, doctor?"

"Fleur will be fine. Her temperature is down, and her body now nicely hydrated, she still needs to get her strength back so I'm feeding her intravenously. Bit of sunburn here and there, lots of mosquito bites, one or two tick bites, but nothing we can't fix. She may have hit her head on something, she seems confused. Nasty bump and a bit of bruising but I've sorted that out. She has low blood pressure, I imagine she probably always has had, hence her inclination to faint under extreme stress."

De Klerk glanced at her file in front of him. "Can you tell me anything about her. I know you brought her here but where does she come from. I need to complete her paperwork; we need to contact her family so they can come and collect her when she's discharged. Do you have any idea at all where they live?"

Blake ran his hand through his short hair and shook his head. "No, I've no idea where she comes from. Not from this country. She's English that's all I know and hasn't been in the country very long. I found her out in the middle of the bush, all alone. I have her suitcase in my truck, but the luggage tag only gave me her name, not where she comes from. But my guess is that at some point she lived in England."

Doctor De Klerk frowned. "But if that's so she must be carrying travel documents, her passport for a start. Perhaps we should go through her suitcase and any handbag she was carrying and try and figure out what to do next. I can't discharge her without someone taking responsibility for her?"

Blake looked at him with horror. "Where I come from doc, we would never consider going through a woman's handbag or suitcase without her permission, or unless the police are involved. It's not the done thing.

"Might I suggest we give her a little more time and I'll find out as much as I can. I'd like to go and sit with her for a while, until she wakes up, with your permission, of course."

Blake made his way back to her room and sat down next to her bed. The doctor was right they did need to contact her family. But he needed her permission to do that.

"Hey, Fleur. It's me Blake, come to check up on you. Can you hear me?"

She muttered something and turned over, her hand instinctively feeling for her handbag on her chest. Opening her eyes she stared at him in confusion.

He frowned. "I found you in the bush, remember?"

She struggled to sit up. "I'm not sure, but I can't remember your name. Where am I?"

He could hear the panic in her voice. "It's all right, stay calm, you're quite safe. I brought you to a hospital. You're doing well but the doctor has given you some heavy medication, it will take a while before it works its way through your system. You have a bit of a bump on your head which is making you a little confused."

He hesitated briefly. "Listen Fleur, we need to find your family, they need to know where you are. The doctor won't release you from the hospital unless someone takes responsibility for you. You need to be looked after for a while before you find your feet again. You must have your passport somewhere, travel documents, your destination details, where you were supposed to be staying?"

Fleur fumbled with the zip of her bag, then flopped back on her pillow, her eyes closing. "My medical bag was stolen with all my personal documents."

He opened the zip and looked inside. There was a miniature bottle of antiseptic spray, some tissues, a square disc, a lipstick, and nothing else. He searched in the side pocket and found a credit card and a small cream card: *Captain Michael Bennett*, he looked at it curiously, a telephone number with an international code he didn't recognise. Her husband? A relative? There was also a delicate silver chain with a locket attached. The hospital staff had obviously removed it from her neck and placed it in her bag when they examined her.

He looked at it curiously and felt his way around the edge of the locket, it sprang open, and he saw two tiny black and white photographs of two children, not much more than babies. He smiled, there was someone out there who knew who she was. They both had the blueness of identical eyes, even though the photographs were black and white. He closed the locket carefully and placed it back in her bag.

He flipped over the business card and found another number with a code he recognised immediately. The UK.

There was no passport and no other travel documents. He looked at Fleur, but she was asleep again.

"Don't worry Fleur," he said softly. "I'll find your Captain Bennett and let him know you're safe. He'll come and find you wherever he is. Everything will be all right. He'll take you home."

Blake Hemmingway made his way back to his truck, the cream card tucked into his shirt pocket. It was too late now to call the number in the UK, or the other one. He would wait until morning.

He decided to book into a hotel. Tomorrow, he would try and find Captain Michael Bennett using the hotel's phone.

The next morning Blake approached the receptionist. "I need to make a long-distance phone call. You can put the cost on my bill, but it's important – very important."

The first call he tried was the one with an international code he thought might be in East Africa somewhere. He let the phone ring until it went dead in his hand.

The call to the UK was picked up immediately. The Ministry of Defence.

Blake explained he was looking for a Captain Michael Bennett, he had no idea of his regiment, where he served, or where he was now. He emphasised that it was of the utmost importance as he had found a woman in South Africa who was now in hospital and had little recollection of who she was or how she got there. Captain Michael Bennett, he emphasised, was the only contact he had, he had found his card in her handbag. Possibly her husband or a family member? Could they help perhaps?"

"I'm sorry, sir, this information is classified. There is a helpline number I can give you, but you will have to provide a valid reason and identification before someone might be able to help you."

Blake looked at the number he had scribbled down. He picked up the phone again. Explained to the person who he was looking for and why. "I'm sorry, sir, I don't have clearance to give you any information about Captain Bennett. However, if you leave your number with me, I'll pass your message on to the appropriate department and see if they can help you?"

Blake slammed down the phone in frustration. He would book into the hotel for another two nights, visit Fleur, and wait for a phone call which he doubted would come.

The doctor had told him that Fleur was well enough to be released, but she would still need care to heal some kind of shock she had obviously gone through. Had he found any relatives or family that he could release her to?

The answer was no.

Late that night the phone rang in his room. "This is Colonel Mallard. Army headquarters in the UK. I understand you are seeking to find one of my men. Captain Michael Bennett?"

Blake struggled to get his thoughts together. "Yes. Absolutely. I've given the Ministry of Defence all my details. I served in the British Army myself, many years ago."

"Yes, yes, we've checked you out. But I'm sorry to inform you that Captain Bennett, whilst on duty in the Middle East went missing in action, some time ago now. Missing presumed dead. Any information we had from his records was sent to his lawyer in London, but I'm afraid I cannot disclose any more details to you."

"Well can you at least tell me how long ago it was that he disappeared?"

Colonel Mallard cleared his throat. "That's classified information I'm afraid."

Blake slowly put the phone down. What now? Fleur was in no way strong enough to take another emotional upheaval. He thought it might tip her over the edge.

He called his housekeeper, Tapu. "Make up the guest room. I'm bringing someone home with me."

Blake Hemmingway sat in front of the doctor. "I've tried to locate any members of her family, but I've come up with nothing. There's no sign of any travel documents or her passport, I think they were probably stolen, and she was left in the bush to die alone.

"There was a card in her bag with a name and a number. I followed it up and it appears whoever the man was, he was a Captain in the British Army. He went missing in the desert in some God forsaken place; could have been months or years ago for all I know. Missing presumed dead."

He flipped the card over in his fingers. "Despite my reservations, I found the keys to her suitcase in her bag. With no other course of action available to me, I opened it up and went through it. Just the normal things women carry around with them when they travel, clothes, a pair of sturdy safari boots, toiletries and not much else. There was a small leather-bound book in amongst her clothes, I took a quick look, but it was all written in French. I speak a little French myself, but it was way beyond anything I could remember from school. It seemed to be about plants and flowers. There was a pouch at the back of it which held some photographs of some impressive drawings of plants and flowers.

"I'm thinking Doctor Fleur Palmere, came here on some kind of research contract. She told us she was a medical doctor, but perhaps she was a scientist as well. She might not even be English, perhaps she's French, she does have a slight accent now I think about it," he grinned at the doctor, "quite a sexy one actually."

De Klerk frowned at him with disapproval. "So, what do we do now then?"

Blake rubbed the stubble on his chin. "Look, if I can persuade her to let me look after her for a while when she leaves the hospital, would you allow me to take responsibility for her. I can't think of any other solution, but I'm not going to leave her here alone.

"Maybe when she fully recovers, we can start to look for her family. She had a locket in her purse, there were two photographs, black and white, they looked old. I think perhaps she may have a sibling somewhere, but she's the only one who will know who the other child is."

Doctor De Klerk rubbed his tired eyes. The country was in turmoil, changing its course of history. There were riots and unrest everywhere, as tribe went head-to-head with other tribes to ensure they had a fat slice of the cake in the future years. It was no place for a white woman, on her own, with no relatives and no home.

"What do you suggest Blake?"

Blake rubbed the side of his face. "I suggest I take her back to my home, which is about four hours from here. It's far away from any political upheavals, at the moment.

"It's remote, I'll admit that, but I have a helper in the house, his name is Tapu. He can take good care of her until she recovers fully. I'll be there for a few weeks before I must get on with my job?"

"Which is?"

"I work for an international property development company with a huge investment in southern Africa. We source land which is suitable for development, and I go and assess the land and work out a business plan for them. It means I travel a lot, not only to the cities, but out in the rural areas. But it's not only property development. If they find something, in these remote areas, they would like to invest in, with potential, they also invest in the people, making sure they have the permission with the tribal chiefs and, in exchange, if the plans are approved, we build schools and clinics, teach the locals how to farm, set up dairy projects and teach them how to work the land for the benefit of their communities.

"It's been highly successful in the past, backed by many international aid programmes."

Doctor De Klerk looked at him with a bleakness in his tired eyes. "And you assume you'll be able to continue this good work with the country and the turmoil it's in at the moment?"

Blake gave him a confident smile. "Mandela is considered a gift from God, despite his past, he has his people close to his heart. He wants to make his country work. I believe it will be possible."

"Alright Blake. If you'll furnish me with your identity number, your full name and address of where you live, I'll hand over the responsibility of Fleur to you. But only if she agrees. You do understand that don't you?

Blake nodded as De Klerk continued.

"I'll need you to sign a legal document agreeing to become her custodian until her family can be found. I will discharge her tomorrow, make sure she gets plenty of rest and takes the drugs I will prescribe for her."

He frowned. "She not only has low blood pressure, but there seems to be something else which I won't be able to define without some tests. Tell me, does she faint for no reason?"

Blake grinned. "As far as I know, only at my feet."

Chapter Nineteen
The Middle East

The sun dipped low over the arid horizon, casting long shadows across the terrain, the distant rumble of artillery echoed through the valley, a sound that had become all too familiar to the British soldiers stationed there, a haunting reminder of the endless conflict which gripped the region and the exhausted troops.

The days were sweltering, the merciless sun beating down on them, day after endless day, as they patrolled the dusty streets and barren landscape, sweating in their combat fatigues, bullet proof vests, and the weight of their heavy weapons. Dust storms engulfed everything in their path, turning the air thick with grit and sand which dried and cracked their lips and stung their eyes.

Amidst the harsh unbearable conditions, tensions ran high. The threat of insurgent attacks loomed constantly, every shadow seemed to be a potential enemy, every noise a threat.

The air hung heavy with the acrid scent of burning metal and scorched air, the aftermath of a buried explosive device which had torn through the small convoy with merciless precision, a cacophony of screams echoing through the dust choked air.

The scene was a tableau of devastation. The twisted wreckage lay destroyed across the once golden sand, flames licked hungrily at the scattered remains, casting flickering shadows dancing across the now ashen landscape.

Amidst the wreckage, bodies lay in the sand, twisted and broken, their lifeless eyes staring blankly. The screams of pain lost amongst the chaos, the air heavy with the stench of blood and burning flesh.

Michael's medics scrambled frantically amidst the carnage as they fought to save the lives of the wounded, but for many it was too late.

Doctor Michael Bennett with unwavering determination worked alongside his medics, trying to save as many soldiers as he could – there were not many left…

A lone figure lay in wait amidst the rocky outcrops. The sniper peered through the scope of his rifle, his breath slow and steady, watching the British medical officer moving doggedly amongst what was left of his men.

His finger hovered slightly over the trigger as he waited for the perfect moment to strike.

Doctor Michael Bennett fell forward. The sniper smiled. Now there was no doctor to tend the wounded. He took the medics out as well.

Silently the sniper descended from his concealed vantage point.

He moved amongst the dead and dying men, putting a bullet through the head of any of them who still moved.

With methodical precision he collected the dog tags from all the dead soldiers, each one a grim trophy of his lethal skills. Satisfied with his haul, he vanished back into the unforgiving terrain.

He slithered into the shadows of the rocks, leaving nothing but silence and death in his wake.

Ahmed was a humble man and lived a simple life, although now, with the war raging across the region, life was not easy. The British military had changed all that as they arrived with their guns, tanks, and determination.

He and his wife Fatima has not been blessed with children and their families had been wiped out with the bombings. Some of their relatives joined the terrorist groups, desperate for money, stability, and peace which they had always known before the war. They knew if they didn't align themselves with the terrorists they would be shot as sympathisers.

Ahmed had moved high up in the mountains and built a simple structure in front of a cave where they slept at night, taking their goats and chickens with them. Fatima tended the barren ground as best she could, growing vegetables and herbs to supplement their meagre diets. The goats, and chickens, who had flourished in this remote place, provided them with meat, milk and eggs. Enough to survive on until the war was over, when they would return to their village, to their family and friends, if indeed any of them had survived.

Ahmed heard the explosion as it echoed around the mountains and hills. He made his way silently down the steep rocky path towards the mushrooming black smoke, his weathered face etched with concern as he surveyed the scene before him, his heart heavy with the weight of witnessing such senseless violence.

In the distance he heard the low rumble of an approaching sandstorm, the strong winds already whipping up the sand and tearing at the scrubby bushes, the light changing as it started to smother the sun. He covered his face as the determined wind buffeted his body.

He ducked down into the shadows of the rocks as more shots rang out. He glimpsed the outline of the sniper and watched as he bent over each body and removed their identity tags before once again blending back into the landscape.

He waited to be sure the sniper had accomplished what he had set out to do, then made his way towards the bodies of the dead soldiers.

Ahmed shook his head with despair as he saw the young faces of the British soldiers. The roar of the violent wind and swirling sand seeping into their unseeing eyes. The sky now darkening and blotting out the sun with the impending storm, already extinguishing the flames enveloping the vehicles and covering them with sand.

He looked at each one with compassion. They would have family, wives; children in the place they came from, waiting for them to come home.

A slight movement caught his eye. He crouched over the soldier, turning him over. He was dying, he knew, there was nothing he could do to change that. But still he hesitated.

The soldier opened his eyes. They were as blue as the sky above before the storm. Ahmed quickly removed his headdress and bound the shattered remains of the man's arm to staunch the bleeding.

He lifted him onto his back and made his unsteady way up the steep path towards his shack, stopping often. The soldier was heavy, the wind and the buffeting sandstorm, unforgiving. The sand stinging his face, but he knew the soldier he was carrying would be feeling nothing.

Fatima had been waiting for him. When she saw he was carrying the body of an injured British soldier, she clamped her hand over her mouth in disbelief.

"What are you doing, Ahmed? Why did you do this?"

"Hush, woman. I couldn't leave him to die alone. It is not our way. Come we must help him."

She shook her head with despair. "My husband it will bring big trouble. This soldier is British, they will be looking for him. The terrorists will know, they have watchers everywhere. They will come after us. You have put us in grave danger. It is a foolish thing you have done."

Ahmed lay the soldier on a simple cot inside their shack. He was unconscious. "Bring water and your herbs and healing plants, we must try to save his life. Turn your face away as I undress and wash him, bring me one of my robes, it will make him more comfortable after I inspect his body for other injuries. You must take his uniform and bury it deep somewhere. He will look like an Arab with his dark skin. My headdress will cover his light hair. Nobody will know who he is. But I am thinking he is dying."

Long into the night Ahmed attended to his soldier. He had staunched the blood from his almost severed arm. Using the thick paste he used on his livestock, he covered the young man's burnt face, carefully lowering the light gauze over it. He had a high fever; Ahmed bathed his fevered brow with the cool water his wife had brought from the trickling stream that made its way down the side of the mountain.

He stayed with him until dawn as the vicious sandstorm swirled and whipped the sand outside his dwelling. Exhausted he slumped over the cot, a prayer on his lips to Allah to spare the life of this infidel.

Four days later the vicious sandstorm blew itself out. Leaving no trace of the carnage which had taken place. The desert sands once more lay calm and serene, the searing sun finally appeared and there was silence everywhere.

Chapter Twenty

Colonel Mallard looked around the table at his fellow officers. "Captain Bennett has not called in for several hours. I fear the worst may have happened. He's been out of radio contact. We must launch a search and rescue party immediately."

He turned and pointed at the map pinned to the wall. 'This was the route he was travelling, delivering medical supplies to another base some sixty miles away. He and his men never arrived. It's a vast and unforgiving terrain, but I want them back and we shall do everything to find them."

The helicopter pilot broke in. "Sir, there is a ferocious sandstorm blowing in that area. The probability of finding the captain and his men would be impossible. We can't fly in this weather, it's too dangerous. We must wait until it's blown over before we can even begin to start looking for him and his men.

"Even on the ground the visibility would not be possible for a vehicle to try and find them. I'm afraid we'll have to wait until the sandstorm has blown itself out. Perhaps Captain Bennett and his men have taken shelter somewhere to ride out the storm?"

The Colonel ran his hand through his cropped hair. "Perhaps…but at the first opportunity I want boots on the ground to search and find them and you up there in your helicopter, scouring this God forsaken land, until we find them. Is that understood?"

The helicopter finally took off four days later, the pilot looked down on the terrain below him, sand, sand and more sand, endless bloody miles of it.

For two hours he and his co-pilot scoured the area where they thought Captain Bennett and his men might have travelled. There was no debris anywhere, no sign of any vehicles. Nothing.

They flew over the rocky outcrop near where they thought Captain Bennett and his men might have been. There were no signs of any habitation, no signs of any people. Reluctantly they returned to base.

Colonel Mallard was waiting for them. "Well?"

"Nothing sir, nothing at all, the sandstorm covered any trace of any confrontation with the enemy. Sorry, sir, we tried our best. It's a vast area. The mission was impossible."

Colonel Mallard closed his eyes briefly. "I'm not giving up on my men. I'm sending ground troops and transport to comb every area where we think they may have been."

The ground troops with their tanks and vehicles scoured the area, doggedly looking for any clue, any evidence Captain Bennett and his men had been somewhere there. Their troops searched relentlessly amongst the rocky outcrops looking for any sign of life. There was nothing, absolutely nothing, only silence from the unforgiving desert.

Their own Arab desert trackers looked diligently for anything they could find but, as men of the desert, they knew the sandstorm would have buried any evidence in this vast tract of land in a very short space of time. They knew all their own efforts; all the might of the British Army and their sophisticated machines would find nothing.

With a heavy heart Colonel Mallard had to finally accept that all the men, and Captain Bennett, had disappeared without trace. They had not faltered in their efforts to find them. But they had gone.

He finished his report to Headquarters in England, listing all the names of the men and Captain Bennett.

Missing in action and presumed dead.

Chapter Twenty-One
London

Jeremy Foxton signed for the couriered envelope noting from the couriers' label it was from the Ministry of Defence.

"It is with deep regret, as Captain Bennett's solicitor, we must inform you whilst on a tour of duty in The Middle East, Captain Bennett went missing. Extensive searches were carried out and the conclusion has been reached that Captain Bennett and his men were ambushed and the resulting extreme sandstorm during this time made it impossible to recover any bodies.

Captain Bennett is considered missing in action and presumed dead.

It is also with deep regret we have no identity tags or personal effects to forward to you, only a letter from a Doctor Palmere which, unfortunately arrived after he had left on his last mission. You will find it enclosed.

Jeremy sat back in his chair. Shocked into disbelief. But there it was in front of him, Michael had gone, one way or another.

He looked out of his window at the endless traffic making its way through Knightsbridge, he watched the shoppers with their designer bags, their designer clothes, no doubt making their way back to their expensive homes before stopping for a cocktail or a glass of wine in the many trendy bars. They would probably already have plans for dinner at a pricey and famous restaurant. Not for a second would they give a thought to the men who had died an agonising death in a God forsaken place on the other side of the world.

Not for a moment would they be able to comprehend the devastation of grief which would overwhelm the families of the dead men. Wives, girlfriends, children, brothers, sisters, and grandparents.

Their lives torn apart.

Jeremy looked at Fleur's letter to Michael. He would have to let her know Michael had never received her letter. But how?

He was the custodian of not only Michael's estate, but also Fleur's and her sister Helene.

He would give it more time, perhaps a miracle would happen, and they would find them. He knew army HQ would have used everything in their considerable power to find the missing men and their vehicles. For them to have reached the only conclusion possible was what he should accept.

But he wouldn't. He would wait. He wanted proof.

Chapter Twenty-Two
The Middle East

Ahmed looked at the tall figure, dressed in full Arab robes, as he sat silently looking out over the desert, his empty sleeve rippling in the hot torpid air.

He had brought him back to wellness again using the simple traditional medicine his people had always used. This British soldier had no name and had not uttered a word in the many seasons which had passed.

He would bow his head in acknowledgement when Fatima, her face covered, presented him with food. Ahmed knew the man's mind had gone somewhere else, after the war in the desert. This man knew not who he was, or where he came from.

Fatima sat next to her husband on the jutting ledge outside of the cave they lived in. "There is no food left, my husband, we must return to our own people if we wish to live. The war is over, it is said it is safe for us to return to our village. But this British person cannot come with us. The villagers will see us as traitors to the cause of their war. He is too tall and not dark enough to pass as one of us. He cannot come with us. He does not speak our language, and he has eyes the colour of the sky."

Fatima looked out at the tall man in his Arab robes as he gazed out across the thousands of miles of desert in front of him. She had become fond of the stranger with his gentle ways.

"My husband, you must listen to me now. This soldier must find his way back. There is family there to which he belongs. He cannot come with us."

Ahmed made his way to the nearest village, under the cover of darkness, when the air was cooler, and the stars would show him the way. In the soldier's pocket, so many seasons ago now, he had found some money. With the face of a white leader and the name of dollars written on the paper.

He went into the marketplace two days later and sat with the elders as they argued and drank dark coffee and talked about their families. Who was to be married to who, who had died in the short desert war and what was to come. All agreed it was in the hands of Allah, and not theirs to question.

A young boy approached him as the sun was setting. "You want to go somewhere; you are a stranger here. You want to use my camel?

"I have camel, she is old, but she is true to the desert. Where you want to go?"

Ahmed shook his head. "You, my child, are too young to remember the war here in the desert. I wish to find the place where the British soldiers lived?"

The boy grinned at him. "My uncle is knowing these things, if you pay for this camel, I will take you to my uncle for him to show you the way. He will tell me where the place is, and I will take you there."

After the desert war, where many British and Arab lives were lost, the British still retained a base to monitor and advise the government of that country, but mostly to keep surveillance of any unusual movements.

Sergeant Higgins was a born and bred Londoner, far away from home and sometimes bewildered by where he found himself. But he was well trained and did his duty for Queen and country, although he longed for the rain sodden country of his birth, fish and chips out of a newspaper and his local pub. Yes, he longed for the low grey skies and the incessant rain, the green pastures and gentle grazing sheep. Away from the blistering heat and sun of this wretched place where he was now.

He was on duty the day when Ahmed finally found the place he had been looking for. Higgins watched the approach of the camel and its passengers through his binoculars, distorted by the heat waves shimmering and rising from the intolerable heat of the desert. He raised his gun in anticipation of trouble coming his way.

He alerted the four military police at the base as to the approaching Arabs, and Major Jameson the commanding officer. The base was well secured with lookout towers and miles of barbed wire and fencing, it was unusual to see a camel with passengers, he was more used to a military vehicle or two from the other NATO peacekeepers monitoring the area.

The jeep pulled up at the perimeter fence and the entrance to the compound. The Military Police, guns at the ready, watched the camel's slow swaying gait until it sank to its knees and off-loaded a small boy and a wiry looking Arab.

"Halt!" barked Major Jameson. "What is your business here?"

The boy sank to his knees in terror. The Arab approached the entrance to the compound, his hands clasped in front of him. "I come in peace, my brothers. I have someone you are seeking."

Major Jameson looked down at the trembling boy. "Somehow, I doubt that."

"Sergeant? Arrest this man, take the boy, and look after him."

Ahmed's arms were forced behind his back and he was taken into the compound. In a desolate cell he waited for he knew not what.

Sometime later, he was pulled from his cell and presented to the officer in charge of the base. Major Jameson.

"Name?"

"I am Ahmed bin Hama. I live here in the place where this war was fought. When I was young, I went to school and learned the language you are speaking, but only a little."

"So, why are you here now?"

Ahmed was frightened. He had learned this English language but only in a simple way. How would he tell his story now?

The Major looked impatient; his eyes were not gentle. "Come on, man, what do you want? I have other things to attend to?"

Ahmed took a deep breath. He would do the best he could in this other language. "When the war was coming to us here, there was much movement in the place we only knew as a peaceful place. The British and Americans came, and all was ended. There was much killing. My people rose up to fight these foreign soldiers. But my wife and I were simple people, wanting nothing more than to live the way we had lived for hundreds of years. We did not want war."

The Major shook his head with frustration. "Yes, yes, we all know about this. What do you want?"

Ahmed shook his head. "It is not what I want. But it is one of your own who must go back to this land of yours beyond the deserts. It is why I am here. It is what you want I am thinking."

The Major lifted his head, his eyes still hostile. "One of ours?"

"Yes, one of yours. I do not know the name of this soldier. I found him with his other dead soldiers and took him to my cave. My wife Fatima and me, we looked after the soldier who was badly injured. My wife and I must return to our village, but we cannot take this soldier with us. He belongs to you and not to us. We cannot leave him in the cave where he will surely die without care. His eyes are the colour of the sky, not brown like our people."

Major Jameson sat back in his chair. There seemed to be some truth in what the simple Arab was telling him.

"Can you take us to him?"

"It will be difficult. I have travelled through the night for many days. I will try to take you there to this person."

"How do I know what you're telling me is true Ahmed, do you have any proof?"

Ahmed stared at his feet. "Your men took everything from me when they took me to the cell. But with the camel comes something. You must find these things. When the war was on and we found the soldier, we buried his uniform, for we were very afraid of the people who would kill us for trying to help."

Ahmed looked at him. His own eyes now hostile. "It is permissible I pray now, for I am a Muslim. It is time at the end of the day for this."

Major Jameson looked at the man in front of him. He seemed a humble sort, trying to find help for what seemed a British soldier who had gone missing. His duty was to find this man.

Dead or alive.

He nodded. "You may go and pray."

The Sergeant and the Major watched him leave the office. Ahmed made his way to the old camel and retrieved his prayer mat, facing Mecca, he lowered himself to his knees and bent his body forward.

Jameson watched him. In the world he came from religion was a contentious issue; religion had never been simple. He had been brought up as a Christian, gone to the right schools, attending Sunday school as a child, Church on Sundays as required by his public school. But as he grew into an adult, he started to question a religion which had no answers. Faith, yes, he knew everyone needed something to believe in when their lives fell apart. Hope, if nothing else.

He knew it brought great comfort for those who were left behind when there was nothing else but God to believe in, and they would all meet again at some point. But he had found it difficult to comprehend. Yes, the ancient churches still promised hope and an afterlife, centuries after being built. The bible could be found in most hotel rooms, hidden away in a drawer. How could it be, he pondered, that a story two thousand years old could still have such an impact on the faithful?

He watched the Arab called Ahmed, as the sun set, throwing shadows on his prayer mat and he wondered if the man's simple faith made his life easier in this time of terrible war and unrest and kept him steady. He seemed not to need a congregation about him, a man of God in front of him, reading from long lost scriptures, ancient hymns, that still resonated with the faithful. It seemed Ahmed only needed himself.

He, personally, had almost given up. In the world he came from, war had always been about religion. The Middle East was in turmoil, more wars would come, he knew. Oil was the new gold, man had become greedy, it seemed to him, there was no room for religion anymore.

Major Jameson had been briefed by the former Colonel Mallard who was handing over his remote post to the new commanding officer – him. He knew about the missing soldiers who, it had been assumed, were all killed in action during a skirmish in the desert, two years or so ago. Their bodies, or vehicles, had never been found. If there was a chance, any chance at all, maybe one of them had survived and, impossible though it seemed, he had a moral duty to pursue this. But first he needed some proof to ensure it was not another planned ambush of more of his soldiers.

When the sun had set, he ordered food to be sent to the cell where Ahmed was being held and told the sergeant to put the boy in the same cell with him. Once they were safely locked away and accompanied by two military police, he approached the bad-tempered looking camel tied to one of the posts.

"Go through whatever the camel is carrying and bring it to my office. But leave the prayer mat where the Arab put it when he had finished his prayers."

He turned smartly on his heel and returned to his office. Twenty minutes later the two policemen knocked on his door.

"Nothing, sir. Only some bits and pieces these people carry with them when they journey through the desert. There were no arms, no ammunition, no identity papers, nothing to cause any alarm; but we did find this parcel in one of the side saddles."

Major Jameson looked at the crudely shaped parcel in front of him, tied with string and wrapped in some sort of newspaper written in Arabic.

"There's nothing inside of it which feels like a weapon, it feels like it might be clothing of some sort."

"Open it with care, Sergeant, these Arabs are clever buggers, you never know what you may find in it. Could be a venomous snake for all we know. They feel soft as well, until you piss them off."

Gingerly the string was snipped and the newspaper carefully peeled back.

Inside lay what looked like a pile of ragged clothes covered in sand. "Shake this stuff out and lay it on the table. Let's see what we have here shall we?"

Major Jameson sucked in his breath, it was almost impossible to discern the actual colour of the faded cloth but the three rusting pips on the epaulet lying in front of him could only belong to a captain in the British Army, with the four letters next to it. RAMC, they were faded but he recognised them instantly. Royal Army Medical Corps.

Jameson bowed his head for a few moments, then looked up at the two military policeman in front of him. "I want photographs of all of this," he gestured across the table. "Bag and seal all of it.

"At 0500 hours tomorrow morning, I want a full contingent of soldiers and a couple of medics, along with this man called Ahmed, ready to leave the base. The boy is innocent and probably rented out his camel to help Ahmed find our base. Let him and the camel go.

"Ahmed, under guard, will lead us to where he found this soldier and where he buried his uniform. I think he's telling us the truth."

He paused and looked at the soldiers who were waiting for their further instructions. "Treat him with respect and listen to him. It's possible the injured soldier he found in the desert might be Captain Michael Bennett.

"He tells us the man he rescued and cared for was badly injured. It's likely his mind is shattered as well, otherwise he would have found his own way back to us.

"It took a lot of courage for Ahmed to make this journey. You will treat him with the respect I think he is due, do you understand? Work with him and not against him, no matter what your own feelings may be about the situation in this God forsaken place."

Jameson looked out over the endless desert in front of him. "I want our officer back; he needs to go home for any treatment he may require. All of us will be responsible to make sure it happens."

The convoy of soldiers left well before the sun came up the next morning. The boy had taken his old camel and disappeared amongst the sand dunes.

Ahmed sat in the front of the first vehicle in the convoy. Major Jameson at the wheel. He was rigid with nerves with all the soldiers and guns around him, and following the vehicle he was travelling in.

He had travelled by camel all his life, he was not familiar with these army vehicles, he wondered if he would be able to lead these British back to where he had cared for their missing comrade for so many months. The desertscape looked different when not on a camel's unforgiving back.

Major Jameson had immediately contacted his commanding officer in England with the unexpected news there was perhaps an army officer who may have survived an ambush over two years or so ago. He had been given all the information they had. Within minutes he had been put through to Colonel Mallard, his predecessor, who had given him the co-ordinates of the journey Captain Bennett had set out on that fateful day when his entire unit disappeared without trace.

"If it is him, Major Jameson, bring him home. This chap called Ahmed has shown great courage in coming forward, putting his own life in danger. Take good care of him, you hear me? Make sure, if this is indeed Captain Bennett, he is rewarded. I expect nothing less, is that clearly understood?"

The small convoy made its way through the suffocating heat, following the journey the ill-fated one before had been making.

Ahmed had been silent as he looked at the endless shimmering desert in front and all around him. In the distance he saw the wavering mountains and caves to his right.

He stood up a smile spreading across his face, his Arab robes fluttering with the movement of the vehicle, oblivious of the guns now pointing at him from the soldiers behind him.

"We are close, Mr Major, we are close to where I come from. Close to where your soldiers were killed, except for the one I saved."

His eyes searched the terrain until he saw the tiny plume of smoke high up in the mountains and caves.

"My wife, Fatima, she has been waiting for us, to show us the way. See there the smoke? This is our home. Here is where the man we have looked after is now living."

Major Jameson looked up at the barren rocks and held up his hand, the vehicles all stopped. The troops dropping to the ground, their guns ready and waiting, in case of another ambush.

Ahmed jumped from the vehicle and beckoned for Major Jameson to follow him. "You must climb here. Where I climbed with your soldier. It is steep but there is a path, it is hard to see."

Jameson assessed the situation in front of him and made his decision immediately.

"Sergeant Higgins, you come with me. The rest of you stand guard."

He and the sergeant followed Ahmed along the sandy steep path, feeling the sweat trickling down their backs and faces.

They paused for a moment to catch their breath.

"Blimey, sir, look at that?"

Major Jameson looked up. There standing alone on a ledge stood a man dressed in traditional Arab attire. The whiteness of his robes was startling amongst the black rocks and wavering yellow sands.

His breath caught in his throat. The man was tall and still.

"Blimey, sir," Higgins repeated. "Looks like bleeding Lawrence of Arabia, don't he?"

"Lower your gun, sergeant and show some respect. If he meant us any harm he would have a gun pointing at us and be down on one knee. I'm going to move slowly towards him, lower my gun and put my hands up to show him we come in peace, watch my back all right?"

The Major moved slowly up the rocky path, following Ahmed moving towards the man in the flowing robes, holding his hands up in the air. He stopped in front of the tall man.

The Arab stared at him and slowly lifted his one arm in salute.

Speechless, the Major returned the salute and stared at the man's face. Slowly the man removed his headdress revealing long grey hair and an equally long beard and a pair of confused blue eyes.

The Major softened his voice, he recognised the look in the man's eyes, the man was in a state of shock, shell-shocked was the term they gave it in the army.

"Can you confirm your name to me, sir?"

The man stared at him then looked out into the distance as though he might find the answer out there somewhere, he appeared not to glance at the unit of soldiers in their vehicles down below him.

Ahmed came and stood next to the Major. "He is not speaking, sir, he does not know any words. But this is the soldier I found amongst his dead comrades. He is British, what I am telling you is true.

"I will bring him down to you as I brought him up to my place for he is trusting me. He will become frightened if you take him for no reason. He is also only having one arm and one strong leg; the other leg is not good for carrying him."

Ahmed reached for the man's one arm, and spoke softly to him, although he knew his words would not be fully understood. "These people are your people from across the sea. They have come to take you home to your own family where you will be cared for."

Major Jameson looked up and heard the thwack, thwack, thwack of a military helicopter carrying two medics on board coming into land, throwing up billowing hot clouds of sand. It had followed the unit of men from a distance in case there was any trouble.

Ahmed murmured to the man with the empty blue eyes as he slowly helped him down the rocky path, stopping now and again so he could rest his lame leg.

The two medics ran towards him. The tall grey-haired man shrank back, looking wildly around for Ahmed.

Ahmed nodded his head and smiled, gesturing for him to go with the men, holding his hand reassuringly between his own. "Go well, for you are safe now, with your own people."

The medics led him gently towards the helicopter.

Major Jameson turned to Ahmed and shook his hand. "Thank you. You saved his life. I should like to thank your wife myself if it is permissible."

Ahmed shook his head. "This will not be allowed; she must not be seen by other men."

Major Jameson nodded. "I understand, but please thank her."

"What is this man's name Mr Major? Do you know? Where is his home?"

Jameson cleared his throat. "We have reason to believe his name is Captain Michael Bennett. He is from England, but he has another home in a place called Lamu, in East Africa.

"The army will wish to reward you for your kind act of bravery, for saving his life."

Ahmed watched the medics carefully lift his captain into the helicopter.

He turned to the Major. "I have no wish for money from the army. My only wish is to return to my village with my wife. Allah will reward me when it is time.

"I seek only for peace in our land again. *Ma'a as Salama*. Go in peace Mr Major."

Jameson watched him make his way back up the rocky path. He turned to his sergeant. "Make sure the pilot gets some clear aerial shots of the area before he returns to base. In time we will send a team of forensics back here and try to find the remains of the other missing men. Metal detectors will find the vehicles. Stake the place out so we can find it again. Spray paint on one of the rocks as a marker.

"These men must be recovered and returned to their families. They will be given a full military funeral when the time comes.

"Let's return to base, there's a lot of paperwork to be done and arrangements must be made for Captain Bennett to be flown home for medical treatment and a full assessment of his physical and mental condition. It's unlikely he will fight any more wars."

He looked up once more to the rocky outcrop and saw Ahmed raise both his arms high in farewell as the helicopter lifted off and headed back to base, his flowing white robes fluttering against the black rocks behind him.

Major Jameson tried to dislodge the lump in his throat. He knew it was an image which would stay with him for the rest of his life.

An image of hope.

He shook his head. Ahmed may have appeared to be a simple Arab but there was intelligence in his dark watchful eyes. Ahmed would know, as they all did, there were always hidden eyes in the desert, in the caves. As soon as he sent his team back to search for the other dead men and vehicles, the bloody terrorists would go after Ahmed and his wife and kill them.

But he knew Ahmed, and his wife, would already be hurriedly packing whatever they had and disappearing back to the safety of their village, travelling through the dark nights and shadows of the mountains. Taking the memory of the tall man whose life they had saved, despite the dangerous repercussions if it had been discovered they had been sheltering him.

He bowed his head briefly, perhaps there was a God after all. Ahmed and his wife Fatima had given him a sliver of hope in an anxious world which seemed to be full of war, despair, terror and hopelessness.

Chapter Twenty-Three
South Africa

Tapu, Blake Hemmingway's housekeeper, had prepared the guest room for the person Blake was bringing home with him. He had been puzzled by the request to put some flowers in the room and chosen some fiery red hibiscus and placed them in a jar next to the looking mirror.

He had seen the billowing cloud of dust behind the vehicle on the horizon and hunkered down on the generous wrap-around veranda waiting to greet Mr Blake and his house guest.

Blake had chatted to Fleur on the four-hour journey from Graaff-Reinet, he explained his house was in the bush, but Tapu would be there who had worked for him for some years now. There was a town an hour away from the house where, once a week, the local farmers would come in from their various farms dotted around the landscape, and there Tapu would buy meat and vegetables from the back of their vehicles or stalls.

The so-called town was little more than a dusty village. It had a filling station with a tiny shop attached which sold dry goods, a bank, a modest pharmacy, a garage with one mechanic, a pub with a steak house and that was it.

He explained Tapu had prepared the guest room for her, where he occasionally entertained travelling colleagues from his company. He told her about his job, how much he travelled in the bush looking for business opportunities for development. He was away a lot, sometimes for days, sometimes for weeks, even a month or two, depending on where he was needed.

He had been born in England, grew up there in Brighton, was married briefly, but no children. After his divorce he had decided to re-locate to South Africa, a place he had been to many times with his work, and there in the quietness and solitude of the enduring landscape of the bush he had licked his emotional wounds and began his new life.

Fleur made the occasional comment, asked him a question or two, otherwise she remained silent watching the passing arid and hot landscape.

Blake braked suddenly, throwing her forward, but her seat belt held her securely in place. A group of warthogs marched across the road in front of them, their stiff tails held high, looking like a line of businessmen on their way to an important meeting.

Despite herself she laughed. Warthogs always looked so purposeful; she remembered them from her days in Kenya as a child. Down on the front legs, bums in the air, always so busy foraging in the ground.

They passed simple villages where the children waved and ran alongside the vehicle, covering them with dust, as they pulled their toys made of wire, or old supermarket trolleys behind them. The women walking tall with elegance as they balanced wood and water containers on their heads, babies strapped to their straight backs, lifting their hands in greeting at the passing vehicle.

It was a world away from the life Fleur had known, but it tugged at her African heart. "They're happier than us, Blake, they have so little, but what they have is known to them. Their world is safe within their communities, they're more content than we are with our modern world and uncertainty. A world full of greed and power, a world that fights wars to enhance their own lives, a world full of politicians who promise everything and never deliver."

Blake pulled up outside of his house and turned off the engine. "Now listen to me, Fleur, I know you're still a little confused with things – I had a long conversation with the doctor before he allowed me to take care of you until you are fully recovered. Somewhere along the line, from wherever you came from, you must have hit your head on something, he said you'll have some memory loss, but with time your memory would return.

"However long it takes, you're welcome to stay here in the guest cottage. When you're strong enough, you can make your own decisions about what you want to do next. But, meanwhile, I've been given the task and responsibility of looking after you, which, I have to say, will be my pleasure. It can get lonely out here with nobody to talk to…ah, here comes Tapu."

Tapu bounded up to the vehicle and opened the passenger door. A thin woman, wearing sunglasses, stepped down onto the path.

She held out her hand. "Hello, you must be Tapu. I've heard all about you."

Tapu beamed at her. "Yes, it is I, Tapu, here to welcome you to Mr Blake's house. I will take you to the guest room."

Blake nodded to him. "I have her luggage in the back Tapu. Settle her in, her name is Miss Fleur, then we need to unpack the truck and my equipment."

Fleur followed Tapu down a short dusty path, which led to a round house with the thatched roof. It consisted of one room. A double bed, draped in mosquito netting, a round table with two chairs and a room leading off to an outside shower and toilet.

Overhead a rattan fan moved slowly, rippling the sides of the mosquito netting. To the left of the bed, near a window was a square dressing table with a mirror, the bright red flowers Tapu had put there, creating the only splash of colour in the room. Next to it was a rail with coat hangers and underneath a few drawers made of some dark wood.

"I will collect your luggage now, Miss Fur, perhaps you will allow me to unpack for you, it is my job when we have guests?"

"No," she said quickly. "I need to lie down for a while. I can do it myself later. But please bring me some water, Tapu."

He lifted one side of the mosquito netting and hooked it to the top of the frame surrounding the bed. "Your water is here. I will leave you to rest for a while. Now I must unpack the truck for Mr Blake."

"Thank you," she whispered, and sank gratefully onto the bed, taking a long drink from a bottle of cold water she closed her eyes. Once more the greyness surrounding her.

Blake surveyed all the boxes and equipment spread around the veranda. Tapu, with his usual efficiency, was taking the empty cool boxes to the kitchen, returning to sort through the equipment and paperwork which he took through to the study.

He took a long hot shower and sank into one of the comfortable cane chairs overlooking the bush. Tapu brought him a cold beer.

"Will Miss Fur be having dinner with you Mr Blake. She is still sleeping?"

"Let her sleep, Tapu. She's been in hospital for a week or two, she's been through a rough time. Let her sleep for as long as she wants, check on her through the night. I need an early one myself; it's been a long journey; I'll have some toast then I'll be off to bed."

"Very good, Mr Blake. I will myself stay outside the door of the guest house in case Miss Fur wakes and needs anything. I will bring her food if she wakes and is hungry. Miss Fur is a thin person, she will be needing my cooking."

Tapu waited until the sun was setting before tapping gently on her door. Miss Fur was still sleeping. He left the soft night light on so she would not be frightened if she awoke in the dark.

He settled down outside her door. Mr Blake's room was in darkness, he too was sleeping. He would watch over them both.

As the sun rose through the grey and pink dawn, Tapu silently approached her bed. Miss Fur was waking up. "I will bring you tea Miss Fur and perhaps something to eat. The body is needing food I think?"

Fleur turned towards the sound of his voice. "Yes, I need food. Tea sounds lovely."

Tapu could only see the outline of her through the thick mosquito netting. "I will get this for you Miss Fur. Mr Blake is here; I am making his breakfast as well. Will you join him?"

She seemed to shake her head. "No, only tea now please and maybe some toast."

Blake tucked into his bacon and eggs, feeling refreshed and energised after a good night's sleep. "How is Miss Fleur, Tapu, have you checked on her?"

Tapu filled Blake's coffee cup. "Yes, she is also sleeping well. She wishes for only toast and tea. I will take it to her now."

Fleur was sitting outside of her guest room, watching the sun make its way towards the heavens. She had taken a shower and wrapped a large towel around her. Her suitcase still waiting to be unpacked.

She heard Tapu's cheerful voice as he called out to her. "Good morning, Miss Fur, I have brought you tea, some toast and some fruit for your breakfast."

She took off her sunglasses and smiled at him. He put down the tray and poured her tea. "Here, Miss Fur, tea and fruit is good for the digestion."

His voice faltered as he looked at her, his hand trembled and the tea spilled onto the cloth on the tray.

Those eyes. He had seen them before.

Fleur looked at him and frowned. "Why are you looking at me like that?"

Tapu bowed his head. "Sorry Miss Fur, I must leave for a few moments…"

Tapu sat down in his own quarters, his duties to Mr Blake and Miss Fur forgotten. He had been a young boy then, his mother had taken him to town where she lived and worked, this woman with the strange eyes had asked his mother questions about the people in the forest for which she had no answers. He had never seen anyone else with eyes like spilling sea. Mr Blake's guest must be a relative of the woman he had met as a young boy, perhaps even her mother, for she was older than Miss Fur.

He was frightened. The other woman with the same spilling eyes of blue had been looking for something which he and his people had kept hidden from her.

His people lived deep in the forests of the Eastern Cape. For many years the previous government had been moving many of the other clans of San people from their homes in the desert. They had left, some seeking work in other places, others moving together to other hidden places where the government would not find them, but where they could still practice their skills and old traditional ways. Growing their own food and hunting in the shadows of the dark night. But his people were now poor with no desert to call their home, they could not move freely as they had before. He knew there was no future for the San people and soon they would all be gone.

The children born in the forests and towns would forget their old way of life and not learn the traditional skills of the nomadic tribes of San people who had lived in the harsh desert for thousands of years.

Mr Blake had told him this guest sometimes would not remember things. But perhaps there would be things she had heard about and remembered. He would follow her closely and watch to see if she was also looking for the secrets of his people

Chapter Twenty-Four
2005

Fleur paced around the impressive vegetable garden she and Tapu had created over the following years. At the back of Blake's house, they now had chickens which supplied them with newly laid eggs every day and one cow who provided fresh milk. There had been two cows once, but the other one had been taken by a lion in the dark of the night and been carried away into the bush.

Once a month she would go to the market, an hour's drive away, with Tapu and buy their meat and other provisions. Blake had given Tapu his own car years ago, it was old but reliable, the paint faded and its journey through life marked by dents and scratches.

She would leave Tapu to gossip with his friends as she spent three hours at the local clinic administering pills and medical treatments for the long queue of people who waited for her visit every month. The local farmers, their wives and children also waited for her.

Once when Miss Fur was having dinner with Mr Blake, he had gone to her room to prepare the mosquito netting over her bed and had seen the small book with the animal skin covering and opened it but did not understand the writing there. At the back of the book, he had found photographs of plants and herbs, and his heart had beat rapidly.

The guest staying with Mr Blake was seeking what they held secret.

With Tapu's help she had found many things which she recognised from her writings and her mother's drawings. Tapu showed her new plants and leaves his own people used for healing.

She knew he was a San person, or at least had the diluted blood of the San people running through his veins. His eyes were green, his cheekbones high and he had the wiry frame of the people of the desert. His skin was more of a chocolate colour than of an African, and although not old he had a lined face, but it was hard to say exactly how old he was.

Whilst Blake was away on his business trips, she and Tapu would visit remote parts of the Eastern Cape looking for specimens and meeting the local traditional healers.

If Blake were going to a new area they hadn't been to before, Fleur and Tapu would go with him. She would sleep in the back of the truck with Blake and Tapu would roll out his bed and find a suitable spot in the bush to sleep. If an area was known for predators, Tapu would sleep under the vehicle for safety.

In the evenings Fleur and Blake would sit around the campfire, whilst Tapu grilled their meat over the fiery embers and talk about many things, the plants, the country, the politics, the people they had met, whilst under the clear black sky, a canopy of brilliant stars looked down on them.

All around them animals would come out for their nightly hunt, but Fleur had no fear of the spine-tingling roars of the lions, the deep rumbling of the elephants, the bark of a jackal, the sneeze of an antelope, the cackling of the hyena, or the cough of a leopard, she had become used to them and her life in the remote parts of the bush. If they camped near water, she loved to hear the deep belly laughs of the hippo as they made their way onto land to forage along the shores of the lake at night. It reminded her of her childhood at Naivasha.

Now she looked up when she heard a vehicle in the distance, the dust rising behind it as it made its way towards her.

Blake was coming home.

"Tapu," she called, "the boss is back. Is everything prepared for dinner tonight? Did you prepare the French cooking I showed you? Is there plenty of ice for his drink?"

Tapu smiled. Since Miss Fur had arrived, she had changed everything. Mr Blake was a happy man.

"Yes, Miss Fur, all is in order, all is waiting for him with the French cooking with the red wine and much cream."

Fleur ran to the bedroom, took a quick shower, and brushed her hair, letting it hang loose around her shoulders, the way he liked it, then changed into a long pale pink dress, she knew was his favourite.

Dabbing a little perfume around the base of her throat, she ran out onto the veranda and waited for him.

From the moment Blake had met her he had felt responsible for her. For weeks he had left her to put her world back together again, knowing Tapu was always at her side, watching over her.

Blake still travelled, but with the country in turmoil, the new President firmly in place, he didn't worry too much about his own safety, because he carried a gun like many South Africans. But he wanted to be close to her, spend time with her, protect her. He had, of course, fallen in love with her.

Initially she had rejected his suggestion she make the little cottage her own place and work out of there. "I couldn't possibly Blake, I have no money to pay any rent or contribute to other living expenses."

"Listen Fleur I travel a great deal, I'm away more often than I'm here, as you know. You could take care of the place for me, make something of it. Make it your own, buy some chickens, plant vegetables, teach Tapu how to cook, his repertoire is sadly lacking in that department."

He watched her carefully. "My house, well actually it's not my house, it's supplied by the company I work for, is what you might call basic. I don't have time to make it into a home, as you can see. You could help me do that. Let's face it, if you moved somewhere else you would have to pay rent, buy furniture and a car and you wouldn't have Tapu to help you with your research. Plus, you would be a stranger wherever you went. It's not a good time to live in some remote place as a single female, wandering around the bush on your own."

He leaned forward. "At least think about it. Once you've completed your research you can return to the UK and pick up your old life complete with your mysterious cure. Pharma companies will be queuing around the block to get their hands on your seeds, plants, or bits of bark and herbs.

"I think it's a great plan and would suit both of us. We can lead separate lives and you'll be here for company when I make a quick pit stop before heading off again."

He pushed ahead trying to persuade her to stay with him. "Tapu can drive you to town for your shopping, you'll get to meet the locals, maybe even help with the local clinic there. You could make a big difference to a lot of people's lives."

Fleur asked him to give her time to think it through. She knew it made sense. She felt safe here and looked forward to seeing Blake when he returned from his trips around the country and cities.

The one thing that puzzled Blake was her reluctance to open a bank account, although there was one in the dusty town nearby.

"Look, Blake, there's a reason why I don't want to open a bank account, not yet anyway. I have a considerable amount of dollars which I can use when I need cash. I hid them in my suitcase when I arrived in South Africa, the bank will change them to Rand for me at a considerably attractive exchange rate, so I'm not exactly penniless."

He watched her face, the fleeting sadness which crossed it. "Who are you hiding from Fleur Palmere? Will you tell me?" he asked softly.

Alarmed he had seen the tears filling those incredible eyes. "It's the way I want it to be, Blake. I need a new life now. A fresh start. It's better for everyone I know to let me out of their lives and get on with their own. So, let's leave it like that shall we. I don't want to discuss it, and I never will."

Blake nodded. "Of course, I shall respect your wishes. So, what better place to start a new life than right here with me in the middle of nowhere where nobody knows anything about you?

"What do you say to the arrangement I've proposed?"

She smiled at him. "Alright. Yes, it is the perfect place for me right now. Thank you, Blake. I've never been much of a housekeeper or cook, but I'll give it my best shot. But I want to transfer some funds from my lawyer in England, into your account. I'll feel more comfortable if I can contribute."

Blake watched her walk back to the little round house and frowned. What was she running away from? He had a strong feeling it had a lot to do with Captain Michael Bennett. But he wasn't going to rock the boat, he would respect her wishes for a new life – especially now it included him and his home. If Fleur had no wish to discuss her past life and Captain Michael Bennett, he saw no need to tell her he was dead. Their relationship, for whatever reason, was as dead as he was.

Years later Fleur was still there. Their relationship had grown, he loved her and hoped, in time, she would come to love him.

With the new culinary skills, she had taught Tapu they enjoyed many a meal when Blake returned to his home.

If Blake travelled to a decent sized town, or went to Johannesburg on business, he always brought her newspapers and magazines, not that she was interested in those, but she enjoyed keeping up with what was going on in South Africa and the rest of the world. The one magazine she enjoyed immensely was The Spectator. Then, unexpectedly he had brought her a copy of The Lancet, Britain's leading magazine on medicine and science, this she devoured, savouring every article especially the one about a certain Doctor William Mwanga, a Kenyan scientist, who had been working for some years for The Foundation in London, her old company.

Doctor Mwanga indicated his company was on the verge of a breakthrough with a new drug which would change the lives of thousands of patients who were suffering from one of the most puzzling diseases modern sciences had known. He had hinted that combining traditional and modern medicine would produce a cure so desperately needed. In this regard, he had declared, his research was turning to South Africa and its abundance of rare and valuable plants which would make such a cure possible when converted to a parallel synthetic alternative available to all those, and their families, who were hopeful for such a cure.

Fleur sat back in her chair a slight smile on her face. "Oh yes, Doctor Mwanga," she murmured to herself, "but I'm still way ahead of you on this one, if this is indeed what you are chasing. You need contact with the people who know what you're looking for. It takes years to win their trust, they are a tight knit community who covert their knowledge and secrets. I fear you may struggle as, with my brief encounter with you at The Foundation, you don't evoke trust, only greed. You are not from their land; they will not trust you anymore than I did.

"Should the day come when the cure is found and I believe it will be, the accolades will not be given to me, this I have no wish for. The accolades will be given to the people who have always known the cure. The San people of South Africa.

"I'm way ahead of you on this one, Doctor William Mwanga!"

Fleur had eventually told Blake about her life in Kenya, where she had been brought up, her sister Helene who lived in England with her daughter, Lucy. Her mother who had dedicated her life to studying traditional healing. Her love affair with Captain Michael Bennett, which she had broken off so many years ago now and had not been in touch with since.

"You see, Blake, he was the love of my life, but it was an impossible life for both of us, too much distance between us. Once you have loved like that it's impossible to replicate it."

Blake had remained silent about what he knew about Captain Michael Bennett. She had ended the relationship, it was in the past, he would keep it that way. He had no way of knowing how she might react to his decision to not tell her, it might damage their own relationship which was the last thing he wanted to do. He wasn't prepared to take that chance.

Fleur reached for his now familiar hand. "Yes, you can love again but in a different way. A new lover will look different, feel different, his body contours different, his voice not familiar, his sense of humour different, his attitude to life, his character all new. Yes, it is possible to love again, as I love you. It's not the same, I know, but it's as valuable to me as my love was for him. I hope he is happy somewhere; met someone he could marry and have children with. That's my wish for him."

Blake knew that this had been impossible for Michael.

Her relationship with her sister Helene had mystified him for a while. She seemed to have no contact with her, this he accepted for whatever the reasons may have been. People, he knew, made choices to better enhance any new life they were moving towards. He never intruded on what might have happened between the two sisters. Fleur still wore the pendent around her neck. Never took it off. The other child in the photograph was her sister Helene.

As with most couples there were things which remained hidden, of no importance, things which would not make a difference anymore to either of them, would not enhance the enchanted world of falling in love again.

Over time, with the help of his international contacts and the British Embassy in Pretoria he had helped put her past back together. She now had a new passport. A copy of her birth certificate, father unknown.

Blake had suspected all along that in a way Fleur's gaps of loss of memory was self-inflicted. But it would make no difference now. She had chosen to leave whatever it was behind. She had a new life now, with him. Michael Bennett was dead.

Over the years she travelled with him when he was out and about in the bush looking for new projects. Tapu always came with them, showing Miss Fur as he still called her, different terrains, different forests, and hidden places where he collected samples with her and discussed their healing possibilities.

Blake's computer was functional enough for his work. Tapu did not know how to work this strange machine. But he watched Miss Fur looking at her notes and taking her photographs of the things they had gathered. The information written in her book she used on the tapping machine then transferred it to something she called a floppy disc. These square discs she always carried around in the leather bag across her chest.

One evening, as he was clearing the table from the dinner he had cooked, he heard Mr Blake ask Miss Fur if she had found what she had been looking for, for so many years.

Tapu took his time clearing the table waiting to hear what her answer to this question might be. "I'm close to finding what *Mama* was looking for, very close. I know these plants grow deep in the forest, there must be San people there because they're the only ones who would know."

Blake smiled at her. "What's so special about this plant or these seeds, you've never told me."

Tapu had hesitated slightly as he brushed the crumbs slowly from the table, hoping to buy a little time, hoping he might hear something.

Miss Fur had glanced at him. "We'll take coffee out on the veranda, Tapu. Thank you for dinner, it was excellent. I've taught you well."

Fleur waited until he left the room. "I've never shared this information with anyone Blake, my *Mama* warned me never to tell anyone. But now I'm so excited because I know I'm close to finding what she was looking for. She spent her whole life looking for this healing plant. It's not a plant, it's a seed and it's only grown in one place now. If I'm right, the discovery of those seeds is going to have a huge impact on the western world, on medicine and science. Its value is incalculable. It will be worth billions of dollars. It will rattle the big pharma companies, it's the last thing they want to hear about. It's massive Blake – and its dangerous knowledge if it falls into the wrong hands."

Blake stared at her. "So, what is it?"

"If I tell you I'll put your life in jeopardy, one word in the wrong ear and we'll both be in danger. I know it seems odd, but I can't tell you. I can't take any risks. But I promise, when I find those seeds, you will be the first one I'll tell. Because we'll have to find a company we can trust to advise us on the best way forward. Not, and I repeat, not any of the international pharma companies.

"The key, once I've found the seeds, is to see if they can be germinated in different soils, be grown in other countries, be produced in laboratories without losing any of their magical healing properties. If this is possible it can be made available to those patients who so desperately need help."

Blake took a sip of his now cold coffee. "But if this is all a possibility and the same formulae can be reproduced without losing any of its powers, well, it could take years before it will be available to patients, there are many rigorous legal and medical challenges when introducing a new drug to the market."

"Yes Blake. But someone must start somewhere and that's been my mother's and my mission in life. It must never get into the wrong hands, the seeds I mean. Because if they do the pharma companies will bring out their big guns and destroy it, decimate the source of the seeds and anything else in their path, including the San people, who know where these seeds grow, and their way of life. I need to protect these people too. They've been displaced for well over a hundred years now, their nomadic life destroyed, their unique hunting and tracking skills almost lost in time."

Fleur took a deep breath. "I want whichever company I trust with this cure, if this is what it is, to give back to these people what has been taken from them. A bit like the cure itself…

"They need to return to the place they have inhabited for thousands of years. It will be petty cash for my chosen company to commit to buying a sizeable piece of land in the desert, the Kalahari perhaps, and let these people go home and gather their old ways. Without this commitment there will be no deal. They will be the custodians of the cure."

Blake laughed. "Well now you really do have to tell me what this fabulous cure might be. If you can't trust me, who can you trust? Anyway, I know a little about your work but most of it, with all those Latin names is a complete mystery to me. Come on. What are you hoping these seeds are going to do to cure your mystery diseases."

Fleur hesitated, she did trust him, of course she did. It would be a relief to share her research with someone, it had been a heavy load to carry alone for so many years. Now she had almost reached her goal and the excitement of being able to talk to someone about it was overwhelming, intoxicating.

"Alright darling. Of course I trust you, I'm practically bursting with excitement.

"Let's have a glass of wine and celebrate what I hope is the end of a very long journey taken by *Mama* and myself."

For the next hour she talked to Blake and told him everything.

"My God, Fleur, this is huge. If you're right, it *will* be a game changer. What will be your plan of action when you find those berries or seeds?"

Fleur took a sip of her wine. "I haven't really thought much about that part yet. But these San people must be protected at all costs."

Blake looked out into the dark night his mind working rapidly. "Well, let me advise you on what you should do. As you know I work with some of the best lawyers in this country on my various projects.

"One of them is known as the Rottweiler, his name is George Mason. Everyone is terrified of him; he has never lost a case in his life, and I've never won an argument with him. But he gets the job done. I suggest you meet with him; he's based in Johannesburg."

He looked at her steadily. "You must trust him and get some advice from him. He'll protect you and your findings, make sure they're registered to you, until you decide which company you want to trust this incredible information with."

Fleur wrapped the blanket hanging from the chair around her shoulders. "Once we reach that stage, Blake, your George Mason should be able to advise on which pharma company to entrust it to. I would like it to be a South African company, a company who will respect the people who have found the right compound to make the drug I'd like to see created."

Tapu who had been hiding in the shadows, listening to Miss Fur talk, sank to his haunches. He had been right. Miss Fur with her strange eyes must be the daughter of the woman who his people had been hiding from in the forest.

On his last trip with Miss Fur, they had journeyed to a remote village on the edge of the great Karoo region, the ancestral home of some of his nomadic people who had wandered there amidst the vast plains and rugged mountains where rare plants and animal species were found. There was a *sangoma* there, a medicine man, a healer of his people, an advisor to his people. This man was not a San person, but Tapu knew he had San blood running through his veins.

A child in the village had tugged at Tapu's shirt and told him he must bring the white woman to him.

Tapu had tried to make light of it, but his heart was heavy with a sense of foreboding. "Miss Fur, there is someone here who wishes to meet you. He is a traditional healer, much respected by the people hereabouts. He is called a *sangoma,* a healing person like you. I will take you to him if you wish?"

Fleur was intrigued, over the years she had met many medicine men and woman and been fascinated with their way of treating people who looked for mental and physical cures for their ailments.

But it was something bigger than that. Unlike in the western world when patients had been told they had untreatable illnesses, and there was nothing, other than drugs which may give them a little more time, they had accepted it, fought against it, but in the end had given in to it. Others, if they had great wealth, would seek any other possible means of medicine which might extend their lives. Consulting world leaders in medicine who might save their lives if they paid them enough, or so they thought and hoped.

Some patients who had been diagnosed early enough had indeed fought the demons of a disease and gone on to live a normal life, but in the back of their minds they knew the disease may come back, perhaps lying dormant but ready to strike again. So, their lives were only half lived, yes, with hope, that little word again, but also aware whatever disease they had been diagnosed with might creep back into their bodies, if not already hiding there; they had looked death in the face once and fought against it. But they were always waiting, knowing one day it may return.

The rural people Fleur had worked with had a different attitude. They had utter faith their traditional healer would heal whatever ailment they had. The healer had no word for the disease they had, had no idea how long it would take to make them well again. Was the spirit, therefore, stronger than the physical disease? If it were not given a name could the disease be cured by complete faith and trust?

She pursued this aspect with her research. But there was one disease all the people knew about – the slim disease, which the world soon became aware of as AIDS.

Traditional healers knew there was no cure for this; no western medicine would make it go away. This he told the slim ones who sat in front of him, and this the people accepted. They looked for no cure, only towards the ancestors they would soon be joining. There was no traditional medicine, or western, which would help them.

Chapter Twenty-Five

Fleur entered the *sangoma's* round conical hut, it was dark and smoky inside, once her eyes had adjusted to the darkness and the thick smoke which brought tears to her eyes and made her cough as discreetly as she could, she saw the shadowy figure sitting in the middle of the hut, he indicated she should sit on the skin of a long dead animal and remove her shoes.

This she did. Looking around she saw the skulls of long dead animals, abandoned snake skins hanging from the rafters, beads and shells, with many coloured feathers and bleached bones everywhere.

She wiped her eyes and looked up at the *sangoma.* He was an old man, his dark brown skin wrinkled with many lines across his face and body. Around his head and waist, he wore the tails and pelts of leopards, his scrawny chest hung with many shells and beads. Metal bracelets and colourful wooden beads adorned his arms and legs and rattled when he moved, his lower body covered in some kind of soft leather pelt from yet another dead animal.

The *sangoma* looked at her for a long moment then cast his eyes down and lifted the bag by his side. He crouched down on his haunches and gently shook it before releasing the contents of bones and wood in front of him. He stared at them, saying nothing, but his lips were moving. He scooped them up and threw them down again.

He rocked back and forth then stopped moving and looked straight at her, his legs now stretched out in front of him, the bones and beads between them. Fleur could feel the strong aura of energy around this strange man.

He spoke softly and Fleur leaned forward to catch his words.

"*Mama* doctor you have travelled far, you have looked for many answers to the questions you seek. It is better if you do not find these answers. They bring danger to you. This the spirits have told me."

He poked his finger amongst the bones. "You must return to where you come from, across the sea where your people have their own medicine. Ours is not for you to give. It is for us to give if we so wish."

Once more he looked at his bones and bits of wood. "I am knowing you would come here to look for what she was looking for; she with the same eyes. Your ancestor."

Fleur sucked in her breath. "My mother came here. You met with her?"

"Your mother met with me, *mama;* she with the same eyes. People who seek for something come here to me; it is not me who looks for these people who are needing help."

Fleur was speechless, not wishing to intrude on this wise old man's thoughts and words with the spirits, this old man who had met her mother.

Carefully the old man gathered his bones and replaced them in his old worn pouch.

He looked at her. "Your ancestor has gone now to another place in Africa. She is no longer here to help you with what you are looking for. The spirits tell me, your mother perhaps, you must stop this looking.

"There are two people sharing your life now, one is a good man to be trusted with watching you. There is someone coming for you, *mama*. This person will take all from you. He is already known to you."

The *sangoma* stood up, seemingly exhausted with his contact with the spirit world, then he disappeared into the dark shadows of his hut.

Realising their meeting was over, Fleur stood up, badly shaken, and made her way out of the gloom and smoke of the hut and into the bright sunlight and fresh air.

Tapu was waiting for her. He hurried towards her; his face creased with worry. "Come Miss Fur, there is a hotel not far from here. It is better you stay there this night and not in the truck. Your face is very pale… I will get the hotel to call Mr Blake, I am thinking he must come now from wherever he is in Johannesburg. He will take care of you as both of us have always done."

Tapu took her to the simple hotel, taking the money card from the bag around her neck he presented it the receptionist. "This person is Doctor Palmere, as you can see here from the money card. She is unwell and needs to sleep. Someone will come for her tomorrow."

The receptionist looked at her potential guest. She did indeed look unwell, her eyes unfocussed, her face pale, almost as though she was in some kind of trance. "Would you like me to call a local doctor?"

Tapu gave her a proud smile. "No. She is a medical doctor herself. She needs to sleep. I am thinking her mind is tired. Her partner will be here tomorrow if I can be permitted to use your telephone?"

The young receptionist took her guest to her room, herself. Tapu padding along silently behind them.

"Here we are Doctor Palmere. Lie down for a while, it's a hot day and you probably need to rest for a while. She turned to the anxious man next to her. "What is your name?"

"I am Tapu. I have worked for Mr Blake and Miss Fur, who are together for many years now. When Mr Blake is travelling, he trusts me to look after Miss Fur. This is what I must do, it is my job."

The receptionist, Magda, made up her mind immediately. "Listen Tapu, you seem like a good and caring man. I'll order food for you and Doctor Palmere, so long. You can use the phone and find her friend. I want you stay here in the room next to the doctor's, I will give you the key so you can watch over her until he arrives. If you need anything at all just call me. My name is Magda – okay?"

Tapu looked at her and his smile softened his face. "Thank you."

Tapu had spoken to Blake. "I am thinking, Mr Blake, I will take Miss Fur back to our house. She will tell you what happened. You must finish your important business in the city, and we will see you when you come home."

Blake had agreed with him. "Okay, Tapu. Take her home, she'll tell me everything when I get back."

Chapter Twenty-Six

Doctor William Mwanga, the Kenyan scientist, who had taken over from Doctor Fleur Palmere, had been busy mapping out his own future since he had joined The Foundation.

Much as he disliked the South African botanist, Hansie, he could turn out to be a valuable person for his new company.

Doctor Mwanga, two years ago now, had registered his own company in the land of his birth, Kenya. His family there were wealthy and knew all the right politicians and businessmen to open the right doors. He called his new pharmaceutical company Mediken. He was the sole shareholder and Chairman of the company, his brother, a scientist himself, disseminated the information William sent back to him from The Foundation, in London, building his own data base for the future.

Once he was appointed Head of Research, Mwanga had sent his assistant, Hansie, back to his homeland, South Africa, on a regular basis, to pursue various projects, all involving his skills as a botanist. He knew his country better than most; the world of game lodges and game rangers was tight. Everyone knew everyone else in the industry.

Doctor William Mwanga waited for his moment, which came sooner than he expected. He had been building up his pharma company, with his brother in Kenya. Storing valuable information he gleaned from his work with the big company he now worked for. But so far, he was not trading.

His timing had been perfect. Now he looked at the surly face of his assistant, Hansie, across his expansive desk.

"So, you want to leave this prestigious company permanently, and return home, is this correct? You have given in your notice, I hear."

The South African nodded his head. "Yup, despite everything I want to go home. Been here in London for far too long. I'll look for a job as a game ranger, I want to be back in the bush, amongst the wild animals. Too much wildness here in London. It's become a nanny state where the police seem unable to do anything in case they upset someone, and I hate the weather. Need to go back home before I get too old."

Doctor Mwanga nodded his head. "Yes, I can understand this. I also wish for my own country often. Your country South Africa is struggling with the changes which have come, a lot of hostility and anger towards the old apartheid government. The Black people want their land back which includes the game lodges. You'll find it difficult to find a job until things settle down."

He gave Hansie a satisfied smile. "Tourists are turning their back on a longed-for safari in your country, in fact Kenya is benefitting from this, the tourists come to us now, for we are a peaceful country with extraordinary landscapes where the game roam freely. The crime and corruption in your country has tainted your tourism industry."

The game ranger nodded gloomily. "Yes, I know, we've all seen the movies produced there, *Out of Africa*, being the smash hit it was, it turned tourism around in your country. Tourists have turned their back on what we in South Africa have to offer. Wild animals are not feared as much as the violence, crime and killings, the pure anger of the people of South Africa, of all races."

Doctor Mwanga fiddled with the pen on his desk. "If you're interested, I may be able to offer you something in South Africa. Away from the hot spots in the cities, out in the bush."

Hansie looked at him suspiciously. "I will require you to sign a confidentiality agreement with the company I have formed in Kenya – Mediken. I am prepared to pay you well and offer all the benefits other companies in the industry offer."

Hansie frowned. "I know you don't like me, but I'm not a fool Doctor Mwanga. You've been passing all the information we have worked on here to your own company in Kenya. Is that what you're telling me. Are The Foundation aware of this?"

Mwanga grinned. "Of course not. That's why I'm offering you a good job.

"See here, we've both been working on traditional medicine in Africa trying to ascertain how we can take this medicine and turn it into something synthetic to sell to the millions who are looking for cures. We've done well. However, there's one person who is working out there on her own. She's way ahead of the pack, shall we say."

He polished his glasses. "From what I can gather from my various contacts, she's close to discovering with all her research over the years since she left London, a cure for one of the most mystifying diseases the western word has seen. There seems to be no cure for it – but I think our Doctor Fleur Palmere is close to finding it."

Mwanga leaned back in his executive chair. "The information I've gathered from various sources, which shall remain anonymous, is that she's looking somewhere in the Eastern Cape. It seems the San people, in only one area, have what I'm looking for."

Mwanga continued. "I want you to find where she's living. Who knows she might remember you and be pleased to share any progress she's made."

Hansie frowned. "Am I getting this right? You want me to track her, use my contacts in the safari world, find out what she has found out? You said you'd heard she was in the Eastern Cape somewhere, that's a damn big area to try and find someone in. But it can be done, might take a few weeks?"

"Precisely. You will be well paid. So, what is your answer?"

The South African botanist, Hansie, had many faults, had failed so many times in his life, had never had enough money to live a lifestyle he dreamed about. But even so what the man across the desk seemed to be asking him, turned his stomach.

Mwanga shuffled some files on his desk. "Get on the first flight to South Africa and track that woman down." He said gruffly.

"So, what exactly are you asking me to do?"

Mwanga looked out of the window, his expression blank. "Whatever is necessary. Find the woman and see how she is doing with her research, that's all. There will be a large bonus in it for you.

"Nothing sinister about that is there?"

Chapter Twenty-Seven

Fleur pushed up her glasses and rubbed her eyes. The next time she and Blake went to a decent sized town she needed to have her eyes checked. Too much close work with the computer and the expensive microscope Blake had bought for had taken its toll on her eyes.

Blake had converted the spare bedroom in the house into a modest laboratory. Here Fleur kept all her samples, her notes, specimen jars and research books. Every night, without fail, she locked the door with a sturdy padlock, much to the amusement of Blake and Tapu.

Blake came up behind her and rubbed her shoulders. "Come on, darling, dinner's ready. Let's eat outside tonight, it's a beautiful evening, crisp and clear. Tapu has started a fire which will keep us warm whilst we eat. The table looks beautiful, as beautiful as you, with all the candles and lanterns. Tapu has even put hot water bottles on the seats and blankets over the chairs for when it gets cold later."

Blake and Fleur sat and ate, looking out over the bush, the candles flickering with the cool breeze, the fire with its embers keeping them warm as they sat outside, hissing and spitting as it shot flurries of sparks into the night.

Fleur twirled her wine glass and watched the starburst of light coming through the glass from the fire. "Are you frightened of dying Blake?"

He laughed. "No, of course not, when you're gone, you're gone. Nothing to be afraid of, you won't know anything about it. Losing someone you love is the hardest thing. The one that's left behind pays the price for loving too much."

Fleur looked at him thoughtfully. "It's not as simple as that, Blake. "You see in my world, science is tantamount to religion. Science is based on fact, unlike religion which is based on pure faith with no credible answers.

"Religion and science in their pursuit of knowledge, truth, and understanding have certain parallels. Science is based on scepticism, the search for the unknown, searching for truth and answers to questions, not so different from religion, you see."

Fleur wrapped the light blanket around her shoulders. "Religion involves accepting certain beliefs, but people are also searching for the truth and answers. They want proof. Sadly, they will never find it. But science will present truth, whether people want to believe it or not."

"Come on Fleur, let's talk about something else, why be so gloomy on a perfect night like tonight?"

Tapu cleared their plates away and brought the coffee out.

Blake thanked him and wished him goodnight. But Tapu stayed where he was.

Blake smiled at him, slightly bewildered. He released a moth from his glass of wine. "Is something wrong, something you want to talk about?"

Tapu nodded his head. "It is permitted I may sit here with you both. I have something I wish to say."

Fleur glanced at Blake and felt her stomach contract with something she didn't understand, a sense of foreboding perhaps.

Blake grinned at Tapu. "Not going to resign, I hope. What would we do without you?"

Tapu perched on the edge of the chair. "There are some people who wish to meet Miss Fur. They have what she is seeking, but they are afraid. I am the only one who is permitted to take her there. We are from the same clan; I don't know exactly where they live but I have been given directions so I may find them."

Fleur felt the excitement bubble and burst within her, she had always known Tapu was holding something back as they searched the bush and the mountains for hidden plants and herbs.

Blake looked baffled. "Why didn't you mention this before Tapu? Miss Fleur would never harm anyone, you know that. Why haven't you told her this?"

Tapu shrugged. "It was not my decision to make, Mr Blake, it could only be made by the elders of these people who have this knowledge. I will show her the way."

Fleur lay in Blake's arms, her ear against his chest, the warmth of his now familiar body keeping her warm and feeling safe.

"I must go with Tapu, darling, he knows after all this time what I've been looking for. He's been watching me from the moment he met me. I also think he's been in touch with these hidden people for a long time now. I must go with him. He trusts me, as I trust him."

Blake pulled her close and ran his fingers through her thick hair. "Of course you must Fleur, of course you must. There's a big meeting in Port Elizabeth this week and I have to be there, all the directors from Geneva are going to be present, including the Chairman, so I'm not sure what's going on.

"Tapu said the place he wants to take you to is somewhere near the coast. He hasn't told me where exactly. There are thick forests there, almost impenetrable, this is where these people must be living now, the people who know what you and your mother have been looking for. You'll be safe with him, I trust him. As he trusts me."

He stroked her back. "I checked the location on my map where he wants to take you to and I've come up with a plan, because I'm now as intrigued as you are."

He grinned at her. "But I have a plan. There's a place on the Wild Coast. The Wild Coast stretches hundreds of kilometres, it's called Safe Harbour, a simple rustic hotel, apparently, and a ridiculous name because there is no safe harbour there. But you go off with Tapu. I'll have my meeting with the directors. We can meet up at the hotel, far away from everyone and everything, no problems there, no violence, no politics, it's almost like another world. Let's have a couple of days, take a much-needed break and you can tell me all about your trip with Tapu. Have to say I do need a break, need to wind down a bit, been feeling a bit tired lately – must be getting old. I'll see you at the hotel on Friday."

Blake looked at the ceiling and took a deep breath. "I need to tell you something. Something I've kept from you for years. It's been weighing on me heavily for some time now, and we need to discuss our future."

Fleur propped herself up on her elbow. "Gosh, this all sounds very mysterious, why don't you tell me now?"

He pulled her towards him. "Because I can't. It needs to be the right time in the right place.

"Once Tapu's dropped you off at the hotel, let him bring the old car back here. I'll join you there and we can travel back together in mine. If for any reason I should be delayed, well, you take the time out, use the Safe Harbour phone and call Tapu to pick you up, okay?"

Fleur lay quietly next to him, listening to his heartbeat which she had always known as steady and constant. She frowned slightly. Yes, he needed a break, his heartbeat was no longer as steady as before, skipping a beat now and again. Or perhaps he was apprehensive about the meeting and their own future.

Two days holiday was what was needed. She would travel with Tapu and see what he wanted to show her. She and Blake, hopefully, would have two glorious days together away from everything. She was more than intrigued with what he wanted to tell her.

"You know something, Blake, you should take Tapu with you in the future, he speaks English, Afrikaans, and Khosa, it would be good to be seen to have a local assistant in this new South Africa, I think it's a great idea.

"What do you think – good idea?"

Blake nuzzled the back of her neck. "Go to sleep, darling, we both have a big day tomorrow, but, yes, it *is* a splendid idea. Let's discuss it some more when we have the time at the beach."

What Blake hadn't told her, as she slept peacefully next to him was that TLI, the company he had worked for, for so many years, had decided to close their operations and investment in South Africa. The risk, and the politics in the country, were too high with no guaranteed long-term investment. They wanted him to move somewhere else to ascertain whether there were potential markets elsewhere for investment.

He had a tough decision to make.

He knew Fleur would not leave South Africa, not now she was so close to finding what she had been searching for. She would either come with him or he would have to resign. It would mean the company would take back the house where they lived, the vehicle and everything else. Tapu would have to find another job somewhere.

He tried to imagine not working, moving somewhere else in South Africa. He wasn't ready for retirement. He couldn't imagine sitting around some house in suburbia playing the classic husband whilst Fleur carried on her work. He knew the relationship would not sustain such a shift in circumstances. He knew he would change, become restless, discontent, and bored.

His whole life in South Africa had been spent driving around the bush looking for potential investment for his company. It was a life he loved, the only life he knew, until Fleur came along and enhanced it even further with her presence.

He wasn't a wealthy man by any means, he needed to keep making money. Setting up from scratch somewhere else, buying a house, furnishing it, a vehicle and all the other things up until now the company had provided; living a domestic life was not an option.

However, if Fleur had found the cure she had been searching for, she would take the world of medicine to a level thought to be impossible. She would be famous; her life would change immeasurably, and he would be left floundering in her wake.

Blake slid out of bed, careful not to disturb Fleur, and went out to the *stoep*. The sky was as black as pitch, not a star in sight, the wind hissed, growled, and whipped around the house as if it too wanted to find which direction to go.

He knew the meeting he would have the next day, before he met Fleur at Safe Harbour, would define his future. He wasn't sure their relationship would survive such a huge shift in circumstances.

His success with the company over the years had never factored in a family a wife, or any personal life come to that. No, his success was based on the fact he was always available to go anywhere at any time for as long as it took.

He went back to the bedroom and watched her as she slept, gently pushing back the hair from her face.

He had made his decision.

He would have to hold his nerve and focus on what had to be done to secure his future. If sacrifices had to be made, so be it.

Chapter Twenty-Eight

Tapu nosed the old car as far as he could into the thick forests with the backdrop of mystical mountains, with their rugged secret cloudy peaks.

"We must leave the car now, Miss Fur. We will have to walk and climb from here; it is far, I think, but your boots will help. I have been here as a child many years ago but cannot remember the way. Someone will be coming soon, watching for us to show us. Ah, here is this person."

A young man seemed to appear from nowhere in the dense forest and beckoned for them both to follow him. He wore the beads and pelts around his body of his people, his brown face already lined by the harsh landscape and the ancient look of his tribe.

Fleur looked around as she followed Tapu and their guide through the dense forests; she could see deep valleys and the lush vegetation all around. The darkened forest with its impressive tree canopies let only slivers of sunlight through, but her eyes soon became accustomed to the dark shadows.

In the distance she could hear water either from streams or waterfalls. The towering yellowwood, stinkwood and Cape beech trees were enormous, it would be an easy place to get lost in.

After half an hour's heavy walking and climbing they came to what seemed to be the foot of a mountain peak.

Here the forest cleared, and she saw the first signs of human habitation. Basic round reed huts were clustered around a circular area containing a low bricked fireplace. Beneath the shadows of a huge yellowwood tree, six brown men stood up. They wore some sort of leather band around their caps of tight curls, over their chests were beads and shells, a short skirt of soft leather covered their lower torso, around their ankles were brightly coloured beads and wood, reaching to their knees.

Tapu held up his hand in greeting and gestured for her to sit on a tree stump. He walked towards the men. They all sat in a circle, she could hear them talking in their strange language of melodious murmurs and rapid clicks.

Fleur eased off her light backpack and sipped from her bottle of water.

Tapu gestured for her to come and join the San men. "They are not speaking English, Miss Fur, but I will translate for you. Puso is the head man, he speaks a little of your language, but not much."

It was hard for Fleur to gauge the ages of these men, they all had the dry lined skin of the desert people, their bodies creased by age and weather, but were strong with no signs of any fat. Their eyes clear and penetrating. Puso looked taller and stronger than his clan, younger. She thought perhaps he had some mixed blood running through his veins, Zulu perhaps. He handed Tapu a small cotton bag.

The men stared at her and muttered and clicked to each other. "They know why you are here Miss Fur; they have known for many months you would come."

He glanced at them briefly and took a deep breath. "They wish to give you a gift of the seeds you have been seeking. In exchange for this they only wish to be left in peace. Puso tells me others are also seeking this information. You will never be able to find this place again, for it is well hidden and known only to the people who dwell here."

Fleur nodded. "You must give them my word no harm will come to them. But should these be the seeds I have been searching for, they will be rewarded. These seeds, as you know, are very valuable. But I wish to see proof of their gift, this is what I'm looking for."

Tapu translated this for the desert men who talked amongst themselves and nodded. The head man clapped his hands softly.

Emerging from the huts came the women. They too wore the beaded necklaces, the ankle bracelets, and the short skirts like the men. Their bare breasts hung loose almost touching their wrinkled stomachs. They were a darker brown in colour, their hair plaited with beads and tightly held back with some kind of leather strap. Behind them came a few younger women and a clutch of toddlers.

They nodded to their men, clapped their hands softly in greeting to Fleur, before settling down beneath another tree, their legs straight out in front of them as they talked and laughed amongst themselves and busied themselves with their baskets of brightly coloured beads, threading and fashioning them, looking up at Fleur now and again and smiling shyly at her, their hands covering their mouths.

The younger women had disappeared into the forest carrying their empty baskets, leaving the older woman to watch over the little ones.

Fleur studied the women. They all seemed to be in good health, none carried any weight or wore glasses, they all had their own teeth as far as she could see, from their smiles; their faces were animated as they laughed and talked together. It was true their faces were lined, as well as their bodies. But as she watched them come out of their huts, she saw no sign of discomfort in the way they walked, their backs were slightly stooped but this she had put down to the fact the women were the ones who traditionally went out into the forests and deserts to forage and gather the fruits and berries for their families, bending from the waist as they filled their baskets.

Fleur looked at Tapu. "There are only a few young women here?"

He nodded. "The others have all gone from these mountains looking for work in the towns and villages as my mother once did. Here they clean the hotels and houses who pay for this work; they sell their beadwork in the marketplace. When these men go to look for their wives, they find them in the town, claim them as their own, and then return here. When the women become too tired to work in the town any longer, they come back here and stay as part of their own community."

Fleur frowned. "So, how old are these women here Tapu, do you know?"

He smiled at her. "They are all grandmothers; each one is over seventy years old, some even older. They do not count their years, time means nothing to them, only the passing seasons."

Fleur looked at him with astonishment. "But they seem so much younger, the way they're talking to each other and laughing, doing their fine beadwork, not needing glasses. How can this be?"

Tapu reached into his pocket and withdrew the small cotton bag which Puso had given him. "These are the seeds from the sacred trees which keep their minds young, they remember everything. Sometimes perhaps a little muddled, but it is rare. This is what you have been seeking, as are others. It is a gift from the people here."

Fleur's hand trembled as she reverently took the bag of seeds from him. Excitement flooding through her veins. She finally had in her hand what she had been searching so long and hard for, through the long years.

"Tapu would it be possible to examine one of these women."

He shook his head. "This will not be possible, Miss Fur. These men do not like anyone to touch their women. You will have to trust me what I have told you is true. You have found what you have been seeking.

"These women when they reached the last of their monthly cycle have been using these seeds, a part of one every full moon. It does not make their bodies like a young woman again, but their minds are not damaged by age. Each of these grandmothers can remember everything they have learned in their life. They are not forgetting anything."

Fleur stared at the women. "What about the men. Do they also take this seed at a certain time in their lives?"

"Yes, Miss Fur, this they do. When it is the right time for them, they decide this themselves."

He glanced briefly up through the trees. "We must go now. It is time to leave these people and return to the car."

Looking slightly bemused, Fleur followed Tapu back down through the trees and rocks. She had wanted to thank the men for their gift, but when she looked to where they had been sitting, they had all gone, melting back into the landscape, their women had probably returned to their huts, their laughter and chatter still being carried on the other sounds echoing around them.

Only Puso and another man stood there. "He will come with us, Miss Fur. He is the guardian of the seeds."

By the time they reached the car, Fleur was out of breath, the heat after coming out of the shade of the forest was intense.

"How long will it take to get to the hotel, Tapu, I want to fling myself into the sea, it's so hot now."

"Maybe two hours Miss Fur, but I know a way through the bush, which is much quicker than the big main roads; dirt roads and tracks only, but not so comfortable. Puso and one other will come with us for a short time, then I will drop them off – he has San business to attend to. Will this be in order?"

Whilst he drove, Fleur examined the seeds in the cloth bag. She tried to tamp down the excitement flooding through her body.

Puso, speaking to Tapu with the strange rapid mixture of clicks and musical sounds of their language, indicated where they wished to be dropped off.

In the late afternoon Tapu and Fleur arrived at the rustic looking hotel called Safe Harbour. In the distance Fleur could hear the rumble of the sea as it hurled itself against the rocks. For as far as she could see there were scrappy bushes and miles and miles of yellow sand dunes and not a soul in sight.

She put the precious seeds in the bag across her chest and turned to Tapu. "It will be dark in an hour or so, you should be on your way. I'm going to check in then take a long walk on the beach. I have a great deal to think about."

Impulsively she hugged him. "Thank you Tapu – for everything. I'll see you back at the house. Mr Blake should be here tomorrow afternoon if he hasn't been delayed. I think we all need a break. Don't forget to water my vegetables and feed the chickens, you hear?"

Tapu climbed back into the car and started the engine. A figure emerged from the front of the run-down hotel, or perhaps it was the high wind, the sea and other elements which made it look weathered and old.

Tapu got back out of the car and waited for the man to approach. The man smiled at her. "You are Doctor Palmere, yes?"

She nodded her head. "Yes, we've booked a room for two days?"

"My name is Thomas, your friend is coming tomorrow, yes?"

"Yes, that's correct."

Thomas wiped his brow with his sleeve. "Your room is prepared, the owners go overseas for three months' when it is out of season here, and I am running the place. This can be a self-catering place, or simple meals are served in the restaurant. When the owners leave, we close the hotel, you will be our last guests before we close, then I will be going back to my family."

Fleur looked slightly confused. "There are no other guests here?"

"No. But all is ready for you. You will be safe here tonight and then your friend comes tomorrow. There is a night-watchman who will be available should this be required. I have filled your fridge with food which should be enough for the two days you are staying. There is no electricity here but there is a generator. It comes on when darkness falls and turns off when the next day is light."

Fleur looked concerned. "When are you going?"

A big smile creased his face. "My wife is close to her time for not one but two babies. I wish to be with her when they are born, but I must leave here now. I am asking if your driver will take me to the nearest place where I can take the bus to the clinic where my children will be born. Then we shall all return to our village, but I will not be returning to Safe Harbour. I wish to be with my wife and the children. When the owner's return they will find a new manager."

Fleur turned and looked at Tapu. "He's not my driver Thomas, he's my assistant. It is he you must ask and not me."

Tapu looked concerned. "I am not happy to leave the Doctor here alone even for one night. I will want to meet with this night-watchman who will watch over her before I give you a lift into town."

"Please bring him to me now. If he is suitable, I will give you this lift."

Thomas hurried back inside the hotel and returned with the night-watchman. "This is Kingston, he has been here many years. He is a Zulu, but this we cannot hold against him. I myself am a Khosa. The Zulus are fine warriors. Doctor Palmere will be well looked after. He is on duty from eight at night until six in the morning. He too will be leaving for his home tomorrow, but your friend will be here so all will be well, and you will be safe. I have put you in chalet seven. Take care when you walk on the beach doctor, do not swim in the water, it is very dangerous and has many sharks. When you leave, a friend of the owners will come and lock up your chalet."

Tapu looked Kingston up and down, noting the short spear he was carrying, his blanket draped across one shoulder, deciding Miss Fur would be fine for one night until Mr Blake came to be with her.

"Come, Thomas, I'll take you to the bus. The birth of babies is a gift from the Gods, you must be there for this."

Fleur looked around the room. Like so many guest houses and hotels out in the bush and in remote places, it was round, painted white, with a conical thatched roof. As promised Thomas had filled the fridge with food and water, even a bottle of wine.

She was weary and even though she longed to take a walk on the beach she knew it would be better to take a rest. It had been a highly emotional day.

There was still much work to be done. If she were right about the seeds she would have to register her discovery legally. She had already started the legal procedure some months before.

Blake had suggested she use their company attorney, George Mason, one of the top legal guys in the country and an expert in international law.

Fleur had spoken to George at great length on the phone, emphasising what she had found was only used in traditional medicine by one tribe, as far as she could ascertain. He had assured her, under the circumstances, she had no obligation to report her findings to anyone as she had funded her own research without contributions from any pharma or research company.

This, she had told him, she could prove by producing her mother's leather book with all her own findings in Kenya and Fleur's ongoing determined search to follow the trail her mother had left for her.

Therefore, she could claim the discovery as her own and let George Mason sort the rest out. He would be able to recommend a reputable pharma company, or research company in South Africa to entrust with her work. He would ensure she was protected, and the San people who had made all this possible.

This was another project Fleur had become passionate about. The San people and the right to own some land of their own, preferably in the desert where they belonged, and not allow the government of the day to move them on when they felt like it, to a place they could never call their home. There would be more than enough money to achieve this, once she had ascertained the power of the seeds and how they could be harvested to produce the cure she had been looking for.

George Mason told her he would handle this as well. So, all her bases were covered. He asked her to put the facts down and send them to him and he would begin the legal process of registering ownership of the success of her, and her mother's research, and ensure all the rights belonged to her, should this be the case.

George had paused momentarily. "Be very careful with this information Doctor Palmere. It puts you in a vulnerable, and dare I say, a dangerous position. What you have discovered, should it fall into the wrong hands, could have disastrous consequences for you. That is, of course, if you find these seeds or plants and they hold that vital information.

"Also, if you are correct in your assumptions, and research proves this, then the particular area where the seeds grow will need to be protected. I shall have to think about how this can be done."

He scribbled some notes onto his legal pad. "Have you shared this information with anyone else?"

"Only Blake, Mr Mason, he knows."

Fleur bit the end of her pen thoughtfully. The conservation and harvesting of the seeds would have to be carefully monitored, now she had found them, and seen the results with her own eyes with the women in the forest this morning.

Could they be planted in a similar environment, perhaps in a laboratory and still retain their powerful elements? Could they be cultivated, without losing that power, and made available to the millions of people who looked so desperately for a cure for their illness?

She would take a nap then make something to eat from the supplies in the fridge. There was cheese, fruit, cold meats, eggs, bacon, bread, and milk.

Chapter Twenty-Nine

The next day Fleur woke refreshed, she made herself a mug of coffee and sat out on the patio watching the sea. It would be peaceful until the tide turned, and the tumultuous furious waves came thundering back to shore.

For the next two hours she made notes in her book, remembering everything she had learned on her trip into the deep forest the day before. The cotton bag of seeds next to her. The place was eerily quiet with no other guests and the hotel now closed. She would be glad when Blake finally arrived to keep her company.

He would be here soon; she wasn't sure of his time of arrival, but she knew it was Friday, and today was Friday. He would be with her, and they would have two glorious days together, away from everything and everyone. Hopefully, he would not be delayed.

After a lunch of cheese and grapes she decided to take a long walk on the deserted beach. The tide was slowly turning, the wind gusty, blowing across the sand dunes, the sun was hot. She sat on one of the sand dunes, watching the sea, and thought about Michael Bennett, as she so often did. She hoped he was happy, as happy as she was. She had loved him and knew she would never love that way again.

She loved Blake in a different way. He was a good man, caring, loving, and accepting she had a past she didn't wish to talk about.

She thought about her sister Helene and her little daughter Lucy, living what she hoped was a fulfilling life in the house in Lymington.

That life seemed so many years ago now, as it was. A life she had chosen to leave behind.

She scanned the beach looking for Blake. She knew once he arrived at the hotel, he would come looking for her; knew she would only be on the beach.

Fleur stood up and stretched as she looked at the sea again, then she turned to head back to the hotel. She saw him in the distance and started to run towards him, her feet stumbling and tripping in the soft sand, impeding her progress.

"Blake! Blake!" She rummaged in her bag and found the cotton seeds in their cotton pouch, her voice carried away on the strong wind. "Look, my darling," the tears of joy ran down her cheeks. "I've found it. I've found the cure."

The sand whipped into her eyes, the heat rising from the sand the fine spray from the surf, distorting his image.

He lifted his hand in greeting, as she tried to increase her speed. There he was. "I've found the seeds; I found the seeds!"

As he drew nearer, she rubbed her eyes briefly and watched with horror and disbelief as he lifted his gun and shot her.

Chapter Thirty
England
1993

Captain Michael Bennett had been air-lifted out of the desert and returned to England.

During the first year back, he had spent time in a military hospital in London. The doctors and specialists had repaired his missing stump of an arm as best they could, before fitting a prosthesis.

But his shattered mind would take longer. He was moved to a rehabilitation centre, run by the military deep in the countryside of Wiltshire. What once had been a private country house was now a centre for army personnel who were suffering the deep trauma of seeing and being through too much of the many wars raging across the world.

Jeremy Foxton, Michael Bennett's solicitor, had, of course, been informed of the discovery and recovery of his client, but had been advised not to visit until the army surgeons and the treatment Michael would have to go through to try and repair his shattered mind was completed.

Michael Bennett had been told he was suffering from severe trauma and sometimes memory loss. He sat in his wheelchair and looked across the green and peaceful countryside of an English summer.

He looked down at his new arm. With the ongoing daily appointments with psychologist, psychiatrists, and the constant care of the nurses, he slowly had flashes of memories, but he couldn't put them in any kind of order. His most vivid memory was looking at dead soldiers all around him covered with sand – this memory he couldn't erase from his mind.

He was talking coherently now, and the doctors considered he was making good progress, although he was distracted at times.

Michael sat looking over the gardens and the green and verdant fields of his country. It was, the doctors and nurses agreed, when he seemed to relax, looking at what he described as *fleurs*.

One of the nurses had asked him why he always wanted to sit in one place near the flower garden. She knew the French word for flowers was *fleur,* but he had only shaken his head in despair.

Michael spent many months at the rehabilitation centre, he had frequent flashes of memories now. The medical team decided his solicitor, who had kept in touch every week, insisting on an update, should be allowed to meet with him.

The medical team had agreed there was no more they could do to enhance Captain Bennett's life; time would be the great healer. He was to be discharged from the centre. His military career was over. He could walk now, although with a heavy limp.

Michael sometimes had unexpected flashes of his past. A place somewhere as old as time; he knew he had lived there. Another flash, but fragmented, was a dark-skinned man, a man who he had stayed with in a cave somewhere. This man's name he did remember.

Ahmed.

Jeremy Foxton met briefly with the doctors and staff who had looked after Michael for a year now, before making his way out onto the lawns of the hospital searching for his client.

It was a glorious summers day, the warm sun filtering through the boughs of the many trees in the grounds. Other patients, some in wheelchairs, others walking slowly around accompanied by a nurse, or a visiting relative. Michael was sitting alone on a bench under a chestnut tree, one leg stretched out in front of him, a sturdy walking stick propped against the side of the bench. No longer wearing his uniform, he appeared to Jeremy to have shrunk in size since the last time he had seen him, his once blond hair now grey.

He hurried towards him. "Michael, my dear chap, it's so good to see you again, so very good!"

Michael turned at the sound of his name and looked at the man wearing what looked like a very expensive suit and a red bowtie.

Jeremy held out his hand and shook Michael's gently. "You've been through a terrible time. I was informed you went missing in action and presumed dead. To see you sitting here makes me very happy indeed. You do remember me, I hope?"

Michael gave a wan smile. "Yes, I remember you Jeremy, not everything, but I do know you've been our family solicitor for many years. It's good to see you again.

"Let's take a walk around the grounds, I'm getting stiff sitting here, I need your advice on a few things."

Jeremy stood up and reached for Michael's stick. "Don't do that Jeremy," he said tersely, "I might have lost my arm and a bit of my memory, but I'm quite capable of moving around on my own, I'm not going to fall over if that's what you're worried about."

Much to Jeremy's surprise, Michael had recovered a lot of his memory, there were gaps, and he put this down to the severe trauma his friend had suffered, the things he had seen. It was natural for the brain to block out traumatic events.

Michael limped along beside his solicitor, looking up at the abundantly leaved trees, the sunlight filtering through. "So, when you heard I was missing in action; dead. What did you do? Wind up my estate, let everyone know I was dead? Did you tell Fleur?"

Jeremy looked at the grass and flowers, busy with bees and butterflies, feeling the warm sun on his face. "Actually, no I didn't. There was no proof, it was an assumption the military had made. Solicitors always want proof, and I had none. I wasn't prepared to do anything but hope, and pray, you would be found. And I was right," he said triumphantly, "because here you are, right in front of me."

Michael lowered himself down onto another bench, exhausted by the short walk they had taken.

"What did you do with my estate?"

Jeremy grinned at him. "Absolutely nothing, old boy. Paid your bills where necessary. Made sure the place in Lamu was paid for, Ali was paid every month and collected his money from Peponi. The monthly amount you stipulated was paid into Fleur Palmere's account, every month…what is it, Michael?"

"Fleur. Where is she? Do you know? I must find her, I must."

Jeremy looked at the broken man in front of him. "The army sent me what little it seemed you had. There was a letter there from Fleur. I have it in your file. But it never reached you, you were in in the desert somewhere. It was returned to me by the army."

Michael leaned forward expectantly. "Did you open it? What did it say? Where is she now?"

Jeremy flinched at the intensity of the question. "Of course I didn't open it. Now listen to me, Michael. You're being released from here. The army, of course, will give you all the support you need, social services will find a temporary place for you to live. However, you will still need the army doctors to monitor you and take care of you."

He paused. "But I have known you and your parents for a long time now. You need more than tea and sympathy; you need to regain your own health and mind in the real world.

"I have a small apartment, not far from my rooms in Knightsbridge. I want you to come and stay there. You need to leave the terrible world of war behind and start a new life. I want to help you.

I was very fond of your parents, as I am of you. You have more than enough money which I have invested for you. You'll be all right. You need time to adjust to a new life which is waiting for you."

Michael rubbed his aching leg. "I need to find Fleur. That's all I want. I can put my life back together with her beside me."

Jeremy looked at him. "I'll try to help you find her. But you must remember a lot of time has passed, years in fact. My thinking is she's back where she belongs in Africa, but I have no idea exactly where."

Michael nodded enthusiastically. "Yes, she'll be in South Africa! I knew she was going there. She was going to pursue her research, initially staying in a safari camp, in the Eastern Cape, but she wasn't exactly sure where it was."

Jeremy rubbed the side of his face. "Could be a little harder to find her, she could be anywhere now. But first, we must get you settled in London, in my apartment, get you used to the real world again. I've been told you'll be able to leave here at the end of next week, and I'd like you to at least spend a few months with me, we can go through all your affairs, bring everything up to date and we can begin our search for Fleur."

Michael looked at him. "The allowance I asked you to pay into Fleur's account each month, she would have used it, had it paid into her account in South Africa. Surely that would tell you where she was?"

Jeremy shook his head. "She did ask for an amount to be transferred to her, but that was some time after she arrived in South Africa. The money was to be paid into the account of a B. Hemmingway. She gave me the bank details and I made the transfer to an account in Johannesburg. It was the only transfer I ever made for her."

"What about her sister, Helene, and her daughter Lucy. They must have kept in touch. Did you make any contact with them when I went missing?"

Jeremy shook his head in frustration. "I did. Helene assured me Fleur, she told me, went to South Africa and they'd not been in touch since. They don't have the kind of first-class postal system we have here. She had no idea where her sister was."

Jeremy Foxton handed over the letter to the man sitting opposite him.

Michael had read it not once, but twice, sitting in front of him. He pushed it back across Jeremy's table, then sat back and squeezed his eyes shut for a few moments.

Jeremy read it through, and his heart sank. Her written words would crush the man in front of him, more so than he was now.

Michael rubbed the scar on his face. "Fleur kept me going you know when things were bad. She was the one I thought about. But it appears from the letter, she too left me, along with my life. Some years ago. There's no date on her letter. Thank God I didn't know."

Michael glanced at the letter again. 'But she said she would always know where to find me – in Lamu. But I guess that was too long ago now, things will have changed, she will have changed, as I most certainly have."

A screaming siren ripped through the air from the road outside and Michael flinched. Jeremy had kept a close eye on Michael who was now staying in his apartment next to the offices. He had watched him limping down the road, going into Tesco's; it had not gone unnoticed Michael was affected by loud unexpected noises. Once he had watched him, when an engine had backfired, crouched on the ground, his purchases scattered around him, his hands over his head. People had walked past him assuming he was probably drunk. One or two had tried to help but he had screamed at them in terror, and they had edged away, not sure how to handle the situation.

Jeremy sat in front of Michael who was looking at the restaurant menu with disinterest. "My best advice to you, my friend, is to get out of London. Get out of England. This place won't heal you. You've tried to adapt, over the last few years, to a different life, here in London, but I don't think it's working for you. I know the army has supported you, offered you various clerical positions, tried to help you adapt, but it's not working for you is it?"

Michael shook his head in despair. How could he be a doctor again with only one hand?

Jeremy perused the menu. "You should go and spend some time in Lamu. You still have your place there; Ali is still there; nothing has changed. This is the wrong place for you to be. Lamu will soothe your mind. Ali will look after you, as he always has. This so-called real world is not what you need now.

"Your military career is over. You've been badly damaged by other people's wars. Go back, Michael, go back to where you were happy. I'll try to find Fleur. But time changes everything…"

Michael nodded his head in agreement. "I don't want to be here in England anymore. What was it for anyway? I'll go back to Lamu, find some kind of peace. As for Fleur, well, I will always love her. But her letter told me there was no future for either of us. That's the part I don't understand at all. She loved me, I know that. What happened to that future. What made her change her mind?"

"I can't answer that question, Michael."

Michael stared out of the window of the restaurant, watching the never-ending traffic, the taxis, the buses, the endless procession of pedestrians and the rain slashing against the windows, he didn't want to be part of it any longer. He had fought other people's wars, and it had brought him nothing but pain and grief and cost him the woman he loved.

"Yes, Jeremy, I'll go back to Africa. People assume it's a violent and dangerous place, but for me it's always been peaceful. A place from long ago when things were calmer."

Jeremy nodded his head in agreement. For people like Michael, England was no longer a place of safety, there was too much noise for a fragile mind, such as his friend had. He needed to be in a place where he could heal his mind, a place where it was peaceful, away from the cars and buses, the jackhammers, the scream of sirens and the incessant noise of vehicles and people.

Lamu, he knew, had no vehicles at all, only donkeys and gentle people. The peace on the island only disrupted when the Muezzin called the faithful to prayer, but it wasn't intrusive. Michael still had a full life ahead of him.

But he would not find that life in the land of his birth.

Chapter Thirty-One
Lamu

Ali had spent some years looking after the house in Lamu. He collected his monthly wages, sent by Jeremy, from Peponi as he had always done when Michael was away on various postings around the world; places Ali had never heard of. Jeremy had told him the doctor was coming home.

He sat outside on the veranda his eyes watching for Michael's arrival. He had prepared everything in anticipation for this day he had waited so long for.

But what he wasn't prepared for was the stooped man who limped so badly as he made his difficult way through the sand to the beach house. One sleeve of his shirt tucked neatly under what was left of his arm, the other carrying a small suitcase.

Ali hesitated for a few seconds. Could this be Doctor Michael, who was unsteadily making his way towards him. Yes, it was, he recognised him now. But still he waited until Michael reached his house, only then did he go forward to greet him.

"It is good to see you again, very good, I was thinking perhaps you had forgotten your home here with me. Come and sit and I will bring you some refreshment."

Ali could see clearly his doctor had lost an arm and the use of one leg. He shook his head sadly. Where could it be a war was so bad to lose an arm and a leg, for your hair to go white and crush your body into a different shape – for what was this worth fighting for in a foreign country which wasn't your own?

Michael sank into his favourite chair and looked out over the gentle lapping waves, the African sun warm and soothing, seeping through his tired and shattered body, it was a peaceful place to be. He rubbed the aching stump where his arm had been.

Ali brought him a glass of freshly squeezed lemon juice and placed it on the table in front of him. He folded his hands in front of him, shocked by the changes in the doctor.

"I am thinking your body needs rest. I will look after you, as I have always done over the years you have been coming to Lamu. All will be well with Ali to see to things. You will become strong again."

Michael shook his head. "No. Ali, that's impossible I've lost my arm and my leg is useless. How could I possibly become strong again?" he said bitterly.

Ali frowned at him. "You are missing an arm and a leg which is not working so well, this I see now. But I have two of each, between us we have three arms and three legs, this is a gift from Allah. For do you know anyone else with three arms and three legs?"

Despite himself Michael smiled at Ali's clever observation and faith. Ali continued. "I will shop and cook as I have always done. I will share these arms and legs with you. Why would you need any more now you are home again?

"When you are wishing to go to the hotel where the white people go for drinking, you are only needing one arm for this drinking, and this you have. I will give you one of my legs to help and I will bring you home. I am thinking perhaps you will be staying here for a long time, yes?"

Michael nodded. "Yes, I'm not going anywhere Ali. I'm going to make this my permanent home now. Tell me," he said hopefully. "Has Doctor Palmere returned here over the past few years?"

Ali shook his head. "I have not seen her here; she has not returned. But you have, and all will be well. Perhaps one day she will hear you are back in Lamu and will come and look for you?"

Over the following months that rolled into years, Michael adapted to his new life. Every evening Ali would walk with him to Peponi where Michael would mix with the old, retired hunters, who carried almost as many scars as he had. Some had been mauled by lions, charged by elephant, or buffalo; each one of them with many stories to tell, accepting the injuries as part of the big adventure of being a professional hunter in Africa in the days long gone now.

Michael slowly began to accept what had happened to him, the loss of his young strong body, as his friends around the bar had accepted what had happened to them.

Here he began his new life, falling into a routine where Ali would cook and care for him. Every evening, he would walk with him down to the bar where he would meet up with his friends.

These old Kenyan pioneers and hunters had accepted the price they had paid over the years. To live a wild dangerous, and wonderful life, in a country they had always called their own. They wore the injuries from charging elephants, buffalo, lion attacks and all the other dangerous encounters as a badge of honour – they had survived. Michael's enemies had been unknown, but in the end a price always had to be paid for a dangerous and unpredictable life.

He had survived, carrying his own badges, from different kinds of predators who hid amongst the caves, the sand-dunes, and the craggy mountains in a place far away. The army had been his life, and he had given it to them for Queen and country.

Ali always waited for him outside the bar and walked him back, sometimes more unsteady than others, to his house on the beach.

One evening Michael had been sitting on his veranda looking out over the sand and the sea, hearing Ali preparing his dinner. He felt he was being healed and knew he had finally come home, away from all his thoughts of the wars he had fought. But there was an emptiness deep inside of him, for the woman he had loved and lost, but not given up on. He still looked for her. Waited for her. She would find him again.

The sun was beginning to set, turning the sea from turquoise to a carpet of gold and pink. He took a sip of his gin and tonic and felt himself relax. A dhow drifted past, seagulls wheeled, dipped, and screeched behind it, hoping for some scraps to come their way from the fisherman's haul of the day.

That's when he saw her walking slowly along the beach, her dark hair twisting in the soft wind, heading his way.

He levered himself out of his chair and reached for his sturdy cane, his heart pounding in his chest.

Fleur.

She had come back to find him! He stumbled out over the sand calling her name which was whipped from his lips by the wind.

"Fleur! Fleur!"

The woman looked up. She saw a man staggering towards her, waving his cane, and laughing.

She turned and fled, moving away from him, seeing him as a threat.

"Wait, Fleur. It's me Michael. Wait. I know I don't look the same, but it's me. I've been waiting for you. I knew you would find me, as you said you would. You knew I would be here.

"Don't run away…please don't run away from me."

Michael watched the woman running and stumbling away from him. The tears rolled down his face. She had, he thought, taken one look at him and seen someone she had once loved so much, and turned her back on him because of how he looked now: an old broken crippled soldier.

He sank to his knees and fell forward, feeling only the warm sand sticking to his wet cheek, and closed his eyes. The memories flooding back. The wonderful times with Fleur in London, and the nightmare of what he had been through.

He heard someone calling his name, but he was tired now.

Ali was at his side. "It's all right doctor, I am here, it is Ali. I will take you home. Come, you must stand up now. I will help you."

Michael opened his eyes and saw through a haze of intolerable pain, and loss, a face he recognised.

"Ahmed! You didn't leave me behind." He reached out with his hand. "Take me with you... it was better with you when I had no memories."

Ali kneeled and frowned, not understanding. "Come I will take you home."

Michael sighed, his final breath barely making a ripple on the fine sand next to his wet face.

Chapter Thirty-Two

Doctor Michael Bennett's body was flown back to England. His funeral was attended by Colonel Mallard, his former Commanding Officer, and Major Jameson, who had taken over from him, some of his fellow officers, the nurses and the medical staff who had cared for him, and his solicitor, Jeremy.

Major Jameson, now retired, sat through the service, his mind going back to Michael out there in the desert when his unit was blown up by terrorists and how the Arab, Ahmed, had saved his life and cared for him.

Although Colonel Mallard had been determined to find the bodies of his soldiers and bring them home to England, circumstances had prevented it. The terrorists were once again active in the area where the men and their vehicles had been buried by the four-day sandstorm.

Army Headquarters had decided it would be too dangerous to be seen by the terrorists if soldiers brought in equipment to find the men; they would have been picked off, one by one, by snipers hidden in the mountains and desert. It had been explained it would be impossible to identify the murdered men as the sniper, according to Ahmed, had removed all their dog tags and two years had passed since the incident when they found Captain Bennett.

The army would erect some kind of memorial, a cairn, with the men's names listed. They were not prepared to lose any more good men to a war they knew they couldn't win.

Major Jameson thought back to the mid-sixties when he had served as a young officer in Aden. Soldiers, women, and children of military families caught up in bombs and grenade attacks, had been buried in the desert, in a placed called Silent Valley. A desolate, but peaceful place, surrounded by barren rocks, but immaculately kept and bravely flaunting the Union Jack, the crosses startlingly white against the dark rocks. He knew now, after the British had withdrawn from Aden, recognising another war in the Middle East which they could not win so many years ago now, those simple graves would not have been cared for, as before. The flag would have been torn down, the graves and their crosses, carefully recording their names, now completely covered in sand, and surrounded by silence and the soft whispering of the desert winds, who had cared for nobody for thousands of years.

He remembered the lone figure of Ahmed as he lifted his arms in farewell to Captain Michael Bennett, who he had risked his life to save, as he was carried away by helicopter, back to the country of his birth.

Sadly, Jeremy set about winding up Michael's estate. The house in Lamu would have to be sold. Ali would be well provided for in the future.

Michael had requested the money Jeremy had invested for him over the many years he had been away fighting his wars, be left to Doctor Fleur Palmere. This would be invested into her account which Jeremy had looked after each month when Michael had deposited money into it.

Jeremy would have to find her and inform her of her inheritance and of Michael's death. It would not be an easy task.

He retrieved Fleur's will from his cabinet and carefully read through it. It was simple enough. Before she left for South Africa, she had instructed Jeremy to put her house in Lymington, plus all the contents in her sister Helene's name. This he had done. If Helene pre-deceased Fleur, everything was to be left to Lucy.

He had only met with Helene twice since Fleur had left to continue her research. Her own will had also been simple and straightforward. Helene had left everything to her daughter Lucy.

Jeremy smiled, how the years had flown past. Lucy would be all grown up now.

Jeremy had tried every means at his disposal to find Fleur Palmere, but every lead led him nowhere. He hired a private detective who had been recommended by someone in South Africa, but after months of searching, the private detective had reported back to Jeremy that he knew Fleur was working in remote parts of the country which had made it impossible for him to track her down. As he had explained, she could be anywhere, and South Africa was a vast country. Had she been living in one of the cities he would have found her, but there was no trace of her in Johannesburg, Pretoria, Cape Town, or any of the other cities.

Sighing with frustration at the detective's report, Jeremy had no choice but to wait for Fleur to contact him and he would be able to tell her the news about Michael's death.

He had diligently put a notice in various newspapers in South Africa, the UK and Kenya, announcing he was seeking her whereabouts. But there had been no response from anyone. He had searched in other countries and placed an announcement in their newspapers. Zimbabwe, Zambia, Mozambique, Kenya, and Namibia.

There had been one response from Zimbabwe.

Dear Mr Foxton,

I saw your notice in the newspaper here in Bulawayo. At first it didn't mean anything to me until I saw the name Doctor Fleur Palmere, which I recognised.

I don't know how many years ago it was now, because I was only maybe two years old. But a Zimbabwean man, called Simon, left me here in Bulawayo in a safe place, with his grandmother. I had no recollection of why I was placed there. Simon left South Africa; he had been working there for some twenty years at a camp site. When I showed him the notice in the newspaper, which you had placed, he told me about a European woman who appeared at the camp site which had been closed. He was leaving the next day but managed to take care of this woman in the brief time he had shared with her.

Her name was Doctor Fleur Palmere. He told me she had recently arrived in South Africa to continue with some kind of research, but clearly something went wrong, and she found herself alone in an abandoned camp site. The reason he remembered her so well is she gave him money so that he could return to his own country, Zimbabwe. She asked only one thing from him, that he would give life, courage, and hope, to a young child who now lived in Bulawayo.

This young child was me. Poppy.

Simon died some years ago. I had known him all my life, he was the only family I knew.

He gave me the gift of hope. This, he told me, was what Doctor Palmere had wanted for me, although she didn't know me, I never met her. But clearly Simon remembered her well, if only briefly.

Still to this day, I miss him and the gift he gave me of hope.

He told me the place where the camp site was, obviously not there now, was called something like Waterfall, well, that's how it sounded to me. It was in somewhere called the Eastern Cape.

I do hope you find her. I think she must have been something quite special.

Poppy.

Some months later Jeremy received a letter from his private detective.

There was a small piece in the newspapers here (see enclosed) about a scientist who went missing whilst on a field trip in the Eastern Cape. It appears she was in an area called the Wild Coast, a vast rugged area, stretching for thousands of kilometres. Apparently, someone reported her missing. This is a remote area, and no body was found.
Could this possibly be your Doctor Palmere?
South Africa as you and the world know is in a frenzy of excitement with the new president being sworn in, and the change of government.
I'm afraid the article was a little lost in all the other big headlines. But I thought I should let you know.
Unfortunately, I will not be able to help you in the future as I am emigrating to South America.
I wish you luck in your search for the doctor and I'm sorry I was unable to find her, despite all my efforts.
Sincerely,
Bill O'Hara.

Jeremy sat back in his chair and looked out of the window. The whole situation was getting more complicated. He had absolutely no idea what move to make next trying to find Fleur Palmere, to let her know about Captain Michael Bennett, or her inheritance.

Chapter Thirty-Three

Lucy Palmere had been brought up in the quaint town of Lymington. She had been a happy child although puzzled as to why all her friends had fathers, and she didn't seem to have one.

But her life was predictable and steady. Her mother, Helene, was a teacher at the local school and involved in all the aspects of life living in a small town.

Lucy, like all schoolgirls, visited her friends' houses, as they did hers. But their houses were different. Her friends commented on the strange Lamu lamps, the furniture with the wild animal printed cushions and the pictures on the walls of places they could not imagine.

Lucy, of course, was brought up in the house, it was what she was used to. But when she went to their houses, they had hunting prints on the walls, pictures of villages, English landscapes; the furniture was the same in all the houses, the chintz covered chairs and sofas, bland comfortable cushions in muted tones, dining room chairs with no Zebra stripes, no paintings of predators or elephants on the walls, and heavy curtains at the windows to keep out the bitter elements of inclement weather.

Her mother had explained to her, when she was old enough, that her family had come from Africa, a place called Kenya. Her sister, Lucy's Aunt Fleur, had given them the house and all its contents.

"But where is Aunt Fleur. Why have I never met her? Where is my father, what's his name? All my friends have grandparents, do I have any?"

Helene had held her close. "Your Aunt Fleur is in Africa. She's a scientist, trying to find cures for illnesses. Your great grandparents were French, they lived in Nice, in France. All gone now, of course."

"But who and where is my father, mummy. I want one, like all my friends have. Where is he? Why doesn't Aunt Fleur ever write to you. Did you have an argument or something? Your mother was my grandmother. But where is she now? What happened to her?"

Helene knew this question would come at some point. "Darling your father was gone before you were born. He never met you. Your Aunt Fleur," she gestured around the house, "she gave all of this to us before she went back to Africa. Your Aunt Fleur was going to be out in remote parts of the bush. We both decided to take our own paths and agreed that we were close enough not to need to be in touch all the time,

I had no address for her. She wanted to go back to Africa where she was born. She said she would never come back to England."

Lucy frowned. "Yes, okay. But what was my father's name. You have the same name as my Aunt Fleur. Did you not marry my father?"

Helene's smile faltered as she looked at her daughter. "No, I didn't."

"Why won't you tell me anything?"

"Because, my darling child, it won't make any difference. It won't make any difference at all. He's gone. Your grandmother, my mother, died many years ago, in Kenya."

Lucy stared at her mother. "I don't believe you. Sisters always keep in touch, my friend's mothers have sisters, they come to visit, why can't you tell me the truth. Because what you're telling me is I have a father, and you don't know his name. I never met my great grandparents, you never took me to France to meet them, and they never came to visit us here. I have an Aunt Fleur, and you don't know where she is, and you never write to each other. You don't have an address for her, but she certainly knows where you live because she gave you her house."

Helene shrugged her shoulders. "Darling, I know it all sounds a bit odd, but there are many people who lose touch with their parents and siblings, it's not that unusual."

Lucy shook her head. "No. I don't believe you; you're not telling me the truth. But one day, when I'm old enough I'm going to go to Africa and find my Aunt Fleur. I have a lot of friends here and it hurts me when they talk about relatives, grandparents, aunties, uncles, brothers, and sisters. I don't seem to have anyone – only you. My friend's ask me about my family, and I have no answers. I want to know about my relatives. I need to know where I come from."

Helene went to put her arms around her daughter. "Come on darling, you're so young, as you get older relatives are not so important, you'll see. You'll build your own relationships, fall in love, have your own children and all your questions will fade away as you build your own family."

Lucy pulled away from her, abruptly. "I want the truth that's all."

Helene heard the door slam behind her daughter and sank into a chair. Her daughter was growing up, as a teacher she knew children asked many questions, and as a teacher she could always answer them.

But for her beloved daughter she knew it would be impossible to give the child the answers she seemed to be so desperately searching for. - *Impossible.*

Chapter Thirty-Four

Lucy was in her twenties when her mother, Helene, died. It was sudden. Her mother had shown no signs of being ill. But one morning she had gone into the garden and fallen forward and died. Lucy had one more question which remained unanswered.

When someone falls, they put their arms in front of them to protect themselves. This her mother had not done, her arms were by her side. Lucy had run out into the garden, screaming her mother's name, she turned her over and saw only a small sliver of blood seeping from her nostril.

The doctor had told her, her mother had a sudden heart attack, there were no other symptoms her doctor could attribute to her sudden death. He had known Helene since she arrived in Lymington, and he had no cause to speculate it may have been anything else. The end had been so sudden that he had surmised her mother had not felt a thing as she had fallen on her face, she was dead seconds before she hit the garden path. He knew his patient had been prone to fainting attacks, he had put this down to low blood pressure. Helene had refused to have any of the tests he would have liked her to have.

"My mother, and my sister, have always been the fainting types. We just got used to it, that's all, thought it was normal. So, forget about any tests, it's something that obviously runs in the family. Probably our unusual childhood, or something. The hot sun – I have no idea."

Lucy had decided not to go to university although she had all the qualifications needed. She wanted to stay with her friends and the people she had been brought up with. Her retired teachers were still here, the butcher, the woman who ran the local bakery, the coffee houses and delicatessens, the small shops selling clothes, the shoe shops where she had been fitted for her school shoes as a child, now stocking fashionable ones. The library which she had been a member of since childhood, the restaurants and, yes, now the pubs, where she met up with her friends, and fell in and out of love, all surrounded by the beautiful and peaceful New Forest with its wild ponies, ancient trees and endless walking paths.

Lucy had applied for a job at the local library and been successful... She loved books, could lose herself in other people's stories, go into another world – escape.

Jeremy attended her mother's funeral, as did most of the town who had come to love this teacher from a place far away called Kenya, which she rarely talked about, if at all, and her sudden and inexplicable death.

Helene would have been happy to know that in the end she had been loved by so many, something she had craved for since she was a young child, when she had felt so terribly alone, and not part of anything.

Lucy had never met Jeremy before, but after the service he had stood beside her as her mother was lowered into the ground.

He introduced himself.

"I'm Jeremy. Your mother's solicitor. I've taken it upon myself to book into a guest house here. When you're ready, we need to meet up and go through your mother's will. It's hard to lose a mother, but I'll help you as best I can."

He was taken aback when she removed her dark glasses and held out her hand. She had the same startling eyes as her mother.

He handed her his card. "Please call me. I'd like to see you whilst I'm here in Lymington. I'm sorry to intrude on your grief, but there are certain family matters which need to be addressed?"

Lucy's curious eyes hardened, as though the blueness of them had faded and now they looked as hard as ice.

"Family matters? I didn't realise I had any. According to my mother there were only two of us in this family, and now there is one. What possibly would you wish to talk to me about when you say 'family' matters. I don't have one."

Jeremy smiled at her. "Perhaps I may call upon you tomorrow. I have all the family files with me. I have, of course, your address. Would ten tomorrow be appropriate?"

Lucy's eyes softened. "Yes, of course. Now perhaps I'll find out if I have a real family somewhere."

Jeremy watched her walk through the wooden gate of the churchyard. He sighed heavily. How much would he be able to tell her? He had watched her through the service and saw little or no emotion in her at all.

He arrived at the house in Lymington at the appointed time. Lucy told him to make himself comfortable whilst she made coffee.

Jeremy felt he had walked back in time. The entire house looked as though it came from somewhere else. He looked at the Kenyan feel of the place and knew, although Lucy probably didn't realise it, this was her family whispering to her from a place left long ago.

Lucy poured his coffee as he looked around. "Yes, I know, it all looks a bit odd in a place like Lymington. Very foreign. But apparently, I have, or had, an Aunt Fleur. She gave this house to my mother. But since I've never met her, never even received a Christmas card from her, I have no idea who she was, or where she is, or even if she is alive."

Jeremy cleared his throat. "Perhaps we could move to the table and start with the paperwork. You clearly have many questions about your mother's family. Perhaps I'll be able to help you a little."

He unpacked his briefcase. "How are you, Lucy. You seem to be coping with things, if I may say so?"

She looked at him with those incredible eyes which might tell him everything – or nothing.

"I feel numb. Lost. I'll miss her, of course, but I never felt connected to her. As I grew up, I felt there was always something missing, almost as though she was living her life, but I was in the shadows of it. It's difficult to explain."

She laughed. "I have, of course, fallen in and out of love, but it seemed a periphery thing. Not deep enough. Something was always missing as though I'd never learned the levels of different kinds of love. I always felt I didn't have a solid base to work from, I felt disconnected somehow."

Jeremy winced. Where to begin?

He looked across at the girl in front of him. He had, over the years come to some conclusions of his own, but he had no proof of anything. He always needed irrefutable proof before he made a final decision.

He cleared his throat as he shuffled through his files. "Your mother, Helene, left everything to you, this house, all the contents and a modest sum of money. However, there is a problem here. Unless I have proof of your Aunt Fleur's death, I can't legally handover this house and the contents because it still belongs to her. Your mother would have inherited everything if her sister had died. I must have proof you see."

Lucy held up her hand. Jeremy halted in mid-sentence. "Where is my Aunt Fleur? If she is still alive then nothing here belongs to me right, that's what you're saying isn't it. If anyone knows where she is it must be you? So where exactly is she. You must have informed her of her sister's death?"

Jeremy closed the file and rubbed his tired eyes. "I don't know where she is. I can't find her. I've tried for many years to locate her. I think she's in South Africa, but I have no proof of this. I have no proof that she's still alive. I'm sorry Lucy. The last time I saw her was before she left for Africa – that was twenty years or so ago."

Lucy's eyes filled with tears reminding him of the sea rushing to shore. "I must find her; she seems to be the only other member of the family I know I'm related to. It's important to me because right now I have no family at all."

Jeremy leaned across the table and handed her his handkerchief. "I do understand that, Lucy. Let me give it one more try. I'll do my best to find her for you.

"This story goes back to your grandmother, Christiana Palmere who lived in Kenya. Did your mother never talk about her own mother?"

Lucy shook her head. "Not really. She told me my grandparents lived in France, and they were dead, but they were not my grandparents, they were my great grandparents. My real grandmother, Christiana, lived and died in Kenya. Why do relatives lie about their past Mr Foxton?"

He smiled sadly. "Normally because they want to hide things. Sometimes they don't want the truth to be known."

Chapter Thirty-Five
2019

Jeremy shook his newspaper and turned the page. He had retired from the world of law and now spent his time strolling through the parks of London, dining at his favourite restaurants in Knightsbridge and spending time at his Club.

His newspaper of choice had always been the *Telegraph.* At the weekend there was always an article by one of their top journalists, Jack Taylor. He had worked for the newspaper in London for many years, his speciality had always been what they now called 'cold cases'.

Jack Taylor, it would appear, had now re-located, and lived in South Africa, from there he sent his stories of life in the new South Africa. Jeremy had always enjoyed reading his columns, his astute observations of life there now, and the cold cases he had followed up, four of which had been published as best-selling books. Jack Taylor could not ignore the politics in that country, but he kept them light, concentrating more on the gritty stories of life for the people of that country as they came to terms and accepted, or not, their new life under a black government.

Jeremy reached for his coffee, still wondering, all these years later where Doctor Fleur Palmere had ended up. Lucy, he knew, was still working in the library in Lymington. They rarely kept in touch, she seemed to have given up on finding her Aunt Fleur, despite Jeremy's determined efforts to find her. He hadn't seen her again for eight years or so, she would be nearly thirty now he calculated.

He glanced at the clock on the wall. It would be getting dark soon, the trees were bare of leaves, the nights closing in preparing for winter, the pavements slippery and wet with red and gold leaves, lifting and dropping again with gusts of cold wind, the people he observed from his window wrapped up in the uniform of the day, puffer jackets…

He reached for his cane and hauled himself out of his chair. A quick walk, well, perhaps more of a stroll, then a drink at one of the wine bars, maybe one or two people might glance his way and embark on a conversation, he hoped it might be so, maybe someone he recognised.

He shrugged on his heavy warm coat, wrapped a scarf around his neck, wriggled his fingers into his gloves then ventured out.

The icy wind was more than he could take. He gave it ten minutes before stopping at a favourite wine bar and restaurant, with its warm and welcoming glow of soft lights, the busyness of life within there.

No longer feeling comfortable on a bar stool, he removed his coat and scarf, sank into one of the comfortable chairs and opened his newspaper with a flourish. He shook his head at a waiter who approached him, brandishing a menu.

"No, nothing to eat, thank you, perhaps a glass of red wine."

The waiter's smile disappeared, and he frowned at him. "To sit here, sir, at one of the tables, well I'm afraid they are only for our diners?"

Jeremy shook his newspaper with irritation. He had been coming here for years but it seemed now it didn't mean much anymore. He took the menu, stretching his aching back. "Alright, bring me the French onion soup and whatever it comes with."

The waiter disappeared and he looked out of the windows, already steaming up from the warm bodies inside. Things were changing, he knew that. His years of coming to this bar and restaurant, his years of loyalty and support for the owners, their courteous acknowledgement – well it seemed to have gone.

The place had clearly changed ownership. He was only another person off the streets looking for the familiarity and comfort of many years with the friendly owner, who had valued his patronage. The new owner clearly didn't have the same philosophy or values. It was all about money, no time for idle chit-chat, no time to spare for a loyal patron. No, he thought sadly, just get as many people as possible in and out again in the shortest possible time.

His onion soup was exceptional, he paid his bill and shrugged on his coat – feeling the new world had left him behind. He didn't want to imagine the yawning years ahead where elderly people didn't count anymore, had become invisible, had no apparent value, nothing to offer this brave new world. He was seventy-eight.

But Jeremy Foxton had always been tenacious – he never gave up. He returned to his Knightsbridge flat and after lighting a fire, closed the heavy curtains, then surrounded himself with the soft lights of the place, with music playing softly in the background. He picked up the newspaper again.

Jack Taylor.

Jeremy knew he had no great story to tell. Only a missing scientist…he looked up at his bookshelf and saw the large leather book which had belonged to Christiana Palmere, still wrapped in the crude sacking where it had been found in Naivasha, in Kenya, so many years ago. Now belonging to Doctor Fleur Palmere, who he had spent years looking for.

He sipped at his brandy and thought back. Captain Michael Bennett who had fallen so deeply in love with Fleur in Kenya, who had fought wars that were not his own, been lost for two years in the desert and then been found.

But where was she?

Chapter Thirty-Six
Hazyview – South Africa.
2019

Ex-Detective Inspector Piet Joubert drove fast along the dirt road leading towards Jack's cottage leaving a billowing cloud of red dust behind him, almost obliterating the last of the rays of the sun of the day.

Hope, his labrador, stuck her head out of the window, her pink tongue flapping behind her smiling face, bits of her fur floating back inside, joining the already fur covered upholstery and sticking against the windows.

"*Ag*, man, Hope, can't you keep your mouth closed at least. You're slobbering all over the place here, enough already with the fur, but the spit is too *bleddy* much."

Piet parked under the tree and let Hope out of the car, she ran towards Jack's cottage eager to see if he had anything for her to eat – biltong was something she loved, and Jack always had some for her.

Piet frowned. Jack was invariably sitting outside on the veranda of his cottage as the sun went down, enjoying a beer, his bare feet propped up on the wooden balustrades, either on his phone or tapping away on his computer, doing his column for the *Telegraph* in London, his braai smouldering in the shadows of the garden, soft grey plumes of smoke rising into the darkening sky. But there was no sign of him.

Piet let himself into the simple but tastefully furnished cottage, although it was still summer, there was a slight chill in the air, a fire burned low in the sitting room, the faint sound of music penetrated the air, otherwise there was silence. Winter was on its way.

"Hey, Jack! Where are you, my friend. Why are you hiding yourself away in there. Haven't seen you for a week or so? *Braai is* going, I see. What's for dinner?"

Piet, in the old days, before the new government had taken over, had been a senior serving officer, a detective, in the South African police force, based in the Eastern Cape. He had been nudged aside to make room for the young and aspiring Africans who had worked for him.

It had been a bitter pill to swallow, but he was an intelligent and astute man, saw the changes coming and had taken, with great reluctance, early retirement.

He had met Jack years ago when the top English journalist, then based in London, had come to his town in Willow Drift, in the Eastern Cape, re-tracing the footsteps of the daughter of an ex-British Ambassador who was looking for her.

Piet, like many Afrikaners of a certain age, resented the intrusion of an Englishman chasing the same story he had chased himself; and failed to solve. The Afrikaners had a deeply embedded dislike of English people. After all, the English could always go home and take what they wanted from his beloved country, leaving them with the debris of it and nowhere else to go.

Piet and Jack had formed an unlikely friendship, despite their differences, solved the case, and against all odds become firm and close friends.

Piet Joubert never missed an opportunity of having a stab at the British, but Jack, with his public-school background and long successful career dealing with cold cases, let him get away with it; to him it was all history. However, Jack was swift to come back and make comparisons with the British and Afrikaners and defend his own country when necessary. But mostly Piet's observations made him laugh aloud as they were usually spot on.

They had worked on other cases together – a unique team, given the circumstances, allowing Jack into the complex world of South African politics and problems as they stood today, standing back as a British journalist and assessing the entire situation. Jack knew he had limitations, and one was the language. He didn't speak Afrikaans so many doors were closed to him when dealing with the authorities. With his public-school accent, and wild mop of blond hair he stood out as a classic Englishman and a journalist to boot.

He had learned a few words from Piet, his favourite being *voetsek*. Initially he thought it was a favourite name for all dogs and cats, used liberally, but he found out it was an expletive, and meant something completely different, but he liked to use it where necessary. It was a useful word especially with the screeching noisy hadada birds who seemed to think it was fun to wake everyone up at dawn and spend the day digging up their gardens. He had decided these unattractive birds, with not one other tune in their scrawny grey heads disliked flying and therefore wished to let everyone know this was so.

It was the same with the vervet monkeys who galloped across his tin roof looking for food, the word *voetsek* seemed to work with them as well, as they scrambled for the trees somersaulting through the branches, glaring at him and baring their teeth. He was always careful to make sure he closed and latched the fine netted door when he went in and out of the cottage, he knew if the monkeys gained access, they would trash the place looking for food. However, *voetsek* didn't seem to work with mosquitoes, spiders, insects, ants or snakes. They carried on their business and ignored his swearing.

Jack found the Afrikaans language intoxicating, the descriptions of things, the colloquialisms unique to the country and the ability of the people, of all religions, colours, and backgrounds, to laugh at themselves and adapt to the swiftly changing circumstances in their country.

The laughter of the Africans, the exquisite singing which needed no orchestra or song sheets to sing from. The sound of their clear pure voices as they celebrated or mourned, or simply sang when the mood took them, softy clapping as they swayed to the sounds of their own voices. Even when they were angry about the lack of basic facilities in the rural towns, water and power cuts, they still seemed to be able to bring song and dance to their riots, protests and strikes. Africans, he had decided, liked nothing better than a big funeral. There they would gather in their finery, their large hats, their songs, and their dances – like Ascot, he mused; it was a real day out. Nothing sombre or sad about a good old South African funeral.

Even the mine workers who worked in the darkness underground had their own dance. The almighty thunder of the gum boot dance which shook and vibrated the ground beneath the male dancers' feet, their beads and animal skins quivering and swinging as they slapped their boots in unison. This was the famous dance of the mine workers who came from near and far and didn't speak each other's languages, but they communicated with each other, underground, by slapping their boots.

Jack had thought they had earned a place on Britain's Got Talent, but they were hard working men who lived and worked in darkness far below the crust of the earth, they had no such time for frivolities such as that. They worked long and hard to earn money to send back to their families, some who lived far away in other countries in Africa.

One case they had been following had led them to the town of Hazyview, a vibrant safari town, and the portal to all the spectacular beauty of the famous Kruger National Park with its world-renowned luxury lodges, game, and spectacular backdrop of sunsets, as the skies turned blood red, and the predators came out to perform their dance of death. The giraffe was an unforgettable sight as they made their languid gracious way through the bush, their unmistakeable outline there for all to see, their tall necks like periscopes towering over all the other animals, gazing down with disdain, like disapproving aristocrats, at the guests out on their sunset safari drives. An iconic image that epitomised Africa and nowhere else.

The bush, to Jack's mind, was where animals ruled the land and not people. A peaceful place with no politics, where man did not rule the world and its finances. Of course, the predators came out at night and there was indeed violence, but in the scheme of things, a peaceful place. The animals only took what they needed in their pursuit of food.

The lions were spectacular hunters. The male of the pride would sit and watch as his lionesses formed their unique pincer movement as they surrounded their prey, bringing it down and killing it swiftly with a deep bite to the jugular.

After the male had taken his fill, he would graciously allow his females to enjoy the fruits of their labours. The pride would gorge on their kill then saunter away, their pale cream bellies round and full, their muzzles bloodied. The hyena would then move in, the vultures biding their time high up in the trees, their dark feathers cloaking their bodies like a shroud, their scrawny pink necks and savage beaks waiting for their moment, goose-stepping on the branches with impatience. The undertakers of the bush.

Although, to Jack's mind, the vultures were ugly buggers, he knew when in flight, they were as graceful as any of the eagles, falcons, and other birds of prey, who graced the African skies, their shadows on the land as they hovered on the thermals, their sharp eyes missing nothing as they floated hungrily over the bush.

A bit like people, he mused, once young and beautiful, then as they grew old and unattractive (not all of them, of course), they became bitter and discontent at what the world had thrown at them. But in their dreams, they could fly like the vultures, not ugly, not old, but in their prime, becoming as perfect as they used to be as they soared above the earth they had always known.

There was no malevolence in the world of predators. They did not kill for any kind of religion or power. They were simply what they were. Existing and following the instincts going back thousands and thousands of years.

Following a case, Piet and Jack had based themselves in Hazyview, staying in a hotel called The Inn, run by an Englishman, called Hugo, who used to sell dreams of safaris as a tour operator, based in London. Hugo had given the whole thing up and decided to live in South Africa himself. Instead of selling the dream, he now lived it himself and had done so for more than twenty years.

The Inn was a humble place to begin with, only a house with a few bedrooms; Hugo had bought the place and extended it into one of the most popular hotels in the area.

Hugo had met them both staying at the hotel, pursuing their story, and offered Piet Joubert a job as his Chief Security Officer. Piet had jumped at the offer of a steady job, a cottage in the grounds, free meals and all the other perks Hugo had offered him in what was a troubling time in South Africa. Plus, the deciding factor was that he could leave the worst tempered and ugliest cat he had ever encountered with the new owner of his struggling security company in Willow Drift.

An ill-fated love affair had left Piet with a labrador puppy called Hope. He thought, as she grew up, she might amount to something; elevate his new position. But, in his words, she was hopeless, not the guard dog he had hoped would enhance his position with his new job. As a guide dog for the blind, she would be hopeless as well, no matter how well trained, dragging her owner into any restaurant where she could smell food. As for a sniffer dog hunting for drugs at an airport, well she'd be useless at that as well, not bothering with narcotics but searching for anything that smelt like biltong or other delights she was partial to.

Jack had fallen for the dog himself. "If you keep calling her Hopeless, she'll develop mental issues, Piet. The guests absolutely adore her, yes, okay, she is useless at her job as a guard dog, but the guests love her."

Piet had scowled at him. "What's with this *bleddy* mental issues *kak*, Jack. You watch too much television. A dog is a dog, it doesn't think like you, nor does any other animal. You Brits, and not only you Brits, try to turn a domestic animal into some kind of baby with fur. In America it's a fashion accessory, load of crap, if you ask me.

"Dogs having birthday parties, with cakes and balloons, wearing collars with diamonds, ribbons in their fur, dressed in stupid clothes, frilly pink skirts, and suchlike. Rich people leaving a fortune to their dogs and not their children. World's gone mad, my friend."

He scratched his chin. "Sure, I understand people love their pets, of course I do. Normally when humans have let them down. Parents put their own lives on hold and devote themselves to bringing up a child, or children, spend a fortune on their education, go through all the fights and arguments with them as teenagers, the kid buggers off to Australia, never to be seen again – *shoo,* what was the point of it all I ask myself, but then again I never had children. A dog, like Hope, is enough of a challenge for me, even though she is clumsy and forgets her manners sometimes."

He fondled his dog's ears. "At least she'll never leave me, didn't cost a cent to educate or train, as sadly you can see. But she'll stay with me until death do us part, well, as long as there's plenty of food around. But*, man,* it's confusing for an animal being dressed up as a child and taken around in a chauffeur driven car, having its *bleddy* nails and hair done in a salon and wearing a hat and sunglasses.

"That's humans for you Jack. Poor *friggin* animal doesn't know what it is anymore, all its basic instincts are killed by trying to be someone's child dressed up in the latest fashion.

"Gimme a lion or a cheetah any day, they know who they are and what their instincts tell them. If they're hungry they go out and kill something, they don't sit there waiting for the butler to bring their designer food on a *friggin* silver platter."

The guests loved to see Hope's smiling dolphin face as she stumbled around after Piet, stopping to greet all the guests, sitting outside their rooms enjoying a sundowner, in the hope they may share their snacks with her, especially if they had biltong.

Plus, the dog seemed to love rugby or pretended to. If there was a big game on and the Boks were playing, well, she was right there in the middle of the rowdy fans, lifting her golden head and howling when the Boks scored a goal. Politely helping herself to whatever was going in the way of snacks, as the fans slapped each other on the back and stayed focussed on the huge television screen. What was not to love about her?

Jack had laughed. "Her public relations skills are unsurpassed. When Hugo pushes the delights of his hotel to the world, on social media, who do you think is right up there with pics of the rooms, the grounds, the staff – Hope, that's who. All the guests who book want to meet her. Okay, she does disgrace herself now and again, lurking under the long tablecloths if there's a *braai* going on outside, stealing stuff, but that's a labrador for you. They have two things in their lives: love for their owner and love for food, oh, and sleeping, of course."

Piet had grinned sheepishly; he loved his dog, hopeless or not. She never stayed asleep in her basket in his cottage when he went to bed. In the middle of the night, he would find her snoring away next to him on his pillow, her jowls quivering, and he found some comfort there. Putting his arm around her he knew he would sleep well. He couldn't imagine Hope with red toenails. She didn't have diamonds around her neck, only a bright coloured collar of beadwork made by the Ndebele people.

Now Piet looked around, wondering where Jack was. Hope came out, a large piece of biltong clamped between her jaws.

Jack appeared from what he called his 'Ops Room,' his spare room, and gestured for Piet to help himself to a beer. He was on the phone, turning his back on Piet he continued his conversation.

"Alright Mr Foxton, I'll do some research, see what I can come up with. But we're talking many years ago now. It's hardly a cold case, no bodies found, no murder reported. But I'll investigate it for you."

Piet was already busy with the *braai*. He had found the racks of ribs in the fridge, along with some lamb chops, *sosatis,* and a loaf of garlic bread wrapped in tin foil. There was no salad to be seen but he'd found a bowl of baked beans heavily doused with something that smelled like braai sauce and whisky, plus two large potatoes wrapped in foil.

Piet looked up at the sky. It was still light enough to see Jack's garden. A tepid breeze caressed the leaves on the trees changing them to a softer feathery green, etched with shadows. A golden shower of flowers cascaded over one of the walls of the garden amidst the tenacious bougainvillea which clung to the walls, their red, purple, white, and magenta flowers, dull with dust. When the rain came it would wash away the covering dust of the days gone by and reveal a stunning palette of colours.

Against the now bruised and threatening sky, the clouds, their underbellies purple with the promise of much needed rain, remained stationery. Birds made their way home to roost, their wings startling white against the gathering darkness of the sky, as they dipped and swooped on their flight to the safety and shelter of the trees.

Piet pulled the *braai* from the shadows of the garden and placed it under the cover of the veranda. There was a big storm coming. He could hear Jack still talking to whoever it was, it sounded intriguing.

Jack was not one to spend hours on the phone. He shrugged, unless it was one of his new girlfriends, in which case he would spend more time than usual chatting someone up. Jack was a very attractive man, and women were drawn to him like moths to a flame.

Piet lit four hurricane lamps on the table outside. With the storm would surely come Eskom, who would wipe the electricity out with their usual efficiency. He checked the food on the *braai*, turned over the ribs, *sosaties*, and chops and sat back with his beer.

The air was still, not a leaf or frond moved, suddenly he felt a coolness in the air where seconds before it had been unbearably hot and humid. He looked around the garden, a slight movement here and there, otherwise only silence, no birdsong either, as if they too had had enough of the heat of the day, but the stream at the bottom of the garden still gurgled as it made its merry way to wherever it was going.

Then came the slight creak, he looked up at the now heavy swollen purple clouds, it felt as though the plops of rain now staining the edges of the veranda had come from nowhere. The sun had disappeared to another place, a grey darkness beginning to fill the sky.

He screwed up his eyes as a dazzling rip of lightening tore through the brooding skies, followed by a deafening clap of thunder, behind it came a low and ominous roll of more thunder.

In seconds the rain came roaring down like a waterfall, thundering on the tin roof of the cottage, bouncing like a cavalcade of hard dried peas and dancing on the veranda before entering the grounds and joining the rest of the bushes, plants and trees in their frenzy, the wind bending and turning their anger on anything in their path. The rich smell of wet earth assailed his nostrils, and he breathed in deeply. The dirt road to Jack's cottage now flat and sodden.

Ah, the smell of rain on hot earth, the smell of rain on the hot tarmac roads, there was nothing like it, or the sound of it on a tin roof. The smell of a *braai,* a tradition every weekend, the grey clouds of smoke rising listlessly into a warm evening as families gathered. The men grouped around the fire, sipping from their bottles of beer, talking rugby and politics. The women, chattering and laughing in the kitchen, preparing the salads, and watching the children as they splashed around in the pool. A sense of history, something they had always known.

For every South African who had left the country, the smell of a *braai* on a hot summer's night evoked irreplaceable and unexpected senses, of memories of a place they would never forget, an avalanche of feelings, taking over the memories flooding through them; of a place they had always known, even though they had moved to another country and tried to adapt. Sometimes it brought them to their knees in grief as they stabbed at the meat and sipped from their bottles and looked up at an unfamiliar sky, a leaden sky perhaps, longing for the home they had left so far behind, blaming the smoke of the fire for the unexpected stinging of their eyes.

Hope, like most dogs, didn't like thunder, she crept under Piet's chair, with what was left of her soggy stick of biltong tightly held between her jaws.

Piet checked the *braai*. All was well there, the wind had not blown their way. He sat and watched nature in all its raw beauty, and he knew he could never live anywhere else. Here man had no control whatsoever and it suited him well. The slashing rain washing and sweeping the hidden beauty of the leaves and flowers, removing the dust and man-made pollution of their cars and everything else essential to them. Now showing their true colours, the leaves and plants had their grey and brown dust removed and revealed the deep green colours they could breathe and call their own.

The thin rivulets made their way through the garden, snake-like they disappeared into the stream. The thunder grumbled off into the distance. Once more there was silence, only the incessant soft plopping sound of the remaining raindrops on the canvas awning, their long streams of water finally petering out to a trickle. The normally tranquil stream now seemed to roar with the elevated level of its water as it sped its way through the bush.

Then the lights went out.

Finally, Jack appeared. Piet had cooked their dinner to perfection, despite the elements.

"*Jeez* Jack, thought you were never going to finish that call. New woman in your life perhaps?"

Jack seemed preoccupied, ignoring the question with a smile, as he looked at the retreating storm. "You know something, Piet, nights like this, evenings like this, well, they'll stay with me forever. The violence of the storm, the rawness of it, but the knowing it – Mother Nature. Bigger than all of us, makes one feel a bit humble."

Piet laughed. "Humble? *Nah*, it's what it is, known it all my life. I don't do humble. You feel a bit down or something?"

Jack ignored him and continued. "I mean look us at here, in the middle of the bush, the sounds and noise all around us, the raging storm, the smell of the meat cooking, we have light, despite Eskom, we have food. How much more does a person need?

"Oh, okay, Eskom strikes again. No power, just as well I finished my long conversation."

Piet handed him a plate. "Dig in, my friend. Yup, we don't do the baby stuff with the weather here, no soft sweeping rains and fog covering everything in sight, like in your country, for week after week, months sometimes.

"*Nah*, when we have a storm, we have a proper grown-up one, plenty of the wet stuff, plenty of noise and the wind blows everything to hell and gone, that unforgettable smell of rich wet earth – what's not to love about a violent storm in Africa? Mother nature at her furious best. Answers to no one."

They polished off their dinner, tearing off the meat from the ribs and chops and sinking their teeth into the warm garlic bread. Hope sat next to the dying coals of the fire and pretended to be most interested in the aftermath of the storm, listening to the drops of rain pattering on the canvas awning, her eyes sliding towards any leftovers which might come her way. Jack always left dog biscuits in her bowl in the kitchen, not that she cared for them but ate them anyway. She had her eyes on the main chance of some decent meat, even some garlic bread if push came to shove.

Jack threw her a piece of garlic bread which she caught in mid-air. "So how are things at the hotel, Piet. High season is almost over but the weather's still good, well, apart from tonight, are you busy?"

Piet wiped his mouth with the back of his hand. "*Bleddy* Brits are still hanging around, moaning and complaining. Game drive this evening was cancelled, caused a lot of muttering and gloomy faces.

"Some woman complained about the ants outside her room, said they hadn't been mentioned on the website, wanted to change her room. I couldn't be bothered to tell her they live here; go wherever they want to when they want to. She also complained bitterly because a fly landed on her sandwich when she was having lunch in the garden and said the travel agent hadn't mentioned anything about flies in Africa either.

"Spiders are lurking around, some as big as saucers, fortunately they don't like the guests any more than I do sometimes, so unlike me they can scuttle away, hide behind the curtains in the rooms or under the bath."

Piet scraped a smear of butter from the garlic bread from his safari boot. "Tell me something, Jack, why do some of those Brits bring their own food with them. Their own tea and flat round biscuits. What's wrong with ours? *Jeez*, I'll never understand them, although I have to say they get stuck into our wines hey, probably numbs them from the reality of being in deepest darkest Africa, surrounded by wild animals, and what's with the chips? They want *bleddy* chips with everything, even breakfast."

Jack laughed. "Look, Piet, not all the Brits are the same. Hugo's place appeals to the average tourists, his room rates are acceptable, and he attracts the tour operators, eager for their commissions and their bus loads of middle-class travellers. Those guys want to have fun and have an adventure, but they also want the comforts of home, hence they bring their own tea and biscuits."

Piet grunted. "Don't know why they bother to come then. If the lot I saw tonight was having fun, I'd hate to see them when they're not. Complaints, complaints, complaints. The pool is too cold, the sun is too hot, the biting mosquitoes, also not on the website, although they are advised by their tour operator to take anti-malaria pills. They think that's enough to warn off the mozzies, stop them biting them. Mozzies want blood, they take it; don't care if the victim is a Brit, an Italian or a German. Blood is blood."

Piet started to laugh. "Last night was good. Hugo had put Bunny Chow on the menu, knowing the Brits like their curry. Some of the guests freaked out thinking a cute dead bunny was going to pop out of a loaf of bread smothered in curry. Best laugh I had this week."

Jack seemed to be only half listening to Piet's stories about his guests.

"Okay, my friend. Being an ex-cop, I know something's on your mind, and it doesn't seem to be a woman. What's up. Who was on the phone and why do you want to know if I'm busy at the hotel?"

Jack brought two more cold beers from the kitchen. "Well, I'm not sure what to make of that phone call. First it was from Harry's personal assistant Bella. There might be something in it, but it seems doubtful to me. There was no meat to the story she told me.

"But it was the story from a solicitor called Jeremy Foxton, who she finally put me in touch with this evening, who made me think. Although there were no dead bodies, no murders in his story.

"It was about a woman who went missing, a scientist, some twenty years or so ago, here in South Africa.

"Apparently her roots started in Kenya decades ago… it might be worth following up Piet."

Chapter Thirty-Seven
2019

Jeremy Foxton had pulled Christiana Palmere's large leather book from the shelf. He had nothing to lose, but perhaps might get some answers to the story which had started so many years ago.

He had explored every avenue open to him over the years and come up with no answers. He knew technology had advanced at lightning speed and he was simply not up for it.

He needed help.

He phoned *The Telegraph.*

"I wish to speak to the editor of your newspaper, Mr Harry Bentley. My name is Jeremy Foxton. I'm a solicitor. I have a case which I have pursued for many years but been unable to solve."

He was put through to Harry's personal assistant, Bella. He repeated his story. "I'm sorry Mr Foxton, Mr Bentley has a busy schedule, as you can imagine. Perhaps you would let me know a little about your story and where it takes place?"

Jeremy cleared his throat. "It's in South Africa. A story which started in Kenya in the sixties."

Bella listened carefully, making notes. "I'm afraid, as I told you, Mr Bentley is not available, he's on holiday overseas now. Won't be back for a couple of months. However, we do have another top journalist here, his name is Stefan de Villiers, he's a South African and works with Jack on his stories out of Africa. Perhaps he'll be able to help?"

Jeremy was quiet for a moment. "I would like to speak to Jack Taylor. I've followed his stories for years. He's the one I wish to speak to if Mr Bentley is not available."

Bella smiled into the phone. "Jack Taylor lives in South Africa now, but still one of our top journalists here at the newspaper.

"Perhaps it would help if you would tell me what it is you're looking for."

Jeremy took a sip of his brandy and looked at Fleur's mother's leather book lying in his lap."

"I am the custodian of a family called the Palmere's. I have handled their estates for many years. I know the history of the family from when they lived in Kenya. Their daughter, Fleur, moved to South Africa in the late eighties. I have been unable to find her since. She was a medical doctor but became a scientist. I don't wish to discuss anymore at this stage. But there is a substantial estate here which I would like to wind up, but it won't be possible unless I can find out what happened to Doctor Fleur Palmere."

Bella twirled her fingers through her hair. Harry would kill her if she let a potential story slip through her fingers. "Mr Foxton, let me contact Jack Taylor and tell him of your concerns about Doctor Fleur Palmere. They're having a little trouble with power cuts and the internet in South Africa now. But I'll try to help. Your story took place many years ago, but Jack Taylor has an excellent reputation for delving into old stories, cold cases we call them now. Leave me your phone number and I'll get back to you. Over above the power cuts and interrupted internet in South Africa there is a time difference, of course.

"But I'll contact Jack and see if he would like to speak to you?"

Jeremy smiled. "Oh, he'll be most interested indeed. This story goes back a long way. Something happened in South Africa, years ago. There are many questions as to what happened to Doctor Palmere, but it seems no answers.

"But it goes back before Fleur arrived in South Africa…that's where it all started you see. In Kenya. In a place called Naivasha."

Chapter Thirty-Eight

Piet rubbed his hands together as he listened to Jack's recounting of his conversation with Mr Jeremy Foxton.

He threw another log on the fire. "Not much meat on this story, my friend, as you say. A British scientist goes missing twenty or so years ago somewhere. Her name was Doctor Fleur Palmere, with roots in Kenya. By all accounts she was wandering around the country looking for plants and herbs. Maybe she switched careers and wanted to be some kind of celebrity chef using different stuff to improve your British so-called cuisine. Let's face it, Jack, it isn't up there with the best you must admit. Deep fried *bleddy* Mars bars served with curry and chips." He shuddered at the thought.

Jack frowned, only half-listening. "Jeremy told me he had a large book, leather bound, handwritten. Fleur's mother lived in Kenya, died there actually, but she kept a record of everything she discovered about traditional medicine. She wasn't a scientist, a botanist, or a doctor, just an amateur, but clearly extremely intelligent.

"Her daughter, Fleur, was a medical doctor but for some reason she turned to science. Following in her mother's footsteps she pursued a career in traditional medicine, she added her discoveries to her mother's. She worked for a pharmaceutical company in London and suddenly left the company and the country for South Africa."

Jack took a sip of his beer, tapping his fingers on the side of the table. "There is a story here, as you say without much meat on it. But supposing she had discovered something, or had a theory, which would change the world of the big pharma companies? If she had, it would be in the leather book. It could be valuable research."

Piet nodded. "For the vast majority of rural South Africans that's all they know. They have their traditional healers, their faith and hope in whatever they are told or given in the way of traditional medicines, and they get better, well not all of them of course, nothing was going to cure AIDS at the time. What are you thinking here? That this Doctor Fleur found the cure for AIDS?"

"No. I don't think so. But she may have stumbled onto something else."

Piet stood up. "Better get back to the hotel. Are we going to take this case on then, my friend?"

"Yup. Because it goes back many years, it's worth a follow up."

Piet rubbed his hands with glee. "So, what's your first move, we have bugger all to go on so far? Like looking for a grey hair on the beach."

Jack scratched idly at a mosquito bite on his arm, then leaned forward and fished a moth out of his drink. Other insects, attracted by the light, sizzled, and burned on the hot glass, dropping on the table in front of them.

"I think this calls for a quick trip to the UK. I need to meet the solicitor, Jeremy Foxton, and get the background on this Doctor Fleur Palmere. I need to see Harry as well; been a while since I saw him last, and I'd like to spend a bit of time with my folks. They won't be around forever."

Piet's head jerked up, a look of horror on his face. "Hope you're not harbouring any hopes I'm going to make a trip to the UK with you – still trying to get over the last one. Did nothing but *bleddy* rain the whole time, ruined my favourite pair of safari boots. Didn't like the funny food you lot eat over there, didn't like that solicitor either, him with the fancy suit looking down his pointy nose at my accent – calling me Joe Bear like I was some kind of circus act."

Jack laughed. "No, I don't think Harry would approve two first class tickets, last time they were paid for by the client, this time I'll be in premier class – on my own."

Piet was more than relieved. "You'll see Harry, of course. Give him my best. You'll no doubt be meeting him at his *larney* White's only gentleman's club with all those other dusty aristocratic members, sitting in their fat leather studded chairs, sipping their port, fancy walking sticks leaning against their chairs, shaking their newspapers in irritation if anyone sneezes or laughs too loudly."

Piet grinned. "All those posh accents, no cell phones allowed, no business discussions, no politics, and no women allowed right? Don't know why anyone bothers to be a member. Bet they wouldn't let me join with my fine Afrikaans accent, not that I could afford the mind buggery annual membership fees. Thinking back, I don't recall seeing any dark faces around when Harry took us there, only tanned ones from expensive holidays in their homes in the Caribbean or South of France. Why was that, Jack?"

Jack was not going to rise to the bait. "White's Gentleman's Club is one of the most exclusive clubs in London. Been going since 1693. It can take years to get membership there and you must come from a certain titled background and be approved by all the other members. I don't think you'd pass that test, mate. Women are not allowed, you're right, even today. That's how it is Piet. Wouldn't bother to apply for membership if I were you, not a hope in hell you would even be considered."

Piet snorted. "Not my kind of place, I can tell you that. All those ancient paintings of old members glaring down at the newcomers no doubt, finding them not quite up to snuff. The dress code, not allowed in if you're not dressed by some fancy Savile Row bespoke tailor or have handmade shoes. Load of rubbish, my friend.

"*Nah*, give me Hugo's place open to anyone, no racial profiling, no gender profiling. We love our women here. We can dress in *slops,* shorts and shirts, wear whatever we like. Rugby with its enormous screen in the bar attracts all sorts of different people and all are welcome, if they are rooting for the Springboks. But we tolerate the Australian, Brits, and New Zealand supporters if it's a big match against their teams; adds some spice and excitement.

"That fancy club in London would have been burned to the ground here in South Africa on the day it opened. Not politically correct in our so-called Rainbow Nation, can't go calling a club 'Whites' – not on, my friend, we are all apparently equal now, no more of that apartheid sounding stuff – ah well, whatever. Gone are those days."

Piet whistled for his dog, putting on his battered baseball cap. "Right then. I'm off. Anything you want me to do this end, so long. Want me to give Bertie a quick ring, see what he can find about the missing doctor, if she is in fact missing. Might be dead even."

Jack stood up. "Nope, nothing to go on now but I will have when I get back. So, go back to your disgruntled guests and make the most of them. I plan to leave in the next day or two as soon as I can book my flight. I'm thinking I might fly back via Kenya, where this whole story started. Should be gone about a week or so, but I'll keep you up to speed when I have more information about the mysterious Doctor Fleur Palmere, who disappeared without trace so many years ago."

Chapter Thirty-Nine

Bertie poked at his fire, he was out in the bush, fishing next to a lake, taking a much-needed week off. He too had been side-swiped by the new government. For years he had worked for the old government in the department of Home Affairs. Keeping a data base of everyone who came and went into South Africa, technology had advanced, and he had embraced it with his unique skills as a computer expert. He knew then, in the old days, technology would be taking over the laborious paperwork of years before.

He had met Piet Joubert at a university in the Free State and they had become close friends. Piet was studying forensic science, and he, Bertie, was embracing the new world of technology. Their careers, their ambitions, at that time, were poles apart.

Piet had gone on to become a highly respected detective inspector with the South African police department. But both their hopes and dreams had been nudged aside when the new President of the country, Nelson Mandela, had come into power.

The new government had recognised Bertie's unique skills with technology and kept him on. But not within the government's home affairs department. They paid him as a private consultant knowing he was one of the top experts in the country when it came to technology.

This gave Bertie the opportunity to go out there and set up his own network for a private club; all the members worked for various governments all over the world, they by-passed all the red tape and exchanged information quickly and efficiently. There was no other private club like this one. Information was exchanged, no names mentioned. They could hack into data bases and produce the information required on anyone, anywhere in the world. Without any government approval. They were a tight and secretive group of world-class computer scientists.

Each member knew, obviously, where the other members lived in the world, but none knew which city or town or the members' surname. Safer that way.

Each request for information had to be approved by all the members, and the person requiring the information, normally a private detective, or ex-police, had to be known and trusted by a member of the group who was asking for the information on an individual or company somewhere in the world.

Like Piet he was in his late fifties although he still looked like a bit of a geek, a relic from the past, with his John Lennon glasses, his thinning hair tied back in a ponytail and torn jeans. He had known for some time that Artificial Intelligence was coming and would make a massive impact on technology. He knew it would be brilliant for medicine, science, and other professions, but could easily be abused in the wrong hands, it would have to be tightly regulated which would be an almost impossible task. He wasn't sure for how many more years he'd be able to keep up, even though he knew his skills with technology were exceptional.

So, here Bertie was, trying to switch his brain off and relax. He had left his state-of-the-art phone locked in his safe in his small, rented room, along with his computer. This was also Bertie's office. He brought his own personal simple phone with him, in case of a family emergency.

He lit a cigarette and looked out over the placid lake and the trees and bushes surrounding it. The sun was starting to set, throwing the silhouettes of the darkening trees into sharp relief around the water's edge. The still water turned to gold before being shot through with pink and red, birds made their silent way home to roost, sending not a ripple across the surface.

He hadn't caught a reasonably sized fish for his dinner, so rummaged in his cool box for a curl of *boerewors* and a piece of steak, throwing them on the fire and watching the grey smoke dissipate into the darkened sky. He sat on the tailgate of his *bakkie* and looked up at the stars as he puffed on his cigarette, sipping from a bottle of beer, feeling himself relax and falling back into the warm and safe days when he was a young boy, out on the family farm, when the world was a calmer place with more hope than an anxious world could imagine today.

He looked out at the darkening landscape, the trees, the mountains, the placid lake, the chortling of the hippos as they made their way to the edges of the lake where they would forage through the night. Deep in his soul and heart he knew the human landscape was changing, but here, beside the lake, listening to the night sounds of Africa which he had known all his life, he knew nothing would change what he was observing and feeling now.

Yes, the world of technology was outpacing most people, all trying to keep up with a changing and unpredictable world, all anxious and worried that if they didn't keep up, they would be left trailing behind. The tech language was introducing words they had never heard of, didn't understand. This would heap more stress on certain age groups, creating mental trauma and a sense of being scuppered in this new world they were facing. A world they had contributed to, fought wars for, brought their children up in, and the grandchildren, then been left floundering.

The world they had known all their lives was being fragmented, forcing them to think differently, adding more and more stress when they were confronted with hysterical media spitting out all the bad news from across the world.

He took another sip of his beer as he sat in this world he had known as a boy. A different world from the one he was in now as one of the best tech guys in the country.

He preferred where he was right now. A place unchanged for hundreds of years. A place where he felt safe in his mind and memory.

He finished eating, washed his plate in the lake, stamped out his fire and crawled into his *bakkie,* pulling up the tailgate, dropping the heavy tarpaulin and securing it against anything nature wished to throw at him during the night.

He didn't bother to undress; he climbed into his sleeping bag and lay listening to the silence of a South African night in the bush before falling into a contented sleep.

Chapter Forty
London

Jack had spent a pleasant weekend with his parents in Somerset, enjoying the cool and blustery weather of the countryside, the familiarity of his family home, his mother's cooking, and visiting the local pub with his father. Now he was on his way to see the retired solicitor Mr Jeremy Foxton in Knightsbridge, at his rather smart looking premises.

"Ah, Mr Taylor, how good of you to take the time to come and see me, a long journey, I fear? Do come in. Bit of a bite in the air; something you have become unaccustomed to I would imagine."

Jack shook Jeremy's hand. "Not really," he grinned at the smiling, kindly face, of the solicitor, "only about seven thousand miles, even though everyone thinks Africa is hot, which it is, it can get damn cold in the winter there, I can tell you.

"I needed to see my folks and visit my editor, Harry Bentley. I'm also anxious to hear your story about the missing doctor, it sounds intriguing."

Jeremy lowered himself into his chair and placed his cane next to him. "Would you care for something to drink. I make terrible coffee but a dab hand at mixing a gin and tonic?"

He pointed to a silver tray on a side table. "Or, perhaps, you would do the honours, this cold weather is not good for my joints, whilst I go through the file of what little information I have."

He reached for his file as Jack busied himself with mixing the drinks. Placing one next to Jeremy he settled into the chair opposite him and took a sip of his gin and tonic, swirling the ice cubes and slim slice of lemon with his finger.

Jeremy ignored his drink. "As I explained to you on the phone Mr Taylor…"

"Please call me Jack, Mr Foxton."

Jeremy glanced up briefly and smiled. "You must call me Jeremy then.

"As I explained on the phone and gave you the brief background on the Palmere family, well, there's far more to it, in my opinion. As you know like a doctor and patient relationship, the same exists between a solicitor and his client. Everything remains confidential."

He took a sip of his drink. "However, there's a lot more to this story. I am, of course, privy to this information, not all of it, but I think it would be useful for you to know a little more about the Palmere family. I have made the decision to tell you what I know because I can't think of any other way of finding out what happened to Doctor Fleur Palmere. It's impossible for me to believe she disappeared into thin air in South Africa, or perhaps in a neighbouring country and was never heard of again."

Jeremy flipped through his file. "Fleur was born in Kenya but educated here in the UK. She was a qualified medical doctor and turned to researching traditional medicine. Her mother, Christiana was also researching plants and herbs etc. in a place called Naivasha in Kenya. It was her mother who was at the beginning of this story. She discovered something and Fleur, her daughter, carried on this research. She left the world of medicine to pursue something she thought was more important."

Jack felt the familiar fizz going down his spine. There was a story here. An intriguing one.

"Fleur worked at the Chelsea and Westminster hospital, here in London, as a medical doctor. She joined an international pharma company wanting to change her career path. She left there abruptly and flew off to South Africa. It was the last we heard of her."

Jeremy lifted a one-page letter from the file. "All of this, of course, is highly confidential. But I advertised in newspapers all over Africa looking for Fleur, this was the only response I received."

Dear Mr Foxton,

I saw your notice in the newspaper here in Bulawayo. At first it didn't mean anything to me until I saw the name, which I recognised.

I don't know how many years ago it was now, because I was only maybe two years old. But a Zimbabwean man, called Simon, left me here in Bulawayo, with his grandmother, in a safe place. I had no recollection then of why I was placed here. Simon left South Africa; he had been working there for some twenty years at a camp site. When I showed him the notice in the newspaper here, which you had placed, he told me about a woman who appeared at the camp site which had been closed. He was leaving the next day but managed to take care of the woman in the brief time he had shared with her.

Her name was Doctor Fleur Palmere. He told me she had recently arrived in South Africa to continue with some kind of research, but clearly something went wrong, and she found herself alone in an abandoned camp site. Simon told me she had been planning to stay in a safari camp somewhere else but when she got there it didn't exist. Someone dropped her at the camp site and drove off leaving her there.

The reason he remembers her so well is she gave him money so he could return to his country Zimbabwe. She asked only one thing from him, that he would give life, hope and courage to a young child who now lived in Bulawayo.

This young child was me. Poppy.

Simon died some years ago, but I had known him all my life, he was the only family I knew.

He gave me the gift of hope. This, he told me, was what Doctor Palmere had wanted for me, although she didn't know me, I never met her. But clearly Simon remembered her well, if only briefly.

Eventually I found out about my parents and my siblings, but Simon kept me close, he didn't want me to re-live such a horrific time in my life alone, without him.

Still to this day, I miss him and the gift he gave me of hope.

He told me the place where the camp site was, obviously not there now, was called something like Waterfall, well, that's how it sounded to me. It was in somewhere called the Eastern Cape.

I do hope you find her. I think she must have been something quite special.

Poppy.

Jeremy handed Jack another report from the detective he had hired.

There was a small piece in the newspapers here (see enclosed) a scientist had gone missing whilst on a field trip in the Eastern Cape. It appears she was in an area called the Wild Coast.

This is a remote and very large area, Mr Foxton, no body was found. Perhaps she was swept out to sea, that coastline is particularly dangerous even if you are a strong swimmer, it is also renowned for its high presence of sharks. I don't know.

It sounds to me as though it could possibly be your Doctor Palmere. Her disappearance was reported to the local police, but she wasn't found.

South Africa as you and the world know is in a frenzy of excitement with the new president being sworn in, the country had *finally been accepted on the world stage after decades of isolation and sanctions.*

I'm afraid the article was a little lost in all the other big headlines. But I thought I should let you know.

Unfortunately, I will not be able to help you in the future as I am emigrating to South America.

I wish you luck in your search for the doctor and I'm sorry I was unable to find her, despite all my efforts.

Sincerely,
Bill O'Hara.

Jeremy closed the file. "I, personally, think Fleur found something of vital importance. Something which might have changed the world of medicine and science."

He stood up and went to his bookshelf, carrying something wrapped in frayed sacking. Carefully he extracted the large leather book from it.

"Fleur left this with me, her mother's book with all her years of research in the bush. Fleur told me she had added some annotations of her own. She left it with me for safe keeping."

Jack leaned forward in his chair. "May I have a look, Jeremy, it looks old, something one should perhaps wear cotton gloves for to preserve it."

Jeremy handed it to him. "It's all written in French, there are some exquisite drawings in it."

Jack's French was excellent, but he didn't have any knowledge of African plants and herbs. He studied the pages. "Can't make head or tail of it to be honest, the drawings, though, are exceptional. I would imagine this journal is extremely valuable in today's world. I see in places the handwriting, written above the drawings is different. These must have been done by Fleur who researched the Latin names for the plants."

Jack closed the book carefully and handed it back to Jeremy who wrapped it reverently in its shabby piece of sacking and placed it back into the bookcase, before returning to his chair and taking another sip of his drink.

"Jeremy, you said Fleur left the world of medicine and worked for a pharma company here in London before leaving for South Africa, or perhaps returned to Kenya where she was born, to pick up where her mother left off. Do you know which pharma company it was?"

"Yes. It's more than your average million-dollar pharma company. The Foundation is an eminent, highly respected old city company. It ploughs back its profits into research. To get a position there you must be highly qualified, a leader in the field of medicine and research. That's who Fleur worked for. I followed this up as well, but it led me nowhere with all the Data Protection laws we have today. I couldn't find anyone who would, or could, give me any information on what Fleur was doing there. One can only assume it had something to do with traditional medicine in Africa judging by the leather book I showed you. But that was decades ago, Jack, where will you begin with this story?"

Jack smiled at him. "At the beginning, of course, where every story starts. I happen to be rather good at old stories."

Jeremy took a last gulp of his drink and carefully placed his glass on the table next to him.

"Fleur had a sister called Helene, they both grew up in Kenya, and were sent to boarding school here, to finish their education, financed by their grandparents who lived in France.

"Helene, according to her sister Fleur, had a problem with abusive substances, drink and drugs and suchlike. I know Fleur took her away from London, somewhere in the north of England and tried to put her back together again. I assume she must have been successful at weaning her sister of the stuff destroying her health.

"Before Fleur left for Africa, she came to see me. Her sister had given birth to a daughter, she wanted to adjust her will to accommodate her new niece, Lucy."

Jack looked at his notes. "Any idea who the father was?"

Jeremy shook his head. "According to Fleur, it could have been anyone. By all accounts her sister, how can I put this, was a party animal. She moved in a fast circle of drinking, drugs, and relationships.

"Helene has since, rather unexpectedly, died, which has put me in this difficult position for winding up the estate. Lucy will inherit everything if I can get some proof that Fleur is indeed dead. Until then my hands are tied."

Jack shifted in his chair. "Would it be possible for me to meet Lucy, Jeremy?"

"Oh yes, I'm sure it can be arranged, but the problem is she never met her Aunt Fleur, or her biological father come to that, so she's as confused as I am about her long-lost family. I need to wrap up this estate. That's why I need your help."

Thoughtfully he tapped his empty glass on the table.
"I think Fleur was murdered, Jack."

Chapter Forty-One

Harry Bentley was more than delighted to see, Jack, his top journalist, now back from Africa, appear at his office door. Still tall, straight-backed, and sporting his traditional navy-blue braces and matching bow tie, the man never seemed to age. He was the most respected newspaper man in the city, indeed in the country, and had been for years.

"Jack, my boy, good to see you. Looks like you have the potential of a new story, apart from your usual out of Africa columns our readers enjoy as they chomp through their cornflakes, muesli, and porridge, peering out at yet another gloomy day of fog and rain. You bring a bit of sunshine into their lives. Days gone by when all was well in the old colonial world, when you could have a big fry up for breakfast not bloody berries and yoghourt. Memories, my boy, that's what you bring them – irreplaceable memories of days long gone.

"I've booked a table at Rules, oldest restaurant in London, as you know, for lunch. You might like your *braais* over there in South Africa, stars twinkling in the sky, lions roaring around the bush, mosquitoes partaking of your blood, but you can't beat a good Shepherd's Pie at Rules. Far more civilised and the service is superb. I will start with a dozen oysters.

"Now give me what you have after your meeting with Jeremy Foxton. Think I met him once or twice at my club. Can't say I remember him, but you, no doubt, will shine the spotlight on him with your next story.

"Now we have, of course, delved into the past of Doctor Fleur Palmere. All medical and scientific stuff, her profile etc. But we have no more than that. Nothing about the woman herself, where she went, but obviously Africa. Nothing on her personal life, as you would expect.

"Fill me in on what you have so far?" He slid an oyster down his throat and smacked his lips with approval.

So, Jack did. "The thing is, Harry, we have little or almost nothing to go on here. It will be impossible to get any personal details on Fleur Palmere with all this Data Protection stuff now. However, I do know someone who will be able to bypass all of that and dig deeper than we can. His name is Bertie. Piet and I have used him before on other cases. He can dig into any data base and produce the goodies. In his hidden world Data Protection is something he has little regard, or respect, for."

Harry looked absolutely horrified. "A hacker you mean? Good heavens, my dear boy, that's strictly against the law as you know. You and your chum, Bertie, could be the demise of the newspaper if it ever emerged we had allowed this to happen and sanctioned it."

Jack smiled at him. "Well, it's always worked before. We've used Bertie often. How do you think we solved all the other cases?"

Harry looked carefully around the intimate dark wood panelling, plush velvet seats and cosy fireplace of the restaurant, wondering how many other secrets and stories had passed between the diners over hundreds of years.

He raised his arm for the bill and busied himself with checking it.

"We never had this conversation, Jack. All this hacking and bypassing the Government's red tape can have disastrous consequences for any newspaper in the UK these days. It's been the demise of some of them."

He tucked his credit card back into his wallet and smiled at Jack. "Go after this story, my boy, use whatever it takes. If this person you mentioned has a surname, I don't want to know what it is, you hear me."

Jack shrugged on his coat. "Sure. Even I don't know what his surname is, where he lives or anything else about him. But he will dig deep if Piet and I can give him enough information, and he'll help us find out what happened to Fleur Palmere, we have nothing to go on. But Jeremy Foxton showed me the letter I told you about, from someone in Zimbabwe called Poppy.

"This, Harry is the starting point. I need to know when Fleur arrived in South Africa, how she found herself in a deserted camp site, and try to follow her journey until she vanished.

"If she did indeed find something of great significance, her life would have been in danger, especially if there were other interested parties after the same information. Jeremy thinks she may have been murdered.

"My plan is to meet Helene's daughter Lucy and see where it might lead me. I want to go back to Kenya and try and find her grandmother, Christiana's, old home. It was a long time ago, I know. But there may be some old retainer there who might be able to help me."

Harry wrapped his scarf around his neck. "Bit of a stretch, my boy. So many years ago. Don't imagine you'll find much left. But you never know."

They walked along the street together muffled up in their warm coats and scarves. "There's something I need your help with, Harry. Do you know anyone at The Foundation, someone who worked there twenty or so years ago?"

Harry thought for a moment, dodging a mother with her screaming child in a pushchair, her knuckles white on the handles, a look of utter exhaustion on her face.

"Well of course I do, dear boy. The Chairman, Sir Malcolm Clements, member of my club. What do you need to know, I'll give him a ring when I get back to the office."

"I want to know, Harry, what Doctor Fleur Palmere was doing there and why she left so suddenly. Also, who worked with her on whatever she was researching and where they are now. Can do?"

Chapter Forty-Two

Jack arrived at the library in Lymington at lunch time the next day. The librarian was busy with her members so he wandered around the aisles of books until he could see Lucy was free. He approached her.

"Hello Lucy, I'm Jack Taylor. Mr Foxton said to expect me. I'm a journalist and he wants me to find your Aunt Fleur."

Lucy looked up and he was astonished by the colour of her eyes, the blueness spilling into the whites. It was her only redeeming feature. Her hair was caught back in a bun, faint lines already appearing on her face, her clothes a little dull. A long grey skirt and sensible grey cardigan buttoned to her neck. A plain woman who obviously did not care for how she looked, but her eyes were incredible.

"Mr Taylor, I was expecting you, but I don't know how I can help you, or how you can help me."

She gestured around the shelves of her library. "Books are my life now. Other people's stories of days gone by. I never found my own life in any of them. Memories that's all there are left here."

Jack could feel the loneliness emanating from her. The disconnect from her mother and the cloudy thoughts of a past which she seemed to have no interest in or had given up on getting answers to.

Jack leaned on the counter. "I'm going to follow this story of your grandmother, Christiana. I want to find your mother's sister, Fleur, your aunt. Find out what happened to her. It's important."

"Well, you go right ahead Mr Taylor, I'm not sure I'm interested anymore. I was, when I was young, but there were no answers then and no answers now. I live in my own world and it's enough for me, it must be. I never wanted to marry or have children. I didn't exactly have any role models for happy families."

Lucy stamped a book with somewhat unnecessary force. "There are no answers to why my mother died so suddenly, something else she left for me to find out for myself. I think it was a hereditary thing. So, I don't think you have anything worth following. End of story."

Jack sighed. "I'm sorry you feel like this Lucy. It must have been difficult growing up and not knowing who, or where, your family were, especially your Aunt Fleur."

Lucy piled some books onto a trolley, ready to be returned to the shelves of the library. Jack was alarmed to see her eyes fill with tears.

"Yes, especially my Aunt Fleur. I was desperate to know her. Know where she went and why she cut herself off from her sister, my mother. I want to know, more than anything, who my father was, why he never contacted me over the years. He may be out there somewhere; unaware I even exist. But I must have had a father. Perhaps he's still alive, it's possible. Perhaps he has a new family, maybe I have stepbrothers and sisters; I'd like that. A connection to something, a tenuous link maybe. But I simply don't know, and don't much care anymore.

"Have you any idea of what it was like for me Mr Taylor?"

Jack shook his head, because he had no idea what it must be like to not know any of your family or where they came from and what happened to them. He had only ever known the love and security from his own parents, and a home which had been passed down through the generations.

Lucy reached for a tissue in her sleeve. "Mr Foxton tried to console me with the fact someone had cared very much for my Aunt Fleur, as she did for him. His name was Captain Michael Bennett. My mother told me she had never met him, but he and my aunt were planning to get married and live in a place called Lamu.

"Well, that never happened according to the solicitor. Captain Bennett was killed in some place in the Middle East and my Aunt Fleur took off for Africa sometime after, or maybe before, I simply don't know. It's possible she died of this hereditary disease which seems to run through the female line of a family I never knew."

Lucy's face softened. "I like to think they are together again. As a lover of books, especially love stories, the happy ever after ones, I think my Aunt Fleur must have been heart broken and I hope she went back to Lamu to live with her memories of him."

She piled more books onto the trolley. "But, according to Mr Foxton, she didn't do that. She went back to Africa, but not Lamu, and was never heard from again, no contact with her family, including me. What kind of a person was she, Mr Taylor, to do something like that?"

Jack picked up one of the books then put it down again as he considered his response to her question. "I know you love books Lucy, but sometimes things are not always as they seem. Families have their secrets. Their reasons for not revealing the truth.

"I'm going to find out what happened to your Aunt Fleur, and I promise you I will tell you what I find. But you have yet another hurdle to jump. If it turns out your Aunt Fleur is no longer alive, you will inherit your mother's house and according to Mr Foxton, a considerable amount of money which Captain Michael Bennett, left for Fleur Palmere."

He paused for a moment. "What will you do with your inheritance, should this be so. Have you made plans for any of it?"

Lucy looked out of the library window, watching the rain slivering down the glass. "What kind of plans could I make Mr Taylor? I have nobody to leave anything to, quite frankly. But in this town of Lymington where I have lived all my life, where I have friends and familiar faces, well I'm thinking I will leave everything to various charities here…" her voice trailed off.

Jack leaned across the counter and took her hand in his, squeezing it gently. "Don't give up Lucy. I'll find your Aunt Fleur. My partner and I have already managed to find out more about her. It's true she disappeared somewhere in South Africa, but we're following information we now have. I'll find her. Find out what happened to her.

"You may yet still have one member of your family left and perhaps she'll want to meet you and fill in all the gaps you've been missing since you were a child. It's something to hang on to Lucy – despite everything."

"Jack!" Harry's voice boomed down the phone. "Quick call must catch my train if it ever arrives. Spoke to Sir Malcolm at The Foundation. He did a bit of digging for me. It would appear Doctor Fleur Palmere worked for the company for years until they brought in a new assistant, Doctor Mwanga from Kenya, bright young researcher, but he and Doctor Palmere pretty much fell out the day he met her, or so it appeared. A conflict of interests apparently. She left before heading, he presumed, back to Kenya where she was born.

"Doctor Mwanga, in time, took over her position, did a decent job apparently, but he returned to Kenya a few years later. Perhaps she and this Doctor Mwanga met up again, who knows."

"It seems Doctor Mwanga was feeding back the information he was working on, to his own company in Kenya, so he was let go shall we say. I'm afraid that's it, all the information I can garner for you. Hope it helps. Highly confidential of course."

Jack winced as a shrieking police siren roared past him. He waited a few moments. "How big was the team she and Mwanga worked with Harry. Any idea of who they were or where they came from?"

"No, no idea of their names, my boy, came from all over the world, all specialists in their fields.

"This smells like a good story, Jack, dirty tricks in the pharma industry. Get on it will you. Need another good story out of Africa. I know you're going to Kenya, keep the bloody expenses down you hear me, with all this social media, the world of print is struggling.

"Cheerio, must dash, train to catch."

Chapter Forty-Three
Kenya – Naivasha.

Jack waited patiently at the offices of the French Embassy in Nairobi. He flicked through a magazine and looked up when the French *attaché's* secretary approached him.

"So sorry to have kept you waiting, *monsieur*, please follow me."

The harried looking French official, half rose from his chair and shook his hand.

Jack greeted him in fluent French. "Good of you to spare me the time. I'm looking for some information about a French woman called Christiana Palmere. She lived in Kenya during the sixties, with her two daughters. In a place called Naivasha?"

The *attaché* raised his eyebrows. "You are with a British newspaper the *Telegraph*, yes?"

Jack nodded. "Yes. I'm following a story about this woman Christiana; there's a considerable estate involved here, and the family solicitor thought you might be able to assist. I understand she died here, and it would be useful to know what the circumstances were, if it would be possible?"

The *attaché* tapped at his computer. "A long time ago *monsieur* Taylor. I will try to assist you, please give me a few moments."

Jack waited patiently. "Ah, yes, I've found her here. Her given place of residence on our records was a place out in the bush near Lake Naivasha. No address as such – they don't seem to have them there."

He frowned. "*Madame* Palmere, it would appear was some sort of scientist, studying traditional medicines and herbs, but, alas, she was bitten by a snake and died shortly afterwards. This was confirmed by a priest in a nearby village who signed a document stating this indeed was the case.

"Her housekeeper, a Mr Noah Kamanti, who, it would appear, accompanied her on her research, reported her death to us here at the Embassy. He buried her himself, close to her home."

He peered at the computer screen and frowned again. "However, this presented a problem for the Embassy, as he only reported her death sometime after she died?"

Jack sat forward. "Yes, that would have presented a problem. Did he give any reason why he waited so long?"

The *attaché* shook his head. "It would appear Mr Kamanti, who brought *Madame's* will with him, and by all accounts the petrified body of the snake who killed her, was specific in her instructions. He was to wait. Mr Kamanti said he had put the document from the priest with her other personal papers and forgotten about them, such was his grief."

The *attaché* mopped his brow with his handkerchief and continued, seemingly as fascinated as Jack was with the story. He glanced back at his computer.

"We contacted the family of the deceased in France not knowing how to deal with the situation. Under Kenyan law we were obliged to inform the police and have her body exhumed and examined for signs of any other reason for her death, other than death by a venomous snake bite. Not uncommon in Africa. But in France we have different laws."

Jack nodded. "Yes, I know."

The *attaché* continued. "Unless a family insist on a post-mortem, none is required. As a French citizen she came under our own laws here in Kenya. We informed the Kenyan police, as a matter of course, but they had little or no interest in what they considered was a tragic death. They seemed not inclined to pursue the matter after having interviewed Mr Kamanti and accepted the letter from the priest.

"Her parents, who lived in the South of France, were informed and insisted their daughter's wishes should be adhered to as per her will."

He shrugged his shoulders and sat back in his chair looking puzzled. "An odd case *Monsieur,* without any doubt."

He smiled. "But I have learned over the years, many odd things happen in Africa. Where there are no answers to many questions."

Jack pulled his notebook from his pocket and made some notes. "I should like to visit her home in Naivasha if that's possible. Perhaps there are some employees still living there who may remember her?"

The *attaché* shook his head. "It is most unlikely. But, of course, we efficient French did visit her bush home in Naivasha. According to her will, she left everything to the housekeeper and his wife," he glanced down at the computer again, "Patience and Noah. They will be old now, of course. But I will give you the directions to where they are living, where *Madame* Palmere lived."

"What about her two daughters, Fleur and Helene. What happened to them?"

The *attaché* lifted his shoulders slightly, his hands spread out in a gesture of indifference, a *Gaelic* gesture indicating a sense of resignation and acceptance.

"*C'est la vie,*" *Monsieur,* there is nothing here of their whereabouts now, but both came for their mother's funeral, but, alas, she had already been dead a year and already buried.

"*Bon chance, Monsieur* Taylor. I have learned from my years here in Kenya, nothing is ever as it appears to be."

Jack negotiated his way down the dry rutted path and pulled up outside a decidedly derelict bush home. Goats nibbled on dry grass, chickens pecked listlessly at the ground and there was silence all around the house. In the distance Lake Naivasha glittered in the hot midday sun, he recognised the sound of the snorting and grunting of hippos, the occasional splash as a fish eagle, with its haunting cry, swooped down on its prey, a glint of silver as he soared back into the wide blue sky above, holding a plump squirming fish.

Jack could see a few old colonial homes in the distance, one he recognised as the Djinn Palace as it was once known, steeped in history from the days of the aristocratic whites who held their wild parties there, now the respectable home of a family who had contributed so much to the economy with their growing of roses in vast numbers which were flown out of Nairobi every night, to grace the shelves of florists, and supermarkets, all over the world. A thriving world class business – a far cry from the house's wild and decadent past. But still it stood, elegant and white, its architecture superb, steeped in history, a sentinel to its past and all it had witnessed.

Christiana Palmere's simple bush house had not stood the test of time. The old, thatched roof had collapsed in on itself, the hand-made bricks crumbling and turning to dust around it. Birds and reptiles had built their own homes, their nests, where Christiana had once lived with her two daughters. Only a skeleton of the place was left.

To the right of Christiana's decaying house, Jack saw a traditional round house with a sagging thatched roof, its walls marked with bird droppings streaking down the walls alongside the stain of red earth from the splashing rains.

He headed towards it but not before a bent figure emerged from its dark depths leaning heavily on a stout walking stick.

"What is it you are wanting, *Bwana*? There is nobody here anymore. You have perhaps lost your way?"

The old man smiled at him but was sadly lacking in teeth. "It happens to us all, *Bwana*. We all lose our way in the end."

Jack held out his hand. "My name is Jack Taylor. I work for a newspaper in London. I was trying to find out where Christiana Palmere once lived. Where she died and where she is buried?"

The old man frowned. "Why would you want to do this. It was a long time ago, many years now?"

Jack smiled at him, saw the filmy milk white of his eyes. "Yes, it was a long time ago. But she had two daughters and now a grandchild. I would like to know what happened to her. Are you Noah?"

The old man looked at him, giving him a broad gummy smile. "Yes, I am Noah. But there is nothing left here for you to find. What is it you are seeking?"

He gestured for Jack to sit on the log outside of his humble home and lowered his tired and broken body next to him.

Jack swatted the persistent flies away from his face. "I know what happened to her; you went to the French Embassy in Nairobi and reported her death. I know she's buried here. Is your wife, Patience, still here with you?"

The old man looked up quickly. "You know a lot about the family, Miss Christy, her children, the *totos,* and my wife's name. But there is nothing left to say now. Patience, my wife, died some years ago. She is buried next to Miss Christy, when it is time, I shall join them there, this is my wish. There is nobody left to bury me. I will know when the time is coming, and I will go there and wait. It is a beautiful, peaceful place, *Bwana*. Come let me show it to you."

Jack walked slowly alongside Noah as he made his careful, but painful and unsteady, way towards the only family he had ever known.

"Here they are *Bwana*."

Jack's breath caught in his throat. The modest sloping hill was a carpet of glorious colours; flowers, plants and herbs lacing the landscape and cascading down the undulating slopes of the hill.

He waited a few moments trying to make sense of how this wonderful carpet of colour could align itself to the dry and dusty landscape around it. It was the most glorious gravesite he had ever seen in his life.

"How can this be Noah, these extraordinary colours, the flowers and the plants?"

Noah indicated Jack should sit on the humble log in amidst all the glorious colours and wildflowers. "This is my special place to sit,

Bwana, where I come often, but you may sit here if you wish, as my guest.

"You see where you are sitting the white stone with the name and numbers? This is where Miss Christy is buried. Her daughter, Fleur, made this sign in stone, in memory of her. At that time there were no flowers, no colours here."

Jack stood up and looked down at the simple plaque Fleur had organised in memory of her mother.

For our mother, Christiana Palmere. I, Fleur, will follow your path.

Jack frowned. It appeared to him Helene was not inclined to follow the same path. It seemed they had followed different ones, and Helene had not been part of the journey. There was no mention of her on the plaque.

Noah was watching Jack as he returned to his own favourite tree stump where he had invited Jack to sit.

"You see, *Bwana*, when Miss Christy died, I took all her samples, everything we had gathered over many many years, and I buried them with her. Her life's work. Some years later, these buried plants, herbs, and flowers, found their way back to the surface of the ground, seeking life again as they knew it before. This is what you are seeing now in front of you. You see, she still lives on, with everything we discovered."

Jack pulled out his phone from his top pocket. "It's magnificent. Noah, you've done a splendid job looking after Miss Christy. She would be very proud of you.

"Would it be alright if I took some photographs and one of you, if I may?"

Noah shrugged his shoulders. "This you may do *Bwana*. Perhaps the *totos*, might wish to see where their mother is now and how it is looking, also Patience who was their nanny so many years ago. They are well?"

Jack looked at the hopeful eyes of Noah. The man was old now, he had carried the Palmere family for most of his life, loved and cared for them. It wasn't necessary to tell him Helene was dead, and Fleur had been missing for years.

"All is well, Noah. They would wish only the best for you."

Chapter Forty-Four

Jack returned to the Norfolk Hotel in Nairobi where he was staying. He had one other person he needed to find and talk to, Doctor William Mwanga, Fleur's chosen assistant at The Foundation in London. He would be in his sixties now, possibly a little older. The chances of him still living in Nairobi where, as far as Jack knew he came from, were good, especially if he was still in the world of medicine and science. He had done a quick search on the internet and only found he was a medical doctor and had numerous business interests in Kenya.

He checked the time. Coming up for five. The Lord Delamere bar would be a good place to start, plenty of the locals came there for a sundowner or two before heading home, he remembered this from his last stay here at The Norfolk.

The tourists were easy to pick out, but he wanted a local, preferably in their sixties. Someone who knew the town and the local people who lived there, maybe a tour guide or game ranger. They would know the doctors in town in case one of their guests needed medical attention, or pills of some sort for a bug they had picked up on their safari. He took a seat at the busy bar and looked around.

He watched a vehicle pull up and disperse a group of chattering Chinese. The driver of the safari vehicle helped them identify their luggage and herded them into the reception of the hotel before wishing them all farewell. He collected his tips and headed for the bar. There were three or four bar stools vacant where Jack was sitting. The tour guide made his way to one of them.

Jack smiled and nodded at him. "Challenging safari?"

The man took a long drink from his glass of beer which the bartender had placed in front of him. Obviously, he was a regular and about the right age group he was looking for, and clearly a born and bred Kenyan with his cropped hair and deep tan, a beaded bracelet around his wrist and a battered khaki cap with a leopard skin trim.

Jack held out his hand. "Jack Taylor."

The man wiped the foam from his upper lip. "Tom Harper, pleased to meet you. No, thank goodness it wasn't a safari I took them on. A day trip around Nairobi to point out all the places of interest. Karen Blixen Museum, the giraffe centre, the elephant orphanage, the boma centre where they can buy art and crafts, listen to Kenyan music, and watch a tribal dance performance."

He shook his head and laughed. "Thing is, Jack, they want to stop every five minutes and get out and take photos. Nothing wrong with that but they want pics of everything, rubbish dumps, dustbins, old trees, holes in the ground, skinny dogs, puddles, supermarkets, trolleys, weird things. They only want to eat Chinese which is all right as we do have Chinese restaurants here, some excellent ones in fact."

He took off his hat and placed it on the bar. "Exhausting day let me tell you. But I love what I do, day trips around the city, meet and greet at the airport, sometimes I fly guests to one of the camps and spend a couple of days in the bush. My brother has a house in Karen, so I stay there when I'm in town; he's a chef, so the food's good."

He signalled for another beer and a top up for Jack. "So, what are you doing here Jack, off on safari as well? Games excellent now and the place isn't too crowded with tourists yet. You'll enjoy it."

Jack smiled at him. "No, unfortunately, no safari this time. I'm a journalist working for the *Telegraph* in London, on a story about a French woman who once lived here, out in the bush. Her name was Christiana Palmere. She died here and is buried in Naivasha."

Tom's eyebrows drew together. "I know the name, but never met her. What's the story you're following. She must have been dead for years."

Jack sipped his beer. "Yes, you're right about that. She had two daughters, one a teacher and the other one Fleur, who was a medical doctor and a scientist, who studied traditional and conventional medicine."

Tom helped himself to a handful of peanuts in a bowl on the bar. "Past tense?" Something happened to her. Why are you in Kenya, what are you looking for?"

Jack also helped himself to a handful of peanuts, brushing down the salt and shells he spilled on his shirt. "Fleur Palmere left Kenya as a child, as did her sister, and ended up in London where she studied medicine before she became interested in traditional medicine. She worked for a huge company called The Foundation. She was highly qualified and, I should add, highly respected in her field. But I can't find her. She went to live in South Africa, where I now live, or maybe she came back to Kenya. She seems to have disappeared."

Jack took a sip of his beer. "Whilst working at The Foundation she was given an assistant, who came from Kenya, to help her with her research. I'd like to meet him and see what he remembers about her work and what she was like to work with. The thing is Fleur Palmere left The Foundation, and this Kenyan doctor took over her position. A few years later he too left and I'm assuming he came back home here. Maybe he can help me track her down. Perhaps she's here somewhere in Kenya. Her family in the UK are keen to know where she is."

Tom waved to someone across the room, then turned back to Jack. "So, do you have a name for this Kenyan guy?"

"Yes. Doctor William Mwanga. Have you heard of him?"

Tom hissed through his teeth. "Everyone's heard of him. Comes from a powerful family of politicians and businessman. Owns a string of pharmacies, medical clinics, and a hospital or two around the country. He's high up on the social scene, seen at all the Embassy parties, around the tables of the chosen few for dinner. A powerful man indeed."

He took another fistful of peanuts. "He's a clever man. All his pharmacies stock both traditional and modern medicines. He's captured the market. I doubt he would remember someone called Fleur Palmere. Easier to get an audience with the Queen than to try and speak to him."

Jack was silent for a moment. "Okay, so he's popular on the social scene and a rich man. But what do the medical fraternity here think about him?"

Tom snorted. "Hate him. He's taken so much business away from their practices. Would be local Kenyan patients by-pass the medical doctors, who, of course, charge for consultations. Instead, patients go direct to Mwanga's pharmacies, and they hand out the pills without a prescription. Of course, scheduled drugs need a prescription from a registered doctor, but he gets around this by putting his name on the label of whatever drug is being dished out and doesn't even see the patient. Highly illegal, but he gets away with it because he and his family are powerful people in Kenya.

"Traditional medicines don't need a prescription, so he's covered there, home and dry. A man who cares not for any patient, and the money keeps rolling in."

Jack tapped his glass on the bar thinking back to the UK where drugs were tightly monitored. You couldn't even get a codeine tablet without a prescription from your doctor.

"See here Tom, I need to meet this Mwanga. Is there any way you can help me? I have a generous budget from the newspaper for this story. We pay well for information."

Tom rolled his bar mat across the top of the bar, back and forth, back and forth, as he thought about Jack's question. The Chinese group he had off-loaded, were not known for tipping well and he needed money.

"We have many extremely wealthy tourists who come to our country, celebrities, internationally recognised names, and sometimes like us lesser mortals they do get sick. In such cases Mwanga always makes himself available. He flies out to the expensive lodges, does a medical examination of the wealthy patient, and prescribes medication."

Tom took a sip of his beer. "Or the lodge might fly the patient to Nairobi where once again Mwanga makes himself available in his rooms. All within the legalities of the country, which protect him against any insurance claims which may be made against him later. Like I said, he's clever. When a person gets sick, whether they be rich or poor, all they want is for someone to take the pain away and make them better, especially if they're Americans out in the middle of the African bush. The game lodges always recommend him."

"Do you think he'd let me interview him, Tom?"

Tom laughed. "Never! He hates the media and any intrusion on his private life. He has plenty to hide I can tell you that."

"Have you met him personally?"

Tom grabbed another handful of peanuts. "A couple of times, with guests from one of the lodges. I make the appointments and deliver them to his rooms, introduce him to the patient then hang around outside until he's finished his consultation."

Jack grinned at him. "You know something, I find myself not feeling too good right now. Would it be possible for you to call him and make an appointment for him to see me? Must be something I ate at the lodge…"

Tom roared with laughter. "Trouble is you look very healthy to me Jack, but I'm sure you'll be able to pull something like this off. Hold onto your stomach, groan a bit, wipe a bit of sweat off your forehead and top lip. I'll find a thick blanket to wrap around your shoulders, which should make you sweat. Especially if you sit in the sun for an hour before your appointment.

"Doctor Mwanga never refuses a patient from a lodge because he charges in cash, double his normal rate. Not a good idea to try and see him this evening, especially after a couple of beers."

Tom hauled his phone out of his pocket and stood up. "Best if I go out into the gardens to make the call, can't have the loud noise of a bar in the background. What name shall I use for you. Jack Taylor?"

Jack nodded. "He might have read a few columns of mine, but I doubt he would associate the name with the poor sick guest sitting in front of him. Go for it, Tom."

Whilst Tom was in the hotel grounds Jack thought about how he was going to tackle Mwanga. He would have to play the part of being ill, and when Mwanga found there was nothing wrong with him at all, he would start asking him questions.

He had been in the room with a lot of low life when he worked in London on his cold cases, including murderers, serial killers, rapists, and such like. Mwanga was hardly likely to leap across his desk brandishing a scalpel and howling for blood if he revealed, which he would have to, he was a journalist with the *Telegraph*. He made a mental note, whatever Mwanga prescribed, should he survive that long, he wasn't going to take it. No way.

Tom returned to the bar. "Okay, all fixed. Appointment at eleven tomorrow morning at his rooms. I'll take you there of course, huddled in your heavy blanket which I will supply. Can't have one with the Norfolk logo showing. I always have blankets in the back of my vehicle for the afternoon safaris, once the sun goes down it can get damn cold in the bush.

"I'll collect you here at ten tomorrow. I'll park somewhere in the sun, and you can get a sweat up. I won't wait with you at his rooms. I've already told him I booked you into the Norfolk because you didn't want to go back to the lodge. Told him I thought you might have malaria and wanted to return to the UK as soon as possible and that I had to get back to the lodge.

"After you have made your miraculous recovery, you can call for a cab to bring you back to the hotel.

He grinned at Jack. "I'll be here in the bar. You can buy me lunch. How does all that sound?"

Jack smiled at him. "Good job Tom, thank you. The newspaper will, of course, make sure you're rewarded for organising this. It wouldn't have been possible without you."

Chapter Forty-Five

Jack sat in Tom's vehicle, a thick blanket wrapped around him, under the blazing sun and the stifling heat of the vehicle with the windows closed. Tom glanced at him. "Getting up a nice sweat there, Jack. Fifteen minutes to go before your appointment. I'm going to turn the heater on and see if we can heighten the colour on your face a bit more."

Jack turned to him. "Actually, Tom, I'm *not* feeling good. My body is overheating, and my blood pressure is going up."

"Excellent, that's what we need. Come on, time to meet the mysterious Doctor Mwanga. Let's go."

Tom ushered Jack into the waiting room of the surgery, there was nobody else waiting to see the doctor. Tom knocked on the door of the doctor's rooms, the door opened immediately. "Ah, it's Tom, isn't it? And this is my patient, Jack Taylor?

"Come in Mr Taylor, come on in and let's see what's wrong here."

Jack looked up at Mwanga in his crisp white coat and the stethoscope loped around his neck.

"Thank you, Tom," he croaked. He managed a shiver and a pathetic cough as the doctor led him inside.

Doctor Mwanga indicated Jack should lie on the leather examining table as he set about checking his blood pressure, his temperature, pulse, and other vital signs.

"You have been taking your malaria pills, Mr Taylor?"

Jack nodded and gave another pathetic cough. Mwanga frowned, asking Jack a few more questions. "Well, your temperature is high but seems to be dropping quite rapidly. Blood pressure is normal, and I don't see any signs of malaria. In fact, Mr Taylor, there doesn't seem to be anything seriously wrong with you. Possibly you ate something at the lodge which didn't agree with you? I'll write a script for you for that."

Jack's body temperature, he knew, had returned to normal, thanks to the air conditioning in the surgery. As he knew, Mwanga would find nothing wrong with him. Time to make his move.

He sat up and swung his legs over the side of the expensive leather examination table. "Feel better already, doc, must have been a bug or something. What a relief."

Doctor Mwanga narrowed his eyes as he looked at his patient who had now settled in the chair on the other side of his desk.

Jack grinned at him. "Someone at the lodge, one of the staff, gave me something to help with the fever, some traditional stuff he said would help with malaria, if that's what I had."

He looked at the man opposite him, in his expensive suit and luxurious surroundings of his rooms. "I understand it's a bit of a speciality with you, traditional medicine against modern medicine?"

"No, Mr Taylor, I combine both, but I do believe that traditional medicine will die out eventually. Patients want a quick fix, and this the modern world of medicine can give them. More and more rural people are moving to the cities to find work. Traditional healers are losing their place slowly but surely.

"I offer both in my pharmacies. But things are changing, health shops are spreading through the world, offering alternatives to modern medicine, expensive ones. People are looking for alternatives. They don't trust modern medicines as they used to. They read the pages of the drug they are going to take, and they don't like the side effects listed, for insurance purposes of course, which seem more frightening than the drug itself. So, health shops are merely picking up on what we call in Africa the old traditional ways. In the Far East, of course, millions still turn to the old cures their ancestors used. It's all about what you believe will cure you in the end."

Jack leaned forward and dived straight in. "Why don't you tell me about Doctor Fleur Palmere? You worked with her at The Foundation in London, didn't you?"

Mwanga's eyes hardened. "Who the hell are you Mr Taylor?"

"I'm a journalist with the *Telegraph* in London, but I've relocated to South Africa where I now live."

He gave the doctor what he hoped was a warm and encouraging smile. "I'd like to know more about Doctor Fleur Palmere, what she was researching. Why she suddenly left The Foundation. Why you also left The Foundation, some years later, under a dark cloud as I understand?"

Doctor Mwanga stood up. "I have nothing to say to you, Mr Taylor. I abhor journalists, always digging to find something to ruin someone's life. I also despise journalists like you who pretend to be someone they're not. I have nothing to say about Fleur Palmere, she was a difficult woman. Impossible to work with as far as I was concerned."

Jack looked up innocently. "Why was that. You were both working on cures using traditional and modern medicines. Did she find something, discover something you saw the potential of and didn't share it with you?

"Do you perhaps know where she is now?"

"Mr Taylor, I have nothing to say to you or your newspaper. I have no idea where Fleur Palmere is now. I have not followed her career and why should I? She is of no interest to me whatsoever."

Jack looked at Mwanga. "I think you have followed her career, because she had found something which would have been of great value to the companies you set up here in Kenya, Mediken in particular.

"The thing is, she seems to have disappeared some years ago now, taking her research with her. Someone obviously didn't want her discoveries made public."

Mwanga was unable to contain his anger. "Get out, Mr Taylor! The big pharma companies follow anything of interest, always looking for the cure. They have their eyes on everything going on around the world, anything they consider might be a threat to their shareholders. I'm afraid you knocked on the wrong door here. I can tell you nothing. If Fleur Palmere has disappeared, well it could have been anything. Nothing to do with whatever she was researching."

Jack stood up. "Was there anyone else working with you and Fleur at The Foundation?"

"I don't recall anyone else. It's a huge company, people come and go…impossible to remember who worked where."

Jack pulled the notebook out of his shirt pocket. "There was a team of scientists working in your department, one of which was a South African, a botanist, do you remember him at all?"

Mwanga glared at Jack.. "From what I gather he went back to South Africa, it's possible he worked with Fleur Palmere on further research. I don't remember his name.

"Enough, Mr Taylor, get out of my office, but not before you've paid my bill for wasting my time. Four hundred pounds, in cash."

Jack slapped down the notes on his desk. "Worth every penny. I'll follow this story, and I'll find out what happened to Doctor Fleur Palmere. Let's leave it there, shall we?"

"No, we won't leave it there. I'm a powerful man here in this country, with many contacts in high places. Should your newspaper print anything, based on your flimsy assumptions, you can be assured my legal team will come after you and your newspaper. Is that clearly understood Mr Taylor."

Chapter Forty-Six

Jack alighted from the dhow which had carried him to the island of Lamu.

Jeremy Foxton had told him about Captain Michael Bennett, the close relationship he had had with Fleur Palmere, the fact they had been lovers and had planned, according to Michael, to eventually settle in Lamu, get married and have a family.

He recalled Jeremy's words.

Thing is Jack, Fleur without warning, left her job with the pharma company. She ended her relationship with Michael by letter. Fortunately, he didn't receive it. He was already in the desert with the army. That's when his unit was ambushed and wiped out.

As I told you, he was eventually found, but he was a different man, a broken man. His mind shattered by what he had seen and what he had gone through.

After a year or so of recuperation in a facility down in Wiltshire, he was considered well enough to go back into the world.

Having been missing in action and presumed dead, his few belongings were returned to me by the army and that's when I found the letter, unopened, addressed to him by Fleur. I didn't read it, of course, not something one does.

I still had hopes that Michael may be found even though the army had already made up its mind he would never return. So, I did nothing about wrapping up his estate. He had left instructions with me before he left on his tour of duty and that I should deposit a certain amount of money into Fleur's account so she could continue with her research. This I did. However, after leaving her mother's leather book with me, she took off for Africa and I never heard from her again. She didn't touch a penny of the money in the account to which Michael had so generously contributed. There was only one transfer she asked me to make into the account of a B. Hemmingway: an account in Johannesburg. This I did. Thereafter she didn't touch the money in the account.

I took care of Michael when he left the rehabilitation facility in Wiltshire. Of course, he was no longer a serving officer in the British army. But his burning desire was to find Fleur.

After giving him the letter from her, saying their relationship was over, well, he was completely broken. More broken than before if that was possible.

It was me who suggested he go back to Lamu, where he had the house which had once held all his dreams of a future with Fleur.

I tried everything to find her for him, but she had vanished. She certainly arrived in South Africa but after that there was no further news apart from the letter from Poppy, in Zimbabwe, and the detective's report, which I showed you.

Jack checked into the famous Peponi hotel and unpacked his safari bag, his main luggage he had left in Nairobi. His room was modern with all the facilities an international guest demanded, but with touches through its rich Swahili heritage of the way it must have been decades ago. He thought briefly he might have preferred it when it was the local watering hole for all the Kenyans who had retired to Lamu after the heady years of a unique social life of parties and big game hunting.

There was a timelessness about it with its lush tropical gardens, coconut palms moving lazily with a whisper and clatter of their fronds, bougainvillea adding splashes of vivid colours of pink, purple and red from their climbing vines, frangipani and hibiscus adding to the kaleidoscope, and in between all this the glimpses of the sparkling Indian ocean beach laid out in front and the gentle, enduring, tidal lapping of the sea on the shore.

Jack made his way to the bar, found a stool, and perched on it. There were guests, tourists, and locals in abundance, enjoying a drink and lunch in these unique surroundings, unaware of the admiring and lingering looks from some of the women sipping from their drinks.

The barman came and took his order for a beer and a crab sandwich. "Are you a guest here, sir, if so, shall I put it on your chit?"

Jack smiled at the tanned, weather worn, smiling face in front of him. The barman, whose name turned out to be Peter, according to the name badge pinned to his unbuttoned shirt, his hair bleached by the sun.

"Yes, I'm a guest, room 23. Tell me, have you lived and worked here for long?"

Peter gave him a broad smile. "Yup. Came here as a young student during my gap year. Got a job right here in this bar and never left, that was over thirty years ago." He shook his head. "Can't believe it actually!"

"I'll be right back with your beer and sandwich in two ticks."

Jack looked around. At one end of the bar, he saw a group of four older men, their faces tanned and lined, thoroughly enjoying the good weather – locals he thought immediately, old buddies maybe going back years. He wanted to meet them.

They seemingly still enjoyed a good life, laughing and joking amongst themselves, their bare feet on the warm sand, wearing well-worn shorts and open shirts, two of them wore faded *kikoi's* wrapped around their waists, their chests bare, a glint of a gold or silver necklace sporting what could be the claw of a lion or leopard, he couldn't tell. The *kikoi* was acceptable apparel in Kenya on the beaches and any other informal setting. Not, of course, at any of the smart Embassy functions, or social dinner parties in Nairobi all those years ago, which were gradually fading in their memories. He thought this way of life was something they preferred. Where they didn't have to play a part but could be what they had become.

One of them wore an eye patch and there were a couple of stout canes, one lying discarded in the soft sand, the other leaning against the bar.

Quite a contrast to the locals he had seen in village pubs in the UK, not so robust, talking quietly amongst themselves, their grey pallor matching the weather outside. Their hopes and dreams a distant memory, not to be re-visited.

Peter returned with his beer and sandwich. "Here on holiday, sir, most people are before going off on safari. Lamu is an interesting town, steeped in history. One of our staff will show you around if you like, let me know won't you?"

Jack held out his hand. "My name's Jack Taylor, a journalist with the London *Telegraph*. I'm based in South Africa now, but still working for the newspaper."

Peter looked around the bar, everyone was happy, no one needing his attention for the moment. He wiped down the top of the bar, took a swipe at a fly, then threw the cloth over his shoulder. "Following a story?"

Jack took a sip of his beer. "Yes, an intriguing one which has some of its roots here in Lamu. You've been here a long time; you maybe know two or three of the people I'm interested in."

Peter laughed. "If they were famous, it's possible, but over the years I've met thousands of people. Princess Caroline from Monaco, Grace Kelly's daughter, has a house here, bit of a scandal with one of her husbands, I do remember that. He was a Prince with a bad temper if I recall. Not sure which one of her husbands he was. But we don't care much here either way."

Jack took a bite of his crab sandwich – it was excellent.

Peter continued, glancing around the bar again. "When 9/11 happened, it was rumoured the local people here, all strictly Muslim of course, knew about it before the media did. But who knows if this was true. Mostly the Muslims who live here are gentle peace-loving people.

"Tell you what. When you've finished your lunch, I'll introduce you to the bunch of guys in the corner over there, they're here all the time. All Kenyans, they retired here to Lamu after their life of high living and hunting. All still comparing their trophies, probably women they bedded and had in common, but no animosity, no pistols at dawn – that's how it was, it was their way of life – lots of women by all accounts."

Peter looked up. "Hang on a sec, need to refill some glasses here." Jack munched on his crab sandwich and waited for him to return.

Peter returned a few moments later. "Out on safari with a famous big game hunter, clients who had paid a fortune to go on a real safari, well, it was fair game, if you'll pardon the pun. Some of the professional hunters, the good-looking ones, even played parts in various films which were made here, when they were much younger, of course."

He topped up Jack's beer. "One of the legendary figures was Bunny Allen, a famous hunter, good-looking and an absolute rebel. He retired here in Lamu. What a character, the likes of which will never be seen again. A golden age when being politically correct was unknown. Those guys lived their lives, ignored what was considered right or wrong and roared through it, living by their own rules if they had any, which is doubtful."

Jack smiled, his kind of people; people with stories to tell.

"Another beer Jack. The lunch time crowd will thin out in an hour or two, the tourists off on their tour of the old town or having a nap before coming back to the bar for a sundowner.

"The Kenyan crowd, like the guys at the end of the bar, normally stay until about five, then make their way home.

"Come on I'll introduce you; they may be able to add to this story you're writing."

Jack moved towards the four men at the end of the bar. Introductions were made and Peter left them to it.

They were genuinely pleased to meet him, a couple of them knew his name from some of the stories he had followed in Kenya, which they had read about. English newspapers were always available in Kenya, a week or so late sometimes, but available, nevertheless.

"What are you chasing this time Jack," a professional hunter called Angus asked, "another story no doubt. If it's about the young and politically correct in England, or politics in general you'll be wasting your time with us, we don't bother with all that nonsense, far more interesting things going on here in Kenya. Beautiful country, beautiful weather, and beautiful women."

Jack gave them a brief overview of Christiana Palmere her time in Kenya, her two daughters who were born and brought up here, and his interest in Captain Michael Bennett.

Angus took a generous gulp of his beer and wiped his hand across his lips. "Mike Bennett? Yes, I remember him. Had a place along the beach here, used to visit in between postings abroad with the British Army, he disappeared for a few years, then appeared again. However, he was a shadow of the man he used to be. Lost an arm and the use of one leg during some war, looked after by the Bedouin, a woman I think, then he pitched up here again."

Jack made a few notes in the book he carried everywhere in the pocket of his shirt. "When he returned from wherever he was injured did he come to this bar on a regular basis?"

Angus adjusted his black eye patch. "He rarely came here before he went off to some godforsaken war somewhere. Probably not encouraged by his commanding officer, loose lips, and all that. But afterwards, when he finally settled here, his houseboy, Ali, used to help him along the beach to this bar, wait for him, then take him home.

"Nice chap, Mike Bennett. Could be a bit vague at times but he seemed to find comfort with us professional hunters, after all, we had all lost bits and pieces of ourselves during our hunting days, he found some kind of comfort in that."

Jack ordered a round of drinks for his newfound friends.

It was hard not to like Jack Taylor, he had a similar background to them, all the right schools in the UK. He was tall, good looking, had a beguiling smile and deep brown eyes, fringed with long lashes, which had been the downfall of many of the crooks and killers he had followed up in his cold cases in the UK. There was also something else about him.

Although the world of newspapers in the UK knew of his reputation, knew how ruthless he could be when he needed information, he had a compassionate side; trying to understand why people committed such terrible crimes, and of course he had to deal with the people a killer had left behind. The debris and the intolerable grief they had to deal with.

Yes, Jack lived in a harsh world of human behaviour, but he had the unique ability to understand why people did what they did and that compassion, even when he was writing a gritty piece for his newspaper, always came through. Women found him irresistible.

Angus took another sip of his drink, the three other men did the same, letting Angus do the talking. Over the years many journalists had come to Kenya and Lamu, seeing if they could drag any more information that had not already been discussed, dissected, and written about for decades. The decadent so called white mischief crowd, if they couldn't find any more information about the key players, they either made it up, or speculated about who had killed whom during those heady days of parties, drugs, and endless affairs of the aristocracy. It seemed, even today, there were no definitive answers.

Angus looked into the distance for a moment... "See here Jack, all four of us were professional hunters. We knew the shape and character of the animal we were after; we knew the risks – if we got it wrong, especially with buffalo, we stood a good chance of being killed. It was heady stuff." He grinned at his three friends.

"I lost an eye, Herbie here had his leg gouged by a buffalo, Matthew was mauled by a lion and lost his arm, and half his shoulder, and Phillip had his guts ripped out by another buff. Unpredictable buggers, buffalo. All badges of honour in the world we lived in. You see, we survived, many other hunters didn't.

"We knew who the enemy was, knew the smell of it, the shape of it, where it lived, how it would react when confronted by a human with a gun. We would follow the spoor of the animal we wanted to find for our rich clients to kill. That's what we were paid to do."

Jack found it hard to imagine a life like that, although he had read all about those heady days.

Angus grinned at him. "Yes, in today's world it seems harsh but that was how it was. You can't change history, can't make a river change its course and return to what it was a hundred years ago. Can't make Victoria Falls, fall in another way. Can't change nature. Impossible. Today I would never kill any animal, big or small, not for any price. Those days of hunting are long gone, but we carry the scars of that time as you can see by our buggered bodies. The memories of those days may have gone for us but not for the animals who were slaughtered by their thousands so their heads or skins could grace some rich American's home.

"No. Wild animals today remember and have a fear of mankind, passed down through the years. That's why they sometimes act out of character. There is still, although rare, fatalities on game drives and the stupidity of tourists out in the wild that cause them."

The sun was beginning to descend casting silver and gold over the colour of the sea, cloaking the vast girth and branches of the baobab trees into an outline which would be etched even more when the lamps discreetly set in the grounds would come on and illuminate their unique shape once again.

Angus rubbed his eyes, lifting his eye patch on an empty socket and putting it back again. "You see, Jack, that's why Michael Bennett came here so often, he was badly injured like us, carrying the scars. But unlike him, we knew what we were looking for. Knew the nature of the beast we were hunting. But Michael didn't know the shape or size of what he was supposed to be looking for, didn't know the nature of the beast, the smell of it, its instincts, its habitat. He went in blind, doing his duty for Queen and country. There was no glory in it for him and he paid the price. He didn't talk about his war."

Angus again adjusted his eye-patch, as he watched the tourists meandering along the beach.

"But he did mention briefly about a woman in his life. Can't remember her name, if, indeed, he ever mentioned it. Although we had many good evenings here, he always seemed a little apart, watching the people on the beach. Almost as though he was waiting for someone."

The other three men nodded their heads. They knew Angus was going to tell Jack about the last evening of Michael's life.

"It seemed he was heading towards the bar here, leaning heavily on his cane when he stopped. His houseboy, as usual, was with him, but this time he was running to catch up with him. For no reason Michael raised his cane and tried to move towards a woman who was walking alone on the beach.

"The woman looked away from the sea and saw Michael coming towards her waving his cane and shouting at her. Well, of course, she turned and fled back towards the hotel for safety.

"The next thing Michael collapsed on the beach, his houseboy kneeling to help him. But it was too late. Whoever he thought he saw, and recognised, seemed to be the woman he had been waiting for. But of course, it wasn't."

Jack made a few more notes. "I'd like to see where he lived. Would that be possible?"

Angus grinned. "Sure, but the place was sold, it's one of those damn bed and breakfast places, sprouting up all over the place here."

Jack took a sip of beer. "What about the houseboy you mentioned, is he still around?"

"Ali? Yes, I see him around. The new owners of Michael's house kept him on, not sure for how long. Always useful to have someone around the house who knows where to go for meat and vegetables etc. How things work and so on. It's the eighth house on the right," he pointed along the beach, "the one with the two tall palm trees in front of it, can't miss it. It's called Rose Cottage, a ridiculous name very much like the people themselves. Ghastly ex-pat couple from the north of England, did a few overseas contracts and now they think they're experts on Africa. They have a fake Coat of Arms next to the name of the place. We might be old, Jack, but we know who's who, recognise a genuine Coat of Arms, the old families to which it belonged. It's who we are, or who we were.

"Even their guests don't like them, not that they have many – word travels fast here on the island. I feel sorry for Ali having to work for them if he still does. Michael was a real gentleman, old school. The couple who bought his place are as common as muck, as they say. Disliked by everyone on the island."

Jack made his way along the beach until be found Michael Bennett's former house. Outside was the sign 'Rose Cottage' hanging next to it was some kind of copy of a Coat of Arms, which the owners hoped would give them some kind of regal air, but it failed miserably, as surely as this bed and breakfast place would. He took a few shots of it and knocked on the door.

A sour faced woman opened it. Her grey hair tightly permed, her solid body blocking his entrance. She looked at him with her piggy blue eyes and downturned mouth. Hardly a welcoming look.

"Yes. What do you want?" she snapped. "We're not expecting any guests today. Do you want to book in?"

Jack shook his head. "No. Not my kind of place. I'm looking for Ali. He worked for the former owner. Is he here?"

She looked at him, one of the few women who wasn't going to fall for the good looks and upper crust accent. "If you don't want a room it's none of your business who works here."

With that parting shot she slammed the door in his face. The hospitality the island was famous for was sadly lacking here.

He shook his head as he walked back to his hotel. Africa today had changed. Those British expatriates who came here on contracts, making lots and lots of money in the old days, then chosen to live here, had no place in this new Africa. They didn't integrate, didn't contribute. They took everything and had no idea how to treat their African staff. They were hard on them, had no empathy with them or their country. Then went back to England with all the money they had accumulated and didn't look back, leaving no legacy, no contribution to the countries they had harvested from. There were many of them, throughout Africa and most of them were English.

Jack was sitting beneath a baobab tree having his breakfast when Peter, the barman, came up to his table. "Chap here to see you, Jack. His name's Ali. Michael Bennett's old housekeeper."

Jack looked up from his bacon and eggs. "Ali? How did he know I was here?"

Peter smiled. "Small island – everyone knows everything here. He saw you at the old house yesterday."

Ali made his way, with confidence, to Jack's table. "I am Ali. I was looking after Doctor Bennett for many years. I heard you had come to the house which is now a British place for guests? Not many though."

Jack stood up. "Yes, I did. Not sure about the people you're working for, they wouldn't tell me if you were still working there. Come and sit. May I order coffee for you, or something to eat?"

Ali shook his head and sat down. "Only coffee perhaps. "I am no longer working for the English people; I found them most offensive. Doctor Michael left me money when he died, it was a good thing he did for me. Now I stay with my wife and my grandchildren, drink coffee in the old square and thank him for looking after me after he was gone."

"Tell me about him Ali? I have heard the stories here, but you probably knew him better than anyone. You were with him for many years, looking after his home, and you were here when he died in Lamu."

Ali sipped at his coffee. "Yes, this is so. I knew him well. He was a good man."

Jack wriggled his toes in the soft warm sand and scooped up the last of his scrambled eggs. "Did anyone ever come and stay at Doctor Michael's house? Friends of his perhaps?"

Ali nodded. "Yes, he welcomed many army and other friends from Nairobi to come and stay here, sometimes he was here and sometimes not."

Jack took care with his next question. "I met his lawyer in London. Mr Foxton. He was in touch with you after Michael died and arranged for his things to be removed from the house before it was sold. Also arranged the money for you which the doctor wanted you to have for looking after his house, his friends and himself."

Ali nodded again. "This is so. But there was little left in the house to sell, some pieces of furniture but nothing else. The lawyer was saying I must take what I wished in memory of my good friend Doctor Michael."

He delved into the skirts of his *kanzu* and withdrew a framed photograph. "This was all I wished to have to remember him."

Jack looked at the photograph. Michael stood in his uniform, a good-looking man with blond hair, his arm around a petite woman, not beautiful, but arresting with her long dark hair falling around her shoulders. By the looks of the brooding sky and the buildings behind them it had not been taken in Lamu. It looked more like London to him.

"Was this his girlfriend?"

Ali took back the photograph and stared at it. "Doctor Michael sometimes brought a woman here, but not often." He wiped the photograph with his sleeve. These women I saw only once."

Jack thought quickly. "But this one must have been special if he kept a photograph of her in his house?"

"Yes. This one was the special one. He told me he wished to marry her and bring her to live here in Lamu. I was most happy with this news."

"So, you met her Ali?"

He smiled broadly. "Yes, I met her. Her mother had died, and she came to Nairobi for the funeral. She came here, but alone, not with the doctor.

"She stayed here with the big book, always reading and sometimes writing in it. I called her *mama,* as I did not know her well enough to address her as Doctor Fur. But this is she.

"This was the only time I met her. She did not marry Doctor Michael. When he returned from his last war he came alone. He was not the same as before. I am thinking his soul had already gone and left nothing behind but emptiness in its place."

Jack held out his hand for the photograph. "May I take a photo of this with my phone. It's important Ali, I'm trying to find Doctor Fleur. She's been missing for many years and I'm trying to find her for her family."

Ali frowned and passed him the photograph. "The evening when Doctor Michael died, I am thinking he saw her walking on the beach. He tried hard to reach her, but she ran away from him. He lay on the sand over there, and this is where he died. He was very confused, he did not know where he was, or who he was – he called me Ahmed.

"The woman he saw was not Doctor Fur, but someone who perhaps looked like her from a distance. Many things, Mr Jack, look the same from a distance, the memory can play tricks. How can it measure distance and time?"

Jack took some pics of the photograph on his phone and handed it back to Ali, who was now standing, ready to leave.

"Thank you, Ali. Your photograph of Doctor Fleur will perhaps help me to find her. It's the only photo we have of her."

Ali shrugged. "I wish you well then. I am thinking Doctor Michael loved her very much. It is possible they are together again at last?"

Jack shook his hand. "It's possible, but I hope not. I need to find this woman and you have helped with the photograph. Thank you."

Ali gave a slight bow and made his way along the beach, back to his own peaceful world, his people, and his family.

Chapter Forty-Seven
Hazyview. South Africa.

Jack arrived back in Hazyview, had a quick shower, and put all his notes and pics in his ops room as he called it. This was his spare bedroom, but he had converted it; putting in a large, long table which ran across one side of the room and an equally large white board where he mapped out whatever particular story he was following. On the opposite wall he had tacked an enormous map of the entire country, one which gave the new names of towns and provinces, alongside their original names.

Working methodically, he pinned up the photo of Captain Michael Bennett and Fleur Palmere and the spectacular grave site of her mother Christiana at Naivasha. On the board he also listed the names of the characters, so far, in what he had learned on his trip to London and Kenya.

Ali, Michael Bennett's housekeeper. A copy of the letter Poppy had sent to Jeremy Foxton, the solicitor in London, mentioning an empty camp site called something like Waterfall where Fleur had met Simon, Poppy's guardian angel. A mysterious person called. B. Hemmingway who Fleur had transferred a considerable amount of money to a bank in Johannesburg. Helene Palmere, now deceased, and her daughter Lucy who lived in Lymington. Doctor William Mwanga who had joined the company Fleur had worked for in London. A place called Jumba which Fleur had mentioned was where she would be working in her last letter to Michael Bennett. A copy of the letter sent to Jeremy Foxton by the South African detective he had hired to try and find Fleur Palmere and that was about it.

He leaned against the wall opposite his chart, his ankles crossed. Pretty much nothing to go on. He and Piet would have to try and trace where Fleur had been to before she disappeared. It wasn't going to be easy but at least they had a location to begin their search – the Eastern Cape. But she could have moved anywhere after that. Could easily have crossed a border into another country like Botswana, Zambia, Swaziland, Zimbabwe, or Mozambique.

Fleur Palmere, as far as he understood, had found something in her search which indicated it was of paramount importance.

Jeremy Foxton's assumption she had been murdered was a chilling thought, and added a different dimension to what might have happened to her.

Jack made his way to the noisy bar at the Inn, the car park was full of locally registered cars. It was a Friday night, Hugo, the owner, would be flat out with his team of bartenders.

Fortunately, one of the bar stools freed up and he slid onto it. Hugo spotted him and waved; he knew Jack would want his usual, a beer. Hugo dodged through his bartenders, his feet bare, his wildly coloured shirt and baggy frayed shorts standing out from the khaki shirts surrounding the bar, carrying Jack's drink aloft. Many of the game rangers from the game lodges frequented the bar on a Friday night and in keeping with the safari atmosphere of the town, a lot of the locals wore khaki as well.

"Hey Jack. Welcome back, although I fear you are going to take my security chief away from the place – you always do if you're away for a while. New story to follow?"

Jack shook his hand. "Afraid so, Hugo. Bit of a tricky story, but a good one."

Hugo smiled. "No worries. Are you staying for the *braai*, we're having a big one tonight. Winter is on the way, so might as well make the most of the last of the balmy nights. Got to go. Busy tonight, see you later."

Jack felt a gentle nudge at his knee, he knew it wouldn't be Piet. His welcome was normally a hearty thump on his back, spilling his beer. He looked down into the soulful dark brown eyes of a golden labrador.

"Hello Hope. Big night for you tonight, lurking around under the long tablecloths waiting for anything coming your way, right? Must say you look very festive with your new collar of Ndebele beads – very smart indeed. Is it your birthday today?"

Piet sidled up to Jack, thumping him on his back, leaning against the bar as there was no stool available. He slapped his cap down on the bar.

"Hey, Piet. Good to see you. What's with the new cap? I preferred the other one, it suited you better. Old and battered."

Piet gave his dog a withering look. "*Bleddy* dog chomped it. I'm not speaking to her at the moment."

Hope put her tail between her legs and slid behind the bar, appearing a few moments later, paws on the counter and a big grin on her face.

"What's not to love about that dog, Piet?"

Piet glowered at the dog and scowled at Jack. "Loved my old cap, Jack, been wearing it for thirty years or so. Hope doesn't care about history and my old cap has seen many things…no doubt she'll be skulking under the tablecloths of the *braai* tonight, smiling and wagging her tail, waiting for some decent meat to come her way.

"Anyways, how was your trip to the land of your birth, that place with its green and pleasant land, according to you and poets, so long. What have you come up with. Still raining over there, as always?"

Jack ignored the jibe. "It was good. I've come up a few things about the disappearance of Fleur Palmere, not much I have to admit. But it seems the starting point will be the Eastern Cape – your neck of the woods but I need your help."

Piet rubbed his hands together. "Excellent. I need to get stuck into something again. I'm brain dead with all the tourists now the season is over. What have you got for us?"

The smell of the grilling meat was hitting all Jack's senses, and he was hungry, very hungry. "Tell you what Piet, let's go and get stuck into the food. I'm starving and feeling a bit weary after the flight.

"I've set up the ops room with everything I have to date. Let's take the night off, enjoy ourselves. Tomorrow could be a challenging day when we look at the board and what I know so far – which is very little. We have a path to follow…"

Chapter Forty-Eight

Piet leaned on the table at Jack's cottage and studied Jack's notes and photos on the big white board, taking a sip of his coffee as he absorbed the little information they had. His policeman's mind taking in every bit of information there.

"Okay Jack, this is what I'm thinking. We need to follow in the good doctor's footsteps. Find out exactly when she arrived in South Africa. Bertie should be able to tell us this without too much trouble. Find the place called Jumba and see if there's anyone there who can help us, although it's unlikely after all these years.

"After this we need to find the place called Waterfalls, the place where the young Poppy told us the Zimbabwean, Simon, met Fleur Palmere, although she did say it was closed. It may still be there but with a new name if someone perhaps bought it. We also need to find out who B. Hemmingway was and why Fleur deposited money into his or her account. That's going to be tricky to find out, Bertie will probably shout at me."

He stabbed at his phone and called Bertie. "Hey, my man, good to hear your voice, how are you?"

Bertie groaned. "I'm fond of you Piet, as you know, but why do I always have this sinking sensation when I hear your voice on the phone. Why do I always know you're going to ruin my day?

"Just got back from a week's fishing out in the bush, feeling nice and relaxed, but in one sentence I know you are going to make me tense, put my blood pressure up. What do you want?"

"Ah, Bertie, I love that welcoming warm tone of your voice when you hear mine. See here, nothing difficult, need you to check on something for me."

Bertie sighed audibly. "I know this is only the beginning and it will lead me into increasing my already brutal workload. Someone been murdered?"

Piet paused. "It's possible. But right now, I need you to check on the arrival date of a Doctor Fleur Palmere who entered the country sometime in the early nineties – can do? We think she was heading for the Eastern Cape so would have come in via Johannesburg or Cape Town."

He heard Bertie tapping away on his keyboard. "Come on Bertie, haven't got all day, maybe put me through to one of those artificial robot *okes* you were talking about, might be a bit quicker."

Bertie snorted. "Maybe the day is coming when I will be replaced by Artificial Intelligence, then what will you do, my friend. No friendly, helpful Bertie on the end of the line, hey. Nobody to shout at. Can't shout at a bloody robot! Also, my friend any *bleddy* AI will never have the personal contacts and access to personal information me and my club mates have. Got it?"

Piet held back any retort. Bertie seemed to be a bit cross.

"Okay. I've got her. Doctor Fleur Palmere arrived in South Africa in the early nineties. I don't have an exact date at the moment. Flew to Port Elizabeth from Johannesburg. Her destination, as required by immigration, was only given as some sort of research camp, I would imagine, called Jumba somewhere in the Eastern Cape."

Piet sighed. "Come on Bertie, you can do better than that. Where is the place called Jumba, I need more information?"

Bertie muttered and swore as he continued to tap away on his computer. "Well, Piet, must tell you the place does not exist. It's not a registered research station, or game lodge, or company. Maybe it was at some point decades ago, a research facility, but if it was, it closed down, the bush would have reclaimed it. Looks like you have a non-starter here. But, hey, good luck. I suggest you ask around a bit. Sounds like one of those scams advertised around the scientific world in those days, offering all sorts of things to eager young scientists' keen to explore our glorious country for hidden secrets. Fake brochure pictures, in those days, empty promises. Now with the internet, potential scientists, can check a place out, but in those days they couldn't."

Piet heard him light a cigarette. "Only hidden secrets we had at that time was who was going to run the country, and it wasn't much of a secret let me tell you. As for your lady scientist, or doctor, there is nothing else my data can tell me. The Eastern Cape is vast, your neck of the woods, but people who live and work in the bush hear about things, who is doing what, good or bad. I suggest you ask around; someone must know something about her and where she went or ended up – probably dead if you think she was murdered. I have no record of her death. Nothing."

Piet looked up at the board. "How about a B. Hemmingway. Got anything on that name?"

"*Jeez*, Piet, gimme a break here. Is that the best you can do? I mean is it a male or a female. Any ID, any idea of where he or she lives in this vast country. What nationality is he or she. Is Hemmingway spelled with one *m* or two?

"*Ag,* Bertie, if I knew any of that I would have told you. I'm thinking it was a man. Fleur Palmere deposited an amount of money into the Standard Bank somewhere in Johannesburg, into the account of a B. Hemmingway, spelt with two *m's*. You should be able to find that surely?"

Bertie snorted. "Okay, now tell me how long ago this transaction took place, I might be able to help you there."

Piet took a deep breath. "Now don't start shouting at me, my friend, but it was about twenty years ago."

He heard the long hiss down the phone. "See here Piet. Twenty years is a *friggin* long time ago. Then it would have been a piece of cake to track the transaction down. But the banks not only here but all over the world have upped their security to a very high level. They have all the hackers, fraudsters and other *skollies* tied down tight. It's nearly impossible to get any kind of information today from any bank anywhere. It's not possible, Piet, no can do."

"*Aw*, Bertie, give it a go will you. It's important. Otherwise, we'll never find this Doctor Palmere. Use those artificial robots, or whatever they call themselves, maybe they can do a better job if you say it's impossible."

He could hear Bertie light another cigarette, heard the intake of his breath as he puffed away and hissed the smoke through his teeth. "I'm the best in the business, Piet, as you know. I'll try and find out who this B. Hemmingway is and where he or she is, can't promise anything with the bank transaction though."

Piet shrugged. "Okay, well thanks for nothing Bertie, next time I'll speak to a *bleddy* robot, probably more friendly. Hey, only kidding, appreciate your help."

Bertie sucked on his cigarette. "I have a bad feeling this is not the last I'm going to hear about your missing doctor…"

Jack had listened to the entire conversation on the speaker phone. He now stared once more at the map on the opposite wall. "Okay Piet. Let's get on the road, hire a decent car, not one of your safari vehicles from the hotel, with no roof, no windows, no windscreen, and tiered seats.

"We need a decent, reliable, and comfortable car, even if I have to pay for it myself. We'll be out and about in the bush, following this scientist working out there doing her research, probably in remote places."

Jack ran his eyes over his board on the wall. "Clear things with Hugo and let's find out what really happened to Fleur Palmere. I've given you her background, we now know what she looked like years ago, and we have a vague assumption from a detective. The solicitor in London told me the detective had told him about a woman who disappeared on the Wild Coast years ago, but it was only an assumption.

"This Captain Bennett seemed to have played a major role in her life. He sent her money every month, none of which she touched, only the one transfer to a B. Hemmingway in Johannesburg. So where was she, and how the hell could she survive with no money?"

Jack leaned further towards his white board. "Did she get a job somewhere? Was someone else sending her money so she could continue her research? I'm thinking she met someone here, someone who believed in what she was doing, perhaps he thought he might gain from her research, another scientist or botanist. Or someone who fell in love with her and looked after her. But who was it. Was it this B. Hemmingway? Did she rent a place from him, or her, somewhere and the money was for renting something from this Hemmingway person?

"More to the point if Jeremy Foxton's assumption was right. Who killed her? Why is there no trace of her whatsoever?"

Piet shrugged. "That, my friend, is exactly what we are going to find out. It won't be easy. It's not like she was in one of the main cities, no, she was clearly a nomadic person, searching for whatever it was she was looking for. She found it, and she paid for it. Possibly with her life."

He tapped his pen against his teeth. "My problem with the whole thing is why she cut her ties with everything in her past. What was she trying to escape from, or perhaps, who was she trying to escape from?"

Piet removed his cap and twisted and turned it, trying to get the stiffness out of it. "That, Jack, is the key to it all. You only do that to protect yourself or, perhaps, protect the people you love, or loved.

"Fleur Palmere had a reason for doing this. For cutting herself off from her past, leaving those she loved behind, leaving no trail behind. She created a new life for herself – we need to find out why."

Chapter Forty-Nine

Jack settled himself behind the wheel of the Range Rover, hired from the company behind the desk at the Port Elizabeth airport, adjusting the seat and the mirrors.

Piet was impressed. "Harry approved this expense, Jack?"

Jack grinned as he turned the ignition on. "Nope. But I'm not going to drive through the unforgiving bush of the Eastern Cape in some cheap vehicle. There's a big story here, not only involving individuals, but my gut feel is it has more international connotations, the big pharma companies – it must be. Everything seems to be pointing that way."

Jack pulled out into the traffic. "Fleur Palmere had found something which was of huge importance. We're up against the big boys here, Piet, not our usual case of finding someone, searching for someone."

He adjusted his mirror again. "Fleur found something. Something which threatened them. That's why it's so difficult to find out what happened to her. She was hiding. Hiding what she had found. There would have been nobody she could have trusted.

"We may live in a world of beauty here, Piet, but out there is another world of greed, power, and money, well, okay, here as well. You only need to ask yourself, how come they can send people to the moon, to the depths of the ocean, how come technology is now so advanced that Artificial Intelligence can come up with unbelievable information gathered over decades of doctors, scientists, musicians, writers, pulling everything together, making huge inroads to how people think and act. That's the bottom line, Piet."

He fumbled in his pocket for his sunglasses. "The world has changed in a short space of time. It's frightening, but fascinating. But at the core of it all are the big boys, the big companies, determined not to relinquish anything despite being confronted with all the evidence in front of them. They will do whatever it takes to keep their shareholders happy and that includes the big pharma companies. They control the world in many ways – everyone wants a cure for what they are suffering. It's human nature to want to feel happy and good and healthy."

Jack changed gear and turned right. "See, I know I haven't lived my entire life in Africa, but it seems to me animals are far more intelligent than we are. They will be the ultimate challenge to Artificial Intelligence because they live by instinct. A wild animal here in Africa, knows instinctively what to eat and what not to eat. Chimpanzees are our closest relatives. If they feel unwell, they'll go and seek some plant, or whatever, which they know will heal them. How do they know this? Even a domestic dog or cat will go out and eat grass if it doesn't feel too good. They seem to know. Artificial Intelligence will never replace basic instinct or emotion. Never. That's all we must hang onto, Piet, the rest is too frightening to contemplate. A world with no emotion or instinct. Animals are much smarter than we are. They will go on, as they have always done, we, however, are at the mercy of technology."

Piet took off his cap and scratched his head. "*Eish*, you sure know how to cheer people up, Jack. But you're right, I know you're right. But this is all to come; now we must find what we're looking for."

They drove from the airport and through the windy city of Port Elizabeth, the endless beaches with their odd, anchor shaped cement barriers against the sea.

"See here, Jack, just to cheer you up a bit, we might have funny sounding accents to the rest of the world and over the years they have hated our politics but let me tell you some amazing inventions have come from this country.

"See those cement shaped objects lining the beaches, they're called Delosse, invented in the sixties by a South African. Keeps erosion at bay, protects the town from flooding; now copied all over the world. Cat Scans, Kreepy Krawlies, which might sound sinister to anyone else, but for anyone with a swimming pool in this country it's a true invention, something else cleans your pool for you, bit like a sort of hoover. Pratley's Putty was used to hold bits of Apollo Eleven together whilst it was out there on the moon – made and invented in South Africa. No South African, or anyone, would be without his can of Q20 for keeping rust at bay, used world-wide now. Oil from coal? Formulated right here. Heart transplants and cataract treatments all started here. They may not like us much for our history, but they sure as hell should be thanking us for what we contributed to medical procedures and all the other stuff I mentioned."

Jack indicated he was turning right again heading towards the bush and off the national highway. "So, what are you trying to say here, Piet? If this Fleur did find something of immense value to the medical profession it would have been discovered here in South Africa?"

"Exactly what I'm saying, my friend. And if this is so, it must remain here. Not sold out to another international country. We have some of the finest scientists and doctors in the world here, yes, many have left and gone overseas, they are much sought after let me tell you.

But thousands have stayed in their country and continue their steady and valuable research. Many are returning."

He looked sideways at Jack. "I like it when good people choose their country over their profession and believe me there are thousands who have stayed here.

"My interest in Fleur Palmere goes beyond what happened to her which of course we must find out and we will. But it's what she found that intrigues me. If she found something here, we must take it as ours, make it our own and show the world we are not all about politics, corruption, crime, and violence. Show the world we still have much to offer, a country to be admired, not only for its incredible beauty, but for the good people, of all races, who dedicate their lives to making it a better place, a place to be admired by the international community."

"Not that the media ever want the feel-good stories...they want death, destruction and all the other bad stuff to throw at their audience."

Jack stopped the car. The dust billowed behind the vehicle, and it had started to rain, thunder rumbled in the distance and the bright blue skies had turned their back, leaving heavy bloated, rain filled clouds on the horizon.

He looked at his map. "We should call it a day Piet. I don't fancy driving around in this. Could be some heavy weather coming up. We haven't passed anything which looked like it might have been a camp site at some point. But there's a lodge about an hour away called The Retreat; I looked it up. It isn't up there with the big lodges, more of a Wellness and Spa kind of place, in fact I've never heard of it, have you?"

Piet shook his head. "Nope. But I'm not really a game lodge kind of guy, don't follow the latest luxury lodge popping up. Not my kind of thing. I'm a cop, Jack, following the trail of the bad guys not flicking through a glossy magazine to see the latest over the top game lodge. They're all trying to outdo the competition with their latest offering of spas in the bush, petals on the pillows, lavender stuffed in your pillowcase, butlers for every room. That's not Africa, Jack.

"Me, well, I would prefer to sit around a bush fire, cooking my chops and *boerewors* and listening to the raw savage sounds of Africa. Not sitting in some *larney* safari camp buffeted from the wildness out there, being served fancy food from another country. What's wrong with our own food, why do we have to import it from *bleddy* France or wherever."

Jack glanced at him. "Not everyone is into eating mopani worms or, what do they call them, ah yes, walkie talkies, that dish of heads of chickens and their feet." He shuddered. "Revolting, if you ask me, not exactly what we call fine dining."

Piet scowled. "Nothing wrong with that on the menu, beats curried mars bars or whatever. Hey, maybe mopani worms and walkie talkies are on the menu tonight – full of nutrition, bet they serve them here!"

Piet laughed and looked out of the window. "The Retreat might be a good start though, out in the middle of nowhere. Maybe the manager might know what else is hereabouts, or what used to be here, and point us in the right direction, because so far, we haven't got any idea where anything is. *Fok* all in fact."

Jack pulled up outside the place called The Retreat. Sheets of rain, hailstones and thunder pounded their vehicle. There were no guards checking names of the new arrivals.

Covering their heads with their raincoats, Piet and Jack ran towards the reception, the thunder booming over their heads, the lightning slashing and ripping across the skies above.

The receptionist looked up and smiled. "You have a reservation?"

Jack wiped the rain from his eyes and face. "No, but judging from the car park, and the weather, I'm sure you can find us two rooms, or if push comes to shove, a room with two singles?"

"I am Innocent."

Piet frowned. "You're innocent? Should we assume you are anything but?"

Innocent looked puzzled. "That is my name, sir. My given birth name."

Piet grinned at him. "Of course it is. Now tell me, is the restaurant here open?"

Innocent gave a wide smile, his perfect white teeth enhanced by his dark skin. "Of course. This is a hotel and a Spa. We have a good menu. Let me give you the keys to your rooms and then you may proceed to the restaurant for dinner."

Piet leaned on the counter. "Now listen here, Innocent. I do not wish to have a celery stick and a nut cutlet and a green drink with bits in it. I want a proper dinner. We've travelled a long way; we are not here to lose weight or embrace a new world of foreign sounding wellness stuff to enhance our lives.

"I don't wish to have hot pebbles placed upon my back, dolphin sounds in the background or a rattan mat to sleep on, with a brick under my head. I most certainly don't want someone treading on my back, banging gongs and chanting. Also, I have no intention of walking around in a dressing gown and snow-white slippers all day. Got it?"

Innocent stepped back slightly. Piet continued. "I want a proper bed. Steak and chips and a beer – can do?" He took his key from Innocent and wandered off to find his room, leaving Jack to the formalities of checking in.

Jack smiled at Innocent. "Had a bit of a bad day, but he'll be alright after he's eaten something. Always a bit grumpy when he's hungry. He can be quite charming sometimes."

Innocent looked doubtful. "If you say so, sir," he said politely.

Piet sank his teeth into an exceptionally good steak and loaded up his fork with golden chips, ignoring the salad placed next to his plate.

"We need to meet whoever manages this joint, Jack, see what it was before it turned into a *larney* hotel and Spa. There's a big interest in the Eastern Cape now. All the game was shot out decades ago, nothing left but plains game and not much of that. But there are landowners and farmers who have a vision to bring back the big five to this area."

He took another bite of his steak and crowded some chips on his fork. "It's an ambitious project. International tourists only know the Kruger Park and the private game lodges in the Sabi Sands. It's going to take a lot of intense marketing to international tour operators to put the Eastern Cape on the map. But it can be done. Anyone who can achieve the re-introduction of the big five to this area, without making it a sort of Holiday Inn in the bush, is going to create a legacy for future generations. I'll tell Innocent we want to meet the manager in the morning."

Jack grinned at him. "Try and put a smile on your face when you ask him, will you. You make him nervous."

Chapter Fifty

The next day the storm had passed, the skies were blue, the sun was warm, the trees, bushes and flowers showing their true colours from the dust and dryness of the day before. Spider's webs perfectly designed glinted like diamonds, hung with wetness between the trees.

After breakfast, Innocent approached them. "The manager of the hotel is here now, should you wish to speak to him. His name is Koos. Perhaps you would like coffee to be served in the gardens and there he will join you?"

Koos was young, perhaps twenty-eight at most. He joined Piet and Jack in the gardens.

"How may I help you gentleman. I'm Koos. You want to talk to me?"

Jack introduced himself as a journalist with the *Telegraph* in London and Piet as his partner here in South Africa. He doubted the young manager would be able to help them at all. He would have been far too young, only a kid, to remember any history of the place.

Koos looked impressed. "You want to do a story on The Retreat, which would be awesome. With all the game lodges, guest houses and everything else going on, we could do with some good international publicity."

Jack smiled at his eager young and tanned face. "The thing is, Koos, to do any kind of story on The Retreat we need to know how it came into being. The history of the place."

Koos took a cautious sip of his hot coffee. "Well, I can certainly help you with that. Many years ago, it was a basic camp site, owned by an Afrikaans couple. Locals left their caravans here and returned every year to spend a week or two taking time out from towns and cities. It was basic then and called '*Waterval*' not that there was a waterfall in sight."

Jack looked at his notes. This was the place where Poppy's guardian, Simon, had worked all those years ago, the place she had named, in her letter to Jeremy, as 'Waterfalls.'

The place where he had met Fleur, the place where she had been abandoned. He tried to imagine it as an empty camp site but failed to conjure up the image. Now the gardens were lush. Trees, bushes, and flowers flourishing from the constant sprays of water and the numerous gardeners working diligently to create an oasis of tranquillity in the harsh bush of the Eastern Cape.

Koos continued. "Things changed, the country was beginning to change, politics came into the picture. Locals became nervous and took their caravans away. The place fell into disrepair and the couple who owned it had no choice but to sell.

"Investors were interested in development, they had hopes for the future of the new government. One company, I can't recall their name, travelled all over the province looking for possible sites for investment."

Koos pushed his empty cup of coffee away. "Hotel chains moved in, Protea, Southern Suns, Sun international, and gobbled up all the run-down hotels with potential. We, however, remained independent, but I'm not sure for how much longer."

Piet leaned forward putting his own empty cup on the table. "How can we find the original international company who researched these places which had potential as hotels and game lodges in the future?"

Koos shook his head. "That I can't tell you. Long before my time. But there must be records somewhere? I can go through to our head office in Jo'burg and see if they can help. They'll be delighted to get some international publicity in an English newspaper."

Koos sprinted off and left Piet and Jack to their freshly delivered coffee. Twenty minutes later he was back with a piece of paper in his hand, looking a little rejected.

"Not much information unfortunately. There was an international company, many years ago called TLI, they had a head office in Jo'burg and Port Elizabeth. Apparently, they specialised in the Eastern and Northern Cape areas. Looking for places which could be ripe for development in the new South Africa. After a feasibility study they looked for investors and property developers. By all accounts they were a highly respected company with excellent credentials, that's why our board of directors decided to invest and developed The Retreat."

Jack was rapidly making notes. "Any idea what TLI stood for?"

Koos shook his head. "Sorry, no idea. Apparently, they closed sometime after the new government came into power. My boss told me things changed rapidly after that. The Africans wanted their land back, but didn't want to pay for it, there were now radical political parties insisting the people's demands should be met."

Koos looked around the lush gardens. "Investors became nervous about getting involved in any deals with possibly a short-term return on their money, or none. Can't say I blame them. Anyway, TLI closed their offices down and left the country. Looked for different destinations – Brazil or maybe Rwanda."

Piet stared into the distance. "*Ja,* we know all about this."

"Suddenly property developers and investors were having to deal with the tribal chiefs. People they had not dealt with before and didn't know how to deal with them or their people. Couldn't speak their language or understand the impossible demands they were making – they wanted what they considered their land back, the radical politicians urging them on. They were not prepared to make any payment – they wanted it all for nothing."

Koos folded his hands in front of him... "Many a small guest house, or fancy country house in the bush and game lodges, hit the dirt. They couldn't deal with all the political dispensations. The deals were non-negotiable as far as certain African politicians were concerned.

"Some of the game lodges came up with a plan. They would rent the land from the Chiefs, who said the land was theirs, belonged to them, belonged to the people now, and pay them every month for the use of the bush their lodges occupied. The Chiefs decided to push for more, they wanted the game lodge owners to rent the animals that traversed through their properties as well. The wealthy lodge owners knew this was the only way they would be able to hang onto the massive investment their families had made over decades. So, they made a plan with the chiefs, and they survived."

Jack watched the birds swooping and dipping through the fine spray of the garden hoses, as Koos continued.

"Unfortunately, many of the lesser game lodges didn't have that kind of money to continue. They couldn't make any kind of deal, so, as they say, they folded their tents, closed their lodges as did the privately owned country hotels and guest lodges. A sad day. A lifetime of dreams and hopes shattered and no return on their investment, or the life they had always known. No inheritance for their families. Nowhere to go next."

Jack looked up in surprise. He knew about the land grabs, the aspirations of the locals but he hadn't been aware of how far the movement had spread. The vast Afrikaner farmlands he knew about but wasn't aware of the other deals being made.

Koos stood up. "The company are super excited about an article in your English newspaper. Let me give you a guided tour of the property and what we have to offer, Mr Taylor. Your stay here will be with the compliments of the hotel. If you would like to experience any of our Spa treatments, which I highly recommend, you must let me know?"

Jack stood up reluctantly. The last thing he wanted was a guided tour and the ominous possibility of lying on a hard floor with hot stones on his back and walking around in a dressing gown. But Koos had given them some interesting information – time to pay the price.

He turned to Piet. "Are you coming?"

Piet tried to suppress his laughter. "*Nah*, you go ahead. After all, you're the journalist. I'll wait for you here in the gardens. I've always been most interested in plants and flowers, as you know, especially recently.

"You go and munch on a celery stick. I'll sit here and have a beer and look at the flowers and suchlike."

Chapter Fifty-One

The next morning Piet was in the driving seat, he reversed out of the car park having no idea of where they might be heading. Jack had his map spread out over his knees.

"Okay Jack, give me some idea of where we're going will you?"

"Right, this is what I'm thinking. Doctor Palmere ended up in a deserted camp site, according to Poppy, or The Retreat as it's called now. She must have met someone there who gave her a lift somewhere. To my mind it must have been someone involved with the sale of the place. Lawyers, bank managers, or possibly the international company TLI. The place had closed, the creditors moving in. Plenty of people around who would have given her a lift somewhere. Nobody would have left a lone female there. So, who exactly rescued her and where did they take her?"

He looked around the deserted bush thinking of the best route to take, then back at the map. "It would have been a town where Fleur could book into a hotel and make alternative travel arrangements." His finger traced a route on the map. "That might have been Graaff-Reinet. There's a secondary road here, the R75. I think we should take that. No point in heading back to the highway, won't see anything that way. But there might be other developments out here in the bush where we could ask some questions. What do you think?"

Piet grunted. "Okay, sounds like a good plan. The R75 it is."

Jack made a mess of folding up his map. "Fleur had a bad experience when she landed in South Africa. Someone with her background would have been devastated to find, according to Bertie, that her safari camp did not exist, and she found herself in an abandoned camp site, The Retreat as it is now called. How she got there I have no idea. She must have been severely traumatised with the sequence of events. According to Poppy, when Simon left the next day, she was alone, maybe she wandered off somewhere looking for help. Or, maybe, someone pitched up and took care of her.

"But someone found her and took her to a place of safety. I'm thinking it might have been Graaff-Reinet."

Five hours later after a bumpy and dusty ride, with the occasional sighting of a herd of golden impala and haughty, bad tempered looking ostrich.

"Hey, Piet, those ostriches remind me of ballerinas, long legs, long eyelashes, slender necks, frilly skirts, don't you think?"

Piet gave him a withering look. "I worry about you sometimes Jack, with your wild imagination. I'm thinking you need to find yourself a girlfriend…sooner rather than later."

They pulled into the old town of Graaff-Reinet.

Situated in the heart of the vastness of the Karoo region, with its quaint Cape Dutch architecture, whitewashed walls, thatched roofs and ornate gables, and the churches with their startling white exteriors and soaring spires. It was one of the oldest towns in the country and rich in its history, attracting tourists from all over the world. To accommodate them the town was awash with signs for hotels and guest houses.

Piet pulled up outside one of them on the outskirts of the town. "This place looks all right, Jack. Need a beer and a hot shower and something to eat, like lamb. This area is famous for Karoo lamb, best in the world as far as I'm concerned."

Jack wiped the dust from his sunglasses and rubbed his eyes. "How do you know that Piet? You've never been anywhere else in the world except for the trip to the UK with me where you didn't stop bitching and complaining about the quality of our food and the weather."

"Just know that's all. See here Jack we passed huge herds of sheep on the way here, no farmers or sheep dogs in sight. The sheep wander around wherever they want to, sticking with their flock, they live on a harsh landscape of scrubland; no sheepdog herds them back to the farm for the night, they live their somewhat short lives out in the vastness of the Karoo. They favour a particular plant called wild rosemary and this is what gives the meat such a unique flavour.

"We shall dine well tonight, my friend, on the best lamb in the world. Now let's check in, have a hot shower and a beer or two before I introduce you to our famous lamb."

Refreshed and relaxed after their gruelling trip through the bush, Jack pushed his plate away. "Phew, you were right about the lamb, Piet, best I've ever had in my life. I was given to understand the best lamb came from New Zealand, but I now must disagree."

Piet smiled proudly. "Yup, best in the world. Like our rugby team, the Boks. But it's also how you cook it, long and slow, like life here in the Karoo. Like this story we're following… going slowly nowhere. Lamb from hereabouts doesn't need to be smothered with foreign spices and fancy names, little white hats on their ribs when they're served.

Chuck some garlic in, bit of wine, bit of salt and that's it. Falls off the bone when it's done. Like I said, best in the world."

Jack took a gulp of his red wine and wondered if he should ask for seconds, damn that lamb was good. If they stayed a second night in Graaff-Reinet, which seemed likely, he was going to have the same again.

Piet pushed his chair back. "Let's go and sit out on the *stoep* and plan the next move. I have a few ideas I want to run past you."

They sat contentedly together as they sipped at their glass of wine, looking up at the crystal-clear heavens above, black as velvet and pitted with stars, the air sharp and fresh, after a hot and dusty day, as night descended once more over the vastness of the Karoo, a peaceful kind of darkness, enduring and endless, like the day that would come tomorrow. Timeless.

Jack dragged his jumper over his head, pulling down the sleeves. Today had been as hot as hell, but now it was cold. "So, what are you thinking Piet? This is your neck of the woods, I'm a bit out of my depth right now I have to say."

Piet held back a yawn; he was tired after the long hot drive. "See here, my friend. If you were a dentist, an engineer, or a doctor, with a load of degrees, and found yourself lost in Africa, what would you do?"

Jack gave it some thought. "If you're talking about our Doctor Palmere and what she went through, I would probably book my next ticket back to London. She most certainly had, by all accounts, a baptism of fire when she arrived in the country."

Piet reached for his glass. "Indeed, she did. Now, if I was a doctor, arriving in a country where everything had gone wrong, and found myself alone in, perhaps, a town like this. I know what I would do, so long.

"I would check into a hotel, pull myself together, and turn to people who would be able to help me. Turn to a world I know. I would have gone to the nearest hospital seeking help. People who would respect me, my profession, and have contacts all over the country. A familiar place."

Piet rolled down his sleeves against the cold of the night. "The medical profession, in this vast country of mine, is a close-knit society, everyone knows someone who knows someone. She might have taken this road seeking guidance in the field she knew so well.

"I don't think Doctor Palmere, whatever state she was in, would have run back to London and, according to Bertie, she didn't leave the country. She was here, following in her mother's footsteps. Looking for something. She would not have given up at the first hurdle or two."

Piet tried to hide his next yawn and failed. "Anyways, that's my theory. We should check out the medical facilities and hospitals in this town and see what we can find. I'm off to bed now, feeling knackered I have to say, must be all the fresh air and the excellent dinner tonight. I'm going to call Bertie and ask him to check out this TLI company, see if we can get a few names to follow up. Also, I need to get hold of a few old mates in the police force along the Wild Coast and see if there are any police reports of a woman scientist who went missing. Be a bit like looking for a grey hair on the beach, but I'm going to give it my best shot. Goodnight Jack."

Jack lifted his nearly empty glass in farewell and sat back in his chair, sifting through what Piet had surmised. He was right. Doctor Palmere would have sought out like-minded people. People in her profession, who would be able to help her and suggest the way ahead.

Jack finished his wine and stood up. The local pharmacies would be the place to start.

Chapter Fifty-Two

The next morning, Jack spoke to the pharmacists in town, asking about the various doctors who worked there, either in private practice or at the hospitals.

Piet was out and about looking up retired police officers, though thin on the ground after all this time, who might remember any reports of a woman who went missing somewhere along the Wild Coast.

They had arranged to meet for lunch at the guest house, which they did.

Jack sat and ravished a fat bun, filled with warm Karoo lamb, he pushed his empty plate away from him, with a satisfied sigh. "So, Piet what did you find out?"

Piet frowned. "Not much I'm afraid. I used my contacts, spoke to a few retired police guys, most of them remembered a British female scientist who had gone missing on the Wild Coast. But you must remember, Jack. It's a vast coastline, rugged and dangerous. There are a couple of police stations dotted along the coast, but because there was no crime there, the police stations were remote, perhaps only with one or two junior police guys manning them.

"Yes, someone reported Fleur Palmere missing, but the police didn't have the resources to carry out an intensive search for her. Which they didn't. So, a cold case, your speciality, my friend.

"Bertie also looked up the company TLI for me. Seems it's an international company called Trans Location Investments. Not much more information than we already learned from the manager of The Retreat. Anyways, they left the country years ago. Another dead end, I'm afraid."

He shrugged his shoulders. "How did you get on in the world of medicine?"

Jack sucked his fingers, still relishing the taste of the lamb. "I went to all the pharmacies in town, and one name that came up time and time again was a Doctor De Klerk. His family have lived here for generations. In fact, they had a farm here on the outskirts of town, one of the oldest families, going back generations. Doctor De Klerk inherited the farm and turned it into a private hospital, which was highly successful. I checked it out."

Unlike the solid square buildings of most medical facilities around the world, forbidding and unattractive to look at, he had found the hospital almost welcoming, despite whatever you were going to confront with your health.

The hospital still retained its old Cape Dutch architectural veneer, the grounds with their well-attended gardens embracing the arc of water from the many elegant fountains creating mini rainbows; ample free parking under the generous boughs of ancient trees and a sense of history still enduring. It reminded him of the long lost "cottage" hospitals of his younger days, dotted around the countryside of England.

Now they didn't exist with your friendly caring GP who your family had known all their lives. No, they were all part of the giant called the NHS, being processed through the system where you had to pay for parking for the so-called pleasure of walking through the security process to get the help you needed. Only a number in the car park, at great expense, and the terrible fear of medical staff who didn't know who you were, who your family were, and what you were there for.

"I've managed to get an appointment with the owner of the hospital, Doctor De Klerk: Told him I was from the *Telegraph* and wanted to do a piece on one of the oldest hospitals in the area which I do. Told him I was bringing my partner, a *fundi* on the area – that's you Piet."

"Appointment at five this afternoon."

Doctor De Klerk stood up as his assistant showed Piet and Jack into his rooms. He stretched his back and held out his hand. "Come in, come in, nice to meet you both. Take a seat."

He shuffled the files on his desk and held one out to Jack. "My assistant," he grinned at them, "my wife to be exact, prepared this for you, it's an accurate account of the history of the area. This used to be a farm belonging to my folks before I re-designed it as a private hospital."

He pointed out of his window. "I still have a modest flock of sheep and some chickens which patients can see from here, helps them feel a little more relaxed, gives the place a bit of a feel of the old farm."

Piet looked around nervously. "*Ja*, doc, all looks very nice, but it's the smell of a hospital which makes me nervous. Hopefully, this is the last time I'll visit you here. Don't like hospitals, takes me out of my comfort zone."

He shuddered. "But there's another reason for our visit. Jack will write a piece on your hospital for his newspaper, with some nice pics of the place, but I'm looking for a bit of information on someone who went missing many years ago. I'm trying to find her."

De Klerk looked up surprised. "You think this person was a patient here, or she worked here perhaps?"

Piet lifted his shoulders. "She might have come here looking for some advice, not necessarily as a patient, but maybe for help. She was English, had only been in the country a couple of days, but got lost in the bush. Someone found her and brought her, we assume, to the nearest town where she could make onward travel plans. That's Graaff-Reinet we think.

"She was a doctor, a scientist. Her name was Fleur Palmere."

Doctor De Klerk frowned slightly and glanced out at his sheep grazing in the last rays of sunshine of the day, their fleece turning from grey to gold. He seemed to be searching his memory.

"Palmere? Yes, I remember her. Perhaps because she was a fellow doctor, an unusual name. Someone brought her here to have her checked out. If I recall correctly, she was disorientated. We almost had to tie her to the bed to be examined. Feisty young thing. Most patients being admitted here are resigned, always nervous. But not that one, she was having none of it."

He leaned forward and buzzed through to reception. "Mariette, will you look up a patient for me called Doctor Fleur Palmere? It was a long time ago, but she should be in the system somewhere. Print out her medical records for me, will you?"

He looked at the two men across from him. "You understand that her records are private. But now you are telling me she has gone missing. I would like to help you if I possibly can."

Mariette bustled in twenty minutes later. "Sorry, took longer than I thought, a long time ago as you indicated, but I did find her for you."

Jack and Piet leaned forward, eagerly awaiting the details contained in the medical report. Jack's foot was beginning to jiggle, which it always did when he knew he was close to getting some information. He crossed his leg and steadied his foot with his hand, excitement slithering down his spine.

Doctor De Klerk flipped through the printout in front of him then put it down. "Yes, Doctor Fleur Palmere was admitted here to this hospital. She was in a highly emotional state, disorientated, as I mentioned, dehydrated, low blood pressure and sunstroke. She had no identity papers on her, no address of any family, or next of kin. That's why I remember her. Nobody seemed to know who she was or how she got here. It seemed impossible as she wasn't exactly a gap year student making her way through the country on a shoestring.

"I tried to get her to answer some questions, even though she was in a state of shock, but she would tell me nothing, either that or she couldn't remember." He paused. "Or perhaps she didn't want to, for her own personal reasons."

Piet frowned. "So, how did she get here? Who brought her in, and when she was discharged where did she go in a country, I assume, she knew nothing about?"

De Klerk rubbed his eyes and replaced his glasses. "I might have seen a lot of bad stuff in my life, gentlemen, a lot of good things as well. But one thing I do recognise is when there is a little romance in the air.

"Although Doctor Palmere was in a shocked state, the man who brought her here, an Englishman, was clearly taken with the damsel in distress he rescued from the bush. He came here every day, if I recall, and watched over her. He tried to find her family with what little information he had."

He glanced down at the print-out. "The only contact he had been able to find was someone called Captain Michael Bennett, he thought perhaps it might have been her husband. But according to him the captain had died somewhere in the Middle East, perhaps long before she came to South Africa."

De Klerk tidied up the printout into an orderly pile. "When Doctor Palmere was well enough to be discharged from my hospital, I knew I would not be able to do this without knowing who she was, where she was going next and who would take care of her in a foreign country. I had a legal responsibility to place her in the care of someone. We didn't have social services then, well not of any consequence. Who would look after her until she was fully enough recovered to take care of herself and perhaps return to her home country?"

Piet watched the doctor closely. "So did this Englishman take her back to England?"

De Klerk smiled as the memories from the medical printout in front of him came flooding back. "No, he didn't take her back to England. He'd been living here for years, working out in the bush. He accepted full responsibility for her, and I released her into his eager custody."

Piet drummed his fingers on the side of his chair. "Okay. But he must have given his name, his ID number, if he lived here and his home address. What was it. Can you tell us?"

Jack pulled his notepad from his shirt pocket, letting Piet lead the conversation.

De Klerk referred to the printout again. "He worked for a company called TLI, he was based here in the Eastern Cape living in a company house out in the bush. This was where he worked from.

"According to him, he and his company were wrapping up a deal, out in the bush somewhere. Apparently, he found this woman, Fleur, wandering around a deserted camp site, completely disoriented. He brought her here to us."

Jack, unable to contain his excitement with the new information, leaned forward. "Where did he take her, Doctor De Klerk, what was the address according to her records and his information?"

De Klerk looked at the bottom of the printout and smiled. "Unlike in your country, Mr Taylor, we don't always have street addresses. The place we have here is what we call an Erf number, a bush address, if you like."

He scribbled the information on his prescription pad and handed it to Piet. "I'm sure Mr Joubert will explain the complexities of it all to you. Now, if you'll excuse me, I must make the final rounds of the day and see my patients. I look forward to reading your article, Mr Taylor, on my family's farm and now our hospital."

Piet held up his hand. "Whoa, hang on a second, doc, you haven't told us the name of the man who rescued Fleur Palmere?"

"His name was Blake Hemmingway."

Doctor De Klerk watched the two men walk back to their car. His thoughts went back to Fleur Palmere. He didn't have the technology then to fully explain some of the things he had discovered. One was the fact that her fainting and blackouts perhaps indicated something else in her blood, something he thought might he hereditary.

The other was something he felt wasn't his place to share with anyone.

Chapter Fifty-Three

Jack strapped himself in as Piet reversed out of the parking area. "What on earth is an Erf number, mate, never heard of it. Is it a sort of South African thing?"

Piet made his way through the quiet town. Settling down for the end of another day, couples sat out on their *stoeps* watching the world go by in front of them. Sundowners to hand.

"Yes, it's unique to South Africa. It's an Afrikaans word meaning an inheritance or a piece of land. This is where the government, for decades, has always been good. Every property has an Erf number, so if you want to buy a house in the leafy suburbs of Cape Town, a commercial building in any city, a holiday home on the coast, a place in the bush, well, they all have an Erf number so the buyer can ensure he's going to get a registered piece of property or land and knows who the legal seller is and can go ahead with confidence knowing the original owners of the land are exactly who they say they are."

Jack mulled the information over and looked at his notes. "Okay, we have one of these Erf numbers, given to the doctor by the now not so mysterious Blake Hemmingway. How will we find it?"

Piet pulled up and parked outside their guest house.

"Easy. Tomorrow, first thing, we go to any estate agency here and say we're interested in it. They'll look it up on their data base, point us in the right direction and tell us more about it, and exactly where it is. Tell us who it belongs to and who owns it now.

"Of course, we already know it had to belong to Blake Hemmingway who worked for Trans Location Investments, or the company who owned it if he was working for them here. Overseas contracts usually come with a fully furnished company house."

He braked to let a skinny dog cross the road in front of them. "I'm thinking Fleur Palmere probably spent some time there, hence the fairly large sum of money she transferred to the account of the said B. Hemmingway. She sounded like an independent woman and probably made some deal with him that she would rent something from him. Fleur was on the hunt for something. Being way out in the bush would have been ideal for her, after all it was what she had planned for her stay in South Africa, a remote place in the bush where she could continue her research. Unfortunately, the place called Jumba went beyond remote, it didn't exist."

Piet picked his next words carefully. "Now listen Jack. Graaff-Reinet is a town I know well, worked on a few cases here over the years, still have a few contacts hereabouts, know the bars where the locals like to drink, the Afrikaners. Might pick up a thing or two. But I'm not going to ask you to join me. You sound way too British, and I'll have to introduce you as a journalist. Not a good mix in the places I plan to visit. Okay with that?"

Jack let himself out of the car. "I'm crushed beyond belief that you don't want me to come with you. We're a team, you and I."

Piet laughed. "Bugger off Jack. Go write your column for Harry, otherwise he'll be bellowing at you again. The hospital will make a good story." He shoved the file De Klerk's assistant, or as it turned out his wife, into his hands.

"I'll see you tomorrow, okay?"

Jack, as he had promised himself, ordered the lamb again, thanking God he wasn't a vegan. He took his glass of wine out onto the *stoep* and tapped out his story for the next column of his newspaper in London. He felt the Karoo was a magical place, timeless. Its stories of the people, the history, the old churches and buildings still whispering through the scrubland, along with the hardy sheep through the harsh winters. The essence of the heartbeat of the generations who had lived and still did, in this unrelenting and sometimes unforgiving landscape with its bitterly cold winters and extremely hot summers. His readers would be able to relate to that. He also had some nice pics of the hospital which would add to his story.

Satisfied with what he had produced, he sent it through to Harry, sat back and thought about the day. They had made considerable progress. Tracked down Fleur Palmere to a hospital in town, finally discovered who the B. Hemmingway was, and this mysterious thing called an Erf which may well take them to the house where he, or both of them, had lived. Although it was highly unlikely, he still lived there, as the international company he worked for had closed and left the country a long time ago.

The next morning, Jack and Piet trawled through the list of estate agents operating in town, finally settling on one.

"Let me handle this Jack, a bloke with a Pommy sounding accent might not cut the mustard as you say. Maybe make them a bit suspicious especially if you'll obviously not know what you're talking about."

They walked towards their car. "So, Piet, what did you come up with from your trawling through the seedy side of town with your countrymen last night?"

"Bugger all, except a slight hangover. Nobody had heard of either Blake Hemmingway or Fleur Palmere. Waste of my valuable time. But, hey, it was nice to rubbish our politicians, in our own language. Had a good time."

They strapped themselves into the car and set off for the estate agency, the oldest one in town according to the locals Piet had met the night before, to find the address of the place which would identify the Erf number supplied by De Klerk.

The former home of Mr Blake Hemmingway.

Chapter Fifty-Four

Tapu, Blake's old retainer, watched with alarm as he saw the curtain of dust heading his way.

Quickly he straightened the For Sale sign in front of Blake's old house which had been lying dormant in the dust for years. Only two estate agents had come during this time. He thought it might be at least some years or so ago, when the international company had been keen to sell Mr Blake's house, or their company house.

A representative of the company had made one visit, after Mr Blake failed to return home. He had asked Tapu to stay on as a caretaker and be there to show around any potential buyers. Sadly, but much to his delight, there had been none. But the company still paid him monthly to ensure the place didn't collapse into the bush in disrepair.

Tapu continued to look after the house; He looked after the vegetable garden which Miss Fur had started and kept chickens, goats and one cow who had supplied milk. Unfortunately, the cow had died but Tapu feasted well on the meat for weeks. For further supplies he went to town where he also visited Beauty.

As was the African way he had counted his blessings, despite his loss of Mr Blake and Miss Fur, he had embraced what the Gods had sent him and got on with his faltering, if unpredictable, life.

But now he was watching the billowing dust following a fast-moving vehicle heading his way and deep down inside he knew his life was about to change once again.

Tapu stepped forward to greet his visitors. One was tall and blond, an Englishman, he thought. The other was without a doubt a cop, or an ex-cop. He knew his life was indeed going to change and he was apprehensive of his two visitors.

"You wish to see the house? It is for sale but there is nobody wishing to buy it. As you can see it is a good solid house. I have looked after it as best I can, for many years now."

Jack and Piet introduced themselves, assuring Tapu they were not estate agents, but looking for someone.

Tapu took a deep breath, knowing he would not be asked to move on if these men were not here to buy the place. "How may I help you?"

Jack looked at him shrewdly. "It seems you have lived here a long time. You must have known the people who occupied the house, otherwise why would TLI have kept you on to look after the place?

"This is where Mr Blake Hemmingway lived; we also believe this is where Doctor Fleur Palmere also lived?"

Tapu's shoulders sagged, this was going to be more difficult than he had anticipated, because he knew he would not be able to give the answers they were looking for. These could *never* be shared with anyone.

Tapu invited them to sit on the *stoep*, the place where Blake and Miss Fur had spent so much time together, enjoying the dinner he had prepared, sharing their thoughts and dreams – but most of all Miss Fur's scientific discoveries, which he himself had played such a crucial part in, and eventually taken her to where the sacred trees were.

And, yes, in his own mind he felt responsible for what had happened and been hidden from the world.

But not from him.

Jack and Piet settled themselves on the dusty sagging cane chairs, Tapu remained standing. Twisting his hands together and looking at them anxiously, but with a certain amount of hostility in his eyes.

Piet gave him what he hoped was a friendly smile. "Don't look so anxious Tapu. Come and sit. We want to ask you a few questions about Mr Hemmingway and his doctor friend. We need your help."

Tapu lowered himself gingerly into the chair but only on the edge of it. "But you are a policeman, sir, I am much afraid of you and your questions. It is true the owner of the house did not say I could live in it, but it is clean and tidy and looked after by me. Will you arrest me now I have told you this?"

Piet studied Tapu's face. Yes, he was indeed a worried man. "I used to be a cop, but I've retired now. I help my friend here, who comes from the same place as Mr Hemmingway, he's here on behalf of the doctor's family who wish to know where she is?"

Tapu frowned. "But how can this be they should wait so many years before looking for her? Miss Fur and Mr Blake went missing a long time ago. I am thinking they are dead now."

Jack sat quietly not saying anything, letting Piet do the talking, he knew these people, this area, it was his turf. He would know exactly how to handle Tapu.

Piet looked down at his hands, then up at Tapu. "But there is no proof of this, my friend, no proof at all, is there. Was it you who reported them missing, or the doctor, Miss Fleur. There is no record in the police files of anyone reporting Mr Blake missing. Why is that?"

Piet watched Tapu carefully, all his police instincts on high alert. He probed a bit further as he saw the man opposite him becoming more agitated, but there was a cunningness about him, he could see it in his green eyes.

"Why didn't Mr Blake report Miss Fleur missing? They were living here together; this we know for a fact. Surely, he would have been most concerned when she didn't come back. Or did she perhaps leave him, and he accepted this?

"You must have been most concerned when he also disappeared. Did they disappear together perhaps? If they did it can only be you who knows the truth about what happened here."

Jack had been watching Tapu and decided to move in with a few questions of his own, perhaps he could smooth the air of tension now surrounding the two men.

Piet was coming across as a policeman interrogating a suspect. Africans had a natural fear and suspicion of the police, thinking they were in trouble whether they were or not.

"Tapu?"

Tapu turned towards him. "Yes, Mr Yak. You have the same voice as Mr Blake, I am thinking you are from the same place across the sea. Also, Miss Fur who had the same voice."

Jack smiled. It seemed no Africans here could ever pronounce his name. But he had grown used to it over the years he had lived here.

"You see, Tapu, Miss Fur, as you called her, did come from across the sea. There are people there who care about her and want to know where she is. What happened to her. We know she came here looking for something, and you know what it was. Mr Blake must also have family there, but nobody seems to be looking for him so perhaps he's not missing but moved somewhere else to live?"

Tapu looked down at his feet, unsure of how he should handle these questions.

"I'm writing a story about your Miss Fur for my newspaper. We pay well for information. But we need to know the truth about what happened to the doctor and Mr Blake. You need have no fear if you tell us the truth, if you know it, that is."

Tapu seemed to shrink in front of them as he listened to Jack's words. He didn't want money for himself; his people were close and had always looked after each other, they would be safe. But he was unsure of what may lie ahead.

He knew what Miss Fur had eventually found might greatly enhance the future of his people who only wanted to return to the desert where they belonged, a place they understood. A place the government had taken away from them. She had promised him and the other people of his clan, she would ensure, in exchange for the seeds, they would be well paid.

Piet moved smoothly in again, this time speaking in Afrikaans, he knew Tapu would feel more relaxed with a language he knew and not another language he had had to learn.

"You people, the San people, who have lived in Africa for thousands of years are a tight and close-knit society. You may live here out in the bush in the old home of Mr Blake, but your people are close and connected. You have a way of communicating with each other, unknown to us."

"If this house is sold, where will you go? The company will no longer pay you should this happen.

"To find this property we went to an estate agency in town. They told us many people are now leaving the big cities and looking for a place such as this, they have some people interested in buying it."

Tapu's face fell with this news, but he knew he could always return to his people, hidden in the forests and start another life. He would have no other choice in the matter.

Piet leaned forward, his voice softening. "But see here, Tapu, we are not here to bring you trouble. We need to know what happened to Miss Fleur and Blake Hemmingway and you know the truth.

"Miss Fleur found something which was important, you helped her with her research. Your own people survive with instinct. The rest of the world don't have that instinct. They rely on science."

Piet continued. "My thinking is that Miss Fleur found what she was looking for and you led her to the people who knew something so important it might change the world of medicine. But your people were afraid it would change their lives, but not in a good way. They trusted her and her words and gave her what she was looking for didn't they Tapu?

"This is why she disappeared or was perhaps killed for the knowledge she was about to make known to the world."

Piet rubbed his face. "You know the truth, Tapu. So why don't you tell us what happened to Miss Fleur and Blake Hemmingway. What exactly happened on the Wild Coast all those years ago?"

Chapter Fifty-Five
The Wild Coast
2005

Tapu, as instructed by Mr Blake, had taken Miss Fur to the dark forests where his people lived their secret lives. There the elders had all agreed they would show the doctor where the secret seeds grew, hidden from the world, the seeds she had spent years looking for. They had asked for nothing in return only that she would honour her words to help them secure a future for themselves, if indeed these seeds she had been searching for had any value.

She had given them her word and they believed and trusted her. Puso, the head of the clan, had shown her where the many thousands of seeds were buried, beneath the sacred trees, giving her a few samples of them.

Tapu, Puso and Fleur had made their way back through the forest until they reached Tapu's old car. Puso, and another elder, had asked for a lift, he said they had business to attend to. At the time, Tapu and Miss Fur had no idea what this business was, but willingly gave them a lift to the place they wanted to go.

Having dropped them off some way from the hotel Mr Blake had booked for Miss Fur, they continued to the place called Safe Harbour.

Mr Blake had told him he had a meeting in Port Elizabeth with the important people in his company who were coming from overseas to discuss the future of TLI. He told Tapu he would meet Miss Fur at the hotel, however, should he be delayed, Miss Fur would call him and ask him to collect her, they would return to their house and wait for Mr Blake.

Tapu had driven carefully over the rutted dirt road, aware of the shadowy outline of a vehicle which seemed to stay behind them, not making any attempt to overtake.

When he pulled up outside the rustic hotel the vehicle seemed to carry on its way, then disappeared.

All his instincts had told him this was not a good place for Miss Fur to be. There were no other guests, and the manager was leaving to be with his wife who was about to give birth to twins. The Zulu night guard had not made him feel any more comfortable. He was old and looked as though he would probably sleep through the night and not contribute to any kind of security for Miss Fur. In the morning, he would be gone.

Much troubled he had dropped Miss Fur off and taken the manager to the bus stop. He comforted himself with the fact that Mr Blake would be arriving the next day or so, and if he didn't, he himself would return and collect Miss Fur and go back to their house in the bush.

As he drove away with the manager of the hotel he had checked his mirror, looking to see if the shadowy vehicle he had encountered on his journey here was still behind him. But it wasn't, and he chastised himself for being overprotective of Miss Fur.

But the vehicle had bothered him.

Tapu had returned to Mr Blake's house and waited for further instructions from him.

A month later Tapu went about his housekeeping duties, happy that Mr Blake and Miss Fur had met up; pleased they were together again and probably extended their holiday for a few weeks, maybe not at Safe Harbour, but had gone somewhere else to be alone together. But the doubts began to form. Mr Blake had always, without fail, kept in touch with him, letting him know where he was and when he would return home.

He had heard nothing.

Now worried he had decided to drive back to Safe Harbour. He doubted Mr Blake and Miss Fur would still be there, but perhaps the old Zulu guard might have returned and would be able to help him.

He drove his old car carefully over the neglected pot-holed dirt road. The sky was dark and broody, the clouds bloated indicating a storm was coming. The grey and white waves crashed against the rocks throwing up a curtain of spray like light sweeping rain. The beach was deserted.

Tapu parked the car and looked around, the rustic hotel was as deserted as the beach, there was no sign of any vehicles, no sign of Mr Blake's big Land Rover.

The wind whipped around the small *rondavels* lifting and pulling at the thatched roofs, seagulls wheeled and dipped, calling to each other their raucous cries echoing through the threatening skies.

Tapu went to the *rondavel* the manager had shown Miss Fur. He tried the door, but it was locked. He wiped one of the windows with his sleeve and peered inside.

His breath caught in his throat.

Lying across the unmade bed was Miss Fur's rain jacket; he recognised it immediately. Next to it was her small rucksack, its flap open, as though she might have been packing, or perhaps she hadn't finished unpacking it.

He searched around for a suitable rock which he used to break the lock on the door. Moving cautiously inside he looked around. It was possible he thought, Miss Fur had forgotten her jacket; but her rucksack told another story, as did the pair of flat shoes lying abandoned on the floor.

Where would Miss Fur have gone without her shoes?

If she had gone with Mr Blake she would have taken her things with her, she would have been wearing her shoes.

The icy wind made his eyes water as he looked down at the deserted beach, and he knew.

Miss Fur had gone down to the beach where she would not have needed her shoes.

Going back inside he collected her few belongings and took them to his car. His heart was heavy with fear as he sat and watched the wild sea. Mr Blake would not have left her there alone; therefore, he surmised, he had not joined her. Perhaps he had been delayed with his business in Port Elizabeth, but Tapu knew, if this was the case, he would have phoned him and told him to collect Miss Fur from the hotel. But he hadn't.

A jagged split of lightening lit up the heavy clouds and the rain started to fall heavily, pitting the beach causing spurts of dry sand to rise briefly, wiping away any trace of humanity and leaving nature to return it to its wild and untamed state.

He went down to the sea, loping across the sands as easily as a gazelle, his eyes searching the sand dunes, the beach and the sturdy tufts of grasses growing between the wild, unforgiving sea, and the dunes.

His keen hunter's eyes spotted the pale cream bag, caught by the wild wind, and tangled amongst the hardy grasses. He sank to his knees as he wrestled it away from the elements.

Doctor Fur's leather bag she always carried across her chest.

It was empty.

A single tear rolled down his cheek. The sea had taken her.

He looked up at the majestic fury of nature and accepted it. But he had one burning question.

If she had walked into the sea with perhaps a burden that was too heavy, a past too difficult to confront, why had she not taken the bag with her? Why take out the contents, the sacred seeds, and then walk into the sea without them. Why leave the empty leather bag behind?

Something else had happened here on the beach.

It wasn't the sea who had taken her life.

It was someone else.

Chapter Fifty-Six

Tapu had made his way back to the main road and headed to the nearest town to report Miss Fur missing.

The town was hardly more than a village with its dirt roads, and he soon found the tiny police station with its cracked blue light flickering outside.

Two young police officers, the only members of the force stationed in this remote area, were less than sympathetic, especially when Tapu told them the European doctor had been missing for over a month.

One of the officers duly filled out a missing person report and told Tapu there was nothing they would be able to do. At some point, they told him, they would check the old hotel out, but as it was now closed for several months, according to Tapu, they had little or no hope they would find anything.

Tapu had not mentioned what he had found, he knew the police would not follow up the case of the missing woman. But if he were wrong and they did, he would be a suspect since he had taken her belongings with him.

He had not mentioned Mr Blake either. What could he tell them?

Tapu had driven back to the house feeling helpless. He didn't know what he should do next. Perhaps someone at the clinic where Miss Fur had worked once a month would know something. He would drive to the town the next morning and see if he could learn anything more.

The clinic was quiet when he arrived, there were no queues of patients seeking her help. The young African woman sitting behind her desk looked up and smiled at him with pleasure. She had always looked forward to seeing him when he brought the doctor there once a month.

She glanced over his shoulder. "You have brought the doctor, Tapu," she said hopefully.

His heart sank, she had not been back then. It had been his only hope although he knew it was a foolish one. Miss Fur would have come back to the house if she had planned to go back to the clinic. How would she have got there is this was so?

Despite his despair, Tapu smiled at the young African girl called Beauty, which indeed she was. He had noticed her many times, as she had him. Then he shook his head.

"I am looking for the doctor, Beauty. It is some time now since I have seen her. Did she tell you if she was going anywhere?"

Beauty gave him a dazzling smile. "Oh yes. She told us she was going away for a while with Mr Blake. We have been waiting for her to come back, as her patients have. The doctor is a good person and does not charge for seeing her patients, she is much loved by them, also the white patients who come from the farms, they also are waiting for her return. Many people have asked when she will come back and where she was. Of course, most of them I knew as patients, ex-patients, or people from the village. But one of them I didn't know, a white man, but he could have been friend or relative. I could only tell him she was going on holiday at the Wild Coast. He asked me where she lived but this I could not tell him. Only that it was out in the bush."

Beauty frowned. "She is coming back, yes?"

Tapu shrugged his shoulders helplessly. "So, she told you where she was going then?"

Beauty smiled at the handsome man in front of her. "Yes. The Wild Coast with Mr Blake, but she did not say where. We were happy to hear this, she was liking this Mr Blake very much, as we did here at the clinic. We wanted them to stay together at their house in the bush, this we knew would mean the doctor would come to us every month and help the people here."

Beauty studied the worried man in front of her. "Has something happened, Tapu. You were always with the doctor, bringing her here every month whilst you did the shopping for her in the market. Why do you not know where she is?"

Then her face brightened. "Perhaps the doctor and Mr Blake went back to their home across the sea, and this is why they are away for so long?"

Tapu shook his head. "Mr Blake would have told me if this was so. But he told me nothing if this was his plan with the doctor. I have heard nothing from either of them for some time now. I'm worried about them."

Beauty thought for a moment. "I am thinking, Tapu, if anything had happened to them, the company Mr Blake worked for would surely have told you if something had delayed Mr Blake and the doctor if she was with him. You are worrying too much; they will return when they are ready. Maybe they have a big family across the sea, and it has taken a lot of time to see them all."

She looked at her watch. "It's time to close the clinic now. Let me walk with you, perhaps have something to eat. We can talk more about this situation. It is good to talk to someone when you have worries like this."

After his conversation with Beauty, Tapu was beginning to feel more hopeful.

He returned to the house and busied himself with cleaning and polishing the furniture. Carefully he wiped the dust from the desk in Mr Blake's study. Satisfied with all his hard work he turned to the telephone; this Miss Fur was most fussy about. It had to be wiped down with disinfectant because it could hold many germs.

He frowned and looked around the study, then back at the table where the telephone always sat with its pen and paper next to it for messages.

Gingerly he held the phone to his ear. There was no sound coming from it. A smile erupted over his face. This is why he had heard nothing from Mr Blake. The phone was broken!

It was possible he had met Miss Fur at the hotel, and then they had made plans to travel to another place to sell their seeds. Mr Blake was maybe thinking the seeds would be safer with him, there were many places in his car where he could have hidden them for safety, safer than in her small bag which she must have thrown away.

Feeling more cheerful he continued with his dusting and cleaning, opening the drawers to the desk to make sure all was tidy and free of dust. He hesitated as he came to the last drawer where Mr Blake kept his private papers; he knew there were things there he should not touch. But the wind had been high for the past few days leaving a layer of dust over everything, perhaps it would be alright to dust down this drawer.

He pulled it open reverently, wiping the dust with a damp cloth, which had seeped in everywhere; and that's where he found the two passports. One for Mr Blake and the other for Miss Fur.

To leave the country he knew these two documents would have been required. Slowly he closed the drawer.

They had not left the country then.

The next morning, he saw the familiar cloud of dust in the distance on the road leading to the house. His heart leapt with joy.

They were back. All the thoughts of what might have happened to both of them dissipated, his maudlin thoughts fled his mind. Here they were, as promised.

He rushed out to greet them already planning another trip to town to shop for food and supplies for their dinner and seeing Beauty, telling her the good news. Perhaps Miss Fur had been so happy to see Mr Blake she had forgotten her shoes and other things.

With a wide smile on his face, he waited for the familiar vehicle to stop, as he waited in the place under the tree where Mr Blake always parked.

His smile faded rapidly as a young man alighted from the vehicle.

"Are you Tapu?"

He frowned, confused. "I am Tapu. But where is Mr Blake. This is his Land Rover, yes?"

The young man took off his cap and knocked it against his leg, small clouds of dust rose from it. He removed his sunglasses and wiped the rest of the dust from his face, then ran his fingers through his hair.

"I'm from the company TLI. My name's Herman, I'm based in Port Elizabeth. This is a company vehicle, they are all the same to look at, but this one is mine, not Mr Hemmingway's."

Herman leaned inside the vehicle and retrieved a bottle of water from which he drank greedily. "Phew, that was a hot and dusty drive."

He stepped onto the *stoep* and sat down heavily on one of the chairs, looking around him at the company house and the grounds. He pulled a notepad from out of his pocket and looked at it, making a few notes without saying anything. Then he looked up at Tapu.

"I want you to show me around the house and the property. I need to make an inventory of the contents."

Tapu looked confused. "What is this inventory word, I do not know it Mr Herman."

Herman sighed. "I need to go from room to room and see what's in it. I need to count the knives and forks, the plates, the kitchen equipment, and anything else in the house, including the guest house and your own quarters."

Tapu looked even more confused. "But why must this be done Mr Herman. Mr Blake has never asked for this?"

"Because Tapu, the company is selling this house. We don't need it now Mr Hemmingway is no longer with us. The company is closing everything down, they no longer have any business in the country. In fact, they are closing all their offices around the world. Now let's get started, shall we?"

"Where is Mr Blake? What is it you are meaning when you say he is no longer with us?"

Herman looked irritated. "Look, I'm only employed by the company, not for much longer though. I joined them a year ago, hoping to work myself up to a good position with them, but that's not going to happen now. They've sent me here to do the inventory before they sell the place."

Tapu knew he could not accept this explanation. Could not be pushed aside like this after all the years he had worked for Mr Blake and looked after his house.

"Where is Mr Blake, Mr Herman?"

Herman shrugged. "I didn't know Mr Hemmingway. I have no idea where he is. He's no longer working for TLI. It's possible he resigned, or maybe the company no longer needed his services as they were closing the company down.

He stood up. "Now, show me around the place and let me get on with the job, will you?"

"Yes, Mr Herman, this I will do, but what will become of me?"

Herman shrugged with indifference. "Not my problem, Tapu. I know the company want you to stay on until the place is sold. Can't leave it standing empty. You'll need to show the estate agents around the place. They'll pay you a monthly retainer until the sale goes through."

Herman diligently went through each room, making a list of contents in his notepad. He came to a room which had a heavy padlock on it.

"We need to open this door, Tapu. I need to make a list of what's inside. Where's the key to the lock?"

Tapu was now totally unsettled, unsure of what to say. "This is the room of the doctor who worked here, a good friend of Mr Blake's. She was studying the ways of our people, learning about plants and other traditional medicines. She always kept this door locked, as you can see."

Herman looked highly irritated. "Well, it must be opened. I need to see what's inside so I can put it in the inventory. Have you got the key?"

Tapu hung his head. Doctor Fur kept all her secrets and research inside the room which was her laboratory. Like so many Africans who worked in a house he knew exactly where the duplicate key was, but he had never used it, respecting her privacy.

"I will get it for you, Mr Herman," he muttered.

He retrieved the key from his own quarters and reluctantly returned to the house. He unlocked the padlock and threw the door open.

Herman's mouth dropped open at the sight of all the bottles lined up on several shelves, the books lining another four shelves. The huge pile of files. On the desk was an impressive and obviously expensive microscope.

"*Shoo*, where the hell do I start with all this lot?"

Tapu, his eyes hostile, looked at him. "You start nowhere Mr Herman. This is the private property of the doctor; it is not part of the contents of the house." Firmly he pulled the door closed and carefully locked it, putting the key in his pocket. "I will remove the doctor's property when the house is sold."

Having completed his task, Herman closed his notebook and returned to the Land Rover. He hauled out a For Sale sign and wrestled it into the ground at the front of the property. Then without thanking Tapu he drove off.

Tapu watched the cloud of dust disperse behind Herman's vehicle before wrenching the For Sale sign out of the ground and hiding it behind a bush, facedown.

Chapter Fifty-Seven

Jack made notes as Tapu told his story, his search for the doctor and what he thought might have happened to her.

Piet was listening carefully. "Do you still have the doctor's things you found in the hotel chalet?"

"Yes. Do you wish to see them, *sah*? I have them locked in her private room."

Piet stood up. "Yes, that might help us. Maybe we could see her private room – would that be alright?"

Tapu shrugged and searched his pockets for the key to the padlock. "Follow me please."

Jack whistled, suitably impressed with Fleur's laboratory and her years of work in the piles of files, the dozens of glass jars with their specimens and the books lining the shelves. The microscope was state of the art and must have cost a ton of money. No way would Fleur simply have walked away from all her work.

Piet was going methodically through the contents of the rucksack finding little of interest. A change of underwear, some skin care products, sunscreen and not much else. Her shoes were lined up neatly next to her desk as if expecting their owner to slip back into them. Her rain jacket was draped over the back of her chair.

Jack discreetly took some pics; they would add to his story of Doctor Fleur Palmere.

Piet finished rummaging around in the rucksack and put it back on the chair. Nothing of interest to help them with their case.

Tapu locked the door after them and joined them out on the *stoep*.

"You would like something to drink perhaps?"

"Do you have anything cold in the fridge Tapu?"

"I have some beer. May I get this for you?"

"That would be good, thank you. Get one for yourself, then we can continue our conversation."

"I do not drink, *sah*, but I will get the beer for you." He brought it through to the *stoep*.

Piet took a sip out of the bottle. "So, Tapu, when you went to report the doctor missing to the police, why didn't you give them the personal affects you found in her room. They might have been encouraged to investigate further?"

"This is true, *sah*, but I was afraid they would think I had killed her and arrest me if I showed them what I had found."

Piet nodded. "Did you kill her Tapu?" he said softly.

Tapu looked shocked. "No! I did not kill her; we had worked together for many years. I liked her very much. Why would I hurt her?"

Jack moved smoothly back into the conversation. "Tell me something Tapu, what do you think happened to the doctor?"

"I am thinking the sea took her. I have no other answer."

Jack made another note, then looked up at the frightened man sitting with them. "You know when this house is sold, you'll have to find somewhere else to live. You won't have a home; you said you would have to go back to your people in the forest."

"I do not know Mr Yak. I myself could not live in a town with much noise and many people and all the lights at night. I come from the desert, from the forests, this is where I will go and live."

Piet drummed his fingers on the side of his chair, then leaned forward. "Look at me Tapu," he said softly. "This is what I am thinking. You knew what the doctor was looking for and where it could be located. You took her there. Perhaps you showed her where whatever she was looking for could be found? Also, there are no shops here, so how do you get your supplies?"

Tapu pulled at a loose piece of cane on his chair. "Mr Blake gave me his old car many years ago when I came to work for him. This I use when I need to. Mr Blake knew Miss Fur would need a car to continue her research, so this I would use when we worked together."

Piet seemed to accept this. "Alright. But I have another question. "You worked with the doctor for many years, helping her with her research, but all the time you knew what she was looking for. You could have shown her years ago, but you didn't did you? I'm thinking it was something hidden deep in the forest somewhere – where your people are living.

"Whatever secret plants or herbs she was looking for was only known to your people so therefore you would have had to have their permission to show her. I'm right, am I not?"

Like so many Africans, Piet knew they sometimes only told you what you wanted to hear. But he knew, from his years with the police, Tapu was holding back on something, but he was gradually breaking him down.

Piet continued. "You took her into the forest and showed her what she and her mother had been searching for. As a scientist she would have wanted to take some of these samples with her to study, so you and your people gave her some. How long ago was that Tapu?"

Tapu shook his head. "This I cannot remember, *sah.*"

Piet looked down at his own notes. "Well, let me help you out with your memory here. It was in August, thirteen years ago. I have this information from the missing person document you lodged with the police.

"But let's go back a few days from that time. The doctor then went to meet Mr Blake, as planned, taking her samples with her. However, there were no samples in her rucksack, so I'm thinking they were so important to her she carried them with her, and didn't leave them at the hotel when she went for a walk, barefoot, along the beach, as you have told us. If she was carrying them with her then she must have had some sort of bag, perhaps one she wore across her body to keep them safe."

Tapu nodded looking wretched. "Miss Fur always carried a bag across her chest. This is where she put the sacred seeds I found for her."

Piet continued. "So, it is highly unlikely she walked into the sea with her precious seeds, is it?"

Piet's full attention was now on Tapu. "You told us she was meeting Blake. She would have been excited at finding the seeds, having some with her to show him. Eager to see him and share her news. Blake knew she was going into the forest with you, to meet your people and see the seeds for herself before they planned to meet at the hotel."

He paused. "They lived together, she would have discussed with him what she was looking for, how important it was if she were right. What a big difference it would make to people who suffered from some disease, and the massive amount of money her research would generate. She would not have shared this information with anyone else, would she?

"She kept all her research locked away in the room you have shown us, which tells me how important her work was and how she trusted nobody. But she did trust Blake and she trusted you."

Jack's foot began to jiggle. He stilled it with his hand. "What are you saying here Piet?"

Not taking his eyes of Tapu, Piet continued. "What I'm saying here, my friend, is that Blake *did* come to the hotel as he had promised.

"It was Blake who killed Fleur."

Chapter Fifty-Eight

Piet and Jack drove back into the dusty town an hour from Blake's old home. There was only one modest guest house which clearly catered to businessmen and not tourists. To say it was basic was an understatement. But it was clean and empty of any other guests. They checked in, had a hot shower, then regrouped under a tree in the garden.

"Nice work Piet, I'm impressed with your analysis," Jack said as he sipped his beer, "how did you work it all out. How do you know you're right?"

Piet grinned at him. "I'm always right, my friend. Like the San people I follow my instincts. They never let me down. I know my people in this country, I know how they think.

"Where you come from, people live next door to each other for years and only nod at each other, nobody really knows anyone. Oh, okay, I know the posh *okes* all know each other, went to the same schools as their parents, probably belong to a *larney* private club, but even then, they only show the best of themselves socially, nobody really knows how they feel deep inside, they don't even know themselves, they play the part until they become the part, and can't remember who they were in the first place."

Jack had fired up his laptop and was now busy downloading the pics he had taken of Blake's house and Fleur's laboratory.

"Anyways, my friend, I think Blake was the killer. Makes sense to me. He meets Fleur, finds her on the beach, kills her and takes the seeds. He knew what they were worth. Probably had a pharmaceutical company lined up to sell them to. Then he takes off, never to be seen again either by his company or poor old Tapu."

He removed a piece of Hope's fur off his shirt. "Blake maybe disappeared across one of our borders here, Swaziland, Botswana, Zimbabwe, Zambia, and jetted off to the Bahamas where a lot of your shifty countrymen seem to find their safe haven. Spain is also a popular destination for dodgy people, Dubai is becoming popular as well, who knows, we'll probably never find him again."

Jack looked up from his laptop and narrowed his eyes. "But surely after all this time, if Fleur had found some miraculous cure for some disease which would change the world, we would have heard about it?"

Piet picked at the peeling paint on his chair. "*Nah*, some big pharma company, or whoever Blake sold the seeds to, would have replicated whatever it was, and sold it as a prescription drug and disguised what it was used for as a traditional medicine in its true, and original, form. More money in that, my friend. Big bad greedy world out there."

Jack watched with impatience as his pics downloaded onto his laptop. The internet signal was weak. "Thing is, mate, those original seeds are still where they were found. Perhaps we might be able to follow this story again, find those seeds and make sure they achieve what the late doctor had always wanted. After all, whoever Blake sold his handful to probably have no idea of the bounty awaiting in the dark forests of the Eastern Cape. I think it's still a story worth chasing.

"Oh, and another thing. If Blake left his Land Rover in Port Elizabeth, which he obviously did according to the young man who came to do the inventory, how did he get to the hotel to meet, and according to you, murder Fleur?"

Piet took a handful of what tasted like very old stale peanuts from the bowl in front of him, he picked out two ants and squashed them.

"Easy, my friend. Probably bought some old beat-up car from a dodgy dealer, paid in cash, no paperwork required, no trail to follow, then went across the border never to be seen again."

A slender woman brought out two menus for them to peruse, her name tag identified her as Goodness. She had green slanted eyes, high cheekbones, her skin the colour of chocolate. A San person.

Jack took the menu and smiled at her. "Hello Goodness. What's on the menu tonight, what do you recommend?"

"Unfortunately, sir, the chef is not here now. But we have toasted sandwiches."

Piet groaned. He wanted steak with chips. "Anything else on offer here?"

Goodness shook her head with regret. "No, only sandwiches."

Jack put the now redundant menu down and looked at her. "My name is Jack; I write stories for my newspaper in London. Have you lived here long, Goodness?"

She sighed. "Yes, all my life, twenty-five years of it. My mother brought me here when she left her family."

Jack could smell a connecting story. "Why did she do that then, it must have been a hard decision to make."

Goodness shook her head. "No. It was the only one to make. That was the way of our people, Mr Yak. The men stayed where they were, and the women, with their children, came here to earn the money. I saw my father maybe three times a year when he came from our family in the forest."

Jack and Piet exchanged glances.

Jack smiled at her. You know, I think we will have the toasted sandwiches. I'm interested to know about your family, perhaps you'll be able to find some time to tell us about the history of this place."

Goodness returned with their meal. They both looked with dismay at the soggy toasted sandwiches and the meagre portion of limp crisps which accompanied the dish. A single leaf of lettuce tried to enhance the appearance of the dish but failed dismally.

Jack attempted a smile, Piet looked thoroughly miserable as he contemplated his paltry dinner. "Thank you, Goodness."

He reached for one of the limp toasted sandwiches. "Would it be possible to show us where your people live? As I said I write for an English newspaper. They pay local people who will help us with a story."

Goodness looked at him and shook her head. "There is nobody there anymore. The Government found where they were living and moved them on."

Jack continued. "Well, it would still be interesting to see the place. Can you take us there?"

Goodness frowned. "Why would you want to see an empty place Mr Yak? As I told you there is nobody there anymore."

Jack was not going to give up and Goodness, he knew, could smell money. "I'd like to take some pics of an original San village."

He reached for his wallet and quickly peeled off several R100 notes. How would you like to help us?"

Goodness eyed the money hungrily. "I have my day off tomorrow. I could take you there, but, as I have told you Mr Yak, there is nothing there anymore. Will you still give me the money although there will be nothing to see?" She said anxiously.

The next morning the three of them set off to see what remained of the place they hoped had once been the home to a tightly knit community and where Tapu had brought Fleur, and where she had been given the seeds from the sacred trees.

Piet parked at the base of a thick forest, ensuring no passer-by would see the vehicle.

Goodness beckoned for them to follow her as she made her way into the dark shadowed trees. It was steep and heavy going, with very little light showing them the way, but she knew the way.

They came to a clearing and Goodness stopped. "This is where my people lived. As you can see there is nothing here except for the old brick fire circle, where the elders would sit and talk, and the women cooked their meat in the evenings.

"The government, when they moved my people on, destroyed all the huts so they would not be able to return."

Jack moved around taking his pics of not much. He could see Piet was as disappointed as he was at the nothingness of the place; no trace of anyone who had ever lived there, only the blackened bricks of the derelict fire circle.

Piet tapped him on the shoulder. "*Ag*, Jack there's nothing here. If the seeds are somewhere hereabouts then it is doubtful Goodness would know what they were or where they were. The people here had no idea of the value of the seeds. It would have been normal for them not to discuss them. They were just there. Harvested like all the other plants and herbs, carrots, beans, and other vegetables, and such like. Tapu *did* know the value of them, knew what Fleur was looking for – and led her here."

Jack looked around the deserted place. Took a few more shots and put his phone back in his pocket.

Jack nodded in agreement. "You're right, but it does add to the story, seeing the place where presumably Tapu brought Fleur to meet his people. Easier for us to visualise what she saw of them and how they lived."

Piet looked at him and smiled. "However, my friend, Tapu is still not telling us the truth, is he?"

Jack looked down at his notes. "He's told us as much as he wanted to, but, I agree, he's still holding back."

Piet wiped his perspiring forehead with his sleeve. "Tapu said when the house is sold, he will move back to the forest where his people live. He might find it a bit lonely, hey, because nobody lives here anymore."

He pushed aside a low hanging branch, as they made their way back to the vehicle. "No point in trying to get more out of him, just now. He's not going to tell us anything. He may well have taken his battered old car and disappeared for a while, frightened we might come back with more questions.

"But you and I, my friend, are going to the beach for the day because that's where all this happened. We're going to the Wild Coast. Might find nothing after all this time, but who knows.

"My mates in the pub remember it as a basic rustic hotel but thought it might have been sold by now – so let's check it out."

Chapter Fifty-Nine

Piet drove down the dry pot-holed road leading to what had been called Safe Harbour. The boom of the sea assailed their ears, through the windows of the vehicle, as Piet came to a stop at what looked like a thriving little community.

Tapu had told them there were only a few simple *rondavels* there but now there were shacks, children running all over the place playing in the dust and sand, smoke rising from fires. Chickens, donkeys, scrawny dogs with their dull fur and bony ribs jutting out, goats, sheep, and a few thin cattle wandered around what had once been the hotel's grounds.

Washing, snapping, and pulled taut by the strong winds, was strung between the shacks, old plastic bags clung to bushes, their logos long gone, and plastic bottles strewn everywhere.

Piet sighed. "Looks like the people wanted their land back and the government gave it to them. The fishing along this coast is good if you don't venture into the sea, but there are plenty of rocky outcrops where fishing would be safe. So, no hotel but we have a fishing village now instead.

"The people should be friendly here, so let me do the talking Jack. Speak to them in Afrikaans, as you can see, they are a coloured community, it will be their language. I'll use our usual trusty story of you wanting to write about a typical fishing village on the Wild Coast.

"Keep your wallet handy, it appears nothing is for free in this country anymore, unless the government give you a big chunk of land for nothing, not going to give anything for free to the likes of us, that's for sure."

Young children gathered around the car, smiling, and calling to them. Jack leaned forward and opened the glove compartment where he always kept a big bag of sweets for moments such as this. The children scrambled in the dust grabbing at them before wandering off, their cheeks bulging.

An elderly man, leaning on a stout stick, approached the vehicle.

"You are looking for something. This is no longer a hotel if you are tourists. It belongs to my people now as you can see."

Piet greeted him in his own language. "My friend would like to take a few pictures of your community and the area around it. If you will allow it. He will pay for these pictures."

Jack was already pulling out his wallet and peeling off some notes.

The old man dipped his head with gratitude and reached for the money. "This will be in order. Your friend may walk around to find what he is seeking. But you are a cop. It is better you stay here in the car; my people will be afraid of you."

Piet watched Jack making his way through the chaotic village with its warren of shacks and laundry. He looked down at the beach; a lone fisherman was perched on a rock waiting to catch fish for his family's dinner. Otherwise, the beach was deserted in all its wildness.

He tried to imagine what had happened here, tried to imagine Fleur walking alone along the beach. He was convinced she had not walked into the daunting, roiling mighty sea. Even he would not have taken a chance like that, and he was well used to dangerous situations.

It wasn't the sea who had taken her. It was someone else.

He had put his money on Blake Hemmingway.

Jack wandered through the community, taking random shots but all the while looking for anything of interest, the children followed him like the Pied Piper.

The old hotel chalets had disintegrated leaving only traces of what they may have looked like. Most had been dismantled, their bricks and thatch used to build small dwellings for the new inhabitants.

Even though he now lived in a different country, Jack's instincts as a journalist were still honed to perfection. His ability to dig deep for a story had never left him, and even though he was mired in a different society with its own nuances, languages, and cultures, he was steadily building his network, with Piet's help. He didn't speak any of the local languages, but he was learning the ways of these people, how they thought, how they felt, their expressions, and their body language.

Now, here, on the Wild Coast, he knew his instincts would not let him down. There was an intriguing story here, and he was going after it with all his unique skills which had put him at the top of his game as a top journalist in the UK.

One boy, probably around twelve, tugged at his sleeve. "You want to buy car? Very old now. It is over there where the bushes are. I will take you."

Jack once more felt the sizzle go down his spine. An old car?

A goat was standing where there should have been a back seat, reaching up on its hind legs to nibble on a bush. It was hard to identify the make of the car or what colour it might have been; the elements had seen to that. The bodywork was pitted with rust, the tyres gone, and anything else which could be removed and used for another purpose, including the number plates.

Jack laughed as he took pics of the wreck of a car. "Have you got keys for this car, if you want me to buy it?"

The boy looked puzzled, then giggled. "This car is not for driving, mister. It is for living in for the goats and dogs."

"Has it been here a long time?"

The boy nodded. "It was here when the government let us come and live here. Already then it was old. The government said we could keep it. The tyres we use for swinging on, the seats are for sitting on in the Chief's house. We play in it sometimes if the old goats are not there. They can hurt with their heads if they wish to be alone, chasing us away with their horns."

Jack ruffled the boy's tight curly hair. "I think this car is not for me. I have a fine one of my own. But thank you for showing it to me."

Jack tapped on the window of the Land Rover and climbed into the passenger seat. "I might have found the car that brought Blake Hemmingway here. However, the state of it leads me to believe it never left what used to be the hotel here."

Piet considered this. "It's possible he dumped the car after killing Fleur. No trace for anyone to follow."

Jack rubbed his eyes and put his sunglasses on. "Then how did he get to where he was planning to go if you're right. This place is very remote?"

Piet grinned. "Uber, of course, or any other driver or taxi service. Don't forget Blake Hemmingway was a planner, a strategist, he would have made meticulous plans. Knew how things worked out in the bush.

"But one thing I'm sure of. He's out there somewhere and we're going to find him. Breathing or not."

Once more they made their way back to the guest house. After a hot shower they re-grouped on the *stoep* relishing their first cold beer of the day.

Jack looked up at the glorious canopy of stars. "Thing is, mate, suppose it had been someone else who was after the seeds and not Blake. Have you factored that in because I have. It could have been someone who followed Tapu and Fleur to the hotel in a beat-up old car and knocked her off?"

Piet nodded, tracing his finger through the condensation of his bottle of beer. "Yes, of course, I factored that in. You're thinking of the Kenyan doctor, Mwanga. If he knew what Fleur was working on before she abruptly left the company and he took over her position, he wouldn't have waited years to come and find her would he?

"Anyways, I checked with Bertie on that one, he never entered the country, never came to South Africa."

Jack frowned. "Okay, but Fleur maybe had a team of scientists working for her right? Maybe someone else knew what she was working on and shared the information with Doctor Mwanga, or maybe kept it to himself, or herself, then sold it out to the highest bidder."

Piet shook his head. "*Nah*, if that were the case why wait decades to follow the trail of Fleur, and where would they have started to look if she were hidden in the bush, out of the public eye in the vast province of the Eastern Cape. She herself didn't know where these seeds could be found when she left the company."

Piet swung the car to the right, avoiding a large pothole. "But see here, my friend, Fleur was secretive, fiercely protective of what she eventually found. She would not have shared that information with anyone she didn't trust. Blake she must have confided in. Tapu is the key to all of this, she trusted him, and he trusted her. We need to talk to him again or wait for him to come to us. I can guarantee he won't be at Blake's old house; he would have taken off somewhere."

Piet took a sip of his beer. "I don't think he'd be running from us. He's gone to meet someone and I'm wondering who that someone might be."

Jack's phone vibrated on the table and his heart sank. Harry.

"Well, my boy, what have you got for me? Your columns are still popular, but where are we with the disappearing doctor?"

"Piet and I, Harry, are sitting in the middle of a town which has more dust than people. We're making progress, but it's slow I must admit. We might be here for another week or so. But we have a few leads to follow, good ones. See here, Harry, this is not London where I had all my contacts. This is the middle of the bush, the internet connection is spotty, surrounded by people who speak a different language, people with different cultures. It's not easy to get them to talk. But we're getting there."

Harry snorted. "Getting where? I want that story, Jack. Staying in fancy hotels and watching the sunsets and animals, eats into the budget I have for you."

Jack sighed heavily. "Hardly that, Harry, we're in a basic hotel, not a tourist in sight, or animals come to that, in the middle of the bloody bush. It's complicated. But Piet knows these people and he's working through the story. You can't intimidate them. You can't pay them big bucks to tell all. They do it in their own time, at their own pace, according to their culture."

Harry paused as an ambulance roared past with all its wailing sirens going, police cars following in its wake. Jack heard him sigh with frustration.

"I wouldn't mind sitting in a dust filled town in the middle of the African bush, right now, with a sundowner to hand," he said sounding grumpy. "Been some kind of incident here, probably back up the traffic and I'll miss my train. Never mind, I'll spend the night at my club, meet up with some old school chums and have a glass or two of decent red before dinner. Cheerio."

Chapter Sixty

Back at the guest house, Piet and Jack re-grouped in the empty lounge. Both carrying their laptops.

Jack downloaded the pics of the battered old car. Piet rubbed his face. "Even Bertie and his robots won't be able to work out who owned this car and where it came from, or how long it's been sitting there rusting away.

"But see here Jack, let's leave the car for the moment. Whilst you were wandering through the fishing village, I went through the images you forwarded to me. Enlarged them as best I could before they distorted."

He peered at his computer screen. "The images you took of Fleur's laboratory. Well, next to the microscope there was what looked like a business card, or a card of some sort. I couldn't work out the details no matter how hard I tried to enhance it. But Bertie with his tech stuff will be able to figure it out for us. It looks like the name might have been someone called George, but I couldn't pick up his surname or his contact details. Anyways, I sent it through to Bertie, he'll come back to me."

Jack took a sip of his beer. "Anything else you spotted?"

Piet tried not to look smug. "Yes. The images you took of the deserted place where Tapu's tribe lived?"

Piet scrolled through them. "Although the place looked deserted, I spotted some sort of structure set way back away from where the people had lived, well hidden. It was a different shape, long and flat, with a dark green roof, melting into the forest. It hadn't been destroyed by the authorities who had moved the people on. Or perhaps it had been built afterwards, that's the only possibility.

"I enhanced it as best I could. Look at this."

Screwing up his eyes, Jack peered at the screen of the laptop. "Need to borrow my glasses, Jack?"

"No thanks. Probably covered in dog hairs and all smeared with the debris of lamb chop grease and *boerewors* because you never clean them."

Piet shrugged. "Whatever. See here, my friend, in that well-hidden structure set back deep in the forest, there is a shape in one of the windows. Not sure what it is, or what it might be, but something."

"Someone who was watching us."

Jack ran his fingers through his hair. Yes, he too could see something, some kind of shadow or shape. But if it were human, how could they survive without food when the village was dismantled, why, if it *was* human, had this villager stayed behind?

Jack was famous for following cold cases, he knew London and the rest of the country like the back of his hand. Knew who would give him information if he needed it, knew how the criminals' minds worked, how to track them down.

But here in South Africa, although with Piet's help, he was already building a network, he was out of his depth. He didn't speak any of the languages of the local people, didn't know the terrain and here he was in the middle of the Eastern Cape having picked his way through a dense forest following the home of a cluster of San people, who no longer lived there, who he knew little about, and didn't understand their ways. How they communicated with each other, their secret lives, or how they thought.

They were a nomadic people, non-political, only wanting to continue with their simple lives like generations before them, going back hundreds of years, if not thousands. The world was changing but they had resisted it.

Jack, when he was doing his research on these people was horrified to read that at some point the bushmen, as they were called then, were hunted down like other wild animals, considered the same.

A triumphant trophy if killed by a hunter of exotic breeds.

"So, what next Piet? Where do we go from here?"

"To the nearest steak house. I need meat."

Chapter Sixty-One

Piet scooped up the juices from his steak, with a piece of crispy roll, and savoured the last of an excellent meal. Then sighed and sat back in his chair.

"You can keep your fancy restaurants in Cape Town and Jo'burg who advertise the best steaks in town, along with the fancy shaped plates and squiggles of the Lord knows what. The waiters with their long aprons and phony accents assuring you, '*you will never taste a steak like this anywhere else in the country*' and trust me they're right on that one. Meat tastes as though it's been in the freezer for years. Not even looking embarrassed as they sweepingly present you with your bill encased in an expensive leather folder with the logo proudly displayed on the front. Like you should be grateful for even being allowed into their precious restaurant.

"The host digs deep into his pockets as he prepares to pay, sweat breaking out on his brow at the mind-buggery price of a pathetic piece of meat we could have out in the bush or in a small *dorpie* for quarter of the price, and ten times better with a mound of fried onions and chips and a fat tip not expected."

He shook his head. "*Ag,* Jack the smell of steaks as you go into a steak house, the smiling waiters, the chefs yelling and laughing over the red-hot coals of the grills, kids running around, no frozen-faced waiters, only happy staff pleased to see you."

Jack smiled. He would never be able to change Piet and his views on the world, but he was right. Businesspeople, and investors, were trying to emanate their final acceptance on the world stage, building *faux* French Chateaus and Tuscan villas, their pseudo-Caribbean places, their fancy restaurants with French names; there was something missing.

The absolute essence of who South Africans were.

Jack and Piet made their way back to the deserted guest house and settled down on the *stoep* to enjoy a nightcap.

Piet eased off his safari boots and placed his cap, laptop, and phone on the table. The townsfolk had retired to bed for the night and the place was silent, broken occasionally by the bark of a dog, followed by another one in the distance.

His phone vibrated on the table, he leaned forward and put it on speaker.

"What have you got for me Bertie?"

"Nothing much I'm afraid. Neither Palmere or Hemmingway ever left this country, and I have no record of either of them dying here.

"The company called TLI, the one Hemmingway worked for, dismantled all its companies around the world, sold off all their properties and assets, and closed. They then moved into the world of information technology, less risk, didn't have to deal with warring tribes and unpredictable governments around Africa, and elsewhere, who promised them everything and gave them *fok* all back after they invested heavily in them."

Piet picked at a piece of skin on his fingernail. "Okay. But here in South Africa to whom did they sell their assets?"

Bertie took another long suck on his cigarette. "The company was registered as a Trust. No trace of who they sold what to whom.

"However, I did manage to enlarge, quite considerably, the shots you sent through. The structure in the forest doesn't look as though it's been there for decades. It's basic but looks functional. The image you captured is a person, but difficult to identify whether a male or a female, African or otherwise, only a shadow."

Piet and Jack glanced at each other.

"The other shot of the card next to the microscope? Well, I captured all the information for you. His name is George Mason. He's probably one of the toughest and most well-known attorneys in the country. No one ever wants to come up against him in a court here. There are no contact details on the card, but it should be easy enough to find him, you'll probably have to trawl your way through dozens of secretaries, para legals, a pack of killer Alsatians, and God knows what else, to even be able to talk to him. Even your chum Jack, with his impeccable credentials and fancy accent, wouldn't be able to penetrate the wall around that man."

They could hear him tapping away on his computer. "But if Palmere managed to penetrate the wall around George Mason, then she must have had something of great importance to earn an audience with him, either in person or over the phone."

He was still tapping on his keyboard. "His fees to handle a case would make your eyes bleed, hey. But, according to her solicitor friend in London she only ever made one transfer from her account to, as we now know, Blake Hemmingway.

'So, it beggars the question that if she did contact George, he would have sent her a whacking great bill before he put the phone down on her, if this was the case. But worth following up by your mate Jack.

He has a better chance of trying to get through to him with his posh *bledddy* accent and being a top journalist from a well-respected UK newspaper. Our Mr George Mason will set his dogs on him to check out if he's legit. Problem is Mason never gives interviews and dislikes the media, so Jack will have to be a bit devious to get around that, something I'm sure he can do, him being a journalist and all.

"What's more, my friend, George Mason was the attorney representing TLI. That's it. Over and out."

Jack grinned at Piet. "Trust me I'll be able to get in touch with George Mason, not sure Harry will approve of the legal fees, but we've come this far so we're not giving up. What thoughts do you have, mate?"

Piet thought for a moment. "We're going to stay here. Each day we'll go out to the house where Blake Hemmingway and Fleur Palmere lived and wait to see what happens. At some point Tapu will return to wherever he has gone. I'm thinking it's the place in the forest with the flat green roof. He won't expect to see us here waiting for him."

Jack looked at him with dismay. "You want us to sit in an abandoned house, day after day, in the hope Tapu will come back?"

Piet gazed over the silent streets of the town... "It's not an abandoned house, Jack. Tapu lives there and I see signs he doesn't live there alone. An empty house has a certain feel. The house doesn't have it. The kitchen has been used, the main bedroom has been used, it doesn't feel like an abandoned place with a caretaker, it feels like a place where people live. Also, there are two different tyre tracks present at the entrance leading to the house, one set heavier than the others. In the living area some furniture has been moved around. There are indentations in the carpet where a chair or two, a small table and other things once stood. They have been moved.

"Tapu offered us a beer, yes?"

Jack nodded.

"Why would he have cold beer in the fridge. Certainly not for himself because he told us he didn't drink?"

Jack stroked his chin. 'Surely you're not suggesting what I think you're suggesting?"

Piet grimaced. "We shall see, my friend, we shall see.

"I suggest you don't contact the lawyer, or barrister, or whatever, George Mason. He will tell you nothing. Waste of money.

"We'll work it all out for ourselves."

For the third day in a row, Jack and Piet spent the day sitting on the *stoep* of Blake Hemmingway's old house.

Then, in the distance they saw the dust cloud which heralded an oncoming vehicle. It pulled up and parked under a tree at the side of the house.

Tapu's ancient old car.

"That," Piet said softly, "belongs to the one set of tyre tracks."

Unaware of the two men sitting in the shadows of the *stoep,* Tapu made his way to the back door and let himself into the kitchen where he began to unpack the groceries he had bought in town.

He heard a knock on the front door. He froze. He hadn't noticed any vehicle parked outside, but then he hadn't been looking for one or expecting any visitor. Perhaps someone had arrived whilst he was unpacking the shopping.

His heart sank when he saw the two men, Mr Joubert and Mr Yak standing there.

"Yes?" he stammered. "You are wanting something more from me?"

Piet took a long hard look at him. "Yes, Tapu. I want the truth. Thirteen years is a long time to hide a secret. You have returned with a boot-load of shopping. We watched you carrying the bags to the kitchen. Way too much food for one person. You don't live here alone that's obvious. So, who were you shopping for? Expecting visitors perhaps? Who owns the other vehicle that parks here?"

Tapu took a deep breath. It *had* been a long thirteen years, and he knew the time was coming when the truth must be told. This Mr Joubert was clever, and he was not going to give up until he found the answers he was looking for. He was already working out what might have happened.

Tapu had played the part asked of him, but now he was tired of the heavy load he had had to carry alone.

He looked at the stony face of the cop. "I am thinking you should come inside. I will tell you what happened and why things are the way they are now. I did nothing wrong, *sah*, I only tried to keep Miss Fur safe from many bad things."

Piet smiled at him. "Then you have nothing to fear, Tapu. I will give you my word on this and so will Mr Yak.

"So, bring us another two beers, as you don't drink, there should be some in the fridge, not so?"

Tapu brought the beers through, his face expressionless.

Piet took a sip and smiled encouragingly at Tapu. "Now, tell us what happened and how."

Chapter Sixty-Two
Tapu
Ten years earlier.

Tapu hunkered down on the steps of Blake's house, he rolled one of his thin cigarettes and blew the grey smoke up into the passive night where it lingered briefly before dissipating. Much time had passed. He had heard nothing from Mr Blake. Miss Fur he thought was dead. The sacred seeds of his people had gone from the bag she always carried close to her chest, the one he had found discarded on the beach.

His knew in his heart Mr Blake had been involved in what had happened. Was it possible he had met her on the beach, that something bad had happened and he had stolen the seeds from her for himself then left the country? But how could he without his passport?

Mr Blake was a good man and had taught him many things over the years he had worked for him. But Tapu knew the power of money, the seeds were valuable, worth a lot of money, this perhaps had made Mr Blake think of keeping this money for himself, to make a different life in another place.

What would happen to him now, what should he do, where should he go? Would he become another bushman specimen to be gawked and wondered at; his proud people reduced to acting out their ancient lineage in a public place, to earn money?

His people had told him tourists were coming here to South Africa and Botswana. Once a year, he had heard, there was a great *indaba* in Durban. Here the tour operators came from all over the world to see what they could sell to their tourists. Always looking for something different; and this they had found.

The San people were put on display in a small cubicle, decorated to look like a reed hut, dressed in their traditional minimal loin clothes, their upper torsos bare save for necklaces of beads and shells, as they rubbed their fire sticks together, did some of their traditional dances and displayed their magnificent hunting skills with moving pictures behind them. Their unique language of clicks and soft sounds were there for all to see, along with their trance dances and other customs.

An ancient people who were now on display, hosted by some game lodge in the Kalahari who promised tourists a unique experience, where these people had originated from.

The San people were ancient and noble, but slowly dying out. Their voices and ways being carried away by the wind that used to blow across their desert homeland, their language almost forgotten as they tried to survive and adapt. The ancient art of his people depicting their thousands of years of history in the hidden caves of this country, a testament to their legacy, had been discovered. Their feast of history embedded for all to see as tourists arrived in their big vehicles to take their photographs of the crude drawings of animals and of his people, and who they had once been.

He looked up at the clear skies above him, the heavy canopy of stars he had known all his life. He too had tried to adapt to this new life, leaving behind all he and his ancestors had ever known, to find work.

Mr Blake had respected his ways, learned from them, and in time he had come to trust this white man from across the seas, learned his ways; learned from him about the world beyond the deserts he had always known.

But now he knew only despair. He had trusted Mr Blake. But it seemed to him Mr Blake had not valued him as much as he thought. But then, Mr Blake could always go back to his place across the sea, whereas he, Tapu, had no-where to go, and an uncertain future in front of him.

He flicked his cigarette into the bush, watching the fiery dying embers falling to the ground, like the history of his people before him.

He would pack his few belongings in his quarters and move on, but he knew not where.

The soft clicking sound made him turn.

The shadowy figure of Puso emerged from the dark bush.

"I see you Puso. What is it you want from me? I have nothing else inside of me to give."

Puso frowned at him. "I am thinking you have. You must listen to my story now, and all will become clear to you."

He hunkered down in front of Tapu. "You remember after Miss Fur had left with her seeds, I asked for a lift for my cousin and I, for we had business to attend to?"

Tapu nodded, miserably. "Yes, I remember this."

"This business was important because we had heard the government was coming soon to our place in the forest. We would have to leave. They said it is the people's land; it belonged to the Africans now. We were not African, so we had to find somewhere else to go, and take our elderly people and family with us."

Puso looked down at his dry, dusty, and cracked feet, pulling the soft animal skin around his shoulders as the cold night air closed in.

"Miss Fur had promised us, in exchange for the seeds, she would take care of us, find somewhere for us to go with the money from the seeds. I trusted she would do this. It was all we could hope for."

Tapu rolled another cigarette, then one more for Puso who dragged greedily on it. Then he continued with his story.

"I was much worried about the seeds and Miss Fur being alone in a remote place by herself. My cousin and I decided to watch over her until this man would join her as you told us he would."

Tapu screwed up his eyes against the acrid smoke from his cigarette. "Mr Blake, his name was Mr Blake, Puso. He was a good man and would have taken great care of her and the seeds."

Puso shrugged. "He did take care of her and the seeds, but not in the way you are thinking…

"My cousin and I found a swift route through the sand dunes and waited through the night. It was the next afternoon when we saw this Miss Fur walking alone on the beach. We heard the sound of a car arriving and made ready to leave, knowing she was now safe."

"Look at me Tapu, for what is coming next is important. Miss Fur started to return to the hotel and in the distance, she saw the man she had been waiting for. She started to wave to him, running towards him, holding up the bag of seeds we had given to her as a gift. Miss Fur stumbled a little in the soft sand, but she was laughing as she ran towards this man who you say was Mr Blake."

The muscles in Tapu's stomach contracted with anxiety. Now he would finally learn the truth.

"This Mr Blake waved to her as he became close to where she was waiting for him. But he was not smiling and laughing as she was.

"In his hand he had a gun. He shot her Tapu. This you must now know."

Tapu put his hands over his face. It was true then; Mr Blake had killed her.

Puso paused for breath. "We might be a forgotten people, Tapu, but our hunting skills have survived over thousands of years. I watched Miss Fur fall into the sand. I drew my arrow from my pouch, my aim was straight and true. This Mr Blake stood no chance against the people from the desert. The arrow pierced his heart with its deadly poison. He staggered briefly then fell to the ground.

"We came to them both. Miss Fur was bleeding from a wound to her head, her blood turning pink with the incoming bubbling tide which greedily awaited her.

"Mr Blake had no chance at all. I took my arrow and let the poison seep through him. I searched his dying body but found nothing of value. But I took what I found anyway."

He puffed on his cigarette. "Miss Fur was not dead. I took the bag across her chest and took back our seeds.

"My cousin and I carried Miss Fur away from the hungry sea. We found a sheltered spot for her amongst the warm sand dunes and used our own medicines to stop the bleeding and make her calm.

"She was light to carry. We used the sticks and shrubs to make a bed for her, we used our animal skins to keep her warm. Then we took her back to our people.

"It was two days before we reached the edge of the forest. We had sent word to our senior women of what had happened. Four of them were waiting for us. They carried her quickly to our village and watched over her with their medicines."

Tapu was overwhelmed with this news. "She is alive then?"

Puso nodded. "She is alive. The sacred seeds are once more with our people.

"But it will take time before she is well enough to return to her house. Until such time she will stay with us. She will be safe. But soon we shall be moved on by the government. Miss Fur cannot come with us. She is a white woman, and there will be many questions. We would be in more trouble with the government than we are now. We would have no answers to any of the questions they would ask, and why we were hiding an injured white woman here. They would take us all away and put us in prison."

Tapu was having a problem confronting all these facts. He was happy Miss Fur still lived, but his heart was broken. Mr Blake was now dead; Puso had told his story, and it must be true. The man Miss Fur had trusted and loved, had betrayed her. He had killed her.

"What happened to the body of Mr Blake, Puso?"

Puso shrugged. "The sea will have taken him. The sharks would come hunting for him – there would be nothing left."

Tapu stared into the cold black sky. "What will happen to Miss Fur then?"

"Deep in the forest, away from prying eyes and government officials, we have built for her a simple structure. It is impossible to see.

We will be moved on, but Miss Fur will stay in her hidden place. There are four elderly women who will tend to her, look after her. Stay with her. This is all my people can do for her."

Tapu stood up. "I must go to her, help her if I can."

Puso shook his head. "No, you must stay here as if all is normal. There are others out there looking for Miss Fur. It is better for all of us she remains hidden, and everyone thinks she is dead. This way she will remain safe."

Tapu stared at him. "But she cannot stay there for the rest of her life. She is not one of us. She is a doctor, a scientist, with a fine education. When she recovers, she will want to return to the life she knows."

He hesitated. "Have you told her you killed Mr Blake and left him for the sharks?"

Puso shook his head. "She is not well enough to tell such things. Miss Fur was badly hurt. She is in another place in her mind. She may stay this way; it is for the gods to decide her fate, not us."

Tapu shook his head. "You will leave her there then. With no one she knows?"

Puso picked a thorn from his foot. "There is no other choice. In a few days now the government will burn our huts and drive us away. If she were found with us there would be big trouble. They would take her away to a white man's hospital where they keep people who have no thoughts in their head. I have heard of these places where they keep people in one room with bars and locked doors, like a prison, and give them medicine which makes them calm and sleep a lot."

Puso flicked his cigarette into the bush. "Four of our women will stay with her, watch over her. My people will move deeper into the forest and find somewhere else to live."

Puso, he thought, looked defeated. But his clan had to live somewhere, find somewhere where they could be safe, away from the prying eyes of the government.

Tapu's eyes filled with tears. "This is the right thing to do then, Puso, the women will take care of her. I will ask one thing of you. When Miss Fur is well enough, I must go to her, perhaps she will remember me. I will bring her back here to her house, I myself will tell her what Mr Blake did to her.

"When this house is sold, we will find another place to live, and I will take care of her as I have always done. But what of the seeds she spent many years looking for?"

Puso stood up. "The seeds must stay where they are. It seems they have brought only trouble and death, and not the cure Miss Fur was looking for. It is best, as with many things in her head, she forgets about them.

"You must wait here, Tapu. One of the women will send word to you when it is safe to come and see her. It will be many months I am thinking. But you must remain here so you can be found if this is so."

Puso disappeared into the dark night. Tapu, broken-hearted, locked the house up and returned to his own quarters, his steps heavy as he tried to digest all the bad news he had been given.

Chapter Sixty-Three

Jack was sitting on the edge of his chair; this was indeed an incredible story. Doctor Fleur Palmere was alive, hidden away in the forest somewhere. By his reckoning she had been there for some years.

Piet's heart softened, but only a little. He liked this simple man called Tapu. He had been plunged, by all accounts, into an impossible situation, but he had remained loyal to the doctor.

According to Tapu, Blake Hemmingway had tried to kill her but failed, and Puso had shot the deadly arrow into his heart and killed him, then taken back the seeds and other things he had found in her bag.

They had taken her to the green flat roofed dwelling in the forest and kept her there. But he still had more questions he needed to ask.

"How long was it, Tapu," Jack said softly, "before one of the women looking after her, sent the message to you that the doctor had recovered enough to see you?"

Tapu scratched his now greying curling hair. "It was many years before someone sent the message I must go to her. I took my old car and drove quickly to where I remembered the old village had been, my heart was light, knowing I would see her again. I found the path back. One of the elder women greeted me in the traditional way and led me to the place with the green roof.

"Miss Fur was waiting for me and lifted her hand in greeting, and I knew then she remembered me, and had sent for me.

"She was looking different. Miss Fur had long dark hair when I last saw her at the old hotel on the Wild Coast. Now her hair was grey and threaded with beads. Her face was old, and there was a scar on her face where the bullet had entered her head. But her smile was the same as she came forward to greet me. Her strange eyes were bright when she saw, and remembered, me.

"I had never touched a white woman in my life, but she came towards me and threw her arms around me. I felt the happiness in her arms and in my heart."

Jack blinked back a tear in his own eyes. "She clearly recognised you, but with her head injury and the damage to her memory, how could this be."

Tapu smiled. "The women had looked after her well. Using our own traditional medicines."

Piet nodded his head slowly and smiled. "The seeds, right? They used the seeds to help her recover her mind and her memories."

"Yes. This is so. This is what they did."

Jack leaned forward. "But in the beginning, she would not have known they were using the seeds, would she?"

Tapu nodded. "This is also so. But she is a doctor and a scientist. As she recovered, and this is what she told me on my visit, she knew she had found the cure of what she was looking for. The seeds had brought back long forgotten memories, not only of what had happened to her, but memories of her childhood in Kenya, memories of someone she had loved before Mr Blake. Of the child of her sister called Lucy."

Piet sat back in his chair. "At what point did you tell her Mr Blake had been killed by Puso?"

Tapu looked up at him. "This is not what happened, *sah*. There are many lies beneath the sand, but the desert will always reveal the truth."

Tapu looked up at the clouds of dust which heralded the arrival of another vehicle. He knew who would be in it.

The Land Rover came to a halt, its driver and passenger alighted, then stopped when they saw the two men standing there.

The man took the woman's hand. "Come on, we knew this was going to happen at some point. Let's find out who these guys are and what they want. It could be nothing except maybe looking to buy the house, in which case they're out of luck, it's already been sold. It might be time to tell the truth about what happened and handle it as best we can."

Tapu looked fearfully at the two men waiting on the *stoep*. He, of course, knew exactly who had just arrived.

The couple mounted the two steps and came face to face with Piet and Jack.

Jack, ever mindful of his manners and upbringing, held out his hand and smiled at the tall man in front of him. "Jack Taylor, and this is my partner Piet Joubert." They all shook hands.

The tall, well-built man had already picked up the very English accent of Jack and the strong guttural Afrikaans accent of his partner. He felt a *frisson* of fear; then a slow acceptance of what he had always known would happen one day. Despite all this he knew everything was in place. Exactly as he had planned it over the last few years.

"Blake Hemmingway. This is Fleur. Perhaps we can help you with something?" He gestured for them to sit.

Fleur was by no means a young woman anymore, her face was lined, her long hair plaited and thread with bright beads, her only redeeming feature was her startling blue eyes, clear and intelligent, defiant almost.

Piet looked hostile. "No. Perhaps you can help *us* with something. We've been working on this case for months now. Trying to work out what happened. You seemed to have left your company TLI and disappeared. By all accounts Fleur died some years ago. There appears to be relatives, family, friends and indeed a solicitor in London who have all been anxious and searched for many years to find her."

Piet continued. "We have interviewed your man, Tapu, he told us a few things which we thought might be helpful, but unfortunately they weren't because although he didn't deliberately lie to us, he withheld the true facts and sent us up a few blind alleys to protect the truth about the doctor, and as it turns out, you as well."

Jack looked at Fleur who was standing behind Blake's chair, her hands resting lightly on his shoulders, her face devoid of any emotion, her extraordinary eyes watching him; eyes he had seen before in her niece Lucy.

Piet continued. "The reason for this, Doctor Palmere, is because your sister Helene died. Her daughter, Lucy, was anxious to find you, her aunt, as was their solicitor, Mr Jeremy Foxton.

"Mr Foxton needs to tie up the estate of your sister. Everything was left to her daughter Lucy. But without proof of your own death, Doctor Palmere, he was unable to carry out his legal duties, after all, it would appear now, you still own the house and contents where Lucy lives. We checked on his behalf and there is no record of your death here in South Africa, but perhaps you moved to another country across one of our borders. Or hiding somewhere?

"Which means, your niece, Lucy would have inherited everything, including the estate of a certain Captain Michael Bennett, which is considerable. However, it is you who will inherit this now."

Fleur's hand flew to her mouth, the colour draining from her face. "Michael? Please excuse me."

The men watched her stumble away from them into the house, her body bent over. Tapu hurrying after her.

Blake looked angrily at Piet. "You might have been a little more sensitive with your news, Mr Joubert. Losing her sister is one thing, finding out the captain was also dead would be too much for anyone to absorb. There are ways of handling things like this. I don't think you gave it much thought.

"Fleur is tough I know, dedicated to her work, her vocation, but she also has, or had, a family and someone from her past who she was deeply in love with, you could have been a little more tactful."

Piet was unrepentant. He couldn't understand why someone like Doctor Palmere could cast her entire family aside to pursue some vocation of her own. How could she abandon them all for her own selfish reasons, good or bad? Noble or otherwise?

"See here Mr Hemmingway, it's true I could have chosen a different way to break the news to her, but sometimes the brutal truth can evoke hidden emotions; emotions that can rise to the surface and lay bare the truth. It's what I want – the truth.

"Doctor Fleur Palmere had little or no regard for what she did to her family by disappearing for twenty odd years and not keeping in touch, it's hardly what I would call a close family relationship. Clearly, she wasn't close to her sister and never met her niece. Jeremy Foxton, searched endlessly for Fleur, at great expense I should point out. It would have been the decent thing to do to let him, and her family, know she was safe and well and living in South Africa. So why didn't she?"

Jack watched the exchange of angry words between Piet and Blake, there was a lot more to this story and being hostile would not solve anything.

He leaned forward in his chair. "Let's calm things down a little, Piet. Give Fleur time to absorb this information. She's been told her sister is dead. A shocking thing for a sibling to absorb even though she had had no contact with her for the past couple of decades."

A few moments later, from a room somewhere, there came a loud, ancient, keening sound of grief.

Jack looked up. "Perhaps you need to be with her, comfort her, Blake?"

Blake shook his head. "No. Fleur is a complex person; she keeps her feelings to herself; she's the only one who can deal with this in her own way, and in her own time. She chose her own path and this she will follow. Tapu will be outside her door should she need anything. But he won't intrude on her grief any more than I will. I would say her tears are more of regret, and not grief.

"Fleur has a soft side to her and a great capacity to love. No one knows that better than I do, not just for me, but for all the others in the world who so desperately need help."

Piet watched Blake before he spoke again. "We had you nailed for killing Fleur Palmere. You were supposed to meet her at the place called Safe Harbour. But it seems this was not so, because here you both are, alive and well, and living in two different places. Here where we are sitting now, and the place in the forest. I'm right, yes?"

Blake nodded. "Yes. It was the safest place for her after what happened on the beach. Someone had tried to kill her, there may have been others with the same intent. But, despite everything, she was more determined than ever to continue her work, especially as she was prepared to try one final experiment, something most scientists and doctors would be reluctant to do. Use the seeds on herself.

"Don't judge her too harshly, Mr Joubert, it was a brave thing, a courageous thing to do. Despite how you have already judged her by the choices she made."

Jack pulled out his notebook. "It seems to me, as a journalist, you have a story to tell. Fleur needs to clarify why she cut herself off from her family in the UK, then disappeared, once again, in some impenetrable forest in the Eastern Cape, letting everyone assume she had died?"

Blake managed a bleak smile. "That's Fleur for you. I always seem to find her in an abandoned place."

Piet wasn't amused by this remark. "See here Mr Hemmingway, you, and the doctor, have messed with many people's lives. Left them in a void they couldn't understand. Now, there's no criminal case here, but you both have a moral obligation to tell your story. Jack and I want to hear that story.

"Mr Jeremy Foxton; the niece called Lucy; Tapu's obvious involvement, but most important of all, how did Doctor Palmere rise from the dead, so to speak, and you by all accounts.

"How could she have done this to her family and why? Who was Captain Michael Bennett who left everything to the so-called deceased Doctor Palmere?"

Piet pointed his glass at Jack. "See here, Blake, Jack followed this story, followed the trail Fleur had left, he knows about her life in Kenya, her relationship with Captain Bennett, her sister Helene and her daughter Lucy – but neither of us can figure out her thinking and why she did what she did – cutting herself from everyone and disappearing."

Piet paused briefly. "Jack went to Kenya, met a few people who knew her, and also Captain Bennett. He went to the house in Naivasha where she and her sister lived with their mother, met an elderly retainer, Noah, who still lived there. So, we know a lot about her, but none of it stacks up."

Blake studied both the men in front of him. Perhaps the time had finally arrived, the story needed to be told. He would tell his story, but it was up to Fleur if she finally wanted to tell hers.

His shoulders sagged, then he straightened up. "Let's go inside and have a sundowner. We all need one after this development."

Blake took a long gulp from his drink and looked at his unexpected guests. "You see, gentlemen, Fleur made a tough decision to leave her family behind and cut herself off from all of them. But she had valid reasons for doing this, hard to understand I know. Even I don't know, although I have my own thoughts on that.

"I found her abandoned in an empty camp site in the middle of the bush. I took her to a place of safety. From what I can gather you both followed this trail, this story. It's why you're here now. Looking for answers and the reasons why we chose to do what we did."

He looked out at the setting sun, the sky turning blood red. "In my own defence I should tell you when I did find her and took her to the hospital in Graaff-Reinet, I did everything I could to try and find her family. She had little or nothing to identify who she was, but I did find a connection to Captain Michael Bennett and learned he had been listed as missing and presumed dead in a skirmish in the desert in the Middle East somewhere – his entire unit was wiped out."

Blake paused for a moment. "Fleur spoke about him briefly; she didn't want to talk about him or her past. She had one goal in her life, a passion, a vocation, if you like, inherited from her mother. She put her research above everything else and I respected that. It's a rare human being in today's world who will sacrifice everything for a cause they believe in.

"Having spoken to her lawyer, Jeremy Foxton, he would have given you all the information you needed to follow her story, to try to find out what happened to her. It would be a fair request for you to tell me what you know, and then I will fill in the gaps."

Jack's foot began to jiggle again. Here was another great story, different from the others he had followed. He wanted it.

"See here, Blake, Piet was a police detective, highly regarded, dogged in his determination to find the bad guys. His questions may seem a little abrupt to you, insensitive in fact, but he has only ever been in pursuit of the truth, to find out what really happened, as I am. Perhaps we should leave things for today. We're staying in a town an hour or so away."

Blake shook his head. "Absolutely not, you must stay here tonight. Tapu has prepared dinner. We need to sort all of this out once and for all.

"Fleur won't be joining us for dinner. Tapu will take care of her, as he has always done, he is dedicated to her, devoted to her.

"Over dinner I will fill in the gaps missing in your investigation. To do this I need your word, Jack, that you will not make this information public, at least not yet. It will become public shortly, but through the mediums we have both worked so hard with and chosen to work with us."

He stood up. "I must go to Fleur now. Please excuse me."

Piet and Jack looked at each other.

"Listen, mate, less of the interrogation, which is instinctive in you. Go easy on them both. If you remain hostile, we'll never learn the truth we have searched long and hard for, as have others. Blake Hemmingway seems a decent sort of a bloke. Not dead after all.

"Fleur is complicated. Most famous scientists, throughout history, seemed to have lived in a world of their own, scorned by society as nutcases. But they forged ahead, disregarding the fact they didn't fit into the normal mould. But they didn't care, you see, because they were different, passionate, focussed and dedicated to discovering the unknown. They didn't give a toss what the world thought about them. They lived, and live, in their own world and nothing else existed, or exists. Normal relationships don't even factor into their other world.

"So, lighten up, mate. There is a story here, a very unusual one, and I want it. If Fleur has discovered something which might shift the world of medicine, then Harry and I want to be the first newspaper to break the story. Then will come the book. The story of Fleur's life which started in the bush in Kenya. It has all the elements of a world best seller. Science, medicine, life in the bush in Africa, a love affair, or two, deserting her family, cutting all ties with them, and the dogged determination of one woman who has possibly found something of great importance which may change the lives of thousands of people in the western world. But we need to tread carefully to get this story."

Piet grunted. "Okay, my friend, I hear you, hey. You take over from here, go chase the story in your own way. But have no doubt I will be right behind you, looking for the truth, as you are. Keep in mind someone tried to kill Fleur, and I want to find out who it was.

"Someone was hunting her down and I want the name of that someone."

Jack tapped his pen against his teeth. "Okay, but clearly it wasn't Blake, who is alive and well. We have yet to hear his story of why he too seemed to have disappeared."

Tapu crept around the kitchen unsure of where they all would go from here. It was getting dark now and he thought perhaps the cop, and his journalist friend would stay the night. He started to prepare dinner, then went and checked the *rondavel* fully expecting it was going to be a long night.

As he carried the fresh laundry to the first place Doctor Fur had stayed in, he looked up. Lightening slashed across the sky; the purple blue clouds heavy with an impending storm, thunder boomed in the distance, he felt it reverberate under his feet. He felt things were going to change this night.

Chapter Sixty-Four
2005

Blake Hemmingway had been called to the meeting in Port Elizabeth where members of the Board of Directors, who had flown in from various places in the world, were congregating, including the Chairman of the company.

The atmosphere was sombre, and Blake knew what was coming. He had heard the various rumours about Trans Location Investments closing down but was not privy as to which countries in Africa this might apply to. But he knew, without doubt, South Africa would be one of them.

The Chairman cleared his throat once everyone was seated. "Blake, you have contributed much to the exploration, the planning and development of many of our investments here over many years. However, it is with regret I must inform you we are closing the entire operation here. It's not viable anymore, the risks too high with dealing with the new government, the local chiefs, and the people.

"However, we would like to keep you with the company with your vast experience and knowledge, plus your negotiating skills and abilities to close deals where everyone is happy with the outcome, including all our shareholders."

He took a sip of water from his glass and cleared his throat again. "We, the board, would like to offer you two other opportunities. Nigeria or Rwanda. We will double your salary, and the position will come with the usual benefits. A furnished home, a generous expense account, a vehicle, private medical aid, a pension, annual leave, and all the other things to make your position more comfortable."

The other board members shuffled through their papers whilst casting furtive looks at Blake Hemmingway, wondering how he would react to this new position he was being offered, and the one which had just been taken away.

Blake took a sip of his bottled water. "If this offer is not acceptable to me, where would it leave me with the company, after working for it for so many years?"

Once more the Chairman cleared his throat. "Sadly, Blake, we would have no alternative other than to let you go. Should this be your choice, you will be well rewarded for your years of service."

Blake stood up. "Gentlemen, I find it impossible to accept your terms. I have no wish to go to Nigeria or Rwanda. Therefore, I resign as of now.

"Please excuse me, but I have another urgent appointment on the Wild Coast, nothing to do with the business of the company. A private and personal thing I must attend to. I do have a private life you know."

The Chairman looked up at him, disappointed he would not be remaining with the company.

"You must cancel this appointment, Blake. The company need to finalise your decision, now you have made it. Our company attorney, Mr George Mason, has all the papers drawn up for you to resign from the company, or, as we had hoped, you would continue with.

"He's expecting you in Johannesburg tomorrow morning to sign everything off. Please ensure you'll be there."

The Chairman looked uncomfortable with his next remarks. "The company house is to be put on the market for sale. Of course, we will give you time to gather your personal effects and remove them from the house as soon as possible.

"You will still have the use of the company vehicle until such time as the house is sold, or perhaps Mr Mason may come up with an amicable arrangement whereby you may purchase the vehicle, and the house if you so wish."

Blake drove to the airport; he would leave the vehicle there and collect it on his return from Johannesburg. He understood through all his years of dealing with big corporate businesses that he was a mere cog in the wheel. Useful for making money for them, but easily tossed aside if he didn't fit the bill any longer or meet their impossible demands for making even more money.

He didn't have a vocation in life, nothing he was passionate about. But Fleur was different. She didn't care about money or power; she cared only for what she utterly believed in. Finding things which she knew would enhance the lives of ordinary people. To him it made the world of business shabby and empty in comparison. A relentless drive for money and power. People cast aside when they couldn't deliver what was expected, the new hungry younger ones promising everything.

Chapter Sixty-Five
2005

Blake arrived in Johannesburg and made his way to the offices of George Mason, the company attorney. Despite the fierce reputation in court, he had found George an amiable, friendly fellow, when he wasn't in court clothed in his scary black robes and white wig and tearing apart the likes of a famous athlete, for the murder of his girlfriend.

A breathtaking court case where he had emerged victorious, after the sentence was delivered. But he hadn't become a celebrity even though the world had watched his spectacular performance in court. He gave no interviews afterwards, declined any suggestions of documentaries, or film offers, which would have made him an international celebrity. He shunned them all.

He stood up as Blake leaned across to shake his hand. "Ah, Blake. Sorry to hear TLI are closing their doors and you're leaving after all your hard work and impressive track record. Take a seat."

Coffee was delivered by Nico, his personal assistant along with two bulging files.

George tapped on his computer, recording their meeting, then turned to the first file.

"TLI have been more than generous with their final package for you. You need to sign off on a lot of highly confidential documents concerning your years with the company.

"They have given me free reign to accede to any demands you may have after your years of service. Take your time to go through it all."

George glanced at his watch. "I need to make a brief appearance in court in twenty minutes time. My assistant will be available to you in our private lounge here. I should be back in an hour or two.

"Nico will serve you lunch, then we can go through any requests you may have, things you don't agree with perhaps. But I would like to wrap this all up this afternoon."

George shrugged on his black robes and adjusted his well-worn wig on his head.

"I have no appearances to make in Court tomorrow. I have kept the day clear to discuss the other matters you want to talk about.

"You have the Power of Attorney from Doctor Palmere?"

Blake grinned at him. "Indeed, I do."

Blake spent the rest of the day going through all the paperwork to tie up his departure from TLI. He made notes in the margins with the things with which he didn't agree. He didn't need the first-class ticket back to the UK, he accepted the more than generous severance packages the company were prepared to offer.

There were two things he wanted, and he would insist this was agreed upon.

He wanted ownership of the house in the bush where he and Fleur lived, all the contents and the vehicle.

He gathered the finished paperwork and put it neatly to one side. He glanced at his watch. Normally he would have phoned Tapu to ensure Fleur was safely ensconced at the hotel. But he had no reason to suspect she might have changed her mind.

She would be there waiting for him. Used to his unpredictable change of plans, as he was to hers. It was there he planned to finally tell her what had happened to Captain Michael Bennett.

Tomorrow he would again meet with George Mason and go through the highly complicated stage of his next plan.

He had the Power of Attorney from Fleur to negotiate the ownership of her research. He himself had taken her bulging file, her discs, and all the evidence of what she had learned, and what she planned to do with the results, and delivered them to George some months ago.

George had ploughed through all the legalities of it and drawn up the final papers which now awaited Blake's signature, on behalf of Fleur.

Fleur had decided which company she would prefer to continue her research and produce the final product which would be made available to the western world.

A small unassuming company based in Tokai, in Cape Town, had been her choice. The group of scientists and doctors who worked there, were as dedicated as she was, to finding ways to heal the world, and not looking to make millions of dollars out of other people's misery and desperation. The findings of her work would, of course, be attributed to her many years of research and analysis and the team she had chosen.

Fleur knew the money made from the launch of the new drug would put the modest company up there with the best in the world. All made, researched, and produced in South Africa.

The big boys in the Pharma companies, worldwide, would be clamouring to claim it for their own companies. They would pay millions for the ownership of the new drug.

Fleur was having none of this. It would be a South African product and remain in the country where it had been found. There would be no negotiations about it. The people she had worked with, the San people who had shared their secrets with her, needed her protection, they would be looked after.

She had already written a tentative article, with her findings and irrefutable claims, for The Lancet, but it was by no means complete. This she had lodged with George Mason.

Chapter Sixty-Six

Blake sat opposite George the next morning. Nico brought them coffee and silently retreated from the board room.

Displayed across the board room table were piles of document, neatly stacked and ready for what would be Blake Hemmingway's most defining moment of his life.

George pulled the first file towards him. "This is straightforward, Blake. All of Fleur's research has been annotated, all the rights belong to her and will remain with her. We have all the legal proof we need here, and it has been recorded as such. The Company she has chosen to pursue the final research have signed all the necessary papers and the letters of confidentiality. They will run pre-clinical trials, register the drug with the appropriate authorities here, then carry out various tests required and look for volunteers who suffer from the disease for the final tests, before it's announced to the world. It's watertight.

"Most important of all, no other worldwide Pharma company may make a claim to say it is theirs, based on their own research."

He glanced down at his notes. "It's Fleur's, and her mother's alone. A company in Kenya tried to claim the research by Fleur's mother into traditional medicine, all started there. But I quickly resolved that. A Doctor Mwanga made a lot of noise, brought in his legal team to try and claim ownership of what could be a life-changing drug. But as Fleur found what she was looking for here, the only place in the world, as far as we know, then the Kenyan's didn't have a leg to stand on."

George reached for another heavy file. "Now Blake, Fleur has appointed me as her attorney here in South Africa. I will ensure she and her discovery are well protected. Her small team of scientists will liaise with me on all their findings. Everything will be legally recorded, and I will handle all the necessary channels the new drug will have to go through before it can be brought to market". ."

Blake was busy making his own notes as George talked.

"Fleur has drawn up a new will, as I'm sure she discussed with you. Of course, her assets in the UK will still be managed by Mr Foxton, her family solicitor. I shall work with him should this become necessary. But not yet, as per her request."

He flipped expertly through the mound of paperwork. "Ah, here it is. You will be the sole beneficiary of her estate here. However, there are provisos which she is most insistent you adhere to.

"A percentage of the profits made from the drug will be paid to you. However, you will only be entitled to said profits once all her other wishes have been carried out and signed off by me.

"Fleur's loyalty and gratitude lie with the group of San people who were pivotal to the success of her finding what she was looking for.

"Once the drug has been approved there will be a great demand for it, from all over the western world where this disease seems to be prevalent. With this will come the large amount of money she needs to buy land for her San people in the Kalahari, so they can go home and know the land can never be taken from them again."

Blake tapped his pen against his teeth. "It won't be easy George, the government own the land. But with my years of experience working in the field and doing such deals, I think it can be done, especially when there will be a huge amount of money offered for it."

He paused for a moment. "The challenge will be to find the land these San people wish to return to and see if the government will be willing to sell it. But I have a few ideas on how to sweeten the deal should we ever reach that stage. In fact, I have a meeting scheduled with the people of the land there, of course, there is never a date made. When they want to see you, they want to see you and you get there as fast as you can, otherwise they don't take you seriously. I'm expecting some kind of communication from them in the next few days. Of all the deals I have done over the past years this is the one of the utmost importance. Not only for me but for Fleur. I've found a place for the people she holds dear, a place where they can be what they long to be.

"The government have no interest in it, it's in the middle of nowhere, no mineral resources, no interest in any kind of development, no potential for anything of any commercial value.

"If I can pull off this deal for Fleur, I have wonderful plans for it which will not intrude on the life of the San people but may well enhance it. However, now I am no longer with TLI this will throw a spanner in the works, and it's unlikely they will deal with an individual rather than an international company. I shall have to discuss this with Fleur and see what else we can come up with."

George took a sip of his coffee. "Have you met any of these San people Blake, the ones Fleur is so passionate about?"

He shook his head. "No. They are a secretive people living deep in the forest in the Eastern Cape. My housekeeper, Tapu, is a San person. These people have an uncanny way of communicating with each other.

"In fact, Tapu has taken Fleur to meet the forest dwellers in the past day or two. They know what she's looking for and will give Fleur the seeds which seem to hold the key to what she wishes to develop. I plan to meet her on the Wild Coast after our meeting."

George pulled another file towards him. "I need your signature on a few documents before you go, everything must be signed off on every page."

Blake laboriously made his way through each document until George was satisfied everything was in order.

"Is that it then George? May I go now?"

George frowned. "Not yet, Blake. Should something happen to Fleur, you inherit everything as per her will, except for her various provisos.

"What provisions have you made should something happen to you? You will be a rich man, the partner of the famous scientist Fleur. You need to get your own affairs in order. You need to make a new will."

Blake rubbed his neck. "Oh God, not more paperwork please. I have a will, TLI insisted on it, but this was years ago, long before I met Fleur and moved into her world."

George raised his eyebrows. "Then let's quickly wind this whole thing up. I have in fact drawn one up for you when I realised how big Fleur's project was. I know you have no family in the UK, you have no children, so who would you like your estate to go to?"

Blake stared out at the Johannesburg traffic, thousands of cars snaking their way home after a day of business in the City of Gold. Like ants on an endless journey of pursuit.

He rubbed his jaw and turned back to George.

"I've spent years in this country, George, it's my home. I love living here and would never consider living anywhere else, hence the offer of TLI sending me to Nigeria or Rwanda was completely out of the question. I love being out in the bush, traversing the country, getting to know its staggering landscape, meeting the people who ask for so little but can only hope for a better future, which is unlikely, out in these rural places.

"Look, how about you choose some charity you can trust and leave whatever I have left to them?"

George smiled broadly. "What a splendid idea!"

He cleared his throat. "My choice, therefore, is a company who give so much to help so many, not only here, but in many trouble spots around the world when disaster strikes unexpectedly. They move in quickly. They're not political, they answer to no government. They ask for nothing – they only want to assist and help in any way they can.

"We live in a highly dangerous world, Blake, countries at war, countless innocent people losing their lives because of politicians' greed for power and money and votes, their complete disregard for the respect of people who only want to live a decent and safe life.

"Yes, there will always be natural disasters, earthquakes, flooding, raging fires which destroy whole communities. Politicians stand before the cameras and say their thoughts and prayers are with the families who have been killed in one skirmish or another, etc. etc. But then the next big story breaks and the people, their communities, left behind in the dust, forgotten as they desperately try to retrieve what they can from the devastation left behind."

An agitated Blake stood up and paced around George's office. "I've been lucky in my life, and now I have Fleur. I'm not a religious man, George. But I do respect other religions. As Fleur once told me there are parallels between religion and science. But it's the goodness in people which seems to be fading. There are good people here in this country. People who are truly making a difference, they are the unsung heroes, trying to make things work. So, you pick a worthy cause, and I'll go along with it."

George slid the final document towards Blake. "Please sign where indicated and my para-legal will insert the name of the company."

"Who will inherit my estate then?"

"The Gift of the Givers. Not a single blemish on their impressive record of giving and helping, for years now, where they can. They have my greatest respect. They are non-political, not judgemental, and not financed by the government, so they don't have to answer to them. They operate from sponsorships and donations."

Blake shrugged. "Fine with me. Now I really must be going. I have a flight to catch."

"Good luck, Blake. Everything is now in order. I will let the Chairman of TLI know you wish to purchase the house in the bush and your vehicle. He won't have a problem with this. I'll handle the transfer of both into your name.

"As per your request, I will hold all the legal documents here rather than courier copies to you. As you so rightly pointed out the information in Fleur's paperwork is highly confidential. It wouldn't do for them to fall into the wrong hands.

"If there are any changes in circumstances you will let me know, won't you?"

Blake shook George's hand. "A most constructive meeting, thank you. Everything is finally in place and now I can get on with the next phase of my life, with Fleur."

George laughed. "Yes, everything is in place, covered legally in every aspect. However, you may not feel so jolly and thankful when you get my bill. My assistant will furnish you with our bank details, kindly settle the amount before you leave. There is also an amount outstanding from the work I did with Fleur, perhaps you will settle this as well?"

Blake rubbed his hands together. "Of course. I'll do it on my way out. Fleur and I need to discuss our future and what we're going to do now I'm out of a job, and the land deal she so desperately wanted for the San people will more than likely not go through, since I no longer work for TLI."

Blake flew back to Port Elizabeth and collected his car. On the windscreen a note fluttered, pinned down by one of the wipers. Feeling slightly irritated he reached for it, thinking it was yet another flyer advertising some restaurant or other in the city.

He was about to screw it up when he noticed it was handwritten.

Blake, please come to the office urgently. I have some information for you. I'll be here until around eight this evening, packing up my desk and other things, like you I shall have to look for another job in another place. All the directors have flown back overseas, and I am here alone, the rest of the staff have gone home.

Maggie

Blake looked at his watch, it was coming up for six o' clock. He could spare Maggie half an hour or so, then he would drive through the night towards the Wild Coast and hope Fleur was still waiting for him there.

Maggie had worked for the company for as long as he had, she would find it hard to source another job at her age. But she had taken time to contact him, despite her own world being turned upside down. The least he could do was swing past the old offices of TLI and hear her out.

Maggie was busy rolling up maps and papers relating to the projects TLI had been involved in over the years, stacking them against the wall.

"Hey, Maggie, looks like you have a lot of things to sort out before you can leave. I'm sorry this has turned out the way it has for you, for all of us in fact. But there it is."

Maggie sat down and rubbed her back. "You found my message then?"

Blake smiled at her. Everyone knew Maggie, and Maggie knew everyone they had dealt with across the country over the years.

"Yes, the least I could do was drop by and say goodbye, see if I could help in any way."

Maggie gave him a bleak smile, as bleak as her future seemed to be now. "No, Blake, you can't help me. I'm afraid, it is what it is, the company has closed down.

"However, I had a phone call this afternoon, from a landowner up near the Kalahari. He wants to sell some land, he's looking for an investor to develop it into some kind of bush lodge, then sell it on to one of the major hotel chains here.

"Look, let me show you where this land is."

Maggie reached for one of the maps on the top of her desk and unrolled it. "Here it is," she circled an area with her finger, "on the edge of the Kalahari."

Blake reached for his glasses and studied the terrain on the map spread out in front of him. His breath caught in his throat.

"This landowner, has all the permissions from the local people and the government to do this?"

"Yes. Plus, the new owner would be allowed a limited amount of hunting on the land, but only plains game, for which there is a quota and hunting permit."

Blake sucked in his breath. It was bloody perfect for what he and Fleur were looking for.

"The thing is, Blake, there are other people interested in this land, but the landowner knows our reputation and wants to sell it to us. But, as 'us' are no longer in business I thought you might be interested in pursuing it under your own personal agenda. It was just a thought. The thing is the landowner wants to see you.

"Everyone knows your reputation in situations like this. Your ability to deal with landowners, tribal chiefs and the government, the sensitive way you handle the negotiations. He wants to see you, Blake, sooner rather than later, to tie down the deal. He has given TLI one week to close the deal before he puts it out on the market."

Blake stared at the map in front of him. He knew he was one of the best at putting these kinds of deals together, but the mounds of paperwork that came into play, once the deal was done, had always been handled by Maggie and the company attorney, George Mason.

"Maggie, I want to go and meet this landowner, win him over and get him to trust me even though I'm no longer with the company. He needs to know all the legal paperwork and permits will go through as they would if I was still with TLI. You know how to do all this; Maggie, I'd like you to work with me on it. I'll pay you of course on a freelance basis. What do you think?"

Maggie's face lit up. "Of course I will, I can do all the necessary paperwork from home. It's a deal. After all, my contacts who I dealt with for over thirty years need not know I am no longer with TLI, do they. Especially if we use the same lawyer as we always have. George Mason?"

Blake hugged her. "Right, I'm off to the Kalahari. Let the landowner know I'm on my way will you.

"I need to let Fleur know I'll be away for some weeks, maybe a couple of months depending on how complex the deal is and who I might have to meet. She's waiting for me on the Wild Coast, I thought I would have to bring her bad news about the land deal TLI was working for in that area, but it seems we've been given another opportunity. She'll understand completely. I've tried to call her, but nobody answers the phone at the hotel, and Tapu isn't picking up the phone at home."

Maggie made a note. "Yes, of course I will. Good luck Blake and have a safe trip, it will be a long and hard journey. The landowner is called Mr Van Tonder. There's a town about eighty kilometres away, everyone knows him; they'll be able to direct you to his farm.

"I shall let Mr Mason know about your hopefully new project and I'm sure he'll be happy to handle the legal side of things once I've processed the paperwork. After all, he is your own personal attorney now, right?"

Maggie hesitated for a moment. "If you pull this deal off, Blake, you will need to form a company, or a Trust, a legal entity for all the paperwork to go through, otherwise I doubt it will happen. An individual with a deal this size won't carry any weight. I can set this up for you, with George's help?"

Blake frowned. "You're right of course. A Trust is what we need. We'll need Trustees. I suggest, of course, one will be Fleur, I will be another, and I would like you, Maggie, and George to make up the Board. I think the Head of Research at the company in Tokai should also be included.

"Should keep you busy for a few more years, better than a microwave supper and staring at the television – what do you say?"

Maggie held back her tears. "I would like that very much, Blake, thank you. What would you like the Trust to be called?"

Blake rubbed his eyes; things were moving fast if he could pull off this deal. "The Naivasha Palmere Hope Foundation" bit of a mouthful I know, but it pulls in the history of where it all started. I think Fleur will approve."

Blake rolled up the map. It was a vast amount of country to cover to get to where this land was, and a huge amount of money the landowner was asking for. But he knew he was going to do it. It would take him two days of hard driving, day and night, but without any doubt he was going to take this project on. He was going to close this deal, even if it took him months, not for him, but for Fleur, and the people who had led her to what she, and her mother, had been searching for.

A place to call their own.

Chapter Sixty-Seven
2019

Blake took a deep breath and reached for his beer. Piet was listening intently, looking for any holes in the story, making and reaching his own conclusions, so far.

Jack was on the edge of his chair making copious notes in his notebook. What a great story this could be; Harry would be as fascinated as he was. They could run a few teaser columns in the Sunday magazine, then write a condensed story of the personal life of the people involved which would, without any doubt, become a best-selling book. But he would have to tread carefully and do some sort of deal with Blake and Fleur so the *Telegraph* would have the exclusive rights to publish before any other magazine, or newspaper, got hold of it.

Of course, magazines like The Lancet, one of the most trusted, influential and highly respected medical publications in the world, would have to know the outcome of all Fleur's work over the years, it would be ground-breaking stuff in the world of science and medicine, but it didn't necessarily mean they needed the personal story of this couple. This he wanted exclusively for his own newspaper.

Piet glanced down at his own notes. "Were neither you nor Fleur worried about not being in touch for several weeks?"

Blake shook his head. "No. Our relationship was clear from the beginning. She went off to do what she wanted to do, and I carried on as I had for thirty years. We understood each other and the importance of our work. We didn't suffocate each other by having to be in touch all the time. When you work in the bush there's no way to keep in touch, no telephone lines, and if there were any, the elephants would probably have destroyed them, of course we didn't have cell phones then, but even so there would still have been a problem with no signal. "This is a vast country, but technology hasn't been able to cover it all, at least not yet, if ever. It doesn't help that Eskom plunges the country into darkness when the mood takes them, but I have a generator, though I rarely use it. It's noisy and intrusive, I prefer to sit out under the stars in silence."

Blake continued. "Our relationship is unique in this way, she goes off, I go off, and we collide now and again – it works for both of us."

An owl called in the distance through the still night and all three men paused to listen, a brief calming moment with nature.

Blake smiled. "It's why I live out in the bush far away from the frantic noise and energy of a city. Fleur and I are happy here. It's peaceful and tranquil. We can be alone together.

"It was a hard and gruelling drive to find Mr Van Tonder and his ranch. He was a giant of a man, with a bushy white beard, hair and eyebrows and piercing blue eyes. He reminded me of Eugene Terblanche, but without the charisma and rhetoric. A fiercely proud Afrikaner. I realised Van Tonder would do things at his own pace and not be pushed around by anyone, legal or otherwise, this took more time, he was close to giving me what Fleur and I wanted, even though I was an Englishman."

Blake looked at Piet. "Mr Van Tonder had lived in the family ranch for generations; he had never married and had no children. But I noticed the tall Zulu man around who managed the farm and the house alongside Mr Van Tonder. His name was Kanu.

"Van Tonder insisted I stay at the ranch whilst we went through the legalities and negotiations of the sale. On the second night there, Kanu served dinner, cleared it all away and came and sat with us outside. He sat comfortably in a chair and poured himself a beer, perfectly at ease with the situation, as was Van Tonder, although he was watching me closely.

"I sensed immediately they had a more personal relationship. It must have been a difficult one, given the history of the country. He would have been ostracised by the local Afrikaners, farm owners, townsfolk etc, and they had probably cast him out as a traitor to their history.

"Van Tonder was tough, but he was sensitive to the situation, and he now realised I had worked it all out.

He shrugged his shoulders. "I didn't approve or disapprove. If you can find love and companionship it should be grabbed with both hands. They had clearly found it."

Van Tonder looked at the Englishman sitting opposite him. "You and I, and our people, have a long and bitter history, the Boers, and the English. I swore decades ago I would never forgive them or do business with them. But I am old now," he glanced across at Kanu. "You can see how I live my life and I'm happy. You accept what you see. You do not judge me for the choice I have made, unlike my own people, hereabouts, who have cast me out."

Van Tonder stood up and extended his hand. "The deal is yours."

Blake smiled. "I won't bore you with the details of the deal I finally pulled off with him – which I did. I secured the land deal which Fleur was so passionate about – it took weeks, with documents going through his attorney, then on to Maggie to process the documents and then to George Mason who stood guarantor for the money I needed and set up the Trust. I travelled to and from Port Elizabeth, to Johannesburg, Cape Town, then back again to Van Tonder, hundreds of documents to be signed off. He was a hard man, but fair, he wanted the deal done and wasn't prepared to wait months for the legal process to work its ponderous way through the system."

Jack stifled a yawn, it was two in the morning, but the adrenalin was racing through his body, he wanted the rest of the story, and he wanted it now.

Tapu brought another tray of coffee in, then sat in the shadows listening to the story Blake was recounting.

"The deal was done, the documents signed, and I wanted to go home to Fleur. She had found what she was looking for, the seeds, and I had bought the land where the people who had given her this gift could now safely go home and live the life they had always known."

He frowned. "I was disappointed when I arrived back at the house, I was desperate to see her and tell her the news. But she wasn't there and nor was Tapu.

"I knew she would pitch up and I hoped it would be soon. So, I waited another few weeks. I checked the telephone – it was dead. I bent down to see if it was connected. It seemed Tapu with his enthusiasm for keeping everything clean had dislodged the connection. I plugged it back in and it sprang to life.

"But still I waited.

"Fleur never came home. There was no sign of Tapu either. The house felt neglected. There was no food in the fridge, only canned tins in the kitchen. The place was dusty, lacking in life.

"It's when I realised something had happened to them."

Chapter Sixty-Eight
Blake

Blake looked across at his two guests and continued. "I knew it would be a hopeless task to try and look for them in this vast area. I didn't have a starting point, only the old hotel called Safe Harbour. I called many times but there was no reply.

"I knew a journey there would produce nothing, as Fleur was only booked in there for two days, and I had been away for many weeks. I nearly drove myself mad trying to work out where she and Tapu might have gone. Had something happened deep in the forest where she had gone with Tapu to seek the seeds? But I had no idea where this might be. Had something happened there to both of them, maybe Tapu had never dropped her off at the hotel?

"Now the phone was working again I contacted George Mason and asked him if he had heard from her.

"Fleur had not been in touch with him.

"George was as worried as I was. Without Fleur and her precious seeds, the deal we had all worked so hard for, everything we had put in place, well, it would come crashing down around our ears, with huge financial consequences."

Blake had been lying on his bed, unable to sleep such was his concern for Fleur and Tapu. It was pitch black outside, he had no perimeter lights, the wind was howling unnervingly around the house, he had no idea what time it was but knew it was in the early hours of the morning.

A strafe of light briefly lit up his room and he sat up, reaching for his gun. A visitor at this time in the morning was not possible, it could only mean trouble. Marauding criminals looking for a soft target.

He didn't plan on being one.

Without putting any lights on, he prowled around his house. The unrelenting wind made it difficult to pinpoint any unusual noise. He checked each room until he came to the kitchen.

He froze.

The handle of the kitchen door was moving. He raised his gun in anticipation then turned the light on. The door opened and there stood Tapu, blinking his eyes rapidly as they adjusted to the light.

"Tapu what the hell are you doing creeping around in the dark, I nearly bloody shot you!"

Blake cast his eyes around behind Tapu. "Where is she?" he said angrily. "Where is Miss Fur? Where the hell have you been?"

Tapu stood transfixed, unable to understand who he was seeing, then he threw himself at Blake's feet, clutching his legs, the tears streaming down his face.

"Mr Blake, Mr Blake, you have come back!"

"Well of course I've come back, I'm standing here in front of you aren't I! Where is Miss Fur, is she with you."

Tapu stood up unsteadily, holding onto the kitchen sink, trying to absorb the reality in front of him. "It cannot be you have returned from the dead."

Blake shook his head, baffled. "Of course I'm not dead. What are you talking about, man, you're not making any damn sense! Is Miss Fur in the car with you?"

Tapu tried to gather his scattered thoughts. "No, Mr Blake, she is not with me. She is safe somewhere, but there was an accident at the Wild Coast. I am thinking I must sit somewhere…"

Blake's fear and anger subsided. "Come and sit, I can see you're shocked to see me, this has never happened before in all the years we have been together. What accident are you talking about? Is Miss Fur in a hospital somewhere if she is I must go to her."

On shaky legs Tapu sank into a chair in the sitting room wondering where to start with his own story.

Blake stood over him. "Now see here Tapu, you're in a state of shock. I know you don't drink, but I'm going to make some coffee and put some brandy in yours, it will calm you down. Then I want you to start at the beginning, when you drove Miss Fur to the forest."

The long grey fingers of dawn announced the beginning of another day.

Tapu had told his story.

Blake was now angry, incensed that Tapu could believe for a minute he would kill Fleur.

"I am most sorry Mr Blake, but someone shot Miss Fur. This man was then killed by Puso, who is the elder of the tribe in the forest. His body was taken by the tide and then the sharks would have found him, as I have told you. What else could we believe?"

Blake took a gulp of his coffee laced with a generous dose of brandy, badly shaken. "So, Tapu, you and everyone else thought I had killed her, or attempted to kill her. But obviously I didn't – so who was this other man?"

Tapu shook his head. "This I do not know. But a car had been following us, then it disappeared. I'm thinking the killer was in this car and this is how he found Miss Fur. Beauty, at the clinic, had told me a white man had been asking after her and where she lived, also where she had gone on holiday. Beauty thought he was a relative or a friend. I am thinking this person was watching for me and followed me."

Blake stood up. "I'm going to take a shower now, then you are going to take me to see Miss Fur. Does she too think I'm dead? Has anyone told her?"

"No, Miss Fur was most hurt and Puso advised she should not be told until her mind was working again. Puso came to see me many seasons ago and told me where they had taken her. It is in the forest. The Government moved all the people and burnt their huts, they have all gone now. But they built Miss Fur another place, deeper in the forest, before this happened. She is there now, four of the older women stayed behind and have been taking care of her.

"Once Puso gave me permission, I myself went to see her. She was different, she is looking different, but she remembered me. I go to her with food and notebooks for her writing."

"So, you know exactly where she is then?"

"Yes, Mr Blake."

"But you didn't tell her I tried to kill her, and was taken by the sea?"

"No, Mr Blake. She was finding it hard to remember what happened. But on my last visit she asked for you – I did not know what to tell her."

Chapter Sixty-Nine

Blake drove at a furious pace, disregarding any traffic regulations, until they came to the edge of the forest.

Tapu indicated they should stop and walk the rest of the way. "Bugger that, Tapu, this is a Land Rover built for rugged terrain, show me the path and we'll drive there. I don't care if there are no roads, the Landy will take us there."

Blake pulled up at the structure with the flat green roof, astonished at how well it was hidden. Impossible to find unless you knew exactly where it was.

Tapu turned to him. "I am thinking it would be best if I go to Miss Fur to tell her you are here. It would not be good to not warn her. She is much better, but I need to go there first, she knows who I am. I will tell her you are waiting outside."

Blake disagreed with him but knew these people had saved her life and cared for her, they probably, he thought, knew her in this new state far better than he did.

He waited impatiently then looked up as she called his name.

"Blake! Blake! Why did it take you so long to find me?"

He smiled, overwhelmed that she was standing in front of him. "I always seem to find you in an abandoned place."

Yes, she looked different. The women of the village had fashioned a long dress for her, made of the soft pelts of antelope, her hair was pulled back from her face and adorned with plaits and beads, her normally pale face and limbs were now kissed by the sun to a light brown. A thin scar ran from her scalp to the edge of her eye.

She rushed towards him, throwing herself into his arms. She smelled vaguely of wood smoke. "Fleur, Fleur, why can I never find you at the Ritz Hotel in London, or somewhere civilised where we can have a cocktail or two, and you arrive by taxi. Why must it always be in some unknown place where no one else can ever find you?"

Fleur disentangled herself from his fierce embrace and took his hand. "Come on into my little house, I can give you a warm beer, I told Tapu to bring me some ready for your arrival, because I knew you would eventually come and find me. No fridge here, no power, but it's heavenly."

The four elderly woman who had been watching in astonishment as this white man plunged into their hidden place in his big car, came forward and softly clapped their hands in greeting.

Blake entered the simple structure which Fleur had made her own, he recognised one or two pieces of furniture from his own house in the bush. Tapu had gone to great lengths to ensure she was comfortable.

Fleur sat across from him and smiled. "Something happened to me on the beach at the Wild Coast, to begin with I couldn't recall anything, or how I got here in the middle of the forest again."

She gestured towards the women. "Without them I would have died. They took good care of me and nursed me back to health using their own medicines. I lost all sense of time as I waited for my body to recover, but my mind seemed to take longer. They gave me seeds, herbs, plants, and goodness knows what else, to help me regain my memory. Gradually I had flashes of recall of my meeting here with the San people, and the miraculous sacred seeds they had given me."

Blake watched her as she talked, tripping over her words and clearing her throat. Obviously, these women she had lived with for so long didn't speak English, but now she could communicate with him in her own language, it was as though a dam had broken and flooded her mind with words.

Fleur reached for his hand. "One day Tapu arrived. I asked him where you were, and he said you were away on a long business trip, but he would let you know where I was when you returned. He told me I had been involved in an accident on the beach and his people had brought me back here. He brought me a few things from the house to make me more comfortable. He brought me food and my medical bag. He talked to me about how he and I had worked for so many years out in the bush. He talked about the seeds these people had given me to help with memory loss.

"That's when I decided I would treat myself, try these seeds out, see what power they had. Tapu reminded me the woman who had lived here only took a small part of them once a month. I decided I would take the risk, without all the medical research and findings. I would be my own guinea pig."

Blake listened to her. "Wasn't this a great risk to take without knowing what the side effects might be, with no science to base anything on?"

Fleur shrugged. "I had nothing to lose. I had to remember and remember I did. I recalled things from my childhood in Kenya, things I hadn't thought about for decades. I remembered my mother's face so clearly, my childhood friends and their names. My sister and how angry she always seemed to be, and the first time I saw the face of the baby, Lucy."

Fleur paused. "I found myself in a unique position. When I was given the seeds, the leader of these San people, Puso, would not allow me to examine his women. But I now had four of them living with me and they allowed me to do this.

"My findings were incredible Blake! None of them showed any signs of ageing although, of course, they were. They had the minds of women in their forties. I knew I had found what my mother and I had been looking for."

Chapter Seventy
Blake
2019

"It was at this point, gentlemen, Fleur and I made our ultimate decision. She knew her research was dependent on the four San women who had looked after her. She wanted to stay with them, learn from them about the bounty the forest offered the western world.

"But she also needed to continue her work in the world of science. But someone had tried to kill her on the beach and we both knew it would be dangerous for her. Whoever this person was, he was not working alone.

"But she looked so different now and we both agreed it would be safe enough for her to continue her work with the four women who lived with her, but also, she needed to forge ahead with the scientists and doctors in Tokai, in Cape Town, she needed to have access to her laboratory at my house and the computer. The internet is spotty to say the least out here in the bush, but we get it now and again, a bit like Eskom's power supply. She needed to meet with George Mason and ensure everything was in place before she let the world know what she had found.

"So, gentlemen, this is what we did for the next four years. Meetings in Cape Town with the small pharma company, meetings with George Mason and then I took her to the place I had found for her San people."

Piet frowned at his notes. "So, did you get in touch with Jeremy Foxton, to let him know Doctor Palmere was alive and well?"

Blake shook his head. "No. Fleur was adamant about that. She was determined to remain in the shadows."

Jack looked up. "So, at what point was she going to tell her solicitor and her family she was still alive?"

Blake rubbed his weary eyes. "I don't know. You'll have to ask her these questions. Why she did what she did and her reasons for it. But I can tell you now, she will not speak to you, especially you Jack. You're a journalist. She wants to do this her own way. Yes, we are ready to launch the results of her research, but she will not speak to any journalist at this point, if ever. George will handle the media, if and when he sees fit. The Lancet will be given the irrefutable facts, but there will be no mention of her name or anything about her life, or where she lives.

"Someone tried to kill her. Fleur must remain anonymous."

Jack frowned. "It would be the decent thing to do to let her solicitor, Jeremy, know she is still alive. You should do this Blake, it's the honourable thing to do. Surely even Fleur must realise that."

Blake glanced at the closed door of her laboratory. "Yes, now you've told me how much time and money he has spent trying to find her it would be the decent thing to do. I'll speak to her."

Chapter Seventy-One

Jack looked through his notes. He now knew the facts behind this extraordinary story which might well change the lives of thousands and thousands of people struggling to remember who they were, and the life they had led before.

He had to sit with Doctor Fleur Palmere and learn more about her, but at this point it seemed impossible.

But Jack had come up against the impossible before. All he had to do was find a weakness in Fleur, confront her with something she could not deny, nothing scientific, but something personal which might break her down and allow him in.

He and Piet had returned to the guest house in town, the next morning. It was noon when they once more congregated in the neglected gardens.

Piet looked around for a waiter in the hope at least some coffee might be available. He needed food.

Like Jack he had spent hours, unable to sleep. He knew the value of Fleur's findings; he knew within days this would be disclosed to the world of science and medicine. From there it would move into a different realm. More tests, more media attention, and so it would go on. But it sounded as though this George Mason had buttoned down everything legally.

But he had a different agenda to Jack's. Jack was after a story about Fleur.

Piet was after the man who had tried to kill her.

An African, wearing a tall white hat, appeared in front of them. "I am the chef in this here hotel. Would you like to order some coffee and breakfast? I have been away but now I am here."

Jack grinned; surprised Piet had not fallen at his feet, like a starving refugee, with gratitude at the promise of some food.

"Bring me everything you have, my friend, chops, bacon, potatoes, tomatoes, eggs, sausages and anything else you can come up with, and lots of coffee."

Jack knew better to dive into the story before Piet had filled his stomach.

Piet leaned back in his chair; he had demolished everything the chef had brought him. Jack had been more sparing with his appetite and settled for the bacon, tomatoes, and scrambled eggs, but couldn't resist the lamb chop.

"See here Jack, I know you'll go after this story, and it won't be easy to get the good doctor to talk. I, myself, am going to pursue the identity of the man who tried to kill her. But I have no leads, no idea who he might have been, but my gut feel is he knew her, and she knew him."

A shadow emerged from the trees at the edge of the gardens. Tapu moved towards them, he tucked a roughly tied parcel under his arm then clapped his hands softly in greeting as he came to them.

Piet looked up in surprise. Tapu was the last person he expected to see, he had spent most of his time hiding from them.

Tapu refused the offer of a seat but hunkered down after carefully placing his package on the table. "Puso has asked me to give you this parcel."

Piet leaned forward. "But why didn't you give it to us when we were at Mr Blake's house?"

Tapu shrugged. "I had not been given permission then. But word has come from Puso, *sah*, from their new place in the desert where he and his people now live. They are most happy to be home where they belong. Puso said it was time to give something back for all they had been given.

"It is our way when we take the life of a living thing. When we hunt an animal with our poisoned arrows, we follow it for many hours, sometimes days before it dies. Then we pray and give thanks to it for giving its life to us. We have great respect for anything we kill.

"Puso killed the man who shot Miss Fur, but he did not give thanks to him. This has been on his mind since that day. He searched this dying man and found some things, also in the bag Miss Fur always carried. Puso was thinking the seeds had not brought life for Miss Fur and her work but had brought death instead. He took them back also with what you will find in this package."

Jack looked puzzled. "But why didn't you give these things in the package to the doctor and Mr Blake?"

"Puso only gave Miss Fur the necklace he took from around her neck. Inside this necklace were two small people hidden from the light. When he saw Miss Fur was not going to die, he placed this necklace once more around her neck so she could still have the hidden children with her. Puso said to give you this package as it was now police business, *sah*."

Tapu stood up and in seconds he had disappeared into the trees.

Piet carefully unwrapped the package and reached for the familiar small green book every South African must carry. An ID book.

He flipped quickly through to the ID number. He stabbed at the number. "See here, Jack, this tells me who this person was, it's all in the numbers if you know how to read them. He was white, a citizen of the country, born here along with his date of birth.

"His name was Johannes Hendricks. He was the man Puso killed; the man who shot Fleur. I need to get hold of Bertie; he'll be able to give me more information about him. Where he lived, what he did and where he came from. The photograph of him is old, hard to tell what he looked like. He was young when he was issued his ID book, he was, of course, much older when he took a shot at Fleur. Probably in his fifties. But there was a connection between the two of them. I will find it. It is highly likely he was called Hansie, a short form of his name."

Piet reached for his phone and sighed with frustration. "*Eish*. No *bleddy* signal. Listen, my friend, my work is done here. I need to get back to Hazyview where I can get a decent signal and call Bertie.

"You stay and chase your story, hey?"

Jack had been turning the two square discs in his hand. "This Johannes, or Hansie, must have been after these as well. In those days before technology really kicked in, Fleur must have recorded her research and findings on one of those old computers. They should be returned to Fleur. I think he might have been the botanist who worked with her at The Foundation."

Jack turned the curled pages of the small notebook also inside the package. "Hard to make out what this is all about, but probably more notes about what she was chasing.

"Yes, I think she did know this Johannes or Hansie. He most definitely knew what he was looking for, but he might not have been working alone. Doctor Mwanga also worked at The Foundation…somewhere along the line he was involved with all of this."

Piet stood up. "Right, I'm out of here. What's your next move, my friend?"

Jack smiled slowly at him. "I have a few ideas. One I know will work, I need to track a couple of people down which will be difficult with little or no internet. But first, I want to compose a message to Fleur… oh, please call Harry and tell him it's impossible to make contact at the moment, but I'll be in touch as soon as I can."

Piet raised his eyebrows in horror. "Are you kidding me? He'll start yelling down the phone from his comfortable leather chair in his fancy club. *Nah*, not doing it Jack. Don't like people yelling at me. But I'll send him an email telling him you're still out in the bush following your story. I'll bring him up to date on what we have so far."

Jack shouted after his retreating back. "Don't get smart Piet and write the whole thing in bloody Afrikaans, he won't find it amusing; it'll put his blood pressure up."

Piet turned around and laughed. "He must have high blood pressure all the time, living in that crap climate where it never stops raining, the trains are late, if they're not on strike and never arrive. Fighting his way through all the commuters trying to get home, and when he does his wife is asleep, a message left on the warming door of the oven saying his dinner was in the dogs. *Shoo*, what a life, hey!"

Chapter Seventy-Two

Jack spent the next day crafting his letter to Fleur. The flagging internet had given him just enough time to find the person he was looking for. He called the number and put in place the next phase of his plan.

He re-read his message to Fleur, deleting, and adding to it.

Dear Doctor Palmere,
I am aware you do not give interviews, for reasons I fully understand.
I'm sure, as a researcher of some note, you will have looked me up on the internet and looked at my profile – or George Mason certainly has done. I have no problem with you sharing this message with him, but it is personal. I know you are a private person, and I respect this.
Yes, I work for the Telegraph, *but I'm based in South Africa now. My forte was following cold cases, finding people who had gone missing and why.*
Jeremy Foxton contacted me in a desperate search to find out where you were and what happened to you. I met him in London, and he told me it was of the utmost importance to find you. Your sister had died, and he wished to wrap up your family estate and ensure Lucy was taken care of. But with no proof of whether you were alive or not, his hands were tied. So, he reached out to me for help.
I started at the beginning, where all stories start, but I wasn't going to follow your career. I wanted to find out more about the woman behind the career. This was you.
I met Lucy before I left, living in the house you had given to your sister. She works in a library in a place called Lymington, which, of course, you know well. She didn't invite me to visit her there, but I knew from Jeremy Foxton it was filled with memories of a place called Lamu, in Kenya, and I wondered what the connection might be between a brilliant scientist and an isolated island called Lamu.
Thus, I began my own journey to find out more about you and who you were as a young woman.
I went to the house where you were born and brought up with your sister Helene. I met Noah. Unfortunately, his wife, Patience, had passed away and was buried next to your mother, Christiana.
Noah took me to your mother's grave. It was a staggering sight of pure beauty. If you agree to meet with me, I will tell you about it and

show you the photos I took of her final resting place and the old man called Noah. Sadly, your childhood home is not how you would remember it, but Noah has done his best. It is still there, and I imagined the laughter and sound of two little sisters skipping through the bush, dancing through the dust in a world which has gone, along with the childhood memories and the footprints you both left behind.

I went back to Nairobi consumed with thoughts of what your childhood had been like, living on the edge of Lake Nivasha. What your mother had been like.

I met a Doctor Mwanga. He had joined your team in London, at The Foundation. Now a powerful, influential political figure. It was not a good meeting. But I will tell you about this if you agree to meet with me.

From there my journey took me to Lamu.

Here I met some of the old local Kenyans who had retired there. They told me about Captain Michael Bennett, who often went to Peponi, the local hotel and bar. I also met Ali. He told me about you and showed me a photograph, taken in London, of you and Michael. He told me Michael planned to marry you and live on the island.

Michael's house was sold after his death. Ali took nothing but the one photograph he showed me. I met with a small group of old Kenyans, professional hunters in their day, and they told me about Michael's last evening before he died. Michael had taken to going to Peponi regularly. He found comfort there. The ex-professional hunters carried their own badges of honour in their damaged bodies, as did Michael with his, although not perpetrated by wild animals, but what the war in the desert had wrought upon him. This I will also tell you about if you agree to meet me. It seemed to me, Fleur, if you don't mind me calling you that, you were the very essence of his life, and he always hoped you would come back to him. This, of course, didn't happen.

I may be overstepping the mark here...but Blake told my partner, Piet, and I, he had found you in an abandoned camp site somewhere in the Eastern Cape. He found a card in your bag which gave the address and name of Captain Michael Bennet. He went to some lengths to find this man to let him know where you were. My gut feel is that he didn't tell you about this, for reasons of his own.

However, Captain Michael Bennett had been reported missing in action and presumed dead.

So, I know a lot about you as a woman, a sister, an aunt, and who you touched in your life. I took many photos as I followed in the footsteps of your past. You might find them of interest.

Unfortunately, I don't have any of your sister, but I do have some of Lucy. Your last living relative.

I give you my word everything I have learned about you, all the people I met who knew you, that I will not publish anything about you without your permission.

I would like to talk to you, to show you the photos I have, show you where your mother was buried and what a glorious sight it was to behold.

Lucy has grappled with her past for many years, wanting answers to so many questions which her mother, Helene, was unable to give her. She is quite alone now and struggling with the many questions about who she is and who her relatives were.

I think you may like to see how she looks now.

I have put all the pieces of the puzzle together and now everything makes sense.

As I said, I may be a journalist, but I have impeccable credentials. I have never published anything in my newspaper without the full consent of the parties concerned.

I would very much like to see you again if you will allow this?

My partner, ex-inspector Piet Joubert has returned to Hazyview where he is pursuing some information about the man who tried to kill you. I am expecting an update on his investigation tomorrow.

His name was Johannes, or *Hansie as he was called, and I think he worked with you at The Foundation.*

I also have some computer discs which belong to you, they were found on the beach where you were shot. I am sure they are immensely valuable. These I will return to you.

All this information I will share with you, should you agree to meet with me.

Finally, your solicitor in London, Jeremy Foxton, although reluctant at first, but desperate to find you, has given me your mother's leather journal. I have it here with me now.

Jack Taylor

Jack read, and re-read, what he had written. Fleur had gone through some hard times over the years she had lived in South Africa, with no contact, as far as he knew, with any of her family.

It would be a rare person indeed who would not be intrigued with what he had offered in his letter. A glimpse of her past, news of her family and what had happened over the intervening years, the photographs, the name of the man who had tried to kill her, and the two computer discs which would hold vital information on her research. She would want those back if nothing else.

And her mother's leather-bound journal.

When Piet had broken the news to her about her sister and Michael Bennett, Jack had had a rare glimpse of the tough, highly successful scientist. He saw the crack in the façade as he listened to the keening sound of her grief which had carried from her room.

He remembered Blake's remark. *"They are tears of regret and not grief."*

He took a deep breath and pressed the send button.

That evening Jack found a restaurant in town, delighted to see Karoo lamb on the menu. He didn't bother to look at what else was on offer. He knew he would be leaving this area soon, would never in his life again taste lamb like this. In fact, he promised himself he would have a double helping.

He drove back to the guest house, where without Piet, he was the only guest, he missed his keen mind and the endless banter. He sat out in the deserted garden and looked up at the dark sky teeming with millions of endless stars, his hands behind his head, his legs stretched out in front of him.

What was it about Africa which through the years had attracted adventurers, pioneers, historians, and farmers from their own countries? All of them, one way or another, had left their mark here, made their homes here, calling it their own.

Africa has promised them nothing, only a harsh landscape of incredible beauty and opportunity. And they had taken it. Putting their own roots down and never leaving, and if some of them did, they never forgot it and longed to return to the place which had evoked such strong emotions.

Lost in his thoughts he was abruptly brought back to the present by his phone rumbling on the table. He snatched it up.

"Hey, Piet. This connection isn't great but give me what you've found out. Where are you?"

Piet laughed. "I'm sitting in my cottage watching television with Hope. She likes to watch the food channel. I have a lot of information from Bertie about this Johannes Hendricks.

"He couldn't hack into The Foundation's scientific research, but he found a way into who had worked there and when. I have more information on Johannes Hendricks who was a highly qualified botanist. He was head-hunted by The Foundation and moved to London to work in their research department. The head of the research department was Doctor Fleur Palmere. She had others working for her, an impressive team.

"Once Johannes, or Hansie as he was called, had obtained his degree, he spent some years at various game lodges as a ranger and a specialist in trees, plants, and such like. The Foundation found him and offered him said job."

Jack scribbled down this information in his notebook.

"*Ag*, Hope, stop *bleddy* drooling will you or I'll change the channel and find the one where abandoned dogs are looking for something called a forever home, then you'll realise how lucky you are.

"Anyways, Jack. Johannes, or Hansie, as she would have called him, worked with Fleur for some years. Then along came Doctor Mwanga from Kenya and everything from that point on seemed to fall apart. Fleur left, Mwanga took her place and worked with Hansie for a couple of years.

"As you told me, Mwanga left under a dark cloud, and went back to Kenya. Around this time Hansie also left. So maybe they had made a private deal between them. Mwanga, I'm thinking, employed Hansie to track and follow Fleur and find out how far she had progressed with her research. Obviously over the years, he had tried to find her, paid for by Mwanga, and when he did – he killed her to get the information Mwanga wanted.

"Bertie had no other information to add. But, hey, Jack, got a copy of the email you sent to Fleur. Damn good I have to say. Yet another woman who will not be able to resist your good looks and messy hair, and that fancy accent of yours and the information you have tempted her with. Even I wouldn't have been able to resist the content. Any response from her?"

Jack pulled his jacket around him; Karoo nights reminded him of the depths of winter in the UK, except they had double glazing, underfloor heating, and roaring fires to keep the place warm, here you had a coat and bugger all else.

"Nothing yet, but she will contact me. The bait is out there, she knows I know all about her. I'll give her a day or two to respond. Then when I meet her, which I know I will, I'll tell her more about Bertie's discoveries – that should do it."

Chapter Seventy-Three

Jack pulled into the drive and parked his car.

Fleur was waiting for him, standing quite still on the veranda, her hands clasped in front of her, a look of resignation on her face.

Her hair no longer plaited with beads, it was cascading around her shoulders, shot with grey. She was wearing a long pale pink dress which moved around her body with the light warm wind which was caressing the bush. Around her neck she wore a necklace of shells and beads, along with her mother's necklace.

"Come and sit, Jack, Tapu will bring us tea." She smiled tautly at him. "Blake is away for a few days, a week or so maybe, I'm never sure how long his trips will take, but it's always been like that."

Jack sat across from her as he sipped his tea. He looked at the woman in front of him, a softer, less aggressive, and hostile version of what he had seen before. Her extraordinary eyes seemed different as well.

He waited for her to open the conversation. She was struggling with a starting point.

He leaned forward and handed over her mother's old leather journal, still wrapped in its simple shroud of sacking.

"This was where this whole story began isn't it?"

Fleur removed the sacking reverently, and ran her hands over the fading cover, the corners of which were starting to turn green with dampness and mould. Thoughts of her mother clearly flooding back to her.

Jack waited awhile as she turned some of the pages before carefully closing it and holding it close to her chest.

"No one really knows me, Jack, but you seem to have turned my world upside down with your email. I have achieved what I wanted to achieve, which I'm very proud of.

"I found what I was looking for, I found, or Blake did, some land for the San people, in the Kalahari. They have all moved there, back to where they came from.

"There are thousands of people who will be given hope with the drug we're now developing."

Fleur sat back in her chair. "A little word – hope. But it's all we have, isn't it?

"A Zimbabwean man, called Simon, used that word when he found me lost and alone all those years ago in a deserted and abandoned camp site. I have never forgotten him, or the baby his grandmother saved, the girl called Poppy and her little white dog."

"I have used the seeds on myself. The drug we have now formulated, works. I'm living proof of it. My job is done. But it was not as successful as I had such high hopes for.

"However, it has come with a heavy price. You see, Jack, people are most resilient, they make their own choices, and they are prepared to pay the price. As I did.

"So, I will tell you my story, but perhaps you'll show me all your photographs first?"

Jack handed her his phone and noticed her hands trembled as she took it and began her long journey home, along the road which had brought her here. She still held on tightly to her mother's journal.

He watched her without speaking, leaving her to her thoughts. He had put the photographs in the order he had taken them.

Fleur was silent as she went slowly through them. She took a deep breath when she saw her mother's final resting place again.

"Oh, *Mama*," she gasped, "what a truly magnificent place to be, in the country you loved so much, with all your own research now living and growing around you."

The tears made their way along the tributary of lines on her face. Jack handed her his handkerchief then sat back, still saying nothing as she made her journey back, through his images.

The photograph of herself with Captain Michael Bennett, the shots of his old house, and the one of Ali brought more tears. She looked at Michael's grave, so far away from Lamu where he had died. It looked a lonely place to be, taken on a dark wet afternoon in the UK.

Not what she had wanted for him. But now she felt responsible for what had happened to him, not the wars he had fought, but the one thing she had taken from him – hope.

She closed her eyes briefly. "Perhaps, Jack, if Lucy will agree. Jeremy Foxton could arrange for one of my tall turquoise Lamu lamps, from my house in Lymington, to be taken to Michael's grave. It will need to be cemented into the ground, so nobody can steal it, and have some sort of eternal light burning within. He'll like knowing I haven't forgotten him. Knowing he's not lying there alone. That I'm still with him. He'll remember the Lamu lamp he brought me."

Jack felt a lump forming in his throat. It was a wonderful idea.

"If Lucy agrees, which will be difficult to explain to her, then I think it's a great idea. Michael will like it – a taste of home – Lamu.

Jeremy, I'm sure will take care of everything. He was extremely fond of Michael and his parents."

Fleur nodded then looked down at the phone. "No pictures of Helene then?"

Jack shook his head. "I was too late, I'm afraid. She had already died. Jeremy Foxton mentioned her extraordinary eyes when he met her. The next shot is of Lucy, your niece. She has the same startling eyes as you and your sister, and I suspect of your mother, Christiana."

Fleur stared at her niece, the strong likeness to the family. She ran her finger lightly over the image of her face and took a deep breath.

"Perhaps, Jack, we should have a glass of wine. I'll need some courage to tell my story. I'll ask Tapu to bring us some. Where is he? He's always around when we have guests?"

Jack bit his lip, this was going to be difficult to navigate. "Tapu kindly offered to go to town for me, there was something I needed. But I know where the fridge is, and I'll bring us both a glass of wine."

Fleur looked up and frowned. "He went off to town without telling me? Most unusual."

She looked up at the golden red sky, another beautiful day in Africa was coming to an end. Fleur felt the greyness gathering around her and fought it, fighting off what normally ended in blackness. There were still things she needed to do, still loose ends to tie up before she could give in to the inevitable.

Jack and Fleur sat out on the *stoep* watching the hot sun sinking behind the trees, accentuating the shape of them. Darkness descended quickly, which it does in Africa, taking the sun and bringing the twilight. She turned to him.

"I will tell you my story, Jack, based on the promise you will not publish any of the details of my personal life without my permission."

Jack took a sip of his wine. "You have my word, Fleur. But your story is not finished yet is it?"

Chapter Seventy-Four
Fleur

Yorkshire, outside of the major towns, was a desolate place and this is why I chose the old farmhouse, out on the moors. Nobody intruded on our life, or the other life which would soon begin.

My sister's life was one of destruction, but I knew, unlike me, she had floundered to try and find love and stability but had failed and turned to drugs and alcohol to lessen the pain of hopelessness.

My vocation then had been to save lives. I knew I had to save her life before she destroyed it. She was my sister, and I loved her.

For months we had talked about the future, mine which was full of hope and challenges, and love; hers which was filled with despair. We made a pact. Helene would only agree to the arrangement if I would cut off all contact with her if she were to live a different life. We fought long and hard over that. But it was the only deal she would agree to, and I too had to agree to it if I still wanted to pursue my career, my passion, my vocation.

Lucy was born on a night which was full of fury. The icy winds blew and screamed around the old, isolated farmhouse as though it was warning both of us of the future ahead, and the crushing consequences of what lay waiting for us.

I took my child and placed her in the arms of my sister.

I didn't see or contact Helene again. I never saw my daughter again.

This was the deal my sister and I had made. She wouldn't have it any other way.

Chapter Seventy-Five
Fleur

Michael was fighting his own wars, as I was with the loss of our child, Lucy. Michael's daughter.

I broke off my relationship with him, knowing he would never accept what I had done. He wanted to marry me, move to Lamu, and have children of our own. I knew he would never forgive me for making the choice I had made. I had given his child away and never told him about her.

But I didn't tell him this was the only reason I was ending the relationship.

I had worked long and hard for my degrees, working relentlessly in the world of medicine and science to follow my own path and find what I was looking for. Sitting on a beach in Lamu, surrounded by children Michael so desperately wanted, having sundowners at some bar on the beach – I couldn't do it. I simply couldn't. In the end it would have destroyed both of us.

And so, I headed back to Africa, leaving my past behind, leaving Michael behind, and upholding my promise to my sister. I would let Helene bring up Lucy as her daughter. It was the only way I could deal with everything. I had to cut all ties with my family, and my daughter.

I shut down my own emotions and followed the path my mother had set for me. I realise now, I left everything who was me behind. Dead and buried.

I achieved everything I set out to do. But I lost the essence of who I was as a person, a woman.

Now, today, I sit across from this man called Jack Taylor, I know the time has come to let go of the scientist and confront my own life.

Jack's photographs had evoked emotions I thought had been long gone. But looking at them I realised what I had lost. Who I was now.

I had found the cure, returned the San people back to their land and their people. My work was done. But where did that leave me?

Right now, looking back down that road, I was alone. I had Blake, of course, but he didn't fill the space or the gaps in my life. Nobody could, only Michael. I loved Blake in a different sort of way. But I had no family of my own.

Fleur now turned to Jack. "So, that's my story."

Jack leaned forward. "As you've told me, you have lived your life, achieved what you set out to do. You have given the world of medicine something unique, they will go on with it, your name will be remembered."

"What's in a name, Jack," she said sadly. "Yes, I will be remembered, but then my name will be forgotten. I ask myself if the price was too high. Who am I now?"

She hesitated. "You see Jack, the seeds I found were indeed ground-breaking, however after all our hard work and our clinical trials, we discovered the seeds were not going to be the complete cure for memory loss. Yes, they helped enormously with extending the memory of the brain, recapturing images of a patient's past with some clarity, but they were not going to be the cure I thought they might be for Dementia. They would merely slow the process down, which was ground-breaking, but not enough."

Fleur laced her fingers together. "It's a blessing not a curse, to forget your past, maybe easier…but not for those who love you, I realise that now from my own life experience. I hurt a lot of people…"

He could hear the despair, the regret, in her voice but still remained silent.

Fleur continued. "I realised then that these desert people must have used something else, or it was in their diet, or simply their way of life, or genetic, or maybe even spiritual. The seeds would not be enough.

"I had given years of my life with great hope I would find the cure for memory loss. I didn't achieve this, but I believe my research has contributed a great deal to the world of medicine. I don't have the energy, or the time, to pursue further research. I'm not young and strong anymore. I have health problems which I believe I inherited from my mother and, I fear, when you mentioned Lucy has health issues, it's something which runs through the female line of our family. It took Helene as well."

Jack was mesmerised with her story but didn't interrupt with any questions of his own.

Fleur took a sip of her wine. "You see, Jack, I have worked out how my mother died. She was aware of the dangers connected to her own work. She knew the seasons of the bush and what they brought with them.

"Yes, she was bitten by a snake, but the snake didn't kill her. At that time of the year snakes are coming out of hibernation, they're lethargic. Snakes don't randomly kill people; they will never attack unless they are threatened.

"My mother was already dead before she fell on the snake who retaliated, which is normal, by biting her.

"My sister, Helene, died very suddenly, without warning, without any signs of a history of ill health. This gave me much to think about."

Jack leaned forward in his chair. "Are you telling me this is a genetic thing, a hereditary thing?"

Fleur nodded her head. "Yes, it must be. So, I may well have contributed to science and extended people's memory for a few years, but I was helpless in trying to save my own family."

Jack took a deep breath as he saw the red dust heralding the approach of a car, hoping his decision would be the right one, and what was going to happen next would not be a complete and utter disaster.

Fleur watched the dust cloud making its way towards them, then turned to him. "I wasn't expecting visitors, is it Tapu?"

Jack took a deep breath and stood up. "Yes. He's bringing someone to meet you."

Tapu pulled up and opened the passenger door of his car.

Fleur stood up frowning. "Who is this woman?"

"Her name is Lucy."

Chapter Seventy-Six

Fleur looked shocked, bewildered and then apprehensive, as Lucy walked slowly towards her, staring at the woman in front of her, not shaking her hand, not touching her. Her identical eyes uncertain.

"Hello, Aunt Fleur. I'm sure you're not pleased to see me, you don't know me do you, never wanted to as you didn't keep in touch with your sister, my mother or me, for the past few decades.

"You look like her though, same eyes, same shaped face…" She faltered and gestured to Jack. "Jack persuaded me to come here. He told me you would fill all the empty holes in my life. Answer all my questions. That's why you've been hiding away isn't it. Not someone who would share her private life with her own family."

Fleur reached blindly for the chair behind her, and sat down heavily, as Lucy continued.

"Although I understand from Jack you've achieved a lot in your life. Given so much hope to the lives of others. Except little to your own family."

Badly shaken by the appearance of Lucy, dressed in her dull clothes, her hair tied back, and her harsh words, Fleur gestured Lucy to sit.

"I'll get Tapu to bring you something to drink. This is all rather a shock to me Lucy."

Jack reached for his phone. "I should head back to town, Fleur, it's getting dark, I have work to do. My editor is waiting for my weekly column, which I'm already late with. I also need to let Jeremy Foxton know the situation as it stands."

He saw the panic in Fleur's eyes. "No, Jack, please stay here the night. You can do your work from the guest cottage which Tapu will prepare for you. He'll bring dinner to you, so you won't be disturbed."

For Jack this was an irresistible invitation. "If you're sure you want me here, then I'm happy to stay a day or two, thank you."

Lucy stared at the woman sitting across from her, a stranger. "When Jack goes back to town, I'm going with him. I have no idea who you are as a person. I thought I would feel excited to finally find my Aunt Fleur, the last surviving member of my family, but I don't feel anything at all. This was a mistake, a big mistake."

Lucy looked at Jack, panic on her face. "Please take me back, Jack?"

He stood up. "Give her a chance, Lucy, she's a good person. She's dedicated her life to helping other people, she'll be able to help you heal as well. Hear her out, it's the least you can do. Then, if you still want to leave, I'll take you back to town, okay? I'll see you both tomorrow."

Fleur stood on shaky legs, leaning down towards Lucy she took her cold unresponsive hands.

"You must stay, Lucy. Give me a chance to get to know you, for you to get to know me, you might feel differently then. You've come a long way to find me and now you have. We're related by blood, DNA, we have the same family history, surely you want to know about that. I don't expect you to love me. It would be an impossible request."

Lucy shrugged. "My mother never told me the truth about my so-called father – I don't even know his name, or where he is, she told me little or nothing about my family. She wouldn't tell me why she never kept in touch with you, her own sister. Blood relations, DNA, it doesn't matter to me anymore. It's all too late, I should have left things as they were."

Fleur sat down again looking at the angry, broken, and lonely young woman across from her. Her whole career in the world of medicine and science had been based on truth, facts, and proof.

She took a deep breath, there was only one way to save this situation, to finally put things right, and she knew she would have to find the moral courage to do it.

She took a deep breath. "Your father's name was Michael Bennett, he was a captain in the British army, a doctor, like me. I met him in Nairobi, in Kenya. We were together for some years, living in London. He went off to fight his wars and I stayed and continued my work as a doctor and then a scientist."

Her voice trembled as she continued, then took a deep shuddering breath. "You see, Lucy, I'm your mother. Not your aunt. A simple DNA test will prove this without any doubt."

Lucy stared at her, the blood draining from her face, she stood up unsteadily, then crumpled to her feet as she felt the greyness and the familiar blackness descend as it had so often before.

Tapu appeared from no-where and together they picked Lucy up. "I will put her in the guest bedroom, Miss Fur, which I have made ready for her."

Fleur nodded, distraught. "She's fainted, low blood pressure. She'll come around in a few moments and I'll take care of her. Please bring me some cold water for her to drink and a bowl with some cloths, the heat is something she will not be familiar with. I'll find her something cooler to wear."

Fleur checked her daughter's pulse, smoothing the damp hair from her forehead. Hardly able to believe she was looking at her daughter after all these years.

Tapu hesitated before he left the room. "Miss Fur, this guest, she is your daughter, yes? She has the same eyes as you."

"Yes, Tapu," she said softly, uttering the words she had never said before. "She is my daughter."

Chapter Seventy-Seven

Jack finished his dinner and continued with his writing. Tapu came to take away his empty dishes. "How is it going with Miss Fur and Lucy, Tapu?"

Tapu shrugged. "European people are complicated, Mr Yak. We people lead a simpler life, we never reject our families. Cousins are welcomed into our clan whether they are cousins or not, blood brothers or sisters, it matters not to us. We are the same people, and this is enough.

"But Miss Lucy is now listening to her mother, trying to understand why she did what she did. It is a lot for a lost daughter to understand. A lot for a lost mother as well."

Talking long into the night, mother and daughter told their stories. Lucy finally had answers to some of her questions. She now knew who her father was, and who he had been. The part the two sisters had played to protect her, and why.

"You see, Lucy, who you thought was your mother, my sister, did the best she could to keep up this charade, for that's what it was. Both of us loved you deeply, but only one of us would ever know you, only one of us could have you and call you her own. That was my sister Helene. She was your mother figure. But I am your biological mother.

"As I've told you, Captain Michael Bennett was your father, and I loved him very much. He too is gone now."

Fleur paused for a moment and took a sip of her wine. "They all go eventually, Lucy, we can't capture anyone, or anything, forever.

"I've told you everything. I've told you the truth. Why I did what I did and my reasons for it. I don't expect you to forgive me, but I hope you'll try and understand."

Lucy exhausted from her long journey to Africa, meeting her biological mother and hearing her story, stood up.

"I'd like to stay with you for a while if it will be all right. I still have many questions. I want to see Jack's photos of my grandmother's past, your past, see what my father looked like. But I need to sleep now. Goodnight…"

Fleur still sat there looking into the night, looking into her past. There was no bond between them, and she knew they both felt that. But Lucy was beginning to soften, she was listening to a story she had longed to hear all her life.

But Fleur had seen something. Something which ran through the blood of all the females of the Palmere family, something running through herself. She knew she would not be able to save her daughter, as she would not be able to save herself.

Chapter Seventy-Eight

At dawn the next morning, Fleur crept into her daughter's bedroom. Lucy was in a deep sleep, one arm stretched above her head. She lowered herself on the edge of the bed and gazed at Lucy's face, seeing clearly, having tried her own memory seeds, a cameo of the tiny face of the baby she had given birth to and seen so briefly, before handing her to Helene. She traced the contours of Lucy's face, the tears running down her own.

Lucy flinched in her sleep. "Mummy," she muttered.

Fleur wiped her eyes; she knew Lucy was thinking of Helene and not of her. It was a title she had not earned, although she would like to have been called it. Just once. It was a more precious title than any of the academic ones she had earned during her career, worthy of so much more.

Fleur returned to her own room and lay on her bed, watching the beginning of a new day, the cold fingers of dawn giving way to the softness of a rising sun and another hot day.

Today, before Jack left, he would show Lucy all the photographs he had taken of her grandmother's grave, of Michael Bennett, her father, of Ali, and the others who had played such a big part in her short life.

Fleur picked up her mother's leather journal, the leather now fading, but still wrapped in the simple sacking Noah had kept it safe in.

"Oh, *Mama,*" she whispered, "what a legacy you have left for the world of medicine, but, oh, what a price your family have paid."

Jack and Lucy sat together, Fleur sat silently, some distance away on the veranda, watching them. Jack with his photographs was adding more to the life of Lucy than she ever could with her stories. Imagination was one thing for Lucy, but bringing the characters to life with his images, meant so much more.

Lucy stopped at the photograph of Captain Michael Bennett. "Can you enlarge this one for me, Jack?"

Lucy looked at the image and her face softened. "He was my father, right?"

Jack nodded. "Yes, he was your father. A fine soldier who dedicated his life to his country. A good man. Life is never as it seems. I know this as a journalist. People do things for what they think are the right reasons. But nobody really knows what they are thinking and why they do what they do.

"He died in Lamu. He loved it there apparently. Personally, I think he should have been buried there rather than the UK, but the Army insisted he be repatriated to England.

"I'll leave you here with Fleur. Don't be too hard on her, sometimes people take the wrong path for all the right reasons.

"You'll meet Blake Hemmingway. He's a good man, he's looked after your mother all these years, and I would say he saved her life.

"I'll transfer all these pics to your phone so you can study them in your own time, they belong to you and your past.

"Blake will take good care of you when he comes home, he'll handle your onward travel arrangements when you're ready to go back to the UK."

Jack looked at her shrewdly. "Are you in any hurry to get back to Lymington, Lucy. Is someone looking after your dog or cat, if you have one? Jeremy Foxton, your family lawyer, will take care of things if necessary."

Lucy hesitated briefly. "No cats or dogs. The library will manage perfectly well without me. I like it here, love the warmth, the high blue skies and the glorious stars at night, the sound of the storms and the burping frogs and other insects after the rain. It's so peaceful, so different. In an odd sort of way, I feel connected to it."

Jack took a sip of his coffee. "Fleur would like one of her Lamu lamps to be placed next to your father's grave, as I'm sure she told you. Will you do this? Jeremy will arrange everything. Perhaps one day you'll go and visit his final resting place?"

Lucy responded immediately. "Of course. I'd like to go and sit with him, talk to him, even though I never knew him, but now I have a picture of him, and know of his love for Fleur, her love for him. It's the least I can do."

Jack watched her as she talked. She seemed softer now, wearing a loose pale blue cotton dress, her hair released from its tight bun and tumbling around her shoulders; more accepting of what had happened in her mother's life. "What do you call Fleur now. You seem easier with her?"

Lucy looked up watching some bird of prey floating on the thermals, she reached for her coffee. "I call her Fleur, because until now her sister was my mother. I feel closer to her because she's been honest with me. There's a tentative bond between us, after all she is now my only living relative. I can see why she made her choices, not that I will ever understand how a mother can give up her child. I admire what she has contributed to the world of medicine and science. She is truly unique. I have never met anyone like her, of course I haven't, after all she is my mother, right?"

Jack smiled at her. "Yes, she has indeed contributed a lot to this world full of its wars and hardships for so many people. Given hope to so many who didn't have it before and didn't imagine it was possible. Through the years she has never asked for anything for herself. But Blake has been a constant in her life for years now, helped her in so many ways. You'll like him, I certainly did."

He tucked his notebook and phone into the pocket of his jacket. "I must be off, or I'll miss my plane."

He paused for a moment. "I like your new look, it suits you, I hardly recognise you from the first time I met you in the library, looking most severe in your long thick skirt and cardigan."

Lucy laughed. "It's Fleur's. I love these long cool cotton dresses. I also like not wearing any shoes." she wriggled her toes. "Look, they're already turning brown!"

Lucy hugged him. "Thank you, Jack, for everything. It's unlikely I can ever repay you, but if I can, well, you know where to find me."

Jack turned back to her. "Actually, there is something you can do for me, it's a small thing, but would mean a great deal to Fleur. You could refer to her as your mother. That one word would be priceless to her and make her happy. Happier than all the accolades and awards she has received during her working life."

As Jack drove back to the guest house, he thought if Fleur would allow him to write her story it would be a cracker, following on from the academic, and telling the story of the person she was – a woman called Fleur Palmere.

Chapter Seventy-Nine

Fleur looked at her daughter. "We have no control of when and where it might happen. If it does indeed run through the female line of the Palmere's.

"I've studied the genetics of the Palmere women. Not my area of expertise really, but I can apply my years of research, and this is the only conclusion I have reached.

"Tapu is leaving tomorrow, he wants to go back to his people in the Kalahari. He'll be gone for a month or so. In a few days' time, Blake will return from his latest business meeting with our lawyer, George Mason, in Johannesburg.

"The past few weeks have given me much joy, a longed-for connection to my own past, to my daughter.

"I have reached the end of my journey, Lucy. The Palmere Curse, as I refer to it, will come calling soon enough."

Lucy watched her mother. She now knew her own life was limited, but with no time scale. It was a very unsettling and frightening thought.

For the next few days, Fleur and Lucy made their plans. They disagreed on some, compromised on others, and eventually printed out what they had agreed upon.

The documents were signed, scanned, and sent through to George Mason in Johannesburg.

"There's one other thing I want to do, Lucy." She reached behind her neck and removed the chain and pendant.

"I'd like you to have this." She opened the pendant. "Here is your family."

She placed it around her daughter's neck and kissed her on both cheeks.

"Time for bed now I think, don't you? Goodnight, my child."

Lucy looked at the black and white photographs of the two little girls. "Goodnight," she hesitated, without looking up. "Mother."

Chapter Eighty
Hazyview
South Africa.

Jack unpacked his bag, poured himself a beer and went to join Piet out on the patio.

"So, my friend, another case is solved. A different one this time. Less crime but more family secrets, not so?"

Jack nodded. "Yes, I suppose so."

"Why are you looking so gloomy then? We found who tried to kill the good doctor, this Johannes guy, or Hansie as we would call him here. Fortunately, the San man killed him. We have no evidence this Doctor Mwanga was behind it all, but he was. But we can't touch him now, we have no proof. The Kenyan government would protect him, no doubt he has friends in high places. Bottom line is he may well be complicit in what happened to Fleur, but he wasn't her killer. But let's leave that there shall we?

"Doctor Palmere found something which would slow down the devastation of memory loss, but not the cure. Plus, the San people have a place of their own now in the Kalahari."

Jack took a sip of his beer as he listened to Piet's overview, not interrupting. "The South African pharma company are well into production now, trials completed. George keeping his eagle eye on everything. Another winner for South Africa, hey!

"The UK lawyer has all the answers he's looking for, he can now process everything. Fleur will be given the accolades she so richly deserves. So, as you say, done and dusted, or as we say here, finish and *klaar*.

"Fleur's complicated path has finally led her back to her daughter, Lucy, and they are now together in Blake Hemmingway's home in the bush. The kid knows who her father was, who her mother is, Blake seemed like a good *oke*, maybe he'll adopt her. What's not to love about a happy ending?

"Fleur has given you the rights to the story of her life, once she has read it, of course. Harry will be over the moon about the final chapter of this story."

Jack was unusually quiet. "I don't think the final chapters are over…"

Chapter Eighty-One

Blake Hemmingway made his way home. The sun was setting with all its gold and red and he was anxious to get there. Darkness descends quickly in Africa and so it was when he pulled up outside of his house.

He frowned as he the approached *stoep*, all was in darkness. Tapu he knew would have lit the hurricane lamps if there had been a power cut, but he knew Tapu had gone to spend time with his people.

He parked but left his headlamps on, which illuminated the ghostly outlines of his house, hiding the single flame of a candle which flickered in the corner of the *stoep*.

"Fleur! Fleur! Why are you sitting here in darkness. Where are you?"

A young woman appeared from the shadows. "Fleur is lying down; she had one of her fainting fits. But she's all right, just resting."

Blake squinted through the darkness. "But who are you. What are you doing here?"

Lucy smiled. "You don't know who I am, but I know you must be Blake.

"My name is Lucy. I'm Fleur's daughter."

Blake flicked on the lights and stared at the young woman in front of him, then smiled.

Yes, the same unforgettable eyes, the same shaped face, her long hair tumbling around her shoulders.

"But how did you get here, who brought you?"

Lucy smiled. "Jack Taylor. I think you know him."

Blake made his way to their bedroom. Fleur was asleep, her face seemed softer. He ran his hand down the side of her face. "You should have told me, Fleur, why did you hide your daughter away and call her your niece?"

Fleur moved at his familiar touch, hearing the same mellifluous voice calling her back to that time so many years ago at the abandoned camp site.

She opened her eyes and smiled at him. "Hello, Blake. Sorry, I fainted again, but you're used to it now."

She rubbed her eyes. "You've obviously met Lucy, my daughter." She smiled, it sounded so odd to say that, but wonderful as well.

Blake was bewildered. "But why didn't you tell me, for goodness sake.

"I would have understood. She's Michael Bennett's daughter, isn't she?"

Fleur looked at him, her eyes steady. "Yes, she is."

"Look, I'm not feeling good at the moment. I need to sleep, but why don't you and Lucy eat the dinner I prepared. Get to know her Blake, it's important."

Lucy looked at Blake, their plates empty in front of them. She smiled at him. "The French know how to cook, Blake, at least it was one nebulous talent I inherited. I'll take the plates back to the kitchen and then we can talk."

Blake looked out at the stars above him. They never changed, but something here had changed, beyond his comprehension. He loved Fleur, she had filled his life for so many years. They had been lovers for a long time, but now he realised he had never really known her. He had had his suspicions about Captain Michael Bennett, knew she had loved him in a way that was different to the way she loved him, had tried to work out her relationship with her sister, but had not produced any answers. Now he knew the truth.

He watched Lucy. She was indeed the daughter of Fleur.

The hurricane lights and candles were always kinder to a face than electricity. He saw in their shadows the face of a young Fleur.

Lucy took a sip from her wine. "I feel, although it's not my place, you should know the story, should know what happened. Fleur has told me everything. It's only fair I tell you."

Lucy had gone to bed; it was late before Blake took to his own. He wrapped his arms around Fleur and pulled her towards him.

"You feel so cold." He pulled the duvet over them, letting the warmth of his own body seep through to hers.

Exhausted from the long drive back home and the revelations from Lucy, he felt himself sinking into sleep, but her familiar body wasn't responding to his. He propped himself up on his elbow.

Feeling uneasy he turned the light back on.

He touched her face, but she didn't turn toward him, as she always had done.

Blake looked at her for a long time, stroking the face he had come to love, had loved so well, trying to hold back what he knew he was confronting. Finally, he dressed again and made his way to Lucy's bedroom, turning the bedside light on.

He shook her gently. "Lucy," he said softly. "I need you to wake up."

Lucy opened her eyes and rubbed them.

Blake ran his unsteady fingers through his hair and took hold of her hand. "Lucy, I need you to come with me. It's Fleur."

Lucy's breath caught in her throat. "What's happened? She was a little shaken up, but just wanted to sleep after she fainted."

She struggled into her dressing gown, pulling the belt tightly around her body, then ran to Fleur's bedroom. Blake held back, she would need time to come to terms with what had happened, see for herself her mother was no longer with them, and say her own private goodbye.

He lifted the telephone in his study and called the hospital in town. The town had grown over the years and the little clinic Fleur had started was now a fully, but modest, functional hospital.

Then he called Maggie in Port Elizabeth explaining the situation. "Please call Mr Van Tonder, he'll know where Tapu is. Tapu needs to know about Fleur. There's no point in him coming back here, by the time he arrives it will all be over. Let his own people celebrate her life and death in their own way. She would have liked that."

Lucy looked down at the woman lying on the bed, wrapped in a duvet, her greying hair spread across the pillow, her eyes closed, her face softer, and she knew.

Then, from somewhere deep inside of her, she felt the rolling waves of grief, of the time wasted, the years gone by – how lonely Fleur must have been without her family around her, without knowing how their lives had turned out. How hard it must have been for her to give her child up, to give hope to so many other people, and leaving herself with none.

Her tears dripped on the duvet. Lucy buried her face in her mother's neck.

"I'm so sorry, mummy."

The words Fleur had so desperately wanted to hear all her life disappeared into the pitiless cold of an unforgiving African night.

Chapter Eighty-Two

Blake saw the lights of the ambulance pierce their way through the night then pull up outside his house. The doors left open at the back, the silent beacon of the red light turning slowly above the vehicle.

The driver and the doctor got out. Six African women stood next to the open back doors, dressed in their nurses' uniform and capes. Their heads bowed, forming a simple guard of honour.

Blake led the doctor through to the bedroom where Fleur lay, her daughter holding her. He gently eased Lucy away from her mother and put his arm around her, leading her away to the *stoep* outside.

"Come Lucy, I'm here, I'll help you through this. The ambulance is here, we need to let them do what they must."

The doctor finished his examination of Fleur and nodded to his driver. The six African women entered the bedroom, carrying the stretcher. Gently they lifted Fleur onto it, placing a pillow under her head.

Softly they started to sing, wishing Doctor Fleur, who had done so much for everyone in the village, now a town, on her next journey to another place. Their voices were soft but clear as they sang her on her way, and carefully carried her to the back of the ambulance and closed the doors.

Blake could hear the fading harmony of their voices. Carried on the endless night until they disappeared with the winking lights of the ambulance, the dust left in their wake.

The entire town turned out for Fleur's funeral. The farmers came from miles around, with their own families, to celebrate and mourn the passing of Doctor Fleur Palmere, who in many ways had made the town what it was today.

In the Kalahari, Tapu and his people gathered. Their fires were lit, the women cooked their food over the hot coals. The men were silent; their creased faces lit by the flames of the fire they stared into.

Then they danced long into the night, hour after hour, remembering this woman called Doctor Palmere, who had given them so much, but asked for so little, only a handful of seeds. The dancers entered a trance-like state, singing as they carried the memory of this woman into their own spiritual world, making her one of their own.

Chapter Eighty-Three

Blake and Lucy sat outside in silence.

Lucy screwed up her face. "I don't know how to deal with all this Blake. I don't know what to do next. What will I do with her ashes?"

Blake looked out into the night, the owls were calling to each other, the night was coming alive with the sounds of the animals as they set about their nightly pursuit of food.

"In a day or two we should go to Johannesburg, meet with George, he's not emotionally involved in this. Let him advise us on the next course of action. You said both you and Fleur had drawn up some agreements between the two of you, and he'll need to have a look at any changes.

"After the meeting we should leave everything to George and Jeremy Foxton. You need some time on your own, as I do.

"You need to return to the UK, come to terms with everything on your own." His voice faltered. "I also need to process this, accept it, and then try to move on without her. Right now, it seems impossible…"

Lucy looked down at her hands, twisting them in her lap. "If it's all right with you, I'll leave her ashes here with you until we both decide what to do with them.

"I'll take the Lamu lamp to my father's grave, as Fleur suggested. She said he's buried in Dorset. Jeremy will be able to assist me there, show me where he is."

She ran her fingers lightly over her grandmother's leather journal. "Fleur wants the journal to be given to the research team in Tokai, she told me they would find it invaluable. We need to take it with us and give it to George Mason, he's a trustee, as you are, of the company producing the drug isn't he, over and above being her legal representative? It will be in safe hands."

Blake stood up. "Yes, good idea. You have a huge responsibility now Lucy, but you're perfectly capable of handling things with George guiding you through the legalities and he'll respect, as I do, any personal requests you may have. He'll consult with Jeremy in London."

Lucy put her arms around him, then looked up at his gaunt face. "I don't want you to feel you've been pushed out of everything, Blake. You will always be a big part of my mother's life and the support you gave her work. I know you loved her, as she loved you."

Blake gave her a wintry smile. "Yes, I loved her. I'm not sure what I'm going to do without her in my life. It's time to sell up here and go somewhere else. I've let Tapu know he should stay in the Kalahari now, with his own people. Like me, there is nothing left for him here. I shall miss him and envy his sure traditional life surrounded by his family."

Blake looked out over the bush, watching the long grasses, the colour of a lion's coat, whispering and swaying in the wind. A flock of Guinea Fowl, with their young chicks, busy feeding from the ground, calling to each other, it was another familiar sound he would miss, but this time they seemed to be calling, as he did in his head *"Come back, come back."* In the distance a small herd of impala grazed as the sun began to descend, spreading a golden glow over the land, with no thoughts of what tomorrow might bring.

He knew he didn't want to stay in the house. He didn't want to live there alone. Fleur had filled all the empty spaces in his heart and now she was gone.

Blake waited until Lucy had retired for the night. They would be leaving for Johannesburg the next morning. Then after the meeting with George, he would take her to the airport for her return flight to England.

He checked the time; not too late to call Jack Taylor in Hazyview.

"Jack Taylor."

"Hello Jack. It's Blake Hemmingway. I have sad news I'm afraid. Fleur died four days ago. Lucy is still here with me.

"I'm taking her to Johannesburg tomorrow to meet George Mason."

"I'm sorry to hear this Blake, a great shock. My sincere condolences to both of you. Is there anything I can do?"

Blake was silent for a few moments. "I know Fleur gave you the rights to publish the story of her life, once she had approved it, along with the photographs of the people who were important in her life, the ones you took in Kenya."

"Yes. I'm well into her story, busy with it now, but this, of course, changes everything, which I fully respect. However, it's a story which should be told, it's what she wanted.

"Her contribution to the world of science, first published by The Lancet, has obviously been of great interest to other medical publications around the world."

Blake rubbed his eyes. "Yes, I know, but not the personal story you're writing. I'd like you to continue with it. Lucy has agreed. As per Fleur's wishes I'd like to sign your story off before you publish."

Jack looked out over his garden, hearing the trickling stream, the deep throaty roar of a male lion, in the far distance, calling his pride together to hunt, nothing but everything had changed. "Thank you, Blake, of course I'll adhere to your wishes. But what will you do now?"

"I will support Lucy in any way I can. Help her through all the legalities and be there if she needs me.

"Fleur is here with me now, one way or another, as she always has been. But there are still the final chapters to be written, Jack. We need to give Lucy some time to do the things she wants to do.

"She asked me to bring her mother's ashes back to her in England."

Blake cleared his throat. "I'd like you to come with me. Then you can write your final chapters. Will you do this for me – for Fleur?"

Jack didn't hesitate. "Of course I will."

Blake's voice broke, and Jack carefully closed off his phone, leaving the man to his own private grief.

Chapter Eighty-Four

Jack and Blake made their way to the final resting place of Captain Michael Bennett, guided by the single flame burning in the darkening afternoon sky.

There, as promised by Lucy, was the tall turquoise Lamu lamp, cemented into the ground with its eternal flame, a small bench placed in front of it. At the base of the lamp was a small plaque.

They both sat in silence. Jack turned the torch on his phone on, and peered at the inscription.

From Lamu. From me. We loved you well. Fleur.

Jack glanced at Blake. Wondering how he would react to this simple sentence of enduring love.

"You okay with this Blake? Would you like some time alone for a while?"

Blake pulled the unfamiliar coat around himself. "No, I'm okay with it. The one thing I have always admired is loyalty and love, sadly cheapened these days. Fleur loved this man, the father of her child. She had a great capacity for love in its purest form.

"She shared her love with me. She accepted what had happened to Michael, although it must have been difficult. I wasn't a replacement for him, I know that. It was more about trust in the beginning. She trusted me not to hurt her, she gave all the love she had left, to me."

Jack switched off his torch, wishing he had known the man whose eternal light would lighten up a little corner of Dorset.

"Come on then, Blake, let's get back to the hotel and have a drink or two, let's celebrate the life of Fleur and Michael Bennett, and the love she gave to you, and face what will be a difficult day ahead."

Blake and Jack arrived at Lucy's house in Lymington the next afternoon. She smiled at them both and ushered them into what had been Fleur's house. It was pure East Africa, although Jack saw the empty place next to the fireplace where the tall Lamu lamp must have stood sentinel, but now had been moved.

Lucy hugged Blake. "You brought her back to me then?"

"Yes. You remember Jack of course?"

Lucy nodded. "Hello Jack. Nice to see you again, even though you turned my life upside down, but in a good way."

She gestured for them to sit. "This house doesn't seem the same somehow, it's too full of complicated memories of my mother and my aunt. Seeing my father's lonely grave made me depressed as well, I feel as though I'm surrounded by unfinished things, if that makes any sense. I don't feel as though I belong here anymore."

Chapter Eighty-Five
Naivasha
Kenya

Fleur's childhood home had crumbled into the bush which had laid claim to it. Lucy looked around, there was nothing here to see which would have given her some idea of how her grandmother, her own mother and her aunt had spent so many years.

Jack turned to Lucy. "Are you ready?"

Lucy nodded mutely. "Yes," she whispered. "As ready as I'll ever be."

Jack led the way to the small hill, which was a riotous carpet of glorious colour, small green bushes, young trees in bud and the pungent fragrance of wild herbs. Almost buried amongst them was the simple headstone which Fleur had arranged for her mother, Christiana.

Lucy hesitated; it was the most beautiful sight she had ever seen. Taking a deep breath, she walked amongst the flowers, trailing her fingers through them, until she reached the simple headstone of her grandmother.

"Hello Christiana, I'm your granddaughter, Lucy, Fleur's child. I've brought her back to you so you can be together again, I thought you'd like that."

Jack and Blake watched as she scattered her mother's ashes amongst the flowers, her mother's necklace, around her neck, catching the light of the sun, the warm breeze distributed them until they disappeared. In the distance the sounds of hippos carried across the lake, the distinctive cry of a fish eagle, mingling with the rustling of leaves and the calls of other birds, and the gentle lapping of water around the glittering lake. Here nothing had changed.

Carefully placing the empty urn next to her grandmother's headstone, Lucy paused for a while with her own thoughts, then turned and beckoned Jack over.

"Where are the graves of Patience and Noah, Jack?"

He put his arm around her. "They're here but you can't see them anymore, Lucy. The flowers and plants have covered their final resting place. It's what they would have wanted. Now, spend a little time here and say your goodbyes, then we should let Blake have some time alone with Fleur."

They watched Blake as he stood alone amongst the wildflowers and herbs, his head bowed.

Lucy turned to Jack. "He looks so terribly alone…What is it about Africa that evokes so much emotion, Jack?"

He smiled at her. "It's hard to explain. I know when I first came here it was like waking up from a deep sleep, feeling more alive somehow, my senses more acute, far away from the smog, fumes, constant invasive noise, and ingrained dirt of the city buildings. I felt happy. I looked forward to waking up in the morning. When I lived in London my whole life was consumed by my job as a journalist, I saw and heard things no human being should ever have to experience.

"But here in Africa, I see the beauty all around me, instead of fighting my way through the London traffic, looking at yet another grey and rainy day, my mind consumed with whatever I was working on at the time, well, now I look up and see the endless blue skies, hear the birds, hear the laughter and song of the people. People seem to *live* here, they don't fight their way through thousands of glum commuters every day, knowing tomorrow will be the same; they don't scuttle back to their small houses at the end of the day, and dread the sameness of tomorrow."

Jack smiled at her. "As I said, it's different here in Africa."

There was silence in the car as Jack drove them back to Nairobi to catch their flights; back to London for Lucy, and South Africa for Blake and himself.

Lucy watched them unload their luggage and stack it onto a trolley. "Blake? Jack? I'm not going back to London, not going back to my house for a while."

She took a deep breath, her mind now made up. "I want to go to Lamu."

Jack and Blake exchanged glances.

"I want you to take me there."

Blake looked at Fleur's daughter. "I think that's a good idea, Lucy, but I won't be coming with you, a step too far for me. But I wish you well if Jack agrees. You don't know this country any more than I do. Let Jack take you. I'm going home."

Lucy hugged Blake. "You'll always be a part of my life, please don't forget that will you?"

Blake stood back and looked at her. "Fleur was my whole life, Lucy, and I want to keep it like that. Just the two of us."

He put his arms around her and held her close. "Go well, Lucy," he said his voice breaking. "Find what you are looking for, as Fleur did. Keep in touch won't you, I shall miss you, you know. You were a great comfort to me over the past few weeks, it was like having a little of her still with me when I looked at you."

He took both her hands in his, his eyes filling with unexpected tears. "I know Fleur will go on because you have so much of her in you. Don't be afraid to love Lucy – your mother wasn't, and when she loved, she loved well."

He hugged her again, then turned and walked quickly away.

Chapter Eighty-Six
Lamu

Jack had booked two rooms at Peponi. Whilst Lucy took a shower and unpacked, he made his way to the now familiar bar.

Peter, the bartender, was delighted to see him. "It's Jack isn't it, good to see you again. Have you finished your story?"

Jack grinned at him; it was like coming home again. "Pretty much, but one more chapter to go. I see those old Kenyan hunters are still propping up the bar," he waved to them, "and I see you have an assistant barman now?"

"Yup, an Australian guy called Rob, on his gap year. Guests love him. Gives me a much-needed break when I need one. I can't believe I'm not a student anymore, I'm in my mid-forties – time crept up on me when I wasn't looking!"

Jack laughed. "Still look like the eternal student to me, life suits you here."

Peter wiped down the bar. "Beer and a crab sandwich?"

Jack shook his head. "A beer, yes, but I'm waiting for someone to join me. I'm going to give her a tour of the island after we've had lunch."

Peter delivered his beer. "New girlfriend?"

Jack laughed. "No, a friend of the family is how I would describe her. Lucy has a strong connection to the island, following in other footprints shall we say.

"Tell me something Peter, the place where Captain Michael Bennett lived, is it still a guest house?"

Peter grinned. "Nah, that ghastly couple didn't make it, don't think they had the necessary warm personalities, or hospitality skills, to attract guests. It's been up for sale for a couple of months now, no bites yet. But someone will buy it eventually, it's in a prime spot..."

His voice faltered as he watched a woman approach the bar. She was wearing a lemon-coloured dress which swirled around her tanned legs, her hair cascading around her shoulders, her feet bare, a straw hat held in her hand.

Peter watched her. "Wow! She's gorgeous and she's heading our way. Is it your friend from the UK?"

He hesitated for a moment. "She looks familiar, but I can't place her. Now, a woman like that I would remember."

Jack watched Lucy approach, and indeed she did look gorgeous. He smiled at Peter. "Perhaps you might remember someone who looked very much like her. I think she would be delighted to meet you, someone who met her mother briefly, Doctor Fleur Palmere, and her father, Captain Michael Bennett."

Peter's mouth dropped open in surprise. "Blimey! I thought Fleur was just one of the doc's guests, I had no idea their relationship turned into a big love story."

Peter looked puzzled. "So, why didn't she return to Lamu with him? I know he was badly injured in some war in the desert and died on the beach here some years later. What happened then?"

He looked thoughtful as he finished polishing a glass, watching Lucy draw nearer. "Ah," he said softly, "he didn't know he had a daughter did he? Otherwise, he would have mentioned it in one of our many conversations."

Jack took a sip of his Tusker beer. "I think that's Lucy's story to tell and not mine. But she'd like to look around the island and especially at her father's house, that's the reason she's come to Lamu."

He turned at Lucy's approach. "Ah, Lucy, this is Peter, he practically runs the place, been here for years. He met your mother briefly and knew your father well."

Lucy held out her hand, "Hello Peter, nice to meet you."

Peter seemed lost for words and held her hand a little longer than necessary before he composed himself. "Yes, Michael came here almost every evening for a sundowner or two. Lovely guy, we all became quite attached to him. His death here was a shock to all of us, as it must have been to you and your mother."

Lucy looked down at the white powdery sand, warm and soft against her bare feet. "I never met him," she said quietly. "I'm here because I want to learn more about him, see where he lived, meet the people who knew him."

"Of course. What can I get you to drink, Lucy?"

Jack smiled to himself. Obviously, an instant attraction between the two of them. An idea was beginning to form in his head.

A good one.

They ordered a crab sandwich, and he was aware of Peter's frequent glances towards them, or rather to Lucy.

They finished eating and Lucy looked at him. "I like Lamu, Jack, in an odd way I feel I belong here, close to my parents and where they met, here in Kenya and my grandmother. I haven't felt as good as this for years, despite everything that's happened over the past few weeks."

Jack smiled at her. "Yes, I can see you like it here, you look happy, it's brought colour to your cheeks, but perhaps it's not only the sun but something else maybe?

"Come on, let me take you over and introduce you to the four guys over there in the corner. They knew your father well and became good friends. They'll be delighted to meet you. Nothing to feel nervous about, they've all led rich and fulfilling lives, I can assure you nothing will surprise them. They've all been through a lot in their lives, lived and loved as they say. They know all about relationships, having had many of their own. I think you'll like them."

The four men rose, as gentlemen do when they meet a woman, and Jack introduced her. For the next hour they chatted easily. Lucy learned more about her father and began to see him more clearly as the old professional hunters regaled her with stories, not only of their own lives, but the life of Captain Michael Bennett, and their close relationship with him over the years.

Chapter Eighty-Seven

Lucy had spent a fascinating hour with the old hunters, then returned to her room for a nap, overwhelmed with everything she had learned about her father. She looked at the small wooden box with the brass clasp, next to her bed, and smiled.

Jack had also returned to his room. He had his columns to write, but more importantly he thought he might be coming to the end of the chapters of Doctor Fleur Palmere's life, through her daughter.

They met for dinner in the early evening. Jack was not surprised to see Peter behind the bar, although it seemed to him that Rob, the assistant Australian bartender, seemed to be doing most of the work.

Time to put the rest of his plans in place…

He gestured for Peter to come over. "See here, Peter, I had a call from my editor at the *Telegraph* in London. There's another story breaking in South Africa, and he wants me to get back there as soon as possible. So, Lucy and I will be leaving tomorrow which is a shame because she's hardly had time to see the island, or even her father's house. I wanted her to meet Ali, but that obviously won't happen now."

Peter looked at Lucy's crestfallen face, trying to look disappointed. But he took the bait as Jack knew he would.

"No reason for Lucy to leave the island. I can look after her, show her around the old town, show her Michael's house, find Ali, if he's still around. As a matter of fact, I have the day off tomorrow, I can show her everything. Lucy can't leave the island leaving everything up in the air. Let me take care of her?"

Lucy quite liked the sound of being looked after by Peter and completing her journey into the past.

"Do I have any say in this at all Jack?"

"Not really, but we'll hear you out. What would you like to do. Come back with me, or stay here with Peter?"

Jack already knew the answer. His plan had worked out perfectly.

Chapter Eighty-Eight

Lucy sipped at her drink as she looked out over the sea, watching the dhows go silently past. She looked around her house, filled with her mother's treasured mementoes which had looked so out of place in Lymington. Here they looked perfect, the intricate lamps, the pictures on the walls. She had re-created her parent's past and made them her own.

Ali had arrived late one afternoon and introduced himself, looking around the old house wistfully. "You will be looking for someone to take care of the house, and you. My grandson is a fine boy, perhaps you would like to meet him and see if he would be suitable to do this work for you? It would make me very happy to know my family still has a connection to Doctor Michael's.

"I remember your mother, she with the same eyes as you, she will be happy to know you are here, where your father lived and died. Of this I did not know then, but now I see it was so, you are the daughter of Doctor Fur and Doctor Michael."

Lucy had sold the house in Lymington and bought her father's old house in Lamu. It was her home now, and she had finally found the connection to her parents and the answers to all her questions over the years - and fallen in love.

Peter was a constant in her life. He had made the island of Lamu come alive for her, and she knew here was the place she wanted to be – with him. Yes, he was older than her, in his mid-forties now, but he had a zest for life on this island, knew everyone, she felt safe with him.

What they had hoped would be a quiet wedding on the beach turned into a rather riotous affair. All the locals swarmed into Peponi to see the couple be married.

Jack had flown in for the wedding, which he paid for himself, even though Harry had been beside himself with the final chapter of Fleur Palmere's life. He had called Jack from London.

"Excellent stuff! Well done, my boy. This one will be a winner. Happy to pay for your trip to Kenya this time."

Jack laughed. "No Harry, for some reason it's something more personal. I'm giving Lucy away and I'm flattered she chose me to do so. The story of the Palmere family was something quite different from anything else I've written."

Jack could hear the roar of the London traffic, a sharp contrast to the couple who now sought solace on the beach as they walked away from the crowds at the Peponi bar. Lucy had looked enchanting in her simple white dress, her long hair decorated with frangipani flowers, the resemblance to her mother quite startling. Peter in a suit, which he probably had to borrow from someone, his long hair tied back for the occasion.

Jeremy, the family solicitor, had travelled from London for the wedding, wearing his expensive suit and bow tie, but within days he was sporting shorts, his legs as white as the sand, a colourful shirt, and a Panama hat. He saw the magic of Africa all around him and wished he had more years ahead, to spend time here in this glorious place.

Lucy had asked him, some months before, if it might be possible to bring back the Lamu lamp cemented next to her father's grave - and Michael.

"I'd like him to come home Jeremy, be with us all again here in Lamu. Would that be possible?"

Jeremy thought about it for a few moments. "It's possible, a lot of legal and military red tape to get through, but it can be done. It will take some time and a great deal of money. But you are his daughter, without any doubt, and your wishes must be taken into consideration. Yes, it can be done. It's something I would very much like to do for you, and for your father."

Lucy had smiled at him. "I don't care how much it costs. I want him to come home again. I want you to bring him back here to us – and the Lamu lamp. He shouldn't be lying somewhere in Dorset, in a cold dark place. He belongs here in a place he obviously loved, a warm place, where he had many friends."

Chapter Eighty-Nine

The night was quiet, a full moon embracing the sea turning it to a carpet of silver. The dhow moved silently through the water with its only passenger, and what she held close to her chest, along with a small wooden box with a brass clasp.

The old fisherman doused the lamps and dropped anchor. There was darkness, stillness, and silence all around. As requested, he had waited a few moments before pressing the play button on the machine the young woman had brought with her.

The haunting song of *"Imagine,"* written and sung by John Lennon, drifted across the water. Haunting words which seemed to be perfect for what she was about to do.

'nothing to kill or die for...'

Lucy listened, her eyes filling with tears, then slowly she stood up. She moved to the front of the dhow and emptied the urn into the placid waters of the sea; she reached for the wooden box with the brass clasp, which she also emptied into the sea.

"I brought Fleur back to you, just a little of her, because she gave so much to everyone else," she whispered to Michael.

Lucy watched as the ashes merged. "She knew she would find you; and here you both are, as it was meant to be.

"You're together again."

She stood there for a while. The old fisherman approached her quietly. "We should return. You have done what you needed to do, and all will be well with my captain. He is at peace now."

Lucy turned towards him, startled, her face wet with tears. "How did you know my father was a captain? How could you possibly know that?"

He turned his creased and weathered face towards her.

"In the desert, during the war now long ago, I helped an injured British soldier. My wife Fatima and myself kept watch over this man and healed him before returning him to his own people from the place called England. They told me his name, Captain Bennett, then they took him home.

"There were many wars to follow. My wife Fatima and myself returned to our village, but in the years to come, this too was bombed and destroyed, my wife was killed. We, the few villagers who survived, became a nomadic people, moving from place to place, but we had heard of the old town called Lamu. It was said it was many hundreds of years old and observed the old traditional ways of the Muslim people. A peaceful place with no fighting, no wars, no guns, no tanks.

"My people travelled by foot, by camel and then by dhow, for many seasons, before we came here, which we made our home.

"I heard about the captain who had been returned here to Lamu, by his daughter, and how she wished to take a dhow out to the sea with his ashes.

"I knew it had to be me who brought you to say goodbye. It is also something I wished to do myself - for my captain."

The old Arab turned his gentle brown eyes to look at the placid sea carrying his captain away, once more.

Lucy looked at him, puzzled. "What is your name?"

"My name is Ahmed."

Acknowledgements

I would like to thank the following for their unswerving support on this long and lonely road called writing. But seeing nearly 1100 wonderful reviews on Amazon, from readers all around the world makes me want to get started on my next story!

Thank you to the readers who took time to write the reviews – each and every one of you are special and I thank you for your support – sorry about the tears…

To be compared to John Gordon Davis and Wilbur Smith is a massive, and humbling, tribute, and thank you for that as well.

To my sister, Jackie who, as usual, held my hand every step of the way. As a librarian her input was invaluable having dealt with thousands of readers over many years. She knows what works and what doesn't.

Mark Baldwin, a friend of many years standing, for yet another stunning cover!

Brian Stephens for doing all that technical stuff required to get this book up on Amazon. I don't have a clue how to do that.

And to all the others who contributed – you know who you are…

*****

If you enjoyed reading this book and would like to share that enjoyment with others, then please take the time to visit the place where you made your purchase and write a review.

Reviews are a great way to spread the word about worthy authors and will help them be rewarded for their hard work.

You can also visit Samantha's Author Page on Amazon to find out more about her life and passions.

Also by Samantha Ford:

The Zanzibar Affair

A letter found in an old chest on the island of Zanzibar finally reveals the secret of Kate Hope's glamorous, but anguished past, and the reason for her sudden and unexplained disappearance.

Ten year's previously Kate's lover and business partner, Adam Hamilton, tormented by a terrifying secret he is willing to risk everything for, brutally ends his relationship with Kate.

A woman is found murdered in a remote part of Kenya bringing Tom Fletcher back to East Africa to unravel the web of mystery and intrigue surrounding Kate, the woman he loves but has not seen for over twenty years.

In Zanzibar, Tom meets Kate's daughter Molly. With her help he pieces together the last years of her mother's life and his extraordinary connection to it.

A page turning novel of love, passion, betrayal and death, with an unforgettable cast of characters, set against the spectacular backdrop of East and Southern Africa, New York and France.

Amazon Reviews

"This book will keep you guessing; that's a good thing. I could barely put it down and one night dreamed about it so much I woke up and read more. It's unbearably sad in some places and wonderfully happy in others. Fantastic!"

"This book takes you on a safari round Africa. It is a compelling story with so many twists. It is beautifully and hauntingly told. The details and descriptions made me feel the heat, smell the ocean and slap the mosquitoes. Thank you."

"I loved The Zanzibar affair. I felt I was there sensing the smells, the sea and the warmth of Africa. The way she weaves the characters into the story is quite fascinating, leaving the reader spellbound and wondering where it's going to end. Always with an unexpected twist. A fabulous storyline and book which I could hardly put down. Highly recommended."

The House Called Mbabati

The Mother Superior crossed herself quickly. "May God have mercy on you, and forgive you both," she murmured as she locked the diary and faded letters in the drawer.

Deep in the heart of the East African bush stands a deserted mansion. Boarded up, on the top floor, is a magnificent Steinway Concert Grand, shrouded in decades of dust.

In an antique shop in London, an elderly nun recognises an old photograph of the mansion; she knows it well.

Seven thousand miles away, in Cape Town, a woman lies dying; she whispers one word to journalist Alex Patterson – Mbabati.

Sensing a good story, and intrigued with what he has discovered, Alex heads for East Africa in search of the old abandoned house. He is unprepared for what he discovers there; the hidden home of a once famous classical pianist whose career came to a shattering end; a grave with a blank headstone and an old retainer called Luke - the only one left alive who knows the true story about two sisters who disappeared without trace over twenty years ago.

Alex unravels a story which has fascinated the media and the police for decades. A twisting tale of love, passion, betrayal and murder; and the unbreakable bond between two extraordinary sisters who were prepared to sacrifice everything to hide the truth.

Mbabati is set against the magnificent and enduring landscape of the African bush - where nothing is ever quite as it seems.

Amazon Reviews

"It is a long time since I have been so absorbed by a novel about Africa. Reading it, I vacillated between willing it to last longer as I was enjoying it so much, and wanting to get through it to reveal the outcome. There can be no greater praise for this novel than its endorsement by the late John Gordon Davis, to whom the novel is dedicated. Anyone who has read any of JGD's novels, in particular his classic 'Hold My

Hand I'm Dying' will understand that Samantha Ford's novel is in the same league."

"What a wonderful story where you have a stormy love affair set in the heart of Africa. It twists and turns as the plot unfolds and you will surely shed a tear or two along the way. For those who have been on an African safari you will not put this book down. Such intelligent and beautiful writing."

"The book is captivating from beginning to end. It takes you on a riveting journey where the story develops and keeps you guessing. Loved it! Didn't want it to end!"

A Gathering of Dust

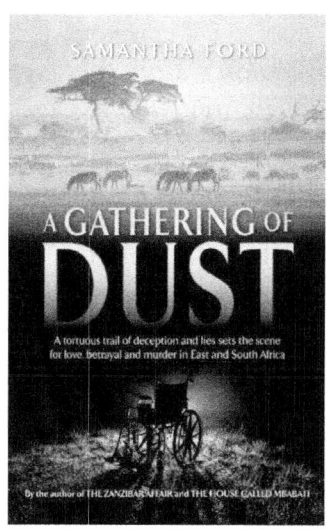

Through the mists of a remote and dangerous part of the South African coastline, a fisherman stumbles upon an abandoned car and an overturned wheelchair.

Thousands of miles away in London, an unidentified woman lies in a coma. When she recovers she has no memory of her past or where she comes from. As fragments of her memory begin to return, the woman has to confront the facts about herself as they begin to unfold. A disastrous love affair in the African bush: a missing husband: and a sinister shadowy figure who knows exactly who she is and where she comes from.

Tension builds as images and secrets begin to resurface from her lost past – rekindled memories that plunge her back into a world she finds she would rather not remember.

Set against the magnificent backdrop of East and Southern Africa. A Gathering of Dust is a fast-paced story of love, betrayal and murder scattered along a trail of deception and lies, with a single impossible truth, and an unthinkable ending.

Amazon Reviews

"What a writer this author is! So cleverly written and with twists and turns you never see coming. I am an avid reader and this authors books are the best I have read in a long time. Her books have everything, mystery, murder, romance, intrigue, suspense etc. etc. Well worth a read."

"My husband knows when I am reading this author's books that there is little that will get my nose out of them. Her descriptives of even the simplest things create such a vivid picture. She has made me fall in love with Africa and her story lines are captivating and intelligently

thought out. I never want to finish one of her books only because I don't want them to end."

"Superb. Absolutely brilliant. I simply couldn't stop reading, turned TV off and just read and read, even ignoring my hubby. Can't wait to read the next book!!!"

"A gripping read, with many gut-wrenching twists and turns. I had trouble putting the book down to eat, sleep or work! Fabulous."

The Ambassador's Daughter

During a violent storm deep in the African bush, a child disappears.

Sara, the ex-British ambassador's daughter, and mother of the child, is arrested.

Twenty years later, journalist Jack Taylor, travels from London to the magnificent landscape of the Eastern Cape, in South Africa, where the unforgiving bush hides long-forgotten secrets of loss, hate, betrayal and revenge.

A staggering story awaits. A deadly secret threatens to destroy the lives of people who thought themselves now safe - a story which has fascinated the media for decades.

Only one person knows exactly what happened on that day - a nomadic shepherd called Eza - but can Jack find him?

Amazon Reviews

"This is simply the best book I've read in a very long time.
This talented lady brings Africa alive.
Wilbur Smith you have some competition…"

"A cracking good story with a totally unexpected twist at the end!"
John Gordon Davis – author of Hold My Hand I'm Dying

"Having read all Wilbur Smith's books, this author ranks up with the best of them. Best read I've had for years!" Peter C. Morgan

A Widow in Waiting

An accident in the Kenyan bush claims the life of Sir David Cooper, the Director of International Trade and Industry for the British Government -a man with impeccable credentials and an impressive family history.

Twenty years later at an auction on a remote farm in South Africa, a young woman discovers two boxes. One, a richly engraved Chinese puzzle box concealing things the late owner had clearly wanted to remain hidden; the other an antique silver box with an intriguing crest.

Jack Taylor, a journalist from London now living in South Africa, and his partner, ex-detective Piet Joubert once more join forces as they try to untangle the mysterious and tragic past of the two boxes and the people involved.

Set against the breath-taking beauty of Kenya and South Africa, this is an irresistible page-turner, laden with unpredictable possibilities. It takes the reader down a trail of deception, secrets and tragedy, culminating in a single impossible truth and an unthinkable ending, which even veteran journalist Jack Taylor had not seen coming.

Amazon Reviews

"Oh my word, what a story. Samantha really knows how to reel one in. Thank you so much for a gripping story. Didn't have a clue as to the ending."OK, so you've heard of Wilbur Smith, so why haven't you heard of Samantha??

One was a millionaire with mega-support, the other is equally as good (better??) when it comes to books about Africa (always with an International 'interest.')Samantha, however, is a dedicated "garret author" with no publicity/marketing Team, and so you can only get her books from Amazon. If you love reading, Africa, mystery.... and don't mind being obsessed with an **"I can't put it down"** *book, get onto Amazon now!" – Philippa J*

"Another fascinating book from Samantha. Her descriptions take you back to Africa! I could not put it down as I wanted to find out what happened! Great read from a great author." – Mrs Jacqueline A Lloyd

"Novel number 6 from Samantha will not disappoint another page turner with more twists & turns than a Rubix Cube, you have just no idea what jumps out at you from the next page. This author also cleverly takes us back to our verandas in Kenya & South Africa with our beers or gin & tonics watching the sun go down. Brilliant writing Samantha keep them coming." – Peter Morgan

Hidden in Full View

An unsigned painting of an isolated farmhouse in the vastness of the South African Free State found in a second-hand shop in London, holds the key to what happened there over forty years ago.

What could possibly link the painting of an old farmhouse and four girls from Cape Town who disappeared without a trace twenty years later?

This sweeping tale is set against the magnificent South African landscape where nothing is ever as it seems. British journalist Jack Taylor and South African ex-detective Piet Joubert follow a frustrating trail until they finally manage to untangle the whole shocking story. The eventual denouement is a case of poetic justice worthy of the appalling crimes themselves.

Amazon Reviews

"I have read all of the African books by Samantha Ford and thoroughly enjoyed each one. Great stories and each one so different. Wish I could have visited there but the stories brought the land to life. Everyone I know who has been there never forgets." – Michelle

"Excellent addition to the collection. Interesting and intriguing. A book you do not want to put down. Looking forward to the next book." – Robin McKenzie

"I have just finished 'Hidden in full view' by Samantha Ford, what an absolutely fantastic book it is, I have read all of Samantha's books and loved them all! The book was so exciting and reading it was like watching a film. I feel I know the main characters now! I am so sad I've finished it!! I hope Samantha will be writing another book soon??" – Jennifer Pegg

Printed in Great Britain
by Amazon